THE VALK

Dead ahead, ho
stars. Just a great
its cloak with e
slowly enveloping Krog's entire uni-verse. When he was close enough to see the blue electric flashes, he knew. He had taken everything into his calculations but the obvious: Iceland's weather. It had found him as the clumsy police could not. He was about to fly into the centre of the most enormous thunderstorm he imagined the world had ever seen.

The rain it carried struck the tiny airplane like a thousand sledgehammer blows loosed at once. There were buffeting winds, and then a violent updraft that caught the Cessna's right wing and flung it over, throwing the aircraft into a roll, and then a dive, and then a deadly spin. Instantly, the instruments were rendered useless, the turn and bank indicator glued to one side. The altimeter dial unwound without pause. Krog's head was pressed against the cabin ceiling with the force of a thousand pounds. He had outsmarted the police, indeed. They would look for his body in the wrong place.

But what about Valkyrie, and all he had discovered? How many millions of people would die with him?

THE VALKYRIE PROJECT

Michael Kilian

Hamlyn Paperbacks

THE VALKYRIE PROJECT
ISBN 0 600 20624 6

First published in Great Britain 1982
by Hamlyn Paperbacks

Hamlyn Paperbacks are published by
The Hamlyn Publishing Group Ltd.,
Astronaut House,
Feltham, Middlesex, England.

Printed and bound in Great Britain by
Cox & Wyman Ltd. Reading

For Fred Little, and for
Patience Abigail Wallace,
of Mount Kisco days.

My thanks to Consul P. Sveinbjorn Johnson and Colonel Christopher Branch for their sage counsel and expert technical advice.

THE VALKYRIE PROJECT

1

THERE WAS NO REASON for the people of the fishing village to fear the shabby little Polish trawler coming up the fjord in the gathering darkness of a sudden Icelandic storm. Certainly none would suspect it carried anyone so unfriendly as to commit murder. Iceland's last "cod war" with England had ended several years before, and Iceland was again quite hospitable to foreign vessels—providing they adhered to its territorial fishing regulations—especially if they were seeking shelter from its frequently violent weather.

The downpour commenced just as the little ship settled at drift anchor a short distance from the village wharf. A few minutes later, the darkness now as much night as storm, three of the crew, dressed in black slickers, motored quietly ashore in the trawler's inflatable. The only one to notice was an old fisherman who had come to fetch a bottle of Brennivin, Iceland's fiery native liquor, hidden from his temperance-society wife in one of the fish-drying sheds. Finding it, he retreated to the shed's recesses and proceeded to forget the strangers, who headed straight up the street for the village grocery.

Two of the trawlermen were Polish. The third, a tall, pink-faced man with a sharp nose and watery blue eyes, spoke the language well and had had a Polish grandmother, but he considered himself thoroughly German. His name was Emil Jahn and he came from Danzig, now called Gdansk, a city he insisted on considering still thoroughly German as well. He found it odd that this project was involving him so much with seafaring vessels. Jahn's military rank was colonel.

In a stretch of near-complete darkness, Jahn abruptly slipped away from the other two, who continued on toward the grocery, and turned into a smaller street, following it until at length he had left the village and was splashing along a gravel country road. Close to the fjord, the road was hazardous on so wet and dark a night, especially for someone who had never traveled it before, but Jahn, as always, had methodically memorized his map.

Iceland is not a pleasant place in which to be lost. The second largest island in Europe, it has few habitations—a population of two hundred twenty thousand scattered over one of the bleakest if most beautiful wildernesses on earth. Reykjavik, the capital, has all of eighty-five thousand people. The village Jahn had just left had three hundred, which made it rather large. The nearest town was two hours' rough drive.

Jahn disliked the isolation, the weather, and—very German of him—the lack of trees, yet he found himself becoming fond of Iceland. The people were hardy, industrious, inclined toward socialism, and indulgent in sex and strong drink. Except for what he considered a regrettable Celtic strain, Icelanders were the most racially pure people in the civilized world, little changed from the Vikings who had first settled their island eleven hundred years before. Their women were tough and independent, often irritating, but inordinantly attractive, in Jahn's mind the finest white women ever produced.

His feet began to slip a little in the gritty mud. Jahn found himself going up a long, steep hill. He thought he could discern through the rain a faint glow of light at the top. All seemed as the map had indicated.

He carried a small automatic pistol in the left pocket of his slicker. But the primary tool that he would use to kill Geir Krog would be an old-fashioned but altogether agreeable device—a pencil-like cylinder five inches long. It sheathed a spring-loaded needle with a payload of a drug that in most cases could stop the human heart within ten seconds. The puncture mark was almost imperceptible and the drug dissipated quickly, detectable only with the most sophisticated chemical analysis. The symptoms were those of a heart attack. Variations of the deadly cylinder could be fitted into umbrella sticks or canes. Jahn usually carried his loose in his pocket. He had used it often, the last victim a man on a crowded tram in Budapest. Very neat. Very pleasant.

Krog would be surprised—indeed, astonished—to have the man he knew only as a Polish engineer named Rozkowski suddenly appear at his east coast hideaway. The East German felt very smug that the Russians had once again had to call him into a situation they themselves had mucked up. They had been very stupid about Krog. They had been very stupid about Iceland from the beginning.

So, of course, had the United States. With their usual disdain for the affairs of small nations, the Americans had paid such little attention to Iceland's case against England in the 1975–1976 cod war that they had come perilously close to losing their wonderfully strategic airbase at Keflavik, along with Iceland's presence in NATO.

All the clumsy Russians had done to exploit this rare chance was to finance some anti-NATO demonstrations by Icelandic leftists. Worse, they attempted a little fish poaching of their own. And worst: under a peculiar arrangement for a NATO country, Iceland imported all its oil from the Soviet Union. Instead of lowering prices to gain a little friendship and influence at that critical time, Moscow increased them to the highest in Europe. It was the same with so much of the xenophobic Russians' international dealings: no subtlety or intelligence; all power and greed.

This attitude was changing, as it must. The Russians now appreciated that Iceland was the most valuable real estate in the North Atlantic. If all went well with Valkyrie, it would soon become—for thirty minutes—the most valuable real estate in the world; perhaps, in the history of mankind.

Reaching the top of the hill, Jahn paused to wipe the rain from his eyes. Off to the side of the road were three small summer cabins, grouped together on a bluff to take advantage of what was in daylight one of Iceland's more majestic views. Two of the cabins were darkened, closed and locked for the season. The third was ablaze with light that flickered as someone inside moved past it. Parked just outside was Geir Krog's yellow Mercedes-Benz. Krog may have been one of Iceland's most brilliant engineers, but he was an abysmal fugitive. This was like dealing with Africans.

Jahn liked Krog, as much as he liked anyone with whom he did such business. In their few meetings, they had discovered a mutual interest in medieval literature and music, and a passion for chess. They had even played a game: Krog had beaten Jahn, but not handily. For a moment, Jahn had toyed with the possibility of demanding a final match. But that dalliance would be so unprofessional as to be idiocy. And there was little triumph in winning a game played while one sat holding a gun.

Circling to keep out of the light, Jahn made his way to the first of the darkened cabins, and then to the next, and finally to Krog's. Crouching by the door, he could hear the clatter of silver and plates from the kitchen. The door, to his surprise, was unlocked. He eased it open and stepped inside, taking out the pistol and thinking of some amusing words with which to announce himself. Then he saw the girl.

He was stunned. Who in hell was she? Very Icelandic, short and slender, well-built, with long pale hair, white skin, dark blue eyes. She wore a thick Icelandic sweater and nothing else, the bottom reaching just to her pubic hair. There was nothing about a girl in the surveillance report. Had he come to the wrong place? Krog's Mercedes was outside.

Jahn's professional instinct was to kill her at once, but he dared not alert Krog, wherever he was, and a shooting murder would complicate things. Yet she had seen his face. He put the pistol back into one pocket and took the cylinder from the other.

Typical of Icelandic women, she was more angry than afraid, which was well, for she might have screamed.

"Who are you?" she demanded in Icelandic. "What do you want?"

"Geir Krog?" he said, stepping forward as he spoke.

"He's not here. Who are you? Get out! You've no right here!"

He would have to kill her quickly, before Krog returned. Obviously, he would return soon. Where in hell was he? He would kill her and they would come back for Krog another time. Soon.

"Get out! Get out!"

Jahn lunged forward, aiming the cylinder at her throat, but he was rattled and off balance, and she was on her guard. In what seemed to him a single sudden motion, she leapt at him, driving her knee into his groin, clawing at his face and eyes, knocking the cylinder out of his hand. Then she began punching at his stomach with her small, hard fists. Furious with himself, Jahn spun her around, gripping her mouth and jaw with his left hand and her arms with his right. The cylinder was across the room, but there was a fish knife on the counter. He dragged her struggling to it, jerked her head up and back, snatched up the knife, and ripped open her throat, twisting her body away from him to avoid the fount of blood that gushed forth as she fell, landing with a thud on her side, her blood a spattered arc on the wall.

He stepped back from the spreading circle of red, his breathing as heavy as an exhausted runner's. There was no time to search the place as planned, nor to wait for Krog. This little mission was a shambles, and there was no one to blame but Emil Jahn. He had undertaken it himself because, so contemptuous of the Russian operation here, he had trusted no one else to do it.

As he wiped his fingerprints from the knife, an idea began to occur to him. By the time he had retrieved the cylinder, fled the cabin, and reached the sanctuary of the outside darkness and the road, he had it fully in mind. Things were not entirely a shambles. It was Krog's girl who had been killed, not his. It was Krog's rented cabin. No one was going to be pounding upon the Reykjavik hotel room door of a visiting Pole named Rozkowski. There were few police in law-abiding Iceland and they doubtless had little experience with murders. They would pursue the obvious. And what was more obvious than a half-naked girl in a man's lonely cabin, her throat slashed in a violent quarrel?

Jahn had not eliminated Krog, but he had certainly inconvenienced him. As Jahn slogged into the village, he made a note to write a stern report on the surveillance team that had failed to inform anyone about the girl. He was beginning to feel pleased with himself again.

He reached the wharf within the agreed-upon time. His men were waiting in the inflatable, a large plastic bag containing groceries between the boat's two seats. Saying nothing, Jahn took his place at the bow. He remained silent all the way to the trawler, as though savoring his thoughts. One rumor about him was true. He derived an almost sexual satisfaction from killing.

2

As HE HAD every night for nearly three months, Jack Spencer ran out of sleep well before dawn, waking sweating and fretful. Someone in the bar of the National Press Club had told him that could be a sign of alcoholism. Spencer had found that very funny.

He sat up, throwing back the sheet, glad of the cool air on his bare skin. The woman next to him did not stir, even when he set his hand on her bare buttocks. Spencer lived in a section of Washington expensive enough to be spared the orange glare of crime-fighting sodium vapor lights, so the light that came through the bedroom window was soft and dim, making her sandy hair seem strangely dark. Spencer stared down at her, unable to remember her name.

He groped his way to the bathroom, and then to the kitchen where to his amazement he found both a clean glass and a bottle of whiskey still half-full. He took both prizes to the living room and lowered his naked body into the cold leather chair by the front window, filling the glass straight to the top.

This was how Spencer got to sleep at night and how he returned to sleep at night. If it constituted alcoholism, he would make the most of it. As his doctors would attest, there were worse problems.

Spencer's wife had divorced him because of his drinking and philandering—or so she had said—which he still found wonderfully funny, for he had been drinking and philandering all his adult life. In fact, he had taken his first drink at fourteen, inexpensive wine sneaked in Joycean fashion from a church altar. He had lost his virginity the following year, to a plump New England high school cheerleader he still fondly remembered. Both seemed simple, harmless pleasures, and he indulged himself in them accordingly thereafter. Once, on a single stroll through Grand Central Terminal, he had picked up three girls, brought them all to the same party, and later slept with each in turn, with no one much bothered about it. He met his wife in similar circumstances. In these predawn awakenings, he often puzzled after the real reason she had left him. He wondered whether it had been something as simple as his getting old.

In his twenties, Spencer had been handsome to the point where young girls called him beautiful and he was sometimes bothered by homosexuals. Now, nearing forty, he had aged greatly. His hair was turning silver and in his lined and weathered face the once-boyish features had taken on a quite melancholy cast. A woman at a party had told him that by age sixty he would look like God. Age sixty. Another wonderfully funny notion.

He gulped the whiskey, clenching his teeth against his stomach's protests. Except for his job, which he had come to despise, there was little left of his life now but drink and sex.

He still could not remember the woman's name.

It had been unusually and irritatingly difficult for Spencer to find a woman that night. He had started in midafternoon on Capitol Hill, a favorite hunting ground, prowling congressional offices ostensibly to chat with sources but with no other real purpose than to acquire a warm female body.

None had been interested. He finally managed to persuade a not very bright and slightly overweight blonde from Indiana to come with him for a drink after the House had adjourned. She had even taken a second—light beer—and then abandoned him for a basketball game. How typical of Indiana to prefer basketball to sex.

Spencer had forlornly tried some other Capitol Hill bars, and then some M Street singles bars, and finally in desperation had sought recourse to one of the embassy parties of the evening, a second-rate affair thrown by a third-rate Latin American legation. The woman with the sandy hair had arrived there perhaps half an hour after him, making an ostentatious entrance. Older than thirty, she must have been smashing in her early twenties but now had to be very careful with her makeup. She wore a short, deeply cut black dress, a thin strand of a gold necklace her only jewelry. Spencer had watched as she kicked off her shoes and began flitting from group to group, talking incessantly and chain smoking, and knew that at last he was spared a womanless night.

It had taken only two drinks. She was a publicity aide for one of the oil lobbies and had talked about her job all the way to his townhouse.

Spencer suddenly remembered her name. Frances.

He was a journalist, the Washington euphemism for newspaperman. He had a good job as newspaper jobs went—foreign affairs and State Department correspondent for the Washington bureau of a large chain of newspapers. As Frances had instantly appreciated, it was an important job, a fitting reward for his years as a correspondent in Vietnam, Mexico, Rhodesia, the Mideast, Russia, and London. He had covered everything from the Cambodian incursion to the Anglo-Icelandic cod war to the Mexican oil find. In the minds of those who ran newspapers, it was logical to promote him to Washington, where his skills and experience in such endeavors as finding taxicabs during street battles in Beirut were squandered covering endless meaningless press conferences called by countless fatuous asses.

Outside on the street, a noise proved to be leaves blown along the pavement. He loved autumn. How kind of the fates to let him have one last one.

He had taken the Washington assignment for only one reason: his wife had asked him to. It was yet another of the continuing conditions she set for the perpetuation of their marriage. Theirs had been a splendid marriage—at the start. Chesley was as beautiful as he was handsome, and much his social superior, a tall, slender woman with long dark hair and perfect manners, the highly intelligent and widely traveled daughter of an old-money Connecticut curmudgeon. He had met her at a London party, in Belgravia. She would never admit to having been picked up, but she had come with someone else, and Spencer had made love to her that night. He had also gotten drunk. Straight gin, right through to the morning. Chesley had taken him back with her to Connecticut anyway. Daddy disapproved but indulged his daughter. A month after they were married, Spencer went on a long patrol with the British SAS in Northern Ireland. Chesley was very unhappy about that.

She proved a surprisingly warm and loving person, especially after they had their little boy. Spencer complied with her every condition, even to being rigidly circumspect about his drinking and painfully discreet about his indiscretions. She left him anyway—abruptly, irrevocably. The divorce court judge granted every demand in her petition. Spencer had not seen her or the boy since June, nor would he until the week after Christmas, the one annual visit that the Connecticut court had allowed him. Christmas.

Perhaps she had married him because he was not her father and divorced him for the same reason.

He sipped his whiskey. Christmas. Would the fates be so kind as to allow him another one of those? What would he do with it?

He sipped again, then gulped, then refilled his glass. That same damned chill had come over him again, the same desperate, terrifying frustration.

It had all arisen from a persistent, savage headache. On a hot, abysmally tropical August Washington day, he had gone to a doctor's office to seek an explanation. The day became weeks: an ordeal of X-rays, scans, blood samples, electrodes, whirring machines, strange laboratory tests, and ultimately very carefully chosen words. He had consulted several doctors, but their words were always the same, as though it were some sort of conspiracy: "Vascular flaw . . . physiological . . . neurological . . . inoperable."

From the doctor he had liked the most, he begged an accurate assessment of his chances. "There is a statistical possibility that you will live a normal lifespan," the doctor said. "You can't ignore that." He was a pleasant man of about fifty, with rather long gray hair, a heavy smoker. "That is, however, a small possibility."

He paused and looked as though he wanted a cigarette. "There is also a possibility that you will die tonight," he continued. "This too is small. The probability lies somewhere in between."

Spencer remarked with some profanity that this was unhelpful.

"Mr. Spencer," the doctor said. "I could tell you the chances are a hundred to one against anything happening to you. But what good would that do you if your case turned out to be that one? If I told you that you had only one chance in a hundred of surviving, what if you proved to be that one?"

Spencer remarked that this, too, was unhelpful.

"We can't predict these things, Mr. Spencer. I'm sorry. We've prescribed medication, a diet, a schedule of checkups. Beyond that, you'll just have to live your life like the rest of us."

"If I were to die within a year," said Spencer, "would you be surprised?"

The doctor slid open his desk drawer and removed a package of cigarettes. He lit one, inhaled deeply, exhaled an enormous cloud of smoke, then stared through it at Spencer.

"No," he said. "Mr. Spencer, I would not be surprised at six months."

Spencer took a week off work after that and was drunk day and night for all of it. He finally compelled himself to recognize the pointlessness of that and made the effort to fashion some sort of life for himself. But it was not life lived "like the rest of us." It was a life utterly bereft of future, a life that ended every day. And the nights were not possible without alcohol.

He had risked his life many times throughout his career—often deliberately. But Khmer Rouge landmines and IRA snipers and storms off the coast of Iceland were dangers that passed. Now he must live with a terrifying danger that could end only with his death.

Still drinking, Spencer fidgeted a moment, then abruptly rose and began moving restlessly through the room. He picked up his wife's picture from the mantelpiece, stared at it, and drank. He took his loaded pistol from the desk and walked with it to the window, letting it hang loosely in his hand as he stood naked watching the swirling leaves.

He had always been peculiarly curious about the experience of killing another human being. He knew an extraordinary number of people who had done it. In Vietnam, some correspondents had gone out with helicopter gunships to shoot VC as a lark. Spencer had gone along once but had no interest in shooting anyone. Merely this overwhelming curiosity about what it would be like.

What would it be like to kill oneself?

Returning his pistol to the drawer with great care, he had a final drink, then went back to stand at the foot of the bed. Frances was quietly snoring. Spencer turned her over onto her back, and heaved himself onto her.

Warm sunlight found him still alive. He had come to rejoice in that morning moment.

Frances still slept. Without dressing, he went to make coffee in the kitchen and, when done, took a cup to his leather chair by the front window. It was against his new rules to drink in the morning, but he poured some whiskey into the strong coffee anyway. It would help him think, and he needed to.

Frances joined him a short while later, having put on an old robe Chesley had left behind. She made a face when he offered her coffee, lighting a cigarette instead. He wished she had not put on the robe, though not for any reason to do with Chesley. Naked, Frances had looked young and vulnerable, appealing. With the robe—her hair disheveled, her bare feet awkward and unattractive—she seemed haggard, almost sleazy.

She exhaled a long plume of smoke into the shaft of sunlight from the window. Then she coughed.

"You're a mean fuck," she said.

"Is that a compliment?" he asked.

"No."

She paused, looking at her hand.

"Yes and no," she said. "You hurt me. You scared the hell out of me. You were wandering around out here with a gun. Are you some kind of weirdo?"

"No. I just drink too much."

He sipped his coffee. There was ample room in the cup for more whiskey, but he decided against it.

"What would you do if you knew when you were going to die?" he asked.

"What?"

"What would you do if you had only a very short time to live?"

She studied him a long moment. Her eyes were roughly darkened from smudged mascara.

"Would you do whatever you wanted to do?" he said.

"I guess I'd do what I wanted to do most," she said.

"Thank you for last night."

"I have to get home," she said, putting out her cigarette. "You can drive me, if you're sober enough. I've got that much coming."

She lived rather near, in one of the old but expensive canopied buildings on Connecticut Avenue near the zoo. She had a roommate, she said—a man, who didn't mind her having other "friends." As he always did with the women he liked, Spencer wondered whether he might ever see her again.

It would require continuing to work second-rate Embassy Row parties. Which meant that he would not. Turning his BMW sedan into the downtown-bound morning traffic, he put her out of his mind. He was putting an extraordinary number of things out of his mind.

The list of committee hearings and press conferences on the Senate press gallery bulletin board was a catalog of trivia. As it was yesterday. As it would be tomorrow.

As he left the gallery, a dark-eyed young girl who worked for one of the wire services looked up from her desk and smiled, earnestly and sadly. There were a great many rumors circulating about what might be medically wrong with Spencer—doubtless none of them right. But he had become a Tragic Figure. He smiled back at her, tragically.

The Capitol's pay phones were much too public. Spencer instead walked over to the Rayburn House office building, following a long corridor to a little-used second-floor press room. As he expected, it was empty. There was a long row of free telephones in booths against the wall, soundproof for the benefit of broadcast reporters. He chose one with a good view of the entire room and slid the door closed behind him. The telephone number was on a dirty, wrinkled card he still carried in his wallet. He dialed it and was informed by an operator that it had been changed. The new number she gave him was answered after only one ring by a girl who merely repeated the number back, saying no more. That much had not changed.

"My name is John Spencer," he said, identifying himself as a correspondent for the newspaper chain in the Midwest.

"Press inquiries are handled by Colonel Fitzwilliam," she said. "One moment, I'll connect you."

Colonel Fitzwilliam, Spencer knew very well, did not exist. It was the name used by all the people in the Central Intelligence Agency who dealt with press inquiries. Spencer wondered why they hadn't given the colonel a new name.

"No, no, no," he said. "This isn't a press inquiry. I've

worked for you before. I'd like to work for you again. Is there someone I might speak to about that?"

"One moment please."

She connected him with a real colonel. He was quite friendly, if circumspect, and invited Spencer to come out to Langley that afternoon. He sounded rather encouraging.

It was an old maxim at the CIA: The best spies are those who want to be spies. And being a spy was what Spencer now wanted to do most.

3

Geir Krog was the only witness to the murder that was supposed to have been his own. He had left his cabin only a short while before, thinking that nothing was amiss and that his American friends were alarmists. With his Mercedes firmly stuck in the mud, he walked to the grocery, leaving Inga to begin the dinner and feeling perfectly secure. At the store he encountered nothing out of the ordinary, except two foreign sailors who made their purchases without paying him any mind. Despite the miserable weather, he trudged back to the cabin feeling peculiarly happy, only to be abruptly halted outside the cabin window by the sight of Inga struggling with a tall man in a fisherman's slicker. Krog heard her body drop to the floor. An hour earlier they had been making love.

Krog was a huge man, a bluff, cheery giant with bright blue eyes and yellow-red hair and beard, who might well have stepped off one of the long ships that had brought the Vikings to Iceland in the late ninth century. A mountain climber who spent much of his free time trekking across Iceland's glacier-strewn interior, Krog had inordinate strength—enough to break the murderer's neck with one hand if he were furious enough, which he was.

Instead, he hurried back into the darkness and dropped to the sodden ground. There was nothing he could do for that poor girl. It was too late—probably too late for him as well. He was in the most serious trouble of his life. And he had been treating this entire business as an intellectual game—just another game of chess.

Krog was frightened, and he was seldom frightened. It was incredible that they could have found him so soon, that they could behave so brutally. The Russians he had dealt with had been clumsy, primitive sorts, but they had been friendly enough. And trusting. Brother socialists.

Yet here was Rozkowski, the gentlemanly Polish engineer who had come to Iceland for the innocent purpose of studying Iceland's hydroelectric techniques. Krog had dined with him, drunk with him, and played chess with him. And here he was in Krog's cabin, savaging an innocent girl like a demented fiend. It was all run together now. So many of Krog's questions answered, so many others raised.

Unless, in this rain and dark, he had made a mistake. It might not be Rozkowski but someone who resembled him, some drunken sex-crazy sailor, or an Icelander gone berserk because of the approaching dark season.

No. It was indeed Rozkowski. He hesitated in the light of the doorway as though listening, then hurried past the unseen Krog, stumbling up the slope to the road.

Krog lay where he was in the rain for another ten minutes, waiting to make sure Rozkowski was alone, wishing he had torn him to pieces. He walked slowly to the cabin. What he saw in the kitchen made him sink into a chair and weep. Krog could not recall the last time he had wept.

He had met Inga only that morning—at the telephone office in the village, where he offered her his place in line. She was a schoolteacher from Reykjavik, visiting relatives here in the east counties. They lunched together, went for a walk in the hills above the fjord, and then stopped for aquavit in his cabin. She had been the one who wanted to make love.

Casual about women, Krog had liked this Inga very much. As became a small person, she was fey and witty, charmingly impish, at once friendly and taunting. She liked his books, and his phonograph records, and his beard. She said she thought he must be one of the giants of Icelandic mythology and asked whether he knew any elves or trolls. He said: "Only you."

Now she lay half-naked, dumped face-down like so much refuse in an enormous pool of her own blood, having committed no crime but meeting the wrong man on very much the wrong day.

Still uncomprehending, he filled a glass with aquavit and sat pondering his circumstance, as he might have one of his engineering problems.

Though he had not taken the Americans' warning very seriously, he had followed their every instruction in precise detail: telephoning the prearranged number, mailing the overseas letter as required, leaving Akureyri at once for this summer cabin, and telephoning again with a prearranged message to confirm his arrival. They had said that they would have him out within the week, and that all seemed well.

Krog had never in his life felt so helpless. His instincts were to do what was required of him by Icelandic law, but he could not do that. The nearest county police were in Egilsstadir, a two-hour drive even in good weather. The village telephone office was closed, and there was no point in seeking help from the villagers. Inga was of a local family and he was a stranger whose presence was already viewed as suspicious. Were one of the local fishermen to see what had been done to Inga, he'd be flayed to pieces with boat hooks, no matter what his explanation.

A woman, liquor, a kitchen knife, the darkening time of the year—it all pointed to the only kind of murder Krog had ever heard about in Iceland. It was as logical as the truth was not.

It would accomplish little to hide Inga's body, even if he could bring himself to do it. Krog could not bear to look at her again. As it was, they'd doubtless have him in a cell in Kopavogur as soon as they clapped hands on him. Ultimately, his best hope lay with the Americans, but not now. He would figure this out—he would figure out many things—but for now he would avoid the Americans.

He wondered whether the Russians might in some way prove to be a help. They were out to kill him, but he could trust them—trust them to act entirely in their own interest. The Icelandic election was a month away. He might yet be able to draw them out with some sort of negotiation. They obviously weren't aware of all the documents—engineering papers in a folder still on top of the one small bookcase in the cabin, the notebooks he had left with a friend in Reykjavik.

Why had Rozkowski left without looking for these things? Inga. Poor Inga had performed a great if inadvertent service for her country. And for him. If he had not met her that morning, he would surely now be dead.

He swore a silent promise of repayment over his glass of aquavit and drank it—all of it. A tiny noise attracted his attention, the ticking of the small portable clock in the bedroom. He looked at his watch with some urgency. Rozkowski might be coming back—with friends. Even if not, providing he could elude the police and find sanctuary, he'd dare not waste another moment.

There was no logical escape by conventional means. There were very few roads in Iceland, especially here in the eastern counties. Even if he could extricate his car from the mud, which he doubted, he would still be only a few hours along the coastal road by the time Inga's body was discovered. The airport at Egilsstadir was closer, but the first flight to Reykjavik didn't leave until late morning. Krog was himself a pilot, but an attempt to steal an aircraft would be a great risk—if there happened to be any parked at that small airport.

Stealing a boat would be quite easy, but pointless. The weather was impossible and the nearest foreign lands were inhospitable Greenland or the Faroe Islands, more than four hundred miles away. The Icelandic Coast Guard had a patrol plane, a helicopter, and six fast patrol vessels. Wherever Krog turned in his mind, he saw himself in the grasp of the Rannsoknarlogregla Rikisins, Iceland's state criminal police.

Krog was a poor spy, but a good historian. It had become clear to him what he must do, terrifyingly clear.

In the olden times, Icelandic justice had been as cruel and swift as any other medieval European land's, with beheadings, mutilation, and torture prescribed for a wide variety of offenses. But the ancient Icelandic legal code contained another punishment that people of those times considered as bad as all the others, if not worse: banishment.

Upon conviction of a crime, the banished person was given the distance of the flight of an arrow, or two or three times that, to flee. Once beyond that distance, he was for the term of his banishment an outlaw. He was denied every protection of the law and could be robbed, beaten, or killed with impunity. He was banned from all human habitation. Any person who gave shelter or succor to the banished was automatically sentenced to the same punishment.

In that harsh and cruel environment, a year's banishment could mean death. There was no escaping Iceland. The visits of ships were rare and celebrated events, and ships stopped chiefly at settled places where a banished person would be killed on sight. The only refuge for the outlaw was the countryside, then as now among the most forbidding the world possessed.

The longest anyone had survived in the Icelandic wild under banishment was seventeen years: Grettim Asmundsson had brought his wife into banishment with him and formed an outlaw band. Asmundsson's sentence had been eighteen years. He died a year before it was up.

The greatest Icelandic outlaw, though, had been the legendary Eyvind of the Hills, a philosophical fellow, Iceland's Robin Hood. One of Krog's heroes.

Now Geir Krog was little different from Eyvind of the Hills. Krog, who thought himself a patriot, who had broken no law and served only what he saw as his country's best interest, was now a banished person. He would be hunted throughout the island, not only by the police but by the men who had come to kill him. He would have to take to the wild and think his way out of this problem from there.

Hurriedly, he changed to warmer clothes and stout hiking boots, filling his backpack with extra clothing, food, and essentials. The last included two books: *Njal's Saga*, the most famous of Iceland's medieval sagas, and the *Edda* of Snorri Sturlsson, the thirteenth-century poet and politician who'd been hunted down and put to death by the king of Norway. Krog added the papers from the bookcase, wrapping them carefully in plastic, and his last bottle of aquavit. He did not neglect to bring his sheath knife, his only weapon.

Before leaving, he took a piece of notepaper and wrote upon it a single sentence: "I did not kill this woman. G. Krog." He set it carefully upon the kitchen table; then, shouldering his heavy pack, he walked out of the cabin without looking behind, heading away from the village, toward the mountains. In the darkness, he saw nothing but Inga's face. And her bloody body. To keep his mind from that, he turned to his puzzle, his game of chess. It was clear now that the Russian endgame was concerned with electricity, massive amounts of electricity, considerably more electricity than might be required for the aluminum plant that was at the heart of Erikisson's naive bargain. To what civilized purpose would the Russians put so much electricity? And why in Iceland? And why the word "Valkyrie"? The Valkyries were spirits of death.

Krog did not know the answers, but he thought he could guess them. He felt colder than he had ever felt in his life.

Commander Richards had gone to the officers' club out of boredom and had left it out of boredom, deciding to return to his office to write a letter to his wife—one of his few escapes.

Richards liked Iceland but despised Keflavik. Clinging to a barren, gale-swept peninsula twenty miles west of the capital at Reykjavik, the navy air base, with its barbed-wire fences and yellow wooden buildings, resembled a prison and functioned as one. That's how the Icelanders liked it. So paranoid were they about the supposed American threat to their old Norse culture that the government had required the navy to shut down its armed forces network television transmitter and hook up its base television sets to a closed circuit system instead. Fraternization with Icelanders was rigidly discouraged, especially between Icelandic women and American enlisted men. Occasionally, a busload of Icelandic girls might be brought to the base for a Saturday night dance, but otherwise there were only glimpses of Icelandair stewardesses when they debarked over at the civilian side of the airfield. Sometimes Richards thought they might all be better off stationed at the air base in Thule, Greenland, where the only temptation was provided by an occasional drunken Eskimo woman, smelling of urine and sweat.

Iceland was a constant and infuriating temptation. Its women were unusually attractive and sexually uninhibited to the point where prostitution was virtually nonexistent. The government regularly reported the illegitimate birth rate among its vital statistics. It had recently risen from twenty-five to thirty percent.

None of this was for the Americans. For them, there were movies, closed circuit television, Saturday night dances, and drunken evenings in the base clubs. Richards' job at least took him around the country, frequently to Reykjavik, and involved him in a number of embassy social functions as well. Still, he had been with a woman only twice in seven months' time. When Richards had first come to Iceland, he had dutifully written his wife once a week. Now he was writing two or three times a week, and his letters were often highly erotic.

Commander Richards was the base intelligence officer. He had just turned forty, but perceptions of his age depended entirely upon whether he was standing or sitting, for he was one of those very tall persons whose height is mostly in his legs. Seated, he seemed middle-aged, overweight, and balding. Standing, he struck people as a younger, brawny man with blond hair. It was rumored that he had been passed over for an early promotion to captain because of his penchant for rumpled uniforms and unpolished shoes.

His pocket beeper commenced its irritating little peeping just as he was opening his door. The base joke was that he and the unit meteorologist were the only ones with anything to do.

Dropping his coat on a side table, unmindful of its slide to the floor, Richards slumped into his creaking chair and called the message center. He sat scowling at the scrambler phone a long moment before picking it up again. It was ridiculous enough that Whelan had been sent to Iceland with the title of embassy cultural attaché as his cover, but for the cultural attaché to be making regular calls to the base intelligence officer was slightly unsubtle. And the Russians listened to everything. The week before, an Icelandic trawlerman had picked up what looked like a rusting World War II relic floating mine. Upon opening it up, they had found a Soviet listening device good enough to pick up the sound of the admiral shaving.

Richards sighed and dialed the long number code. Whelan answered almost instantly and, typically, got immediately to his point.

"I'm looking for funnies," he said. "Yesterday, today, tonight, tomorrow."

"Funnies" was Whelanese for suspicious Soviet naval movements. Richards might have said that all Soviet naval movements were suspicious, except that he must have said that to Whelan a dozen times.

"I'll check," Richards said. "Will you be around?"

"Until you call. Hurry."

"Roger, Roger dodger, over and out."

Yawning, Richards ambled down the hall to the situation watch room, the most interesting place on the base. He had persuaded the admiral to replace nearly all the conventional North Atlantic wall maps with polar ones—graphic reminders of the startling proximity of the Soviet Union to North America across the pole, and of Iceland's extraordinary if too often ignored strategic importance. Iceland sat like an enormous aircraft carrier between Greenland and Norway, an island controlling the only three sea passages through which the Soviets could move their northern fleet vessels into the North Atlantic: the Greenland-Iceland Gap, the Faroes-Iceland Gap, and the Faroes-Scotland Gap.

The fluorescent dark-green screens of the room's video display terminals were the most graphic reminders of all. They showed blips of Soviet and NATO vessels in their approximate positions.

There were many Soviet blips. The northern fleet, the largest and most powerful of the Soviet four, was based just fifteen hundred miles away at Murmansk and adjacent ports on the Kola Peninsula. The northern fleet now included more than seventy combat surface ships—two aircraft carriers, nine guided missile cruisers, seven missile destroyers, and a horde of conventional frigates and destroyers. There were also no fewer than one hundred two submarines, other than sex, the major preoccupation of Richards' Icelandic life.

The NATO blips were sparse: a couple of submarines and a flotilla of eight frigates steaming toward Iceland for a goodwill visit.

Keflavik's principal mission was to monitor Russian naval traffic, which despite the approaching winter was assuming the proportions of a New York rush hour. This was one of the few missions the navy actually had equipment to perform. At its disposal were satellites, surface radar installations, and undersea SOSUS sensors that no one was supposed to know about, but everyone—including, no doubt, the local Saturday night dance girls—did. Recon hunter-killer subs worked the area as well—as did high-flying AWACS 707 jets carrying stuff in their radar domes that Russian scientists could only dream about, and the lumbering low-level P-3 Orion propeller patrol planes, which could drop sound detectors into the heaviest seas and follow a submarine wherever it went. The equipment was so sophisticated it could identify each individual Russian submarine by its engine and other noise "fingerprints."

Richards went to the VDT console of the ranking enlisted man in the room, a very youthful-looking chief petty officer named William Truscott. On the screen, the blip of a Russian "Charlie"-class submarine was being plotted by the computer on a course direct for the Icelandic coast.

"How long has he been on this course?" Richards asked.

"This Charlie?" said Truscott. "Twenty-two minutes, sir. We project him within two miles of the Seltjarnarnes Peninsula in maybe three hours. He's really breathing up our ass."

Truscott was a thin, pink-cheeked, black-haired man of thirty-one who looked twelve years younger and was as pronouncedly neat as Richards was not, though his language was not so pristine. Truscott probably owned twice as many dress uniforms as Richards, and a fairly elaborate civilian wardrobe. He seemed always able to wangle the rare pass or duty assignment off-base to make use of his civilian clothes. Richards had once encountered him in the bar of Reykjavik's Hotel Thor.

"Any others?" Richards asked.

"Nothing this close, sir. That flotilla off Jan Mayen Island has been edging toward us, and we're getting the usual grab-ass to the south."

Richards leafed through the computer printouts in the tray on Truscott's desk. The sub was the same one that had been loitering near Reykjavik a few days before. He went to a scrambler phone and called Whelan.

"We're afraid of a snatch," Whelan said. "This looks likely."

"Do you want me to request some additional patrols?" Richards said. "An intercept? Should we alert the Icelandic Coast Guard?"

"Negative. Let's stay normal. But if that sub gets close enough for a snatch, I want to know. Instanter. What about yesterday? What previous?"

"Nothing nearby," Richards said. "Nothing suspiciously

suspicious. Tonight's the first. He's really suspicious. He's coming at us so straight on he might as well be using his siren and searchlights."

"Always suspect the obvious. I'm going to the admiral's. Call."

Richards returned to Truscott, who was looking through a new copy of *Penthouse* magazine.

"You're sure this is all?" said Richards, studying the VDT screen. "Nothing off the east coast?"

"No, sir. Just some trawlers. They'll be in for a bad night. There's a real mother-fucker of a storm out there."

The dark-green glow of the screen struck Richards as the way the seas in those waters must look. "I'm going back to the officers' club," he said. "If the sub comes within twelve miles, call me at once."

"Aye aye, sir. Sir? This election. Do you think the Communists are going to win?"

"Beats the hell out of me," said Richards.

"Well, if they win, do we all get to go home?"

Richards glanced down at the magazine. Truscott had it opened to a picture of a very beautiful young woman who appeared to be posing for her gynecologist. "Never happen," he said. "No such luck."

The crew of the Icelandic Coast Guard's small patrol vessell *Heimdallur* knew about the storm off the east coast first hand. The one-hundred-seventy-five-foot ship had rounded the cape at Bakkagerdi and was plowing through thick rain and heavy seas on a course due south. The captain, Birgir Ragnarsson, had thought he would make a run past one or two of the major fjords in case any of the fishing craft were in trouble. If not, he would head into one of the fjords himself and seek shelter for the night. They would not be able to tie up in time for dinner—which was just as well, since it was salt cod night and he would prefer a sandwich on the bridge—but they might take some late coffee and ice cream in comfort.

There was an American movie on television. Ragnarsson's crew had earned some relief.

The *Heimdallur* was meeting quartering seas, kicking up a violent explosion of spray and rolling hugely to one side or the other with each encounter. The weather forecast had been for force-ten winds, but these seemed even higher, shrieking out of the southeast and driving the rain almost horizontally across the bridge windows.

The captain perched with practiced ease on a stool bolted to the deck near the starboard windows, sipping as casually from a steaming cup of coffee as though the *Heimdallur* were anchored in some quiet lake. Ragnarsson had a peculiar face, as lined and weathered as one might expect from twenty-two years in the Coast Guard, yet very childlike, even elfin—especially when his humor was showing.

He was wearing slippers, white wool socks, khaki uniform pants, a frayed khaki shirt, and an old sweater—his customary garb when away from shore. Very unmilitary, as his country preferred. Despite its Viking heritage and the fury it had recently shown in the face of the British, Iceland had a pacifist tradition and cherished it. The country had no army; only a four-hundred-seventy-five-man police force. Instead of a navy, it had merely the Coast Guard.

During the cod war, the international press had insisted upon calling the patrol craft "gunboats," but to Iceland they were merely an extension of the police force, and the armaments on the *Heimdallur* were typical: an 1898 Swedish two-pounder deck gun, two World War II surplus bolt-action rifles, and some .45 caliber automatic pistols.

Though commands were regularly rotated in the Icelandic Coast Guard, Ragnarsson had had the *Heimdallur* throughout much of the cod war. He had fired that old deck gun only twice, and just once in anger. Mostly the cod war had been a business of bumpings, rammings, and trawler line cuttings—a nasty business, but something for which the *Heimdallur* was well suited. Launched in 1965, it was the fastest in the Icelandic fleet, as fast as any of the British frigates. Unlike the thin-skinned frigates, the *Heimdallur* was built very much like a tank. A ram from it was not a frivolity. The British had had to bring in four huge ocean-going tugs to compete.

Ragnarsson gulped the last of his coffee. "Mind the drift to starboard," he said quietly to the helmsman. "We don't want to put ashore tonight upside down on some rock."

"Yes, sir."

The man shifted the wheel, edging the little ship closer to the wind. Ragnarsson could instantly tell the difference, though no landsman could have.

The captain had put his second officer, a bearded youth named Throstur, in charge for the evening watch, but with the deteriorating weather Ragnarsson had thought it better to be on the bridge. Throstur was from the rugged Westmann Islands just off Iceland's south coast and an excellent seaman, but Ragnarsson was fussy. He had never lost a crewman, not even in the cod war.

Ragnarsson was one of the heroes of that strange affair, having cut the nets of more British trawlers than any other Icelandic captain save one. The others had fought their war with gruff bravado, bearing down on the British fishermen and frigates like crazed Vikings. Ragnarsson had relied entirely on wile, sneaking into the midst of the British fishing fleet disguised as a small freighter on one night, abruptly appearing out of the densest fog on the next. He was very good in fog.

Ragnarsson poured himself more coffee and then joined Throstur at the radar screen. The radar was set at its shortest and most accurate range, able to detect in detail the smallest rocky islets in their path. A small blip flared with the sweep, then slowly faded until ignited again by the next sweep.

"We've picked up someone," said Throstur.

"So I see," said Ragnarsson. "A little fellow. He seems close enough to Heklafjordur to make it on his own."

"Yes, sir, but he is not making for the fjord. He is heading the opposite way."

It was true. Ragnarsson studied the radar screen, rubbing his chin. By its size and speed, he judged the craft to be a small trawler. But there was no fishing to be done on a night like this; certainly no Icelander would be fool enough to try it.

"Maybe he is trying for another fjord," suggested Throstur.

"No. His course is southeast, directly out to sea. Alter course to overtake him." Ragnarsson leaned back against the bulkhead with his coffee, watching as new navigational numbers appeared on the digital face of the Loran gear. Then he leaned close to the radar screen again. "I wonder who he is, this boy. Is he crazy?"

"Wind's up to force eleven, Captain," said Throstur.

"Probably will go higher," said Ragnarsson. "We won't stay out long. We'll make for Faskrudsfjordur after this. Ice cream and coffee." He drummed his fingers by the edge of the screen for a moment, then on impulse clicked the radar range up to the maximum—fifty miles. Two large blips appeared with the first sweep. The little trawler's course was toward them.

"Well, well, well," said Ragnarsson. "This little fellow has friends. Two big friends."

There had been one of those huge Russian factory trawlers operating in these waters in recent days. Now there were two. Under their fishing agreement with Iceland, the Russians were limited to redfish and capelin, but there hadn't been enough of a catch to keep one of those big factory ships busy for a month.

"Is the radio monitor on?" Ragnarsson asked, still watching the screen.

"Yes, sir," said Throstur.

One of the few pleasures of the cod war had been the radio chatter among the British trawlermen. They talked to one another all day long and far into the night, bantering back and forth in their thick Hull and Grimsby accents as though they were idling in a bar: "fooking fish," and "the fooking weather," and "fooking Icelanders." Now, years later, the radio was mostly silent, in keeping with the dark and empty sea.

In some ways, Ragnarsson missed those Britishers. He lit his pipe.

"More speed," he said to Throstur.

Ragnarsson had once stopped and boarded one of those Russian factory trawlers. He had long been curious about the Soviets' penchant for fishing in strange weather and fishless waters. Catching one excessively close to shore, he had it heave to and went aboard. He found no violations of fishing regulations, no illegal catch, in fact practically no fish at all. The Russians had complained to the Icelandic government, and it had complained to Ragnarsson. The Russians were NATO's enemy, but supplied Iceland with all its oil.

Something blurted forth from the radio monitor—a few quick words uttered in a language Ragnarsson did not understand. After a brief silence, the words were repeated, followed this time by a low, gruff reply.

"What language is that?" said Ragnarsson. "Russian?"

"I think Polish," said the young second officer.

"How do you know Polish? You've never been beyond the Faroe Islands."

"I got drunk once with some Polish sailors in the bar of the Hotel Thor," Throstur said.

"It is expensive to get drunk in the bar of the Hotel Thor," said Ragnarsson. His tone was stern. His feelings were fatherly toward Throstur, whose own father had died when he was an infant.

"They paid."

"Yes? What did they ask you? How we beat the British? If we have a secret weapon?"

"All they asked was how I felt about the Americans."

"Yes? What did you tell them?"

"That I liked them."

"Very good. But in the future, don't drink with Polish sailors. Drink with Finns. They get drunk without asking questions. They get drunk so quickly they are never able to ask questions."

The helmsman called out: "I see his lights, Captain."

Ragnarsson padded in his slippers to the forward windows

of the bridge, peering through the arc of the slowly moving wiper blades. The trawler was off the starboard bow, quite small, rolling and pitching with wide swings of its running lights.

"Come alongside, as close as you can," Ragnarsson said. He went to the radio, tapping the microphone against his cheek for a moment as the *Heimdallur* rose upon a huge wave and turned broadside to the nearing trawler.

"This is Icelandic Coast Guard patrol vessel *Heimdallur,*" he said in English into the microphone. "Do you need assistance?"

There was no response. The two craft heaved and rolled close enough for Ragnarsson to see a brief flare of light in the side window of the trawler's wheelhouse. He thought he saw a face, someone lighting a cigarette.

"He's turning away," said Throstur.

"Stupid fellow," said Ragnarsson. He put the microphone to his mouth again and repeated his message more loudly, in English again, and then in Icelandic. The little trawler lunged on, heeling away, turning its stern to them.

"Son of a bitch," said Ragnarsson. "These are Icelandic waters. Where is their respect? Pull forward of him and we'll come across his bow."

The deck vibrated with the thrust of the *Heimdallur*'s two powerful engines as they accelerated. A great wave immediately cascaded over the bow, rolling over the gun mount and slamming into the superstructure of the bridge, a slab of spray thudding against the windows. Ragnarsson wondered how the little trawler was staying afloat.

"Halloo there!" Ragnarsson shouted into the microphone. "Halloo, halloo!"

No response. *The Heimdallur* had knifed ahead of the smaller vessel and, with Throstur commanding the helmsman, was turning slantwise across the trawler's course.

"Full stop," said Ragnarsson.

With a shudder, the *Heimdallur* settled fully into the water, broadside to the trawler's bow.

"That does it," said Throstur. "He's stopping."

"Halloo, halloo!" said Ragnarsson into the microphone. "This is Icelandic Coast Guard patrol vessel *Heimdallur*. Identify yourself, please, and advise if you need assistance."

There was finally a response, in English.

"We are Polish People's Republic fishing vessel *Waldemar Dulski*. We are on course for Faroe Islands en route to home port of Gdansk. We require no assistance."

"He sounds grumpy," Ragnarsson said. In calmer weather, he would have boarded her.

Throstur was watching the radar screen. The two big factory ships were under way and heading toward them.

Ragnarsson had seen enough. He took up the microphone one last time and said: "Good luck, little *Waldemar Dulski*. It is a very long way to Gdansk. Bye-bye.

"All right," he said to Throstur. "We'll make course for Faskrudfjordur. No, Reydarfjordur. It has better television reception."

"What's the movie tonight?"

"It's a cowboy film—a good one, starring Audie Murphy."

Ragnarsson went to the chart table and made a long entry in his log about the trawler encounter. He would follow it with a routine report, but nothing more provocative. If he was going to get in trouble again for meddling with the Russians, he would wait for an opportunity to really meddle with them.

Magnus Andersson sat uncomfortably at his desk at police headquarters in Kopavogur, outside Reykjavik. He held his throbbing head with both hands as he looked over the front page of *Kvoldbladid*, the largest of Reykjavik's six daily newspapers. There were articles on the forthcoming election, but no news of enough consequence to make him force himself to read any story in detail. Andersson leaned back, rubbing his aching eyes. All Icelanders treasured sunshine, but the glare in the window from the late rising sun was more than he could bear.

As befitted a policeman and an inordinately serious man,

Andersson seldom drank. He had gone months without so much as a bottle of Iceland'a anemic Thule beer. Since his wife's death he had devoted his life to his work and his reading, and alcohol interfered with both.

Last night, he had made an exception. He had planned to confine himself as usual to a glass of wine with dinner, but the host of the party insistently thrust an after-dinner glass of Bisquit cognac upon him. Then, in the living room, Elisabet Bjornsdottir sat next to him, talked with him, danced with him, and so delightfully disconcerted him that he had accepted two more brandies. Or was it three? In any event, he left his car with his host and walked home—rather giddily. It would certainly not have done for a policeman to be arrested for drunken driving, especially the policeman who for the next few weeks would be serving as acting superintendent of the Rannsoknarlogregla Rikisins, Iceland's state investigative police.

Elizabet Bjornsdottir was an extraordinary woman, as intoxicating as the Bisquit. He had encountered her only twice before the party—once at a reception in the Hotel Loftleider and again when he was a passenger on an Icelandic Airlines flight to New York. Elisabet was a stewardess but something more than that, a poet who had published two collections of her verse and an occasional model for Samband of Iceland and other designers.

She was tall, with long legs and neck, and brown hair that she wore very long. Her eyes were a luminescent gray that reminded Magnus of the color of a rushing glacier stream. Her skin was flawless, with a propensity to tan quite rare in an Icelander. The deep neckline of her blouse had revealed the curve of her breast to him once when she had leaned forward for her glass. He remembered that, and the feeling of the touch of her hand on his.

Andersson shook his head free of such thoughts. Of all the men in Iceland who might have attracted Elisabet Bjornsdottir for five minutes, Magnus would have counted himself among the very last. He was thirty-seven and looked much older, with unhappy dark eyes set in a narrow, gray face and dark hair and beard. With his glasses on, he looked quite bookish, and appropriately so. He, too, wrote poetry.

The harsh jangle of the telephone made him start. As he reached for the receiver, he thought the call must be from the hospital where the superintendent was undergoing his operation that morning. Instead, it was some county police official on the other side of the island. The man hesitated, a nervous catch to his voice, then proceeded to relate the details of one of the most gruesome murders Andersson had ever heard of in all his years as a policeman. The circumstances formed something of a familiar pattern, however. A small, isolated cabin. A violent quarrel. The darkening time of the year. And liquor. There had been an open bottle of aquavit near the body.

The local police had identified a suspect—the man who had rented the cabin, a hydroelectric engineer from Akureyri named Geir Krog. Andersson knew of the man. He was one of Iceland's better chess players. Krog had fled but had left his car behind and stolen no other. This was peculiar. There were other peculiarities. The girl's relatives lived in the village but knew nothing about Krog. And Krog had left a note behind, stating simply that he had not committed the crime.

Andersson rubbed his eyes again, letting the telephone line fall silent for a moment. This was going to have to be a major effort. He would have to put detectives in all the airports. Was Krog a pilot? They would have to put up roadblocks on the coastal road. The Coast Guard would have to be alerted. No effort could be spared to apprehend Krog. But there was something bothersome about this.

"Close the road to Heklafjordur and let no one in or out," Andersson said finally. "Keep someone with the girl's family. I'll have detectives there as soon as I can."

He paused. He was in no mood for an airplane ride that morning.

"And I'll come out myself," he said.

4

Laidlaw, Mendelsohn, and Thorn met in what Laidlaw's generation of intelligence operatives referred to as a "safe house." The younger Thorn called it a "spook house." Mendelsohn, in his eerie, metaphysical way, described it as a "sanctum." It was an old white colonial manor house near McLean, Virginia, not far from the Central Intelligence Agency headquarters in Langley.

They were in an ultrasecure room in the basement—a pleasant chamber, paneled and warmly lit. Were it not for all the maps, graphs, screens, and television equipment, it might have passed for a corporate boardroom or a wealthy psychiatrist's office. There was a long table in the middle, and the three men sat in a row along one side of it, the better to share the contents of the single file in front of them. It bore the name "Spencer, John August." It was surprisingly thick.

Bill Thorn was the only one of the three still on the agency's active payroll. Laidlaw had taken an early retirement from the agency four years before and had been called back as a consultant. Mendelsohn, a loyal follower of Richard Helms and a spiritual disciple of James Angleton, had been involuntarily retired in the great purge that had driven those two from their thrones after Watergate.

A large muscular man who had worn a crewcut for much of his life, Thorn was definitely new breed. His background was engineering—three degrees plus six years as a rocketry officer in the Air Force. He was ferociously aggressive and full of jargon, much of it of his own devise. Laidlaw called the Iranians "the mullahs." To Mendelsohn, they were "the maniacal Persians." Thorn called them "the cruds"—not to be confused with the Kurds, whom Thorn called "the milkeaters." Thorn had three children, lived in the Virginia suburbs, rode a racing bicycle on weekends, and had killed a man in Turkey. He was spoken of as being in line to take over the entire Russian section, which his less-macho contemporaries thought wonderfully appropriate.

Hugh Laidlaw was old school, a man whose politics, class origins, and intelligence were well advertised by his appearance. Habitually well-scrubbed and neat, he wore round horn-rimmed glasses and kept his white hair parted in the middle. Much given to corduroy and tweed, bow ties, argyle socks, and brown oxfords, Laidlaw always carried books about with him, or periodicals such as the *New Republic* or *Foreign Policy*.

Laidlaw had come to Washington and the agency almost directly from Harvard in the late 1940s. More than thirty years later, his Rooseveltian and Stevensonian liberalism was still intact. The United States had a mission and all that stood in its way were the Republican Party and the Soviet Union. Possessing an inordinately high IQ, even by agency standards, Laidlaw's views were of course considerably more complicated than that, but those were his basic leanings.

He was at once disgusted, frightened, and fascinated by the Russians. He knew them intimately, having served in a number of posts in Eastern Europe and ultimately as station chief in Berlin. His last job had been overseeing Scandinavia and the North Atlantic. He had retired several years earlier than he needed to, amusing himself since then with the writing of travel books—a pursuit he was sure was proving wonderfully frustrating to the Russians assigned to find some code in them. To his mind, Laidlaw had retired quite honorably. There was nothing in his résumé that had to do with Laos, Cambodia, or Vietnam.

Thorn called it "Nam." Mendelsohn, like the Chinese, referred to "the Lost Provinces."

Mendelsohn, as befitted his age, was from the CIA's oldest guard. As a graduate student at the University of Chicago studying classics, he had drifted into uniform with millions of other Americans in World War II and just as haphazardly drifted into General Donovan's OSS. He had easily survived the transformation of the organization into the CIA and plunged into the Cold War with relish. It suited the dark nature of his intellectual curiosities, and he came quickly to worship his boss, Angleton, even adopting the same rumpled Ivy League suits. Mendelsohn's genius was intuitive and remarkable—and sorely missed. This was the third time since his ouster that he had been brought back to work on a project as a consultant.

The project the three had been assigned to involved an interesting problem. It was called World War III.

On one of the walls was a large framed chart, copies of which could be found in a number of CIA and Pentagon offices. The horizontal measure on the bottom set forth the two decades from 1970 to 1990. The perpendicular was a measure of strategic nuclear capability. The two lines—red and blue—that traveled across the chart reflected the United States' retaliatory nuclear capacity relative to the Soviets' first-strike capacity.

Throughout the 1970s the disparity had remained comfortably in the United States' favor. By 1981 the two lines had converged, with the relative American capability plunging and the disparity turning clearly in the Russians' favor. According to projections, the disparity would remain in the Russians' favor until 1985, when the United States would at last be deploying its sophisticated Cruise and Trident submarine missiles and bringing an MX system into line. Until then it was terrifyingly vulnerable. Naked, in front of the "window."

Using Pentagon jargon inspired by the shape of the lines on the chart, Thorn called this period of American vulnerability "the strategic bathtub." Laidlaw used Helms' phrase: "the window of danger," a wide-open window it would take four years to fully pass by.

Mendelsohn called it "the window of doom."

Thorn glanced at the "window" chart, then looked down at Spencer's file again, frowning. He had just come back from the White House, and he was always frowning when he did that.

"This would mean an end run," he said. "We might be able to pull that on the wimps, but the mossbacks are pretty smart." In Thorn's jargon, "the wimps" meant the Carter administration; "the mossbacks" meant the Republicans who came after.

"Though not, alas, smart enough," said Mendelsohn. "They remain obdurate."

"Yes, indeedy do," said Thorn. "Thick of skull, every one of them. I got up as high as Baxter this time, but he gave me the same old crap. Yes, they buy the 'window of danger.' Yes, they agree that World War III is going to be a come-as-you-are war, and that we're not very well dressed. They buy that the Redskies can take out every goddamn one of our fixed-silo Minutemen and most of our Polaris subs and B-52s whenever they want, that what we face here is like a World War II in which Pearl Harbor is the only battle. What they won't buy is that the Russians will actually do it."

"Did you make mention of the five-city scenario?" Laidlaw asked. Years before, Laidlaw and an Air Force colonel had been the ones to devise that theory: Instead of an all-out nuclear exchange, instead of a preemptive nuclear strike aimed at Washington and our military command centers, the Soviets would use the "window" to eliminate the Minutemen, submarines, and B-52s, but the Kremlin marshals would go no further. Their next move would be to issue an ultimatum: End the war now, on our terms, or our next attack will be on five American cities. If several million New Yorkers were then to be broiled into a radioactive gel, the American President would have only himself to blame.

According to the scenario, the choice would be between surrender and death, surrender meaning the gift of Europe and the Middle East to the Soviets; death meaning simply death.

"Yeah," Thorn said. "He hadn't even heard it before. I swear, these guys are supposed to be paranoid about the Red Menace, but all they ever worry about is guerrillas in Central America."

"What did Baxter say about the five-city scenario?" asked Laidlaw. His voice was very calm and quiet, his words evenly measured. Thorn sometimes complained that Laidlaw talked like a golf announcer.

"He doesn't think the Reds would try it," Thorn said. "We'd still have enough stuff left to paste 'em good, he says. Even if they could keep their losses down to twenty million, that's what they lost in World War II. They wouldn't want to go through that again, Baxter says."

"It is precisely because the Soviet Union survived the war despite twenty million casualties that they would be willing to try it again," Mendelsohn said.

"You tell him that, Freddy," Thorn said. "On second thought, don't. He thinks you're a weirdo."

"I believe in the five-city scenario," Mendelsohn said. "I am devout."

Mendelsohn thought the Russians capable of nuclear warfare because it was natural to their ruthless, xenophobic, misanthropic culture. If a civilized nation like the United States could wage atomic war, as it did in 1945, why have doubts about the bestial Russians?

Thorn believed them capable of pushing The Button because it was the obvious and logical thing for them to do. Their weapons systems were designed for offensive attack, not deterrence. They had a need. Though they exported some oil to Warsaw pact countries and Iceland, their reserves were dwindling. A natural hunger impelled them toward the Mideast. They had opportunity. The "window" gave them that.

They had urgency. The Republicans in the White House were trying to close the "window."

Laidlaw agreed with Mendelsohn and Thorn, but his fear of imminent Russian attack was grounded in something else: the Russians' traditional conservatism.

As with Hungary in 1956, Czechoslovakia in 1968, and Afghanistan in 1979, they acted only when sure of success, only when sure that risk had been reduced to an absolute minimum.

And now the risks attendant to a nuclear strike had been reduced to that minimum, or shortly would be.

"What did Baxter say about the charged-particle beam weapon?" Laidlaw asked.

"Same old mossback crap," said Thorn. " 'Space technology. They can't get one up on a satellite before we do.' I tell you, we're dealing with the same great minds that thought up reactivating all those World War II battleships so admirals will have something big to ride on."

"Saryshagan," Mendelsohn said.

"Yeah, maybe I scored some points on that one. The Chinese are scared stiff about Saryshagan. The White House is interested in that."

"Saryshagan is irrelevant," Laidlaw said.

The concept of directed-energy weapons was as old as Buck Rogers ray guns. One in a stage of widespread development was the laser, a concentrated beam of intensified light that could destroy a missile, satellite, or any other object up to twenty-five thousand miles away. But the laser, being light, could not effectively penetrate cloud cover or even heavy rain. Another directed-energy weapon could, the charged-particle beam. Squirting highly charged particles of atomic matter for thousands of miles in what might be described as a controlled lightning bolt, it was more powerful than the laser and could penetrate anything.

The charged-particle beam required enormous amounts of electricity and could only be fired in a straight, line-of-sight trajectory. But it could shoot down in an instant any ICBM that came its way. It could render the Minuteman rockets, B-52s, and Polaris submarines all but useless. It was the ultimate defensive weapon.

The United States, making up for the neglect of the Carter administration, was now spending a hundred million dollars on charged-particle beam research. A working model had been built and successfully tested in a laboratory in California.

The Soviet Union had one already deployed, a weapon a mile and a half long powered by a huge nuclear reactor, at Saryshagan in Kazakhistan, near the Chinese border. Another one, more compact, was being built southwest of Moscow. Those would deal with missiles fired from the Indian Ocean or Pacific. To reduce risk to an absolute minimum, the Kremlin marshals needed a charged-particle beam weapon that could cover the North American and North Atlantic missile approaches. If Laidlaw's educated guess was correct, they would have one in place soon.

"You did bring up Iceland?" Laidlaw asked.

"Wish I hadn't," Thorn said. "Now he thinks I'm as nutty as you two."

"It's not so preposterous," Mendelsohn said. "When the Murmansk fleet is out, Iceland, Norway, and Sweden are functionally behind Russian lines."

"If Baxter did believe the Redskies were looking for a CPB site up there, which he made maximum clear he does not," said Thorn, "he might buy Finland—"

"Too far east," said Mendelsohn.

"I know," Thorn said. "He might buy Spitzbergen Island—"

"The Norwegians would resist," Mendelsohn said. "The available electricity there is a small fraction of what would be required."

"I know," said Thorn. "But Baxter won't buy Iceland. He won't buy the Reds making moves on a member nation of NATO, especially one where we have a big air base."

"The illogicality of Iceland," said Mendelsohn, "is what makes it so logical."

"I know," said Thorn. "But I am not dealing with logical

people or even illogical people. I'm dealing with the White House. And the deputy is getting tired of my little jaunts over there. He may put me on a short leash after this one."

"You can't get any higher than Baxter?" Laidlaw asked.

"I'm not even sure I can get to him again," Thorn said.

"Then we've no recourse but the end run," Laidlaw said.

"Which brings us back to your interesting Mr. Spencer," said Mendelsohn. He pulled the file folder toward him, arching his brow as though he were about to undertake a critical examination of some painting.

"Give me that back, Freddy," said Thorn. "I'm the one who gives the no-go or go."

Thorn turned first to the photographs in the file, frowning slightly at the first one of Spencer, whistling when he came to one of Spencer's wife. It was an agency telephoto shot, taken of the two of them at a beach. Laidlaw glanced at the background of the photograph, deciding with only a moment's calculation that it had been taken at Cape Cod or the eastern end of Long Island.

"Turn to his reports," he said, when Thorn lingered just a trifle too long over Mrs. Spencer. "They're divorced. She's irrelevant."

Thorn did so, grunting. Laidlaw chided himself silently. In the spy business, nothing was irrelevant. Certainly not beautiful women.

"This guy's been useful," Thorn said, dropping the papers back into Spencer's file. "Really useful."

"That is why he's been brought along this far," said Laidlaw.

"This was really good stuff," said Thorn, thumping on the papers for emphasis. "The Mexican oil find in Tobasco. The Libyan-IRA connection. Fingering that Canadian turncoat in Beirut. How many actual agents have stuff like this in their records?"

"Journalists make the best spies," said Laidlaw. "It's in their nature."

Mendelsohn lit one of his long cigarettes—for some reason, he smoked Virginia Slims—and then smiled his eerie smile.

"Everything Spencer gave us he subsequently put into print in his newspapers," Mendelsohn said. "I don't believe he left out a fact. Not a semicolon."

"Mr. Spencer's penchant for publishing strengthens his cover," said Laidlaw, lighting his pipe in defense against Mendelsohn's cigarette smoke. "He has excellent credibility with the Icelanders. At some point, they're going to have to be convinced of this. They won't believe us. Spencer, they might."

"He covered that stupid cod war," said Thorn, turning to that page of the file.

"He was the only American journalist to do so from the Icelandic side," Laidlaw said. "Many of them think his articles were what persuaded us to lean on our British friends to get out."

"Probably were," said Thorn.

"The gentleman," said Mendelsohn, "is in less than sound health."

"Extremely unsound health," said Laidlaw, reaching for the proper paper in the file. "He has dangerously high blood pressure and a severely weakened artery in the brain. It's inoperable. To complicate things, I think he's an alcoholic."

"What if he keels over in the middle of this?" asked Thorn.

"What if someone shoots him in the middle of this?" replied Laidlaw. "We'll make do."

"You wish to play him as a wild card," said Mendelsohn, exhaling the words in an unfolding cloud of smoke.

"We've no choice," Laidlaw said, "with our other problem."

"The mole," said Thorn.

"Or moles," said Laidlaw.

Mendelsohn grimaced. Worse than jargon was cliché. "You've no doubt whatsoever about this problem," he said. Mendelsohn's questions were seldom uttered as questions.

"We've run a tracer through twice and gotten bumps each time," Laidlaw said. "What happened to Krog was a very large bump. There's a mole on that end, all right. I'm wondering if there's one on this end."

"I'd love to shut it down, good buddy," said Thorn. "The whole enchilada. Especially Whelan. He's put half the damn country on the payroll. But there's that sonofabitching Icelandic election. Anyway, if we lone-eagle this guy, who'll be his control?"

"I will," said Laidlaw, "from here. Iceland has first-rate telephone service. We can use the military if there's really serious mayday."

"I want a backup," said Thorn.

"Karin Nielsen," said Laidlaw.

Mendelsohn arched his eyebrows while lowering his eyelids disdainfully. He disliked the use of women in espionage, except as decoys, or whores.

Thorn rubbed his square jaw with his meaty hand. "No one knows I've got her stashed in Oslo," he said. "She's even off the active roster. But I was saving her for really hot stuff."

"This is," said Laidlaw, "really hot stuff." He made a face as disdainful as Mendelsohn's.

Thorn rubbed his jaw some more. "Okay," he said. "If we go with this guy, you can have Karin. I just have this feeling he'd drag her into the sack and they'd go off the job for a few weeks. I mean, this guy's a regular jackrabbit. How do we know he won't just take his expense money and spend it boozing and getting laid? Damn country's supposed to have some of the best-looking women in the world. The guy knows he's going to die. What a way to go."

"He's been going that way here in Washington for three months now," said Laidlaw. "He's tired of it. That's why he came to us."

Thorn scratched the top of his head.

"Will he buy this Iceland gig?" he asked.

"I hope so," said Laidlaw, "although I presume he'll be disinclined to it. I fear he's seeking a grander gesture. He considers his precarious health an asset. I think he expects to be parachuted into the Kremlin."

Mendelsohn groaned. "Life is but a stage," he said and lit another cigarette. "Death, too."

Thorn looked at his watch—an Eddie Bauer sportsman's underwater model—and pushed back his chair.

"Okay," he said. "Let's see if we have an asset."

Spencer crossed the Potomac into Virginia over Chain Bridge, turning his BMW onto the hilly road to McLean. The trees were still leafy enough to obscure the mansions from the commoners using the highway, giving the feeling of a country forest, not a suburb ten miles from the White House. It was a warm and perfect autumn afternoon, all golden and red against a cloudless blue sky. He reminded himself he should savor such days but could not keep his mind on the weather. He was driving faster than usual, jerking and spurting around the curves, spurred on for once not by escape but by anticipation. For the first time in months, his thoughts had found something happier than the moment.

He had gone for the CIA interview, which was cursory, and then stayed at their invitation for several more, which were not. They had kept him an hour after that filling out forms. Yet at the end they could only shrug and tell him he would have to wait—possibly for weeks. He had been on the verge of flinging himself and his hopes into the whiskey jug again when just two days later the call had come: the cheerfully officious voice of a high-ranking secretary. Could he meet with Mr. Laidlaw at his home in McLean the following afternoon?

Chesley had been horrified—as only Chesley could be horrified—when she first learned of his CIA work. She threatened to leave him if he did it again. In the midst of a screaming fight over it, she threatened to tell his news bureau. The result would have been a loss of his press credentials and his probable firing.

It angered Spencer that this should be so. Aside from minor expenses, he had never accepted any fee for these services. He had never let his association alter the character or the accuracy of his reporting. He knew newsmen who turned the truth upside down and stretched it six miles sideways to suit their prejudices. Half the British journalists Spencer knew were on their government's payroll. All the Soviet ones were. Spencer's only interest had been in helping his country even the odds a little. Yet it was grounds for the sack. The "free press" forever.

Spencer had no idea what the agency would offer him, if it offered him anything at all. He had been told only that the best he could look forward to was some temporary work in which he would go on the roster as a consultant. Spencer told them temporary work would be ideal, but the young bureaucrat conducting that interview had no ear for irony.

Spencer had already obtained a six months' leave of absence from his job. He told his bureau chief what the man already knew—that he had serious health, personal, and drinking problems. He needed time to work things out. He needed help. Would the company object? The bureau chief, as Spencer had expected, responded positively and with great relief. What the newspaper business would not forgive on the sneak, it forgave from the confessed and the repentant. The man gave Spencer his six months' leave with pay.

Following directions, he turned off the Dolley Madison Highway at Langley, passing by the main CIA entrance and continuing for another mile and a half. Then, as directed, he turned onto a side road barely wider than a driveway. The house, when he came to it, was as described: white, very large, with four pillars, set in heavy woods out of sight of any of its neighbors. There were a few signs of neglect about the place. The shiny Mercedes-Benz on the gravel drive indicated they were not to be attributed to a lack of funds. The owner, presumably, was a man preoccupied with other things.

Laidlaw answered the door, introducing himself. He looked wealthy and professorial—and a little eccentric. He had a book in his hand, Richard Nixon's *The Real War.*

Spencer followed him to the rear of the house where they

entered Laidlaw's study, a large but cluttered room with bookcases lining two of the walls and enormous multipaned windows filling the others. They seated themselves in leather chairs to the side of Laidlaw's desk. The stack of magazines on the low, dusty table in front of them had a copy of *Atlas World Press Review* on top.

After a few minutes of easy pleasantries, Laidlaw moved abruptly to the point. They would like to accept his offer. "Would you be willing to go to Iceland?"

Spencer was stunned. His mind had been full of the dusty streets of Teheran, the humid lush of Havana, a hundred other places. When drunk, he saw himself a figure in history. An American Roland. Iceland? He had not been there since 1976. The cod war had ended then, and there had been nothing for him there but the cod war, though he liked the strange little country and, before his affliction, had thought of taking a vacation there.

Laidlaw was that rare person who sat perfectly still, a quintessential example of repose but for the blink of his light blue eyes.

"I was hoping I might be of more use to you than that," Spencer said.

"Oh, there's a great deal you can accomplish for us," said Laidlaw with another quick smile. He shifted his position in the chair and then was motionless again. "Everyone is always so quick to belittle Iceland. You wrote that yourself in one of your dispatches."

"You read those?"

"Yours is a thick and interesting file, Mr. Spencer. Your articles, by the by, were extremely useful. They attracted the attention of the White House, as so little does, and encouraged some high-level twisting of the British arm. Quite frankly, I don't know where we would have been without your stories. We'd been warning for months that Iceland meant its threat to pull out of NATO if the British persisted, but, as happens so often, no one paid us any mind."

"The British are very contemptuous of small countries.

They were willing to destroy Iceland's entire economy just to protect fifteen thousand fishing jobs."

"So you wrote, Mr. Spencer. Very useful." Laidlaw had ever so delicately led him from his path.

"Mr. Laidlaw, I don't think you understand what I had in mind when I contacted your agency," Spencer said, staring down at the table top. "I'm not interested in just helping you out a little on the side, like before. I . . . my motivation . . ."

"You're referring to the state of your health."

Spencer lifted his eyes to Laidlaw's. "I have a terminal illness," he said.

"So you acknowledged on the questionnaire," Laidlaw said. "Though your condition is not absolutely, inescapably terminal. Highly dangerous, but not a closed book."

He pressed his palms together and leaned forward in his chair without shifting his steady gaze. His round spectacles made him quite owlish. "Mr. Spencer," he continued, "if what you had in mind was strapping hand grenades to your body and seeking an audience with some despot, then you'd best hire yourself out to a terrorist group. We are not in the business of assisting suicides. If anything, we would view your physical condition as a liability, as we would—as we do—your, uh, drinking habits. You've been quite helpful in the past, but at the moment you would have to be classified as something of a risk. Quite frankly, your generous offer was met with little interest or enthusiasm. We, the agency, were going to turn you down, I'm afraid. Until we thought of Iceland. We don't even have approval for that yet. Although I don't think there will be any problem."

Spencer wanted a drink, suddenly and desperately. However this interview concluded, he decided he would stop for a quick whiskey in Georgetown on the way home. Maybe two. "I just want to make a contribution," he said. "I'd like to do something meaningful."

"We view everything we do as meaningful," Laidlaw said. "We think Iceland extremely important. The Soviets' northern fleet has more than seventy surface ships, don't you know—more than one hundred submarines. Iceland stands directly in their path. Shall I be melodramatic and take you to my globe?"

It was an enormous globe, very expensive, set in a floor stand in the corner. Spencer shook his head.

"The Soviets," Laidlaw continued, pausing for emphasis, "think Iceland is very important indeed. There aren't many embassies in Reykjavik, but half of them are Warsaw Pact. The Russians have nearly a hundred people in their embassy alone. In per capita terms, that's like their having ten thousand people here in Washington."

"There are Republicans who think they do," Spencer said.

Laidlaw made a face.

"What do you want me to do?" Spencer asked, staring down at the table again. He was thinking hard about Iceland. He had hated the weather, but the country had fascinated him, as had the women. Could the CIA really be all that worried about Iceland? The United States had the air base at Keflavik to lose. And there really were a lot of Russians there.

Laidlaw looked at his watch. It was gold, very expensive-looking, but he wore it on an old leather strap. "It's just past three o'clock," he said. "On weekend afternoons I like to indulge myself with an occasional martini. Would you join me? Or would you prefer scotch? I'm not sure what we have."

"A martini would be very nice right now."

Spencer remained in his chair until Laidlaw had left the room, then rose and began walking about it. The view from the windows was filled with hills and trees. Iceland was forbidding, barren mountains and mossy hills, rocks and swift-running glacier streams. No trees, or at least very, very few of them. His gunboat captain in the cod war had said his favorite place in the world was Hawaii. It was just like Iceland, except that it had warmth and trees.

Iceland. At the time, he had even thought it might be an interesting place to die, to greet eternity, an eternal sort of place. What had prompted that gloomy thought? Would he indeed die there?

The sounds Laidlaw made with his drink preparations were distant. Casually, Spencer went to the man's desk. There was nothing amid the clutter that seemed to have anything to do with Iceland. One file had a green cover sheet marked "EXDIS," the word "Valkyrie" appearing beneath. He opened it quickly and glanced at a few pages. The language was quite technical. There were diagrams and illustrations of what looked to be some sort of laser. What a dull job.

He could hear a martini shaker. Laidlaw had old-fashioned habits. Moving to one of the bookcases, Spencer was astonished to find only the ordinary—classics, a few not very recent bestsellers. Nothing that would be very edifying or useful to someone like Laidlaw. And they were dusty.

He returned to his chair. Beneath the copy of the *New Republic* on the table was a *New Yorker*. Beneath that was a very old copy of a horseman's magazine. The rest of the stack was horsemen's magazines, all very old.

Laidlaw returned carrying a full martini shaker and two long-stemmed glasses on a small, slightly tarnished silver tray. He poured very deftly without speaking. Spencer had not been served a martini in this fashion for at least ten years. He sipped it and found it perfect, taste and icy temperature just as he expected.

"Before we proceed any further," said Laidlaw, resuming his seat, "may I assume at this point that you're willing to assist us in this matter? It won't take long. Two or three weeks, I should think."

"I have two or three weeks," Spencer said. He took another, larger sip.

"My question, Mr. Spencer."

"I'll do it," said Spencer. "Of course. But what is it you want me to do?"

"There's an election in Iceland this month."

Spencer nodded. Laidlaw lifted his eyebrows in query.

"There are only some twenty functioning democracies

left," Spencer said. "I cover the State Department. They keep track of these things."

"Are you acquainted with the political situation in Iceland?" Laidlaw asked. Spencer shook his head.

"The true Communists, the Workers' and Farmers' Party, have a chance to win this one so overwhelmingly they can take the government without a coalition. They can even do without the People's Alliance. Inflation is now running at fifty-six per cent in Iceland. People are getting a bit desperate. The other four parties have had the government and failed. Gunnar Erikisson, the leader of the Communists, has promised to cut inflation in half. We think he can deliver. As you may know, Iceland imports all its oil from the Soviet Union. They've been charging top dollar, but they don't have to. We've reason to believe Erikisson has made an arrangement."

"Cut a deal? For what? To get us out of that air base? Get Iceland out of NATO?"

Laidlaw smiled.

"That's the obvious thing," he said. "The Workers' and Farmers' Party has always vowed to do that. It's a possibility. But I'm not all that certain the Icelandic people would stand still for such a sudden shift in foreign policy. I think the Russians are after something more subtle. They're certainly after something. They've poured ten times the money into this election as they usually do."

"What do you want me to do? Fix the election?"

Laidlaw's smile was reluctant. "We don't do those things anymore, Mr. Spencer," he said. "We confine ourselves to gathering intelligence. That's what we want from you. We would like you to find out what the Russians want, which is to say, we want you to find someone who we think knows what the Russians want."

Spencer stared blankly. He was tiring of Laidlaw's pregnant pauses.

"His name is Geir Krog. He's a hydroelectrical engineer from Akureyri. You remember Akureyri? He's also a geologist, a mountain climber, a chess player of some note, and I think he's a pilot. We have a file, of course. You'll be fully briefed."

"How would he know what the Russians are after?" Spencer asked.

"He's deputy leader of the Workers' and Farmers' Party. He's also working for us. At least he was. You see, unfortunately he's disappeared. There's another complication. He's wanted for murder."

"They don't have murders in Iceland."

"This was a very real and particularly nasty murder, Mr. Spencer."

Spencer had drunk most of his martini. He needed more.

"Why me? I know next to nothing about Icelandic politics. I don't know anything about engineering. I've only been in the country twice."

"You have an association," Laidlaw said. "You took their side in the cod war. They like and trust you for that. You have contacts there. Your presence will be more than plausible. Really, Mr. Spencer, I consider you a godsend."

"Why would my presence be so plausible?"

"You are going to combine business with a vacation. You'll be doing an article on Iceland's success with hydroelectric and geothermal power for *Perspective* magazine."

"You own *Perspective*?" Spencer asked. "Some of the best names in Washington write for that."

"You'll be given a letter confirming the assignment and a check for five hundred dollars. Another two thousand will be paid upon publication. You'll have to write the article, you know. And do a good job. We don't want any doubts cast on your cover."

Spencer drained his glass, setting it down on the table with a pronounced click. He glanced at the pitcher. It was still two-thirds full. "Upon publication," Spencer repeated. "I'm not very flush at the moment, and five hundred . . ."

"You'll be able to draw up to ten thousand in expenses from us, Mr. Spencer. And you won't have to account for any of it."

All Spencer had to do was casually ask for another martini. Perfectly sociable thing to do. Why else the large pitcher?

"What about your own people in Iceland?" Spencer said. "Why can't they find this Krog?"

"They're trying," Laidlaw said, ignoring Spencer's empty glass. "Although I'm not altogether certain I want them to find him. Our operation's been a bit compromised there, I'm afraid. Intruders."

"A mole?"

"Or moles. That's why we want to keep you separate. You'll have to operate entirely on your own."

Spencer felt a little bleak. He remembered being very lonely when he was in Iceland, even though he had been accompanied by a good friend.

"We have some reliable assets elsewhere in the Nordic countries," Laidlaw continued. "If things get really bad, we'll have someone in place to help you. And we'll provide you with a means of comunicating with me. But otherwise, you're a solo, to borrow a phrase from a colleague of mine."

"What about Icelandic intelligence?"

Laidlaw laughed for the first time since the conversation had begun. "Mr. Spencer. Iceland has no army, no navy. Just five hundred policemen and that little Coast Guard. I don't think they have ten ambassadors. Don't worry about bumping into Icelandic agents. They can't afford any."

Spencer looked at the martini pitcher, then decided not to look at it anymore.

"Are you still thinking this over?" Laidlaw asked.

"No. I'll go. I'm your boy."

"The job will have its dangerous aspects, Mr. Spencer, if that sweetens things."

"Weapons?"

"No more questions for the moment, if you don't mind. Everything will be answered at your briefing tomorrow," Laidlaw said. He took a slip of paper from his notecase, writing a four-digit number on it. "Be at this address on J Street tomorrow morning at nine-thirty. Someone will meet you in the lobby and take you upstairs."

They both rose.

"How soon will I have to be in Iceland?" Spencer asked, memorizing the number and returning the notepaper to Laidlaw.

"Soon. Within the week. Perhaps as soon as two days. Presuming we get the final okay. Which I'm sure we shall."

He led Spencer into the hall. At the door, Spencer shook hands and thanked Laidlaw for his hospitality. Then abruptly he said, "Do you ride horses?"

"No, Mr. Spencer," said Laidlaw, with the faintest of smiles. "No, I don't."

As he walked to his car, Spencer took careful note of the weeds growing in the drive. He also noted that the Mercedes had District of Columbia license plates, and, as he twisted his head toward the BMW's rear window in backing it and turning it around, he caught a glimpse of a figure standing in the heavy brush and trees that fronted the road. There were doubtless more. He wondered how the agency could be so clumsy. Where did Laidlaw actually live?

Spencer did stop for his whiskey in Georgetown, at a bar on M Street fashioned after an English club. But he only had one. And he ignored the thin blonde at the bar, although she was alone. He passed the evening soberly, reading about Iceland in some books he had bought during his previous trip but had never opened. It wasn't until just before he went to bed that he had another drink—a very large straight whiskey, just like always.

After Spencer had gone, Laidlaw returned to the study, poured himself another martini, and then rejoined his colleagues in the basement room. Thorn, thorough as always, had the videotaped interview played back again, paying particular attention to the footage showing Spencer's movements in the study after Laidlaw had left to make drinks.

"He passed all the tests," Laidlaw said. "Such as they were."

"Okay," said Thorn. "I'll buy him."

"I do wish he had shown more interest in the particle-beam file," Laidlaw said. "And the word 'Valkyrie.' "

"It was negligent of you not to tell him about it," said Mendelsohn, lighting another cigarette. Laidlaw and Thorn stared at him as though he were not a genius and had never been a University of Chicago classics scholar.

"The most dangerous thing for the other side to know," said Thorn reciting cant, "is what we know."

Laidlaw grimaced slightly as he sipped his gin. He wished Spencer didn't drink so much.

5

GEIR KROG HAD now committed three actual crimes. He had killed a lamb, killed a dog, and broken into a farmer's cottage. By the time his odyssey ended, he was likely to be listed in police records as one of the worst criminals in recent Icelandic history.

The lamb was necessary. He was hoarding his canned goods and taking fresh meat where he could. His hope was that the lamb might not be missed. Icelandic sheep were allowed to wander the country at will, sorted out according to skin markings in an annual roundup. Farmers routinely accepted a few losses.

The dog was unfortunate. Krog had been approaching the cottage at dawn over a mossy meadow when the dog came at him at a bounding run, barking and snarling. Krog could not escape it. He had no wish to fight the dog. It had to be silenced before it summoned its master. As it leapt at him, he caught it in the throat with his sheath knife. It fell, still breathing, whimpering. He stabbed it twice more, horribly reminded of Inga.

As it turned out, the dog was guarding the cottage on his own. The farmer and his family apparently were visiting elsewhere, having padlocked the cottage's only door. Krog kicked in one of the windows. In a quick but thorough rummage, he took some canned fish and vegetables, an extra flashlight, some matches, and what he was most overjoyed to find—a copy of *Kvoldbladid*, Reykjavik's leading paper, only two days old. Geir Krog, high-ranking communist, was amused that he was so happy to have it. *Kvoldbladid* was one of the most conservative papers in the country.

The farmer's cottage was a godsend in another way. Breaking into it would provide unmistakable evidence that he was heading south.

He had been ever since he had fled from his cabin, moving through the hills parallel to the coast road, striking into some mountains to avoid a big loop in the road around the peninsula at Djupivogur, and then descending into the wide mossy valley that contained the farmer's cottage. If he continued in this direction, he would soon enter a barren wilderness and ultimately come upon the huge Vatnajokull glacier. It was good country in which to hide, better country for the police to waste their time searching for him. Making messy tracks as he left the cottage, he continued south until he reached some higher rocky ground. Then he made his chess move, carefully leaving no tracks as he recrossed the valley and headed north.

Now he was camped on the top of a rocky ridge overlooking the long blue lake Lagarfljot. At the far end of Lagarfljot was the town of Egilsstadir. It was where the police might have expected him to bolt to immediately after the killing. But now, several days later, with his having left his car behind and a trail to the south, they might not be expecting him there.

It was near noon, on as clear a day as Krog could remember in Iceland. It would be raining in Reykjavik if the axiom—that good weather on one side of the island meant bad weather on the other—held true.

He had lunched on a meal of canned green beans, lamb, and clear stream water and was rereading the newspaper. Geir Krog was now the most famous name in Iceland. There were pictures accompanying the front-page story—of him, of Inga, and of the acting superintendent of the state investigative police, Magnus Andersson, who had taken over the case. The photograph showed an intense-looking bearded man with dark hair and glasses. One gathered he was quite intelligent, a fit opponent in a chess game. Krog wondered whether he had met him before.

He smiled to himself and then laughed aloud. He had many opponents—Andersson, Rozkowski, and countless, faceless others. He was playing not one but a dozen games, and playing some of them blindfolded.

Frowning, he began to read the news story carefully, wincing at the graphic description of the wound to Inga's body. The article left little doubt that he was the murderer and seemed to treat him as a great danger to the populace. It was a fair presumption, but it angered him, even on his third reading of the article.

They appeared to know only that he had fled on foot into the countryside. They were looking for him everywhere, although for four hundred seventy-five policemen in a country of forty thousand square miles, "everywhere" didn't cover much ground. There was no mention of his note protesting his innocence, no mention of Polish engineers, or Russians, or Americans, or aluminum plants. But why should there be?

Krog read through the rest of the paper, but his mind kept going back to his problem, so he returned the paper to his pocket and took out his map.

He had now ruled out entirely any attempt to escape the country by stealing a boat, no matter how plentiful they were in these eastern fjords. His seamanship was poor, and he knew the Coast Guard would be on him in a trice. His only escape by sea could be as a stowaway on a ship, and ships big enough to hide in docked only at Akureyri in the north and Reykjavik in the west.

Stealing a car to reach either of those places was also pointless. There were seven thousand miles of roads in Iceland, most of them gravel, but only one major highway—the coastal road. Police could cut it anywhere they wished. Trekking on about the wilderness was useless, even if he were able to evade the authorities, because it brought him no closer to a solution of his problem. It was not likely he could evade the authorities for long. Traversing the uninhabited, glacier-strewn interior of the country would be extremely difficult; at this time of year, impossible. He would have to stay near settled areas, increasing the chance of detection and slowing his progress. Reaching even Akureyri could be a journey of weeks.

There was another possibility, one that meant speed and range and opened up a number of opportunities despite its risk: the airport at Egilsstadir. An airplane could take him to the Faroe Islands, and from there to Scotland. Or he might fly to Greenland and make his way somehow to Canada. If he chose to stay, he could reach any point in Iceland by air in two hours. As best as he could recall, there were few if any aircraft based at Egilsstadir. The field was used mostly by the Coast Guard Fokker patrol plane and the two commercial flights from Reykjavik. But there was always a chance. Krog was a sailplane pilot, a very good one, but his experience with powered aircraft was rudimentary. Still, desperation was a wonderful teacher.

He hunched deeper into his parka. The wind had shifted and was blowing cold from the north. He doubted the temperature was much above freezing at this height. Another cold night among the rocks without a fire. He pulled the bottle of aquavit from his pack. Only a little more than an inch of the liquor remained. Eking it out for warmth was becoming a kind of torture. He pulled off the cap and, in a few quick sips, finished it. He was tempted to hurl the empty bottle down the side of the ridge, just for the joy of hearing the angry sound of breaking glass. But such glitter would be dangerous. He slipped the bottle into a crevice in the rocks.

It would be so wonderful to be in Reykjavik—city lights, warmth, hot food, cognac. He had been having fantasies about Reykjavik these sleepless nights, some of them sexual. His friend there, the friend with whom he had left his now-so-valuable notebooks, was a woman. Her name was Evi Kekkonen. A Finn, handsome in a broad-faced way, she operated a leather goods store downtown. They had been lovers once, and friends for years. Occasionally, they still made love.

He would trade all his possessions to be in her warm bed

now. He wondered whether it might somehow be possible to reach her. The police would know or soon find out that she was among his friends. They could not possibly know that she was the only one of his friends that he trusted absolutely, that she was the only one who would truly believe him when he said he had not murdered Inga.

The distant clattering sound struck his ear abruptly, hurrying toward him from the north. Recognizing it, he quickly stripped off his blue parka, bundled it beneath him, and dove for the rocks, grateful for the dull gray color of his thick wool shirt. The clatter increased to what seemed to him a din, but it passed on and diminished without pause. They were not conducting a search but were en route to a search. Grettin Asmundsson, the medieval bandit, may have survived in the wild for seventeen years, but he had not had to contend with helicopters.

The two Russian factory trawlers, having completed a rough voyage around Iceland's south coast, had tied up at Reykjavik, joining a third Russian ship moored at Hafnarfjordur just down the shoreline. Such a flagrant Soviet presence was not out of the ordinary. The Icelanders had come to expect it whenever there were NATO ships in port, and the NATO flotilla numbered eight vessels, a size that more than warranted this large a Russian escort.

Emil Jahn, still disguised as a sailor, stood slouching against the rail of the trawler nearest the NATO ships, his jacket collar turned up and his watch cap pulled down low over his eyes. After the storm had blown over, they had sent the little Polish trawler on its way to Gdansk, just as had been reported to the Icelandic Coast Guard. For a moment, uncharacteristically rattled by the Coast Guard vessel's appearance, Jahn had thought of remaining aboard the *Waldemar Dulski* all the way to Poland. Krog's escape and the girl's murder were not small mischances. But he quickly regained control of himself and continued with the plan, swinging aboard one of the big Russian ships for the return to the battleground. After all, if the Coast Guard captain had suspected anything, he would have boarded. And "Valkyrie" could not wait.

Jahn lit a cigarette in a sailor's way against the wind and leaned farther over the rail, delighted with the scene before him. The NATO flotilla, most of them frigates, were flying the flags of the United States, Britain, Canada, West Germany, Portugal, the Netherlands, and Norway. This was a friendly visit, but they were being greeted rudely. An anti-NATO mob had gathered at quayside, just as Erikisson had ordered, and were raising noisy hell, with a great deal of shouting, swearing, and fist shaking. Some carried signs. One youth brandished a wooden horse's head on a pole, a medieval Icelandic means of inflicting a curse.

The young crew members guarding the gangway of the nearest NATO ship looked frightened, as they should have. The ship was the British frigate *Bacchus*, in the Icelandic view, one of the great villains of the 1976 cod war. Only the British would send the *Bacchus* to Iceland on a goodwill cruise. The Soviets were a lucky gang, and they were most fortunate of all in their adversaries.

A line of policemen came running down the quay, separating the protesters from the ship like a knife. The crowd became noisier and more agitated for a moment, then quieted and thinned as those in the rear began to drift away. The point had been made; the ship cursed. Newspaper photographers had captured much of it.

Jahn picked up his duffel from the deck and, shouldering it, left the trawler and joined the last of the demonstraters as the crowd dispersed into the streets. He trailed along behind them for a block and then slipped into a sailors' bar, a hot, smoky place filled with foreign seamen. He swilled a glass of vodka with the relish of any sailor just off his boat, ordered and drank a second, then wandered off into the town. He spent a sailor's day, even to leering from beneath his lowered watch cap at Icelandic girls. At dusk, he went to a cinema and took a seat in the rear, removing his hat and heavy jacket and wadding them into his duffel. Exchanging his fisherman's boots for a pair of shoes, he left the theater midway through the not-very-good American movie, looking like just another man in a business suit—Rozkowski, the Polish engineer. It was dark and he was not followed. If he had been, there would be nothing at all suspicious about Mr. Rozkowski's dropping by the Polish embassy. He worked, after all, for a state-owned company.

Yuri Gorushchenko had arrived early and was waiting in the basement room, which he had filled with the smoke from his foul Turkish cigarettes. Like many Soviet diplomats, Gorushchenko affected the best Western clothing he could afford, and other capitalist habits, but he would not abandon those awful cigarettes. He had a narrow, rather un-Russian face. He was by far the smartest Russian in Iceland, which was fitting, for he was the ambassador.

"Reykjavik is full of NATO sailors," said Jahn, seating himself across the table from Gorushchenko. The room was dimly lit.

"Seventeen hundred officers and crew," said the Russian. He had a raspy, unpleasant voice.

"It makes it easier to move about," Jahn said.

Without a word, Gorushchenko took an Icelandic newspaper from his lap and dropped it on the table in front of Jahn. The German did not read Icelandic well, but there were pictures on the front page of Krog, and the girl he had killed. She was more attractive than he remembered. "You glory in your efficiency," Gorushchenko said sarcastically.

"I was surprised by the girl," Jahn said. He lifted his eyes to look into Gorushchenko's. "Surveillance said nothing about any girl. I did what was necessary."

"Krog is alive?"

"I presume. I never saw him."

Jahn lit a cigarette of his own.

"And we do not know what he knows?"

"As far as I can determine," Jahn said, "he knows that Erikisson has agreed to the aluminum plant. There's no reason to believe he learned anything more than that."

"And we do not know what he has told the Americans?"

"You tell me, Herr Botschafter," Jahn said, knowing how much Gorushchenko disliked the German language. "I've been at sea. What does our American friend say?"

"Our friend says they are very unhappy about this murder in Washington, but they have done nothing. Here, the Americans have been quiet. The British have been quiet. Everyone has been quiet. Everyone has been going to parties for these NATO ships. Even I have gone to one. Next they will be giving me a tour of the air base at Keflavik."

He smiled. Jahn smiled. Suddenly, Gorushchenko raised his arm above his head and then slammed his fist down on the newspaper. "This Krog should be dead!" he shouted.

Jahn glared at him sullenly.

"He will be soon enough," he said.

" 'Soon enough' is not soon enough!" Gorushchenko said, nearly bellowing. "There is the election!"

He paused to catch his breath, then inhaled from his squat cigarette, exhaling a malodorous cloud that lingered almost motionless in front of his face. Gorushchenko then leaned into the cloud, lecturing Jahn as though he were an imbecile. "Krog could make Erikisson change his mind," he said, this time in a heavy whisper. "Krog has followers of his own. He has friends. This is a small country. Who knows what he might be able to do, what he might be able to tell the Americans? Who knows what he might be able to figure out for himself?"

He leaned even closer. His eyes were slightly bloodshot. "Colonel," he said. "Emil. We have both been involved in extraordinary endeavors, in events of the greatest consequence. This is such a simple matter. How can you allow one dumb Icelander to put it all in jeopardy?"

"I'll have my people in place," Jahn said. "Even if he is captured by the Icelandic police, it will be easy to kill him."

"It was easy to kill him in his little east coast cabin, Colonel."

"Gospodin Ambassador," Jahn said. "The man is being

hunted down as a murderer. He's likely to be shot on sight. Anything he has to say will be disregarded. His effect on the election will be nil. He is neutralized, believe me!"

Gorushchenko pursed his lips and nodded, though not necessarily in agreement. He rose, stretched, and went slowly to a file cabinet in the corner, talking all the while.

"I should not be concerned," he said. "It was not my decision to bring you into this. Now that you have been, our responsibilities are clearly delineated. I am responsible for the political problem and you are responsible for the security problem. Krog was a political problem, but now he is a security problem."

He took a bottle of vodka from the file drawer, filled two small dusty glasses, and brought them to the table.

"I wish you luck," Gorushchenko said, raising his glass. "I look forward to your success."

It was not that pleasantly simple. Gorushchenko knew full well the importance of what they were about. If something went wrong, they would both be shoveling dung in Mongolia. Or graves.

"*Prosit,*" said Jahn, raising his own glass.

Gorushchenko frowned at the word. It was not easy for Jahn being the highest-ranking German in the KGB. It was not easy being any kind of German working with Russians.

Two thousand miles and three time zones distant, in a huge but low-ceilinged underground room, there was another conversation in Russian. The admiral from Murmansk and the KGB general, both just arrived in Moscow, stood circumspectly just inside the door, waiting to be summoned by the group of high-ranking officers busy at the long table at the other end of the room.

"We have your man back in Reykjavik," said the admiral.

"I know," said the KGB man. "The embassy sent a signal."

"Gorushchenko?"

"Yes."

"How do they get along? I understand your man can be difficult."

"He is a professional. He's my best."

"One of my captains said Gorushchenko seemed unhappy."

"I do not tell you how to steer your ships, Anatoly."

The admiral shrugged. "I was in Riga this morning," he said. "Warmer than here."

"I was in Paris," said the general.

The admiral grinned.

"They are so much preoccupied with themselves," said the general.

A young major, brusque and self-important, approached. "The marshal will see you now," he said.

The marshal's expansive peasant face betrayed none of the nervousness one might expect from a man with his colossal responsibilities. He seemed cheerful and contented, as though having just come from a large and good meal.

"Ah, yes," he said, smiling, as he turned in his chair to greet the two newcomers. "The Valkyrie Project. Our little sideshow."

"Our principal sideshow," corrected a party official in civilian clothes seated next to him.

"All goes well with it?" the marshal asked.

The KGB general reached to open the briefcase chained to his wrist, but the marshal halted him with a wave of his hand.

"I have seen all that," the marshal said. "Very impressive. Very impressive. The Premier himself was very impressed with it. Just tell me, all goes well?"

"All goes well, Gospodin Marshal."

"And you, Admiral?" said the marshal, turning his chair a little further to look as carefully into the naval officer's face as he had the general's.

"The project is launched, Gospodin Marshal," the admiral said. "All is on schedule. The Valkyries will soon be flying."

The marshal looked from one to another, his eyes almost merry. Frantic teletypes could be heard in a corner of the room.

"If this fails," the marshal said, "all is not lost. We may consider everything else . . ." he waved his palm up over the table ". . . an exercise, a drill."

The merriment abruptly vanished from his eyes, replaced by a dark scowl. "But, of course," he said, "we do not want this to fail."

"No, Gospodin Marshal," said the general.

"We do not in any way want this to fail," repeated the marshal.

"No, Gospodin Marshal," said the general and admiral together.

"We shall talk again soon," said the marshal, and with that he turned back to the computer projections spread out on the table. On his way out, the KGB general glanced at the huge, brightly lit wall map. Iceland seemed so far out of the way. Sideshow.

Elisabet Bjornsdottir slipped off her robe and stepped naked into the tub in her small bathroom. Hers was an old-fashioned apartment and the tub had been built in the old-fashioned way, square and very deep, with a ledge to sit on. Her long legs were cramped, but there was compensation in that the steaming hot water came to her shoulders. She leaned her head back against the wall tiles and closed her eyes. These fifteen minutes every morning were the most relaxing part of her day.

This one was starting earlier than expected. It would last long, and end for her in the United States. One of the other hostesses had taken ill, and they had called Elisabet at five in the morning to ask whether she would take the girl's place. She agreed, not happily but without much protest. Her plans for the evening had been ruined anyway. She was to have had dinner with Magnus Andersson, but he had been called back to the east coast because of that horrible murder. Her plans had been serious, fantasized to the happiest ultimate conclusion. It was the second time that week that such hopes had been upset by this wretched crime. She had viewed the murderer with disgust. Now she was beginning to hate him.

It was difficult for Elisabet to explain, even to herself, her attraction to this dark, brooding policeman. The first time she had met Magnus she had thought him bookish and somewhat rude. At the Arnasons' dinner party, however, he surprised her by saying something wonderfully wry, and, drawing him out, she found him to be a quite warm and gentle person behind his policeman's brusque façade. Rather than cold, he was shy and rather sad. If he was bookish, he loved poetry—and had read and admired her poetry.

She eased her body deeper into the tub until the water rose nearly to her chin. A sudden rain shower was rattling against the window.

Magnus was a quintessentially Icelandic man. As she grew older, Elisabet came increasingly to value that. Because of her travels, she had dated men from many other countries. Now they tired her, especially Germans and Americans. The harbor was full of foreign trawlers, freighters, and navy ships, and the streets of Reykjavik were consequently full of foreign sailors. One of them, a tall lout who smelled of fish and liquor and wore his watch cap pulled down so far it seemed a medieval helmet, had jostled her on a narrow sidewalk and tried to fondle her bottom.

The thought of that made her shiver despite the steamy heat of the bath. Flying to America might prove to be a good idea. The flight was not to New York or Chicago, as she had feared, but to Icelandair's newest destination: Baltimore-Washington International. Her friend Sonja, who had given up her job as an air hostess to marry an Icelandic-American lawyer named Peterson, lived in Baltimore, and Elisabet occasionally visited her. She thought she might do so again. Icelanders were welcome at any time of the day or night at the Peterson house.

Elisabet opened her eyes. With them closed, she kept seeing that groping sailor with the thin pink face.

By lunchtime, Commander Richards had taken four calls over the secure phone from Whelan, who had news—and questions. The waterfront protest demonstration had been organized by Communists, Whelan proclaimed. What a surprise. The demonstrations were to continue every day as long as the NATO flotilla was in port, he said; then they would switch to the main gate of the base at Keflavik. How amazing. There were three Russian trawlers in harbor, instead of two like the last time. Was that significant as far as the navy was concerned? Oh yes, it showed a fifty percent increase in trawler dockings. Whelan's men had put a make on no fewer than three agents from the other side mingling with the NATO crews. Had Richards' people identified any? Just the usual crowd. The Soviets were not very big on transferring personnel.

Still, Richards had made a point of relaying Whelan's concerns to his admiral, and, to make doubly sure of his grounds for complacency, he checked again with his sources in the Icelandic Coast Guard and Justice Ministry. They said the same: Except for that murder out on the east coast, no one had reported anything out of the ordinary. All was well.

Richards was less annoyed with Whelan than usual. He was, in fact, in fairly good spirits. The visit by the NATO flotilla had given him a great deal to do—professionally and socially. That night, for example, there was a reception at the British Embassy for the officers of the frigate *Bacchus*. Richards looked forward to an opportunity to renew his acquaintance with the wife of the British Embassy's first secretary. She was Danish, formidable in the prow, and apparently fond of fun and games. Iceland being Iceland, there'd be no slipping off down some scented, shadowy garden path. But there were always closets.

On his way to the officers' mess for lunch, Richards stopped at the situation watch room to learn from the duty roster when Truscott would be coming on shift. He wanted to talk with Truscott—in a careful, casual sort of way. Because of the demonstrations, all enlisted personnel had been confined to base, but Truscott had reportedly been seen in Reykjavik the previous night.

6

SPENCER ALWAYS LIKED a drink while he packed. He was being extremely careful with liquor now, especially since he would shortly be off on his mission. But it was an old habit and he indulged it, filling a squat glass with Johnnie Walker Red and ice and keeping it nearby on the night table as he worked. His beaten-up old leather shoulder bag could fit with only minimal cramming under the seats of any airline in the world, even Central American ones, yet carried enough clothing to last a week or more without washing. With the ease of years of practice, Spencer fitted in a heavy-duty L. L. Bean rough country outfit, along with a warm tweed suit for the street. As always, he'd wear gray flannels, a blazer, and a turtleneck on the airplane.

He had an axiom. Success at anything, but most particularly the newspaper business, was largely a matter of being a jump ahead. It could be a very short jump, just so long as it was ahead. To lag behind, if only a little, invariably meant trouble, if not failure. At the moment, he was a jump ahead, or he would be once he mailed the heavy package on the night table. It contained two hollowed-out books in which were carefully packed his thoroughly cleaned and checked pistol, and a box of .32 caliber ammunition. No one ever messed with the mails. Postal authorities the world over routinely delivered diamonds, bombs, and the details of revolutionary plots without knowing it. All he needed was a safe address in Reykjavik. He had not asked Laidlaw for one because Laidlaw had made it more than clear he didn't want Spencer armed.

Spencer had obtained from the Icelandic embassy in Washington a list of knowledgeable people to interview on the thrilling subject of hydroelectric and geothermal power, as well as the names of some helpful types in the Foreign Ministry and one of the local newspapers. If Laidlaw wouldn't give him any contacts, he'd acquire some of his own. There might even be someone around who remembered him from the cod war.

He wished George Peterson were going with him. It was Peterson who had gotten him interested in Iceland in the first place, when at a Christmas party in 1975 he had suggested the glorious adventure to be had sailing out into the midwinter Atlantic in one of those dinky gunboats to play bumper-tag with Perfidious Albion. Peterson was Spencer's lawyer. He and his wife, Sonja, had been among his and Chesley's closest friends. Peterson's parents had been Icelandic immigrants, his father at one time an important Icelandic horsebreeder. Peterson still had some peculiar sort of business dealings in Iceland. He seemed to have peculiar business dealings all over the world.

His phone rang only two times. Peterson and Sonja were home, entertaining a houseguest from—as always—Iceland. Peterson feigned outrage at learning that Spencer was going to Iceland without him, that he was leaving the very next day, that he would not come at once to join them for a farewell dinner.

"You simply have to meet Elisabet," Peterson said. "She's said to be the most beautiful woman in Iceland—now that Sonja's left."

Spencer heard embarrassed laughter in the background. Baltimore was only forty miles away, and the thought of an evening with the Petersons and someone beautiful named Elisabet intrigued him, but he feared how it might end. He had one more meeting with Laidlaw in the morning—on the mall outside the Smithsonian, of all places—and then he had to leave for the airport.

"There's nothing I'd like more," Spencer said. "But I've a lot of work to do tonight, and I . . . I'll need a clear head in the morning. I'm leaving on the afternoon flight from BWI."

"Why the rush?" said Peterson, his voice much quieter. "You haven't explained why you're going."

"It's a rush assignment that just came up," Spencer said. "An obscure magazine is paying me a small fortune to come up with only eight million words on Icelandic energy resources in time for their next issue."

There was a pause. "What about your job?"

"I still have it," said Spencer. "I'm on leave. My precarious health, you know."

"I really should go with you."

"That would be terrific, George, but there just isn't time."

"There are some depositions I need to take in Reykjavik sometime this year. Maybe I'll fly out in a few days and join you."

"I'll be fine, George. Save the six hundred dollars. But I need a favor. They want to mail me some things after I get there and I need an address. I'd use a hotel but I'll probably be moving around."

"They?"

"The editors of this magazine. Some research material."

"Where are you staying?"

"The Hotel Thor, I guess. Isn't that where we stayed in 1976? Right on the main square?"

"Yes," said Peterson. "Austurvollur Square. But why not just have them send it there? The desk people will hold it for you. I once left a hundred dollars in cash on a dresser and it was waiting for me in an envelope when I came back a month later."

"I just don't want to lose this material," Spencer said. "I can't . . . I can't write this article very well without it."

Peterson paused again, a longer time. "I have a client there who takes mail for me," he said. "Just mark it for me. I'll call ahead and let her know it's coming."

Spencer wrote down the address Peterson gave him, being careful to get the exact Icelandic spelling.

"I'm serious about coming out to join you," Peterson said.

"I'll be back before you know it," Spencer said. "This may not take very long at all."

"You'll get to meet Elisabet, anyway. She's going back on that afternoon flight, too. She's a stewardess. Used to fly with Sonja."

"I never seem to do very well with stewardesses. They insist on waiting on all the other passengers, too."

"I'll have her look out for you."

"Great," said Spencer. "Thanks."

Peterson paused yet again.

"Jack," he said. "What are you up to?"

"Just trying to scare up some extra cash. Really. If you'd done your job right I wouldn't have such large alimony payments."

"The judge was less than impartial. Never divorce a beautiful woman."

"*Tak,*" said Spencer, remembering the Icelandic word for thanks.

"*Skal,*" said Peterson.

"*Skal.*"

Spencer hung up. The sudden silence made him feel lonely. For a moment, he fought an impulse to call Peterson back and say he was coming for dinner after all. No. He took what remained of his drink to the living room and settled into his leather chair, opening the folder Laidlaw had given him. The papers inside included a history of Iceland's Workers' and Farmers' Party; a biography of Erikisson, the party leader; a longer biography and notes on Geir Krog; suggested places to look for Krog; and full translations of Icelandic newspaper accounts of the murder.

He read each page three times to memorize it, then tore each up and dropped the shreds into a bucket. He'd burn them before he left. All he'd keep was the English-Icelandic dictionary Laidlaw had given him.

The headache struck as abruptly as a gunshot, a shaft of pulsing pain stabbing from the base of his skull to the back of his eyes. At first he thought he'd suffered a stroke, but there was no numbness, no paralysis, just pain—as bad as that first terrifying headache he'd suffered in the summer. His body responded to it with nausea, panting, a rapid heartbeat, and cold sweat pouring over his face, hands, and back. He hung his head back over the arm of the chair, gritting his teeth and clenching his eyes shut tight.

When, after what might have been fifteen minutes or an hour, he did not die, he slowly sat up and opened his eyes. The pain had not abated much, but his body was adjusting. Dealing with pain was supposed to be Spencer's forté. Had he not once calmly poured disinfectant onto the back of his hand after an automobile crash had ripped it open to the bone?

The medication he had been given was for prevention of symptoms, not treatment. The only instruction he had been given for such an eventuality was to get to a doctor at once. But a doctor—especially his doctor—would only lock him away in a hospital, and there was no time for that.

All his life he had treated headaches the same way. This might be the worst and deadliest of them all, but he would use the same remedy, the universal one. He drained his glass. After another drink, he finished reading and burning the papers. After four more drinks, he staggered to bed.

In the morning he was still alive.

Laidlaw noticed the hangover, of course. He made it clear to Spencer that he noticed and that he was not pleased, but he did not speak about it and went through their business as though nothing were amiss. For his part, Spencer offered no explanation. They just walked along the mall among all the tourists and the joggers, talking quietly.

"Karin will join you soon," Laidlaw said.

Spencer nodded. Elisabets and Karins. He would be a long time between American women.

"You've memorized the addresses and telephone numbers I want you to use?"

Again Spencer nodded. "I hadn't expected one in New York," he said.

"They'll reach me quickly," said Laidlaw. He stopped and

watched for a moment as a jetliner climbed from National Airport past the pinnacle of the Washington Monument. "I'll contact you in a few days," he added. "Sooner if necessary."

They resumed their walk, continuing toward the west.

"I'm running short of time," Spencer said, smiling faintly. "My plane."

"We appreciate this, Mr. Spencer. And I assure you, it's not a trivial business."

"Just stay in touch."

"I mean it. We really do appreciate this."

With his leather bag and portable typewriter secure beneath the row of seats in front of him, and the Icelandair DC-8 leveling out from its slow climb to cruising altitude, Spencer ordered his first drink of the flight—two miniature bottles of Johnnie Walker Red Label poured over ice, with a little bit of water added to the top. He had no idea which of the stewardesses was Elisabet, and although one of them seemed unusually attractive, he did not care. He only wanted to drink, slowly and carefully, drink his way through the black of night above the dark ocean, until he was brought to daylight and Iceland and, for a few weeks at least, a different life.

He picked at his dinner. He read a large part of a paperback novel. He drank. At length, he slept again.

Spencer awoke to a sense of dawn. The cabin lights had been turned off except for the faintest of glows along the ceiling, and the sky outside was still black, but there was a suggestion of pale gray at the forward horizon. Spencer closed his eyes and listened to the comforting, rhythmic hum of the engines. He seemed to be not a mere thirty-eight thousand feet above the sea but hurtling through space, as though outside this world, outside life itself. As though he could look out through that small window and see all of time.

He opened his eyes to see that the gray had spread and was becoming tinged with pink. He would have a brandy. He pushed the stewardess call button. After several minutes, he saw movement at the forward end of the long cabin as one of the stewardesses rose and put on her blue jacket. It was the tall one with long brown hair, the very attractive one. She came silently down the aisle with practiced ease and leaned over the seatback. Even in the cabin darkness, her wide gray eyes were filled with light.

"Yes?"

"A Bisquit, please."

She started to move and then hesitated. He wondered whether she thought he was asking for something else. Bisquit was the quite good brand of cognac Icelandair served.

"A Bisquit, please," Spencer repeated. "A cognac."

"You've already had very much to drink on this flight, sir," she said. Her voice was still near a whisper, but her tone was firm, almost sharp.

Spencer sighed. "Miss, there are no regulations against serving me another drink on a transatlantic flight," he said. "It's my habit to have a brandy at sunrise. I do it all the time, and I've been flying for twenty years. I am in command of my faculties. I've been sitting here quietly, all by myself, not bothering anybody."

She stared at him, her face expressionless.

"Are you Elisabet?" he asked.

"I am Elisabet Bjornsdottir," she said.

"My name is Jack Spencer. I'm a friend of George and Sonja Peterson."

"I know," she said, standing fully erect. "And that is the only reason I am going to bring you a cognac."

Elisabet hurried back up the aisle, furious, glad that the other hostesses were asleep and could not see her face. Sonja and George had spent half the night telling her about this man, his exploits and adventures, the wounds he had suffered, the funny things he had done and said, how handsome he was, what he had done for Iceland. George said Spencer knew all sorts of important people in Washington, that if Senator Derwinski had been elected President, Spencer might have been made an ambassador. Elisabet had been so awed by all this that she couldn't muster the social courage to introduce herself to him. At the beginning of the flight, she had felt shy and flustered every time she passed his seat.

And what did he turn out to be? A drunk. He had sat there steadily consuming alcohol—except for a brief sleep—the entire flight. And now he was at it again. Brandy. At dawn. And how arrogant about it! The typical demanding American. The Icelander must do as the American bids.

Magnus Andersson would be back in Reykjavik that afternoon. Perhaps at last they would have their dinner together. She would never have anything to do with an American man again.

Spencer had paid for only one cognac, but Elisabet had no wish to spend the morning fetching and carrying. For all she knew, he might start clutching at her leg. Smiling to herself, she filled the brandy glass almost to the brim, three or four times what she normally served. If he was bent on arriving in Iceland slobbering and stumbling, so be it. If he wanted to fall flat on his face at the bottom of the steps after leaving, fine.

As always, most of the passengers were young people, dressed in jeans and outdoor hiking clothes, their brightly colored backpacks scattered throughout the cabin. Some of them were beginning to stir. Embarrassed, Elisabet hurried past them with the huge brandy. When she reached him, Spencer was writing in a notebook. He closed it and set it aside, his eyebrows lifting at the size of his drink.

"We are going to be very busy serving breakfast," Elisabet said curtly. "This should last until we land."

He smiled—an exaggerated grin—and said thank you in Icelandic.

She avoided him for the rest of the flight, though she glanced over from time to time to note the progress of the Bisquit. Rather surprisingly, he finished it all, draining the last of it just as the DC-8 was taxiing to the civilian terminal at Keflavik. To Elisabet's astonishment, he got to his feet without difficulty, gathered his belongings together without dropping any, and walked out of the plane and down the steps without incident, strolling to the terminal.

Spencer was the only passenger leaving the plane in Iceland. The others, mostly youths, debarked only to stretch their legs and browse in the terminal's duty-free store, while the aircraft was refueled for the rest of the run to Luxembourg. Iceland's tourist season was short and did not extend to October, the beginning of the darkening time.

Stopping only at the wines and spirits section for bottles of Johnnie Walker and Brennivin at half the price he would pay in town, Spencer walked quickly to customs. As he expected, he was halted only for a glance at his passport and a cheery greeting of welcome. He could have carried his pistol stuck in his belt.

He took the front seat nearest the door of the Mercedes airport bus waiting outside, wanting a clear view. He thought he might have the bus entirely to himself, but then some Icelandair hostesses climbed aboard. Apparently flight crews were changed at Keflavik, but Elisabet Bjornsdottir was not among the women. He guessed she was taking a later bus—deliberately. He didn't care. The only woman who interested him on this trip was named Karin Nielsen.

The driver, a young man in glasses and a black jacket, clambered into his seat, and, with a slight chug, the bus was off, speeding past the yellow American barracks buildings and barely slowing for the Marine guard at the gate.

Lurching the bus onto the paved highway to Reykjavik, the driver turned on the radio and settled into a comfortable slouch for the forty-five-minute drive. The record being played was Icelandic, typically mournful, a woman's cool Nordic voice in a plaintive lament, music to be sad by, music to drink by. Spencer leaned his head against the window, fighting fatigue. Everything was remarkably as he remembered it. Meadows of black lava soil covered with the vivid green of moss. The treeless, rocky coastline. The snow-topped mountains just beyond Reykjavik. Amazingly, there was a bright sun in nearly cloudless skies, and it was warm, nearly fifty degrees.

By the time he reached Reykjavik's Austurvollur Square, it was raining. Spencer ducked up a remembered side street to the English book store, where at unexpected expense he gathered an armload of newspapers and magazines, most of them in Icelandic, and some maps. Then he checked into the Thor. The dark-haired, middle-aged woman behind the desk, whom he vaguely remembered, vaguely remembered him. When he mentioned he had stayed here as a reporter covering the cod war, she remembered exactly.

She gave him one of the best rooms in the hotel, a high-windowed corner room overlooking the square, the Icelandic parliament building, the Althing, and the Hotel Borg. Despite Britain's claim to "the mother of parliaments," the Icelanders had founded theirs in the year 930, before Britain was even a country.

Spencer stood for a moment at his window, fatigue pulling at his back and shoulders like a great weight. He had remembered everything about Iceland except how brightly colored the rooftops were, painted the most vibrant greens, yellows, blues, and reds against the gloom of weather and winter darkness. Nothing seemed amiss on the square or the streets around it, no lurking, trench-coated strangers looking up at his window.

Spencer smiled. There was a considerable difference between being a journalist and being whatever it was he had become. The little work he had done on the side for the agency in the past was only a tiny bit of wading. Now he'd been thrown square into the stormy sea, sink or swim—and all alone.

He pulled a chair into the window's light and then poured himself a scotch with a small amount of water, not wanting to bother with a call to room service for ice. He was frankly tired of drinking. The headache had been adequately drowned. But he needed to keep going for another hour, and whiskey was all he knew that would help him do it.

Reading the local newspapers was an old habit from his travels. There was nothing too interesting at hand here—in fact, his copy of the Paris *Herald-Tribune* was a week old. But there were a few worthwhile items, including a fact-filled article on Icelandic hydroelectric power in the English-language *Iceland Review*. It contained some quotations from the now-fugitive Geir Krog.

With a command of Icelandic that extended to only two dozen words, Spencer wasn't able to learn very much from the morning Reykjavik papers, but they appeared to be filled with stories about the murder, and there was a strong sense that everyone in the country was searching for Krog. Spencer looked closely at the pictures. The dead girl had been very pretty. Krog seemed intelligent and rather likable, a big man with a beard. The file photo the agency had shown him had been of a much younger man.

Laidlaw had had no idea whether Krog was guilty of the murder. That was one of the things he wanted Spencer to find out.

Except for some stories about NATO—one illustrated with a photograph of a Russian cruiser sailing close off the Scottish coast—the English papers bored him, especially the *Manchester Guardian*. Spencer shoved them aside, finished his drink, and dropped onto the bed. He did not awaken until four hours later.

He then found he had no desire for a drink and put all thoughts of that from his mind. There were telephone calls to make, interview arrangements to complete for the next day. He was a newspaperman, after all, and an attribute of newspapermen was that they never wasted time, especially when they were on freelance assignment and paying for the time themselves. Within an hour, he had lined up interviews with the minister of industry and energy, the director of the National Research Council, the director of the National Power Company, and a writer for *Kvoldbladid*, one of Iceland's largest newspapers—the only interview he'd probably enjoy.

Spencer stopped there. It wouldn't do to get his work done

so swiftly. There were others he should interview. For example, for a balanced treatment, he should also talk with Gunnar Erikisson, the leader of the Communist Farmers' and Workers' Party. He had been opposed to expanding Iceland's industrial use of hydroelectric power because of the effect on the environment—or so it said in the article in *Iceland Review*. In view of Iceland's deteriorating economic situation, did Erikisson still agree with that?

Spencer set his watch to Icelandic time—ten minutes to two already. He would have lunch downstairs and then walk to the harbor. If Krog were to try to leave the country, it would most likely be by ship. Spencer hadn't the slightest hope of actually running into Krog down there, but it would be interesting to have a look at all those who might be waiting for him.

It was still raining, a sporadic downpour from low, rolling clouds that occasionally parted for a glimpse of weak sunshine. Spencer lay back upon the bed and closed his eyes. He felt a dull throbbing at his temples but decided to blame it on the whiskey.

Puzzlements. He was awash in them, inextricably enmeshed. It was impossible that he should ever find Krog, or learn whatever it was that Krog knew, or answer any of Laidlaw's other questions. But he might yet learn the answer to one question—the most puzzling of all: why Laidlaw had sent him.

Commander Richards, Whelan, and Emil Jahn all learned of Spencer's arrival within hours.

Richards' section was routinely forwarded a copy of the passenger manifest of every commercial airliner landing at Keflavik, along with the headcount from each departing airport bus. Aside from exchanging weather information, that was the extent of Iceland's cooperation with the American military and NATO. These reports were routinely logged by an enlisted man and then usually forgotten, but, because of the demonstrations and other election-related troubles, Richards had asked that any "funnies," to borrow Whelan's term, be flagged and brought to his attention. Spencer seemed to qualify as a "funny," but nothing particularly worrisome. Richards, his mind occupied with memories of the British first secretary's wife, decided he'd rely on Whelan to check that out.

Whelan had someone at the airport. Whelan had a bus driver and someone at the hotel. Whelan had Spencer's name and profession by his second cup of morning coffee. But that was all he had for the moment. At Laidlaw's instigation, Thorn had gone very high up and gotten permission for a block to be put in the computer at Spencer's name. Whelan's tracer retrieved the usual sort of data the agency gathered on American foreign correspondents, but nothing about any prior service with the agency. Thorn and Laidlaw had decided not to trust any American personnel in Iceland—foreign service or agency—up to and including the ambassador.

There were one or two ways Whelan might have been able to circumvent the computer block, but that would have required first, knowing about it and, second, going to a major center like the United States embassy in London. So he took what came back over the phone and was content with it.

Whelan thought he might have Spencer around for lunch or a drink. Journalists were always turning up something, and journalists liked to talk. Perhaps Whelan might be able to recruit Spencer for a little part-time work on the side. Langley still officially frowned on the recruitment of journalists, but Whelan habitually ignored his home office's frowns. How else could he have acquired such a vast network of informants? And it was Langley that insisted he keep Krog. Krog had not been *his* official mistake.

Emil Jahn was displeased. American journalists were at best a nuisance, talking to everyone and printing whatever they wished. Even if they didn't work for the CIA, as some of them did, their potential for mischief was enormous. They learned too much, especially in small countries like Iceland. Jahn put a man on Spencer immediately, even though he could ill be spared from the hunt for Krog. Gorushchenko was still being ugly about that, though Jahn's people had achieved one small success: they had beaten the police to Krog's house in Akureyri and taken his address book. They were working their way down the list of names.

Jahn would take a look at Spencer himself. American journalists who boarded planes at Baltimore-Washington International made him particularly unhappy.

Elisabet was surprised by Magnus Andersson's hands. There was so much you didn't notice at first, and some things might take years. His hands were extremely clean and soft, perfectly manicured, the sort she'd always supposed a surgeon or a pianist or a flower arranger might have, not that she'd ever known one. She'd never known a policeman before, either, a man who dealt with violent criminals, a man authorized to carry a gun. A man with soft hands.

She touched one, gently, and smiled. He had been brooding again, staring down at his plate. They were in the restaurant of the Hotel Saga, one of the nicest in Reykjavik, having that dinner at last. Except that Magnus wasn't eating. He was a very serious-looking man to begin with. Fatigue, constant travel, and the problems of this case had worn their way into his face, as though permanently. She had hoped—planned—to take him back to her apartment later for drinks and to listen to her jazz records. But he was so tired. He needed to rest.

He took off his glasses and rubbed his eyes, smiling weakly as he dropped his hand. "I'm sorry," he said. "This becomes a fixation."

"You'll find him."

He put on his glasses and took a sip of the red wine he had ordered but not touched. "I shouldn't waste this," he said. "It costs so much these days."

"He can't have left Iceland," she said.

"Krog? No. I'm sure he hasn't. A small advantage of our far remove. I ask myself, how could anyone possibly hide? Yet we are such a vast place—forty thousand square miles. How can anyone possibly be found?" He sipped his wine again and glanced about the room. The huge windows provided a view of city lights stretching all the way to the mountain foothills. Reykjavik looked so much larger at night.

"I have had every one of our men on this," he said. "I think we have worked sometimes more hours than there are in a day. But all we have done is find places where Krog has not gone. He left tracks that headed toward the south and southwest. I thought at first it was a trick, it was too crazy. But now I think that's what he's done."

"It said in the newspapers that he's a mountaineer."

"One of the best. I think he has climbed every mountain in Iceland. That's what I spent most of this week doing, learning all I can about Geir Krog."

"Is he an awful man?"

"I don't think so. That's one of several things that troubles me."

"Several things?"

He seemed to have entirely forgotten his dinner.

"Krog has been a very active man, politically," Magnus said. "There's an election coming up, an election his party finally has a chance to win. Yet he suddenly goes off to a summer cabin in the east counties—in October!" His face was becoming flushed and animated. "This poor girl," he said. "We've established beyond a doubt that he met her only that day. What can someone you've known only a day do or say to make you angry enough to kill like that?"

"Perhaps he has a violent temper."

"Not at all. He is a very rational, reasonable man. According to his neighbors in Akureyri, he was very gentle, good with children. Many very big men are like that. And then there was the note."

"A note? There was nothing in the newspapers about a note." Elisabet took a darting bite of her steak. It was getting cold.

"He left a note behind saying he did not commit the murder," Magnus said. "Very neat and precise. Now what murderer, after a raging act of violence, would sit down and coolly do a thing like that?"

"But who else could have done it?"

"I don't know. There is no one else. The only strangers in Heklafjordur that night were two sailors, and they went straight to the grocery. Everyone else was accounted for. Krog is our only suspect. And I must find him and bring him in. That's why I'm keeping at this so hard. If Krog escapes us, I don't want it to be because I like the man and think him innocent. That is for the Justice Courts to decide."

The evening was reinforcing Elisabet's every initial impression. Magnus Andersson was a very strong, and very good, man inside.

"Let us put the subject aside for a while," he said, smiling and taking her hand. "How was your trip to America?"

"Like any other flight," she shrugged. "A lot of work. I had fun, though. I stayed overnight in Baltimore with old friends. Sonja and George Peterson. Do you know him?"

"The lawyer? Too well. He has helped the defense against me in some cases here. He's an excellent criminal lawyer. I'm glad he lives in Baltimore and not Reykjavik."

The waiter was standing at Magnus's shoulder. "Excuse me, Superintendent," he said. "You are wanted on the telephone."

Magnus grimaced and apologized, touching Elisabet's arm gently. When he returned, the message he repeated was exactly what she had feared. "I have to go," he said. "A farmer south of Oskurfjordur found his cottage broken into and his dog killed. It's Krog. He is heading southwest, it seems. We have a good chance to take him. We need to start the search at first light."

"I understand," she said, making no attempt to mask the unhappiness in her voice.

"I'm sorry. You've no idea how sorry I am," he said. "May I drive you home?"

"No. I don't want to delay you."

"I'll let you finish your dinner, then," he said, putting some large Kronur notes on the table. "May I call you soon?"

"Please. I'll be at home. I haven't a flight for several days."

"I'll call. Forgive me."

She sat for a long time staring out the window, then made an effort to finish her dinner. She had just taken a few sips of her coffee when the waiter suddenly arrived with a glass of brandy on his tray, brimful. She turned angrily and looked about the room. It was Spencer, all right, at a small table by the wall. He gave her a mock salute with two fingers of his right hand and then returned his attention to his newspaper.

She would later wish that she had left the restaurant then and there without saying a word to him. Instead, she took the brandy to his table and set it in front of him. "You ordered this, I believe," she said. "The waiter brought it to me by mistake."

"No mistake," he said. "I always like to return favors."

She had put herself in an embarrassing fix. He hadn't done anything that offensive, and it wouldn't do to be nasty to such a good friend of Sonja's and George's. She could only stand there, feeling ridiculous.

"Please," he said, suddenly very charming. "Sit down. I came here to learn from Icelanders, not quarrel with them."

Elisabet hesitated, then pulled out a chair. This man controlled his charm the way the pilots handled their aircraft. His smile was set just so, his eyes suddenly friendly, inquiring, solicitous. She wondered whether he had ever been an actor.

Feeling oddly shy and uncertain, she still could think of nothing to say. She sat looking at her hands.

"Perhaps we'd best share this," he said, taking the brandy and pouring half of it into his empty wine glass. "Don't be alarmed. I'm not about to go on one of my binges. I'm here to work, and binges aren't much of a help. It's hard typing with your elbows."

She laughed, then caught herself. "You are a journalist, Mr. Spencer? Sonja said you were."

"Newspaperman. People who call themselves journalists remind me of janitors who call themselves engineers. Mine is a humble craft. Snooping. Scribbling. Poking into other people's troubles."

"Have you come to Iceland to poke into our troubles?"

"No. I did that last time I came, when I covered your problems with the nasty British. This time I'm looking on the bright side. I'm doing a magazine article on Icelandic energy. How you heat the entire city of Reykjavik with underground steam. There are some American cities we could do that for. How you have so much hydroelectric power. I've already decided to call you the Saudi Arabia of electricity."

"But we're nothing at all like Arabia. And we can't send our electricity anywhere."

"Doesn't matter," he said. "It'll make a good headline. They may even make it the cover story." He pulled out a notebook and a pen. "But while we're at it, let me interview you. Would Iceland accept a massive intrusion of foreign industry? Is Icelandic electricity as reliable as it is plentiful? What is the megawattage loss in times of drought? Has there ever been a time of drought in Iceland?"

"What is . . . megawattage?"

"A measurement of electrical power. Something to do with microfarads. Or is it ohms? Have you ever heard of Ohm's law?"

She shook her head.

"It's a variation of Murphy's law, I think," he said. "In any event, electricity bores me. I'm only doing this for the money. But it's not enough money. So let me interview you about something more interesting—you. First of all, will you marry me? I believe in taking up the important questions first."

"That's easy. No."

"Well, that ends the interview." He returned the notebook to his pocket and lifted his glass. "*Skal,*" he said.

Feeling a trifle reckless, and nervous, she raised her own glass and politely said, "*Skal.*"

Spencer continued to dominate the conversation, pleasantly but effectively, making jokes, asking questions, holding her with his eyes, never giving her an opportunity to conclude their encounter and leave. They talked of Sonja and George, of the cod war, of Iceland's horrible inflation, of her travels, of cities they had both been to, of museums, of painting, of literature, of her poetry, of her politics, of the election, of the murder, and whether she knew Geir Krog.

"No," she said. "I never met him. We are not *that* small a country."

"Rotten business, that murder," Spencer said. "I'd hoped to interview him. He's supposed to be quite an authority on electrical power."

"Yes," she said, glancing away. To her amazement, she had finished her brandy. There had been so much of it even when divided in half. She felt a little giddy, felt like having another.

"You don't have an inflation problem, you have an inflation catastrophe," Spencer said, reaching for his wallet as he looked at the bill. "We should have saved money by going to Paris." He rose, grasping her arm, keeping in control. "I'll get a taxi."

"I'd like to go home," she said. "I'm tired. Those flights get longer and longer."

"I'll drop you off. I'm sure you're not far from my hotel. Nothing in Reykjavik seems very far from my hotel."

"You're at the Thor? That's just three blocks from where I live."

She didn't really know why she was inviting him in—she would explain it to herself the next day. She offered to play some of her special jazz records for him. They were very old, given to her by her late father. Except for some photographs, they were all she had left of him.

Her father had befriended an American army officer during the United States' occupation of Iceland in World War II. The two had discovered a mutual liking for swing and jazz music, and when the officer was transferred to France at war's end, he started sending back records. Her father's favorite—and now Elisabet's favorite—was Django Reinhardt, the remarkable Belgian-born gypsy jazz guitarist who starred at Paris' Le Hot Club in the late 1940s. Severe burns had left him with only three usable fingers on his fretting hand.

His "Songe d'Automne" was her favorite of all—a plaintive

clarinet juxtaposed with Reinhardt's intoxicating rhythm, music laden with a warmth no season ever brought to Iceland. She put it on and poured two tall, narrow glasses of Brennivin. Closing her eyes, she leaned her head back against the wall.

When he kissed her throat by her open collar, she didn't move. Then he slipped his hand into her blouse. She was not wearing a brassiere. When his fingers reached the nipple, she slowly but firmly pushed him away and stood up. "We're not going to do that, Mr. Spencer."

"So I see," he said. He sipped his drink, without hurry.

"If I invited that, I'm sorry," she said. "It certainly was not my intention."

He was staring at the wall, listening intently to the music, or perhaps just thinking.

"Icelandic women are not what you've been led to believe, Mr. Spencer. That we have sex outside marriage does not mean we have sex all the time. Or with anyone and everyone. If you want promiscuity, go back to your own country."

Spencer finished the Brennivin and set the glass carefully on the table. "I think I like your country better than my country," he said.

"Give my regards to Sonja and George, Mr. Spencer. Good night. Good-bye."

He picked up his raincoat from the chair by the door and left.

The cold night sky was utterly clear, filled with crystalline stars. The temperature had dropped more than twenty degrees since the afternoon. Spencer stood a moment beneath Elisabet's lighted second-floor window. She was playing "Songe d'Automne" again, quite loudly. The sound of it followed him for more than a block down the street. Then it was lost.

Jahn pursued the American with practiced stealth, keeping to the shadows. So the policeman knew the girl and the girl knew the American—and whom did the American know? The search of his hotel room had yielded only the predictable: typewriter, notebooks, whiskey; an Icelandic-English dictionary, two paperback books, no weapons. The stack of newspapers and magazines on the dresser had intrigued Jahn, but he could not divine their significance. Spencer had clipped nothing from them.

A careful man, Spencer. He was making Jahn very nervous indeed. It was a visceral feeling, an itch. Jahn's itches had never failed him.

He could be done with Spencer right then and there. His deadly little cylinder was in his jacket pocket. A few quick steps and this nagging worry would be dispensed with. Jahn struggled with a temporary but intense desire. But the cylinder stayed in his pocket. There were still things about Spencer he needed to know.

The American went straight to his hotel, and Jahn hurried back to his vantage point—not along the street on which the girl lived, but a block away, higher up the hill, a spot that looked directly into her window. Pressing himself back against a wall, he took out a high-powered compact monocular and steadied it against his eye. The living room window lined up directly with the open bedroom door and he found he could watch her undress.

7

WASHINGTON'S BEST RESTAURANT, L'Auberge Chez François, was not in the city but in the rolling hunt country near Great Falls, some eight miles from CIA headquarters at Langley. Laidlaw and Mendelsohn waited there for Thorn, who was uncharacteristically late. The outside terrace had been closed for the season, but drinks were still being served at the benches set out on the inn's parklike lawn. Laidlaw was having one of his long-stemmed martinis, happy with its perfection.

Mendelsohn sipped sickly sweet cream sherry. "Your journalist is in place," he said, another question uttered as statement.

Laidlaw nodded absently, reluctant to interrupt his contemplation of a distant maple tree still in possession of most of its leaves. He associated Mendelsohn with the evil days at the agency and also considered him somewhat daft.

"And Karin Nielsen," Mendelsohn said.

"Not ready."

"She's not ready?"

"I'm not ready to send her in yet. Iceland is a small place, and we've already cluttered it up quite a bit."

Mendelsohn slowly exhaled. The smoke from his cigarette hung around his face like a shroud. "Can our mole identify Karin?"

"I've no idea," said Laidlaw. "Have you?"

"I know our mole," Mendelsohn said, grinning idiotically into his glass.

Laidlaw lifted his eyebrow.

"I know everything about him but his name," Mendelsohn said. "He's a cautious but clever fellow, completely in control. He has access to everything we have in Iceland. He's far ahead of us on this and probably ahead of his Russian chums as well. I think I've the vague outlines of a profile. 'Whatever is unknown is taken for marvelous; but now the limits of Britain are laid bare.' "

"What?" said Laidlaw.

"Tacitus," said Mendelsohn. He leaned back to watch a curl of smoke rise slowly above his head.

"We need his name, Freddy," said Laidlaw. "The Icelandic election is soon."

" 'My heart hath followed all my days, something I cannot name,' " Mendelsohn said.

"Tacitus?"

"Don Marquis."

"This mole is not Archie the cockroach," said Laidlaw.

"He's a professional," said Mendelsohn. "For all his caution, quite elegantly ruthless. Sending Krog off to his sanctum and sending an assassin immediately after. That girl, Inga Gudrun. It's established she wasn't one of theirs."

"Yes," said Laidlaw, increasingly irritated with these statement-questions. "Clean."

"Perhaps I'm wrong," Mendelsohn said. "Perhaps friend Krog is a murderer. Perhaps he killed her before they got to him. Iceland can be like that."

"Perhaps."

Mendelsohn leaned forward and looked down at the grass, the idiotic grin creeping back onto his face.

"Poor Karin Nielsen," he said.

Thorn was coming toward them across the lawn, hunched forward in his peculiar walk, a sort of rapid trudge. "I've got good news and bad news," he said, dropping heavily onto the bench between them. Laidlaw winced.

"The good news comes from State," he said. "The Brits have agreed to take a heap of Cruise missiles. The Krauts will go along, too. But not the Frogs."

"The trouble with giving the French Cruise missiles," said the grinning Mendelsohn, "is that they'd aim them across the Atlantic."

Thorn paused to order a beer from the waitress, a plain woman with a charming smile.

"The bad news," said Laidlaw.

"The bad news," said Thorn. "The White House now wants us to lay off particle beams indefinitely."

"Changing administrations changes nothing," Mendelsohn said.

Thorn paused for an enormous swallow of beer, then set the iced mug on the leveled stump before them.

"Who's doing us in?" asked Laidlaw finally. "The National Security Council?"

"Higher than that," Thorn said, eyeing the departing waitress as a young sailor might. "The exalted national security advisor himself. These guys always resent any intelligence that isn't their own—no matter what it says."

Laidlaw finished his martini, wishing he had thought to order another one. He wanted to keep this conversation going. "Who's fighting for us?" he asked. "The director?"

"Higher than that," said Thorn. "The deputy."

The post-Watergate upheaval in the agency had produced an anomaly: the effective bureaucratic power in the organization was wielded by the agency's Number 2, with the directors functioning in many ways as figureheads, whether they knew it or not. In that respect, at least, the agency knew how to take care of itself. Helms doubtless understood. And approved.

"And?" said Laidlaw.

"I think he's on our side," Thorn said. "Anyway, he'll try to keep us going until the Icelandic election. Which reminds me, there's some more good news."

"The Luxembourgers have agreed to take the Cruise missile," said Mendelsohn.

Thorn frowned. "No," he said. "It's that there actually is someone in the White House who's worried about the Icelandic election: The President's political advisor thinks that, if the Communists win and we get kicked out of Keflavik, it'll look like another Panama Canal and stir up the natives in Nebraska. That'll help."

"Thus does Omaha shape the world," Mendelsohn mused.

"Knock it off," said Thorn. He turned back to Laidlaw. "There's some more bad news. The deputy is not happy about Spencer. He is in fact at ten on a scale of one to ten extremely unhappy."

"But why?" said Mendelsohn. "What could possibly be wrong with an alcoholic Lothario with six months to live and no experience or training floundering about a little country awash with the KGB as a deep cover agent?"

Laidlaw wondered how Mendelsohn could get so tipsy on two sherries.

"It's not that," said Thorn.

"It's the 'no-journalist' rule," said Laidlaw.

"You got it," said Thorn.

Established in the Ford administration, the "no-journalist" rule was another of the reforms foisted upon the agency after the humiliation of Watergate. It made no sense. Every intelligence service in the world used journalists for agents.

"I thought that rule could be bent," Laidlaw said.

"It's being bent," said Thorn. "If it weren't, my first words to you would have been to yank him. As long as this operation stays in house, Spencer stays. But if it gets out to the White House or congressional oversight, no journalists means no journalists."

"Isn't the deputy concerned about our mole?" Laidlaw said. "Isn't he concerned about World War III?"

"He's scared shitless about World War III," Thorn said. "But we're a bureaucracy, you know. Just another bureaucracy. We merely move a little faster than the others. Which reminds me, when do you want Karin? I can't keep her cooling her buns in Oslo forever."

"Not yet," said Laidlaw. "Spencer's just landed. She's only backup."

"I may have to agree with you differently, old buddy," said Thorn, finishing his beer. "If Spencer has to be yanked, she'll go in as our chief asset."

"That wasn't what I planned," said Laidlaw.

"Poor Karin Nielsen," said Mendelsohn, his grin now more melancholy than idiotic. "Such a pretty girl."

Reykjavik's government offices were all within walking distance of one another, but with the rotten weather that day Spencer was compelled to use taxicabs. Most Icelanders spoke Icelandic, one of the Scandinavian languages, and some English. One of Spencer's taxi drivers that morning had proved a notable exception. He had been so dumbfounded by Spencer's request to go to the foreign ministry that, after twenty minutes of forlorn and aimless driving, Spencer finally pointed out the window and shouted, "Ask!" With that, ignoring the pedestrians Spencer gestured to, the driver signaled his comprehension with a broad grin and roared off down the street at top speed, pulling up finally in front of a restaurant called "Askur."

Thereafter Spencer walked, first tolerating the rain, then glad of it, and of the cold, fresh wind. In associating words with cities, Spencer chose "heat" for Washington, "noise" for New York, "old" for London, and "smells" for Saigon. Reykjavik's word was "clean"—crystalline clean, clean streets, clean air. No wonder Iceland had the highest longevity rate in the world. He wondered whether such environmental purity had any beneficial effect on certain cardiovascular ailments.

There was another advantage to walking. He could more easily ascertain whether he was being followed.

On this particular day, he wanted very much to be followed, for these many interviews he had scheduled would amply establish his cover. He could only hope that last ridiculous cab ride hadn't raised any suspicions.

As he started up the steps to the small foreign ministry, a sailor in a dark watch cap and pea jacket stepped from a doorway across the street and began walking quickly away. That morning, as he had gotten into a taxi at the Hotel Thor, Spencer had seen a similarly dressed sailor walking quickly away across Austurvollur Square. Seldom did sailors have such pressing appointments.

By morning's end, Spencer had gathered enough data on Icelandic energy to write the article then and there—an article acceptable to the elite readers of *Perspective*. Icelanders were a serious people, and they took their statistics seriously. Spencer's notebook was jammed with entries about megawattage and kilowattage, geothermal TCALs and brine aquifers.

The picture that emerged was compelling. The country's hydroelectric power potential alone was estimated conservatively at thirty-five billion kilowatts, much of it from just two rivers in the south, the Thjorsa and the Hvita. And the geothermal resources were of the same awesome magnitude. Underground steam heated every building in Reykjavik and in nine other communities. Hydroelectric power accounted for nearly all the electricity used, including the enormous amounts consumed by the huge Icelandic Aluminum Company plant near Reykjavik, Iceland's only heavy industry. If a means could be found to power fishing trawlers with electricity instead of oil, Iceland would have no problems.

The Icelanders could have more than that. They already had one of the highest standards of living in Europe, but they could be rich—as rich as the Saudis. Less than seven percent of these resources were currently being used. Ireland had climbed out of poverty by attracting foreign industry with a pool of cheap, skilled labor on the doorstep of Europe. Iceland could provide infinitely more than that—more than sixty billion kilowatts of cheap electrical power. Electricity could not be exported, but industry could be brought to it. That lone aluminum plant could be joined by dozens more, by all kinds of light manufacturing, chemical firms, assembly plants. Iceland was just seven hundred kilometers from the British Isles. In per capita terms, it could become an industrial colossus.

Icelanders would have to pay a price—in threats to cleanliness, beauty, and health. The Norse culture they had managed to preserve for more than a thousand years would be threatened by every foreign influence imaginable. It was a price no Icelander could bear paying. The construction of that one aluminum plant had caused a bitter controversy.

But the economy was out of control. The inflation rate had defied every government's efforts to curb it and was now nearly sixty percent and was being driven relentlessly upward by the price of oil. Industrialization, new foreign exchange, could change that.

This was Spencer's story, not the vaguely technical piece Laidlaw had suggested. It appealed to the newspaperman in Spencer, and also to the would-be spy. In researching it, he would have ample reason to travel throughout the country—power plants in the north, dams in the south, fishing villages in the east—examining every aspect of Icelandic life, talking to anyone he wished. Including the friends of Geir Krog.

Spencer had talked to seven people that busy morning. In between their statistical discourses on brine aquifers, he chattered, recounting his adventures on his last visit during the cod war, letting the conversation drift to the forthcoming election, to the terrible murder, to Krog.

Every one of them knew Krog by reputation. One, an engineer with the National Energy Authority, doubted that Krog was capable of such a brutal crime but added that Krog, like many Icelanders, fought a drinking problem. He also doubted that Krog had left the country, describing Krog as an intensely patriotic man who would want to resolve this matter within the terms of Icelandic justice. Others thought Krog had escaped on a fishing boat. Another thought he was dead. Yet another expected that Krog, a sailplane pilot, would steal an airplane and try to escape to Scotland.

None of them thought the murder would have any effect on the election, Krog's high standing in the Workers' and Farmers' Party notwithstanding. One minister found the notion vastly amusing. "In an unsophisticated country like yours—that is, there are countries in which a personal tragedy of this sort might influence votes," he said. "But Icelanders, we are a very serious people, very pragmatic about our politics. Murders have little to do with the inflation rate." And then the man became very serious himself, returning the conversation to Russian oil imports. Icelanders were also very pragmatic about the Russians.

As Spencer remembered, the bar of the Hotel Thor was jammed at lunchtime. He paused there briefly, indulging himself with a double scotch for which he paid nearly nine dollars in Icelandic Kronur. There were no sailors in watch caps, no one particularly suspicious. Indeed, a number of the men at the bar looked at *him* with suspicion. No one, not even a Russian, could do that more darkly than an Icelander.

Sverrir Axelsson walked through the entrance of the Hotel Thor restaurant at the precise moment they had arranged to meet for lunch. Though Spencer's age or older, he looked almost boyish—and quite scholarly, pale blue eyes behind thick, black-rimmed glasses. He was a columnist for *Kvoldbladid,* Iceland's largest afternoon newspaper. They had met during the cod war, then again a year later at George Peterson's house in Baltimore. Spencer's articles were read by some two million people; Sverrir's, by forty thousand. Yet Spencer had made a point of treating him as an equal, a true colleague. Sverrir appreciated that.

Nervous, Spencer had another double scotch. Axelsson, very careful about his drinking, contented himself with a beer. The faintest of frowns crossed his face at the size of Spencer's drink. "*Skal,*" he said, lifting his own glass politely.

Sverrir listened as Spencer elaborately—perhaps too elaborately—explained the magazine assignment that had brought him to Iceland.

"You should have no problem finding people to help you," Sverrir said. "All your articles on the cod war were reprinted here."

"George Peterson told me about that," Spencer said, glancing out the window at Austurvollur Square.

There was another sailor in a watch cap. How long would it take them to accept his cover?

"They made George a Knight of the Order of the Falcon for bringing you here," Sverrir said. "There was some talk about one for you."

Spencer grinned, reminding himself of how absurd Chesley would have found that. The Order of the Falcon. "What will you do next?" she would have asked. "Become a Shriner?"

"I was only doing my job," he said.

"That was noted," Sverrir said. "By so fervently championing our point of view, you were merely reporting the truth." He smiled. "But it wasn't that. The problem was that you are not Icelandic or Icelandic-American."

"Not through my own choosing."

"No, of course not. Which brings us to the real reason you've come here. This energy story is just a pretext, an artifice."

"The real reason?" said Spencer, reaching for his drink.

"Iceland fascinates you. You're going to become one of those Iceland addicts. We have quite a few."

Spencer sipped slowly. "You've found me out," he said. "The magazine piece gives me an all-expense-paid Icelandic vacation, and a small profit on top of that. But there's a matter of professional interest to me besides that. This election. Can the Icelandic government really fall to the Communists?"

"'Fall' is too pejorative," Sverrir said. "Ours is a healthy democracy. They're given their chance, and this time they have a good one. The four other parties can claim no success with inflation."

"The Communists have vowed to throw us out of Keflavik."

"Yes."

"Will they?"

"I think that's negotiable," Sverrir said. "But it could be negotiable with the Russians. If Erikisson wins and the Russians suddenly lower the price of the oil they sell us, I think your sailors will have to pack up their duffel bags."

"What if we made a counteroffer?"

"It might be too late. Your State Department is always too late. They were almost too late in the cod war. That base is Iceland's only strategic weapon. We will use it."

The subject of Krog came up, but Sverrir was a professional newspaperman and questions would only alert him. Laidlaw had stressed repeatedly that Spencer was to take no one into his confidence. Spencer intended to violate that order, but not yet.

"I met a really attractive woman on the flight over," Spencer said. "A stewardess. A friend of George and Sonja Peterson's."

"Elisabet Bjornsdottir."

"You know her?"

"Everyone in Iceland knows Elisabet Bjornsdottir, or about her," said Sverrir. "Some say she is our most beautiful woman. She is a stewardess only because she likes to travel. If we made movies in Iceland, she could be our leading—how do you say?—star? Even if she could not act."

"Most American stars can't act."

Sverrir nodded. "We see your movies on our television," he said. "I'm surprised Elisabet didn't leave Iceland long ago to become a model in New York. Or marry some rich American. I interviewed her for *Kvoldbladid* and once she said she became very sad if she stayed too long away from Iceland. Very depressed. How did you two get along?"

"She had me to her apartment last night. To hear her father's jazz records."

"You should consider yourself much honored."

Over Sverrir's objections, Spencer raised his hand to signal the waiter. He could function with three whiskies. Even doubles. It would certainly enhance his cover.

Spencer's last interview that afternoon was an added starter. On a whim, returning from a look at Reykjavik's underground geothermal heating pipes, he decided to stop in at the Althing building and ask to see Gunnar Erikisson. The Communist leader was there, even though the parliament was not in session that day. To Spencer's amazement, Erikisson readily agreed to meet with him. After a stiffly formal introduction, they sat together on a red leather banquette in a window alcove outside the Althing chambers.

Erikisson was an entirely gray man—gray hair, long and wispy; a gray pallor; gray eyes behind gray-rimmed spectacles; gray flannel trousers and a gray tweed jacket; a grayish white shirt; a dark gray tie.

As Spencer expected, Erikisson was both flattered and apprehensive at being sought out by an American correspondent.

He seemed so jittery beneath his grave formality that Spencer decided to be prudent, to choose a neutral, safe subject. Explaining his magazine assignment, Spencer asked, "Mr. Erikisson, Iceland has traditionally resisted any sort of foreign investment or foreign industrial exploitation of its tremendous resources of electrical power. In view of Iceland's deteriorating economic situation, however, do you see any prospect of this changing? I mean, should your party prevail in the upcoming election, do you see any prospect of a different policy? Would you permit some foreign industry here?"

Erikisson looked stricken, as though Spencer had just driven an icepick between his eyes. Though Spencer would not have thought it possible, he grew paler. His eyelids fluttered, and a rapid tic pulled at the corner of his upper lip. His hands began to chase each other around his lap. "I . . . uh . . . we have the one aluminum plant here near Reykjavik," he said. "It . . . it has proved to be of much benefit. I . . . I don't know about . . . Iceland's culture and environment must be—be preserved at all costs. But the working people must, too, be protected. I . . ."

He glanced nervously up and down the corridor, then quickly looked at his watch and jumped to his feet. "I'm sorry," he said. "An appointment. I've forgotten. I'm quite overdue." He shook Spencer's hand. "I am pleased to meet you. Thank you for what you did for us against the British imperialists."

Then he was gone, striding across Austurvollur Square in awkward haste. Spencer had flushed a quail.

Spencer pondered the two telephone numbers Laidlaw had given him. The one in New York for routine calls, and the special one in Glasgow to be used only in extreme emergencies. The New York one was an open line that required that all conversations be conducted in cover. The Glasgow number would patch him into a "clean" line direct to Washington that could not be tapped but had to be used sparingly.

It was time for his daily check-in with Laidlaw. For a moment, he thought of using the Glasgow channel so he could relate more amply Erikisson's extraordinary reaction. But he didn't want to seem rash or hasty—an amateur. Instead, he returned to his room, pausing to pour a Johnnie Walker and water before sitting down at the desk overlooking Austurvollur Square and picking up the phone.

"*Perspective* magazine." The woman's New York accent was harsh.

"Jim Clepich, please. This is an overseas call. From Iceland."

"Oh. Just a minute, sir."

There was a click, another click, and a long wait. Finally, Laidlaw came on the phone, his voice uncharacteristically gruff. "Clepich."

"Jim? This is Jack Spencer, in Reykjavik. Listen. I've started my interviews and everything, and I think now that maybe I want to pursue a slightly different angle."

"What different angle?"

"Well, instead of confining this to the techniques of harnessing geothermal and hydroelectric energy, which is pretty goddamn dull, I thought I'd include more of a human element. I mean, Iceland does have a hell of a lot of electrical energy. But if it were to exploit it, Iceland would have to pay a big price in the way of the threat to its environment and its culture. It's the quintessential dilemma of the era of energy scarcity. The same sort of thing we face in Alaska. I've talked about it with some of the officials here. One of them, Erikisson of the Communists, got really excited. I mean *really* excited."

Laidlaw paused. "Okay," he said, finally. "It sounds interesting—as an angle. But don't let it take over the whole story. Don't lose sight of the main point. Remember, our readers are here in the United States, not in Iceland."

"I'll keep that in mind," Spencer said. "I think I may go out to the country. Take a look at some of these rivers and power plants. They've got a big hothouse complex here, heated with underground steam, where they grow bananas and tomatoes just a few miles south of the Arctic Circle."

"Good. Get some pictures. Don't leave things to memory. How's the weather up there? Are you freezing your ass off?" Laidlaw never swore.

"No, it's much less cold than I expected," Spencer said. "I'm really quite comfortable."

"Good. Stay in touch."

After he hung up, Spencer slouched back in the chair, sipping his scotch as he looked out over the bright rooftops of the city. He had told Laidlaw everything, including the fact that it was not cold—that he was not overly worried about the Russians. Now, as far as he was concerned, his work day was over. He took another sip, a large one.

Emil Jahn's plan for capturing Geir Krog was an old, simple, and effective one: Find someone close to him to take as hostage. But it was not succeeding; they had gone through Krog's address book and made inquiries everywhere, but there was no one that close. Krog was a loner, a man with many acquaintances but few real friends. His parents and brother had moved to Canada years before. He had gone from woman to woman without, apparently, establishing any enduring relationships. His chief passions were his work, his outdoor pursuits, chess, and his politics. No wonder Jahn liked him; they were much the same.

Jahn went through the address book again, circling the names of the nine women who might have had or were known to have had affairs with Krog. Jahn would have his men investigate them one more time; perhaps there were still strong ties. He glanced through the photographs his men had taken. He would like to investigate one or two himself.

His telephone rang. It was the Polish embassy. The consular affairs official would be able to see him now. That meant a summons from Gorushchenko.

The Soviet ambassador was in the same basement room and just as angry as before. Gorushchenko began speaking in his ugly growl as soon as Jahn shut the door. "That fool Erikisson has just been to see me. There's an American reporter here who tracked him down at the Althing for an interview. His first question—his very first question—was whether as prime minister Erikisson would allow foreign industrial development in Iceland!"

Jahn was covered. "His name is John Spencer. He's from Washington. He was here in 1976 to cover the cod war with Britain. He's come again to do a story on Icelandic energy for an intellectual magazine based in New York called *Perspective.*" Jahn paused. "Erikisson is not the only one he's talked to," he said. "This Spencer has spent the entire day interviewing Icelandic officials. The subject was energy."

Gorushchenko squinted at him through his cigarette smoke. "Have you searched his room?" he asked.

"Nothing of consequence."

"Have you run his name through Moscow?"

"He's clean. He's had a number of overseas assignments but has never appeared on an agents list. He's had a few minor CIA contacts, but the kind you'd expect. They're always trying to glean things from journalists."

"Have you checked him out with our friend?"

"Of course. There's nothing. No word from Washington. No attempts at contact. Nothing. The only thing suspicious about Spencer thus far is that taxi ride and the fact that he's come here so close to the election."

"Erikisson is paranoid over this," Gorushchenko said. "He was on the verge of calling everything off."

"Did you reassure him?"

The Russian glowered. "No. I told him he could be assassinated at any minute," Gorushchenko snarled. Then he snorted. "I told him he was getting jumpy; that there was nothing this reporter or any American could do or say to affect the outcome of the election. Everything has been arranged."

"All of which is perfectly true," said Jahn. "Presuming he can still provide the manpower."

Gorushchenko leaned back, exhaling cigarette smoke. "I do not like the idea of this American journalist," he said. "I know that security is now your responsibility but I have rank on you and I will use it if necessary. I want you to contact our friend again and have him run a computer check on Spencer."

"That would be very difficult—and very dangerous—for our friend," Jahn said.

"He's being paid very well," said Gorushchenko. "And in a few more days we shall no longer have need of him. This is important, Colonel. You and I have never been involved in anything so important."

"Yes, Herr Botschafter."

"I want you to keep a very, very, very close watch on this Spencer. And put a man on Erikisson, as well. He's beginning to make me a little paranoid. And this time don't hire a Krog."

Less than three hours later, the KGB's American in Iceland had the information—or the lack of it. The risky computer check had drawn a blank. Spencer was clean.

Jahn, back in his hotel room, telephoned the Polish embassy. "Tell the consular official," he said, "that the answer to his question is still 'no.' "

Geir Krog had been out in the wild for so long that it felt more natural than a human habitation. He had accustomed himself to the cold, the uncooked food, his own unwashed body, and cuts and scratches he found he was able to completely ignore. His hearing had become so finely tuned he could detect the slightest shift in the wind or the sound of a car on a gravel road miles away. Traveling only in the darkness, he found his night vision had improved as dramatically as though he had taken a magic potion. There may have been less myth to Eyvind of the Hills than people thought.

Egilsstadir lay in the middle of a long valley that contained one of the few forests in Iceland. The birch and aspen were scarcely twelve feet high, but they grew thickly and provided ample cover. Krog had been hiding in it all day, watching the lone asphalt runway and small terminal building that constituted the Egilsstadir airport.

It was much like spending a day in a theater, a theater that gave only two main performances—morning and afternoon domestic Icelandair flights from Reykjavik. Within twenty minutes after the aircraft took off again, all would be gone, the terminal deserted, the runway just another desolate place beside the forest, the theater empty.

Except for the policemen. There were two of them, relieved every four hours. One hung about the terminal; the other strolled the perimeter of the airstrip. Krog moved as close as he could. Normally, Icelandic policemen did not carry guns, but normally there were not suspected murderers on the loose. Krog would have to assume that each carried a pistol.

There had been four breaks in the long, dull monotony of hours between the two Icelandair flights. The first was the unexpected—and, for Krog, briefly terrifying—appearance of a Coast Guard patrol plane. It made one low-level pass over the field, then turned and landed. The pilot taxied to the terminal, keeping the engines idling while a crewman ran inside and fetched a package. With that aboard, they flew off, shifting course toward the sea. Krog took a deep, relaxing breath. The Coast Guard visit had nothing to do with him. He was spared a chase, and could continue with his plan. He lay in the woods, waiting.

Around noon, a violent storm roared in from the south, drenching the valley with a cold, unrelenting downpour for half an hour and driving the policemen to the shelter of the terminal. If there had been an aircraft on the ramp, Krog would have seized that moment to steal it. But he had to wait, his clothing slowly drying in the returning sun.

Midafternoon brought what Krog had been counting on, a private plane. A six-passenger, V-tailed Beechcraft Bonanza landed roughly and taxied to the terminal area. Krog rejoiced to see the pilot park it, kill the engine, and tie it down. Not longer after, a speck in the distant clearing sky proved to be a small overhead-wing Cessna 150. Its pilot also parked it and tied it down, but first—making Krog even happier—he stopped at the avgas pump to refill his fuel tanks.

Now the waiting became even less endurable. Krog dared not make his move until the fall of darkness. He stared through the foliage at the afternoon shift of bored policemen, knowing that at any minute either or both the two pilots might return and fly off. The afternoon Icelandair flight from Reykjavik came and went. The policemen changed shifts again. The sun sank and the shadows lengthened. Still the pilots did not come. At last the eastern sky began to darken, the deepening hue spreading overhead like a curtain being pulled by the gods.

Krog got to his feet, painfully, for the first time since sunrise. In his hand he held that rarest of objects in nearly treeless Iceland, a length of wood. A club. *Now I am the compleat Neanderthal,* he thought. With well-practiced stealth, he slipped along through the trees, circling toward the terminal building, again deserted but for the two policemen. One lounged in the doorway, smoking. The other began his walk around the airport perimeter.

They were there in case Krog tried to get aboard one of the Icelandair flights or attempted precisely this—the theft of an airplane. Krog had seen himself described in the newspaper article as a highly skilled pilot. The truth was, Krog had only a rudimentary knowledge of powered aircraft. He was one of the country's leading glider pilots, having achieved two of the three tasks needed for the Federation Aeronautique Internationale's diamond badge. It was international soaring's highest award, and fewer than a thousand had been issued.

That was now moot. He knew only enough about powered aircraft to start them, take them off, and land them. He had little or no experience with their sophisticated navigation instruments or the mysteries of keeping a sputtering engine going.

As he moved through the trees, he weighed in his mind the advantages and disadvantages, the possibilities and limitations of both aircraft. The large Bonanza would have the fastest speed and longest range. With full tanks, it could take him to Scotland. But he had no idea how much fuel had been left in it. The small Cessna, though its tanks were full, could only take him, with a miracle, close to the Faroe Islands. More likely, it could go no farther than Greenland.

And all this at night.

He made his decision.

The man walking the airport perimeter had reached the apron of the runway and turned to the right, heading for the point on his rounds farthest from the terminal. The other, still smoking, started to walk in a counterclockwise fashion around the terminal building. When he had disappeared around the far side, Krog ran from the cover of the trees for the near corner. He flattened himself back against the wall, the length of wood in hand. They had doubtless been on this duty assignment for several days, waiting and looking for Krog, seeing and hearing nothing. They would be bored and tired, irritable, certainly not expecting anyone to steal an aircraft and take it off from an unlighted field after nightfall.

Krog heard the leisurely crunch of the policeman's feet upon the gravel. Tightening his grip on the club, he realized he had no idea how hard to hit the man. Too much force—Krog was a huge man—and he would become the murderer all Iceland so falsely accused him of being. Too little, and he would be captured. He could only guess.

It was a good guess. The man turned the corner and Krog

swung the wood without hesitation, striking the crown of the man's skull with a loud thud and dropping him to the ground in an instant. Krog knelt a moment beside him. He was unconscious but still breathing.

Still holding his club, Krog picked up his pack and ran toward the two aircraft, stopping at the small Cessna. Slashing the tie-down ropes with his knife, he darted for the door, guessing that it was locked, that he would have to break the window and thus alert the other policeman. But the door opened when he pulled the handle! He threw his pack in the opposite seat and climbed inside, feeling cramped in the little cockpit. It would be no problem for Iceland's best electrical engineer to cross the ignition wires. He had started his own and his friends' cars that way countless times. But it was an added complication that could cost valuable seconds, or worse.

He started to fumble with the wires, glancing over the instrument panel outlined in the faint remnants of twilight. There it was in the ignition—the key! Why would a pilot leave the key in his plane? Was it a trap? But why wouldn't he? The police were guarding the airport twenty-four hours a day.

Krog rummaged through his memory for a procedure he had last gone through in a flying lesson six years before—a lesson taken, fortuitously enough, in a Cessna 150. The magneto switches had to go on. The carburetor heat had to go on. The fuel mixture turned to rich. The throttle halfway in.

He pushed his feet on the rudder pedals and pushed the wheel and turned it, making sure the controls moved freely. That would be all the preflight he would have time for. Then he turned the key. The engine coughed, then caught, throwing back a few bright blue sparks of exhaust against the darkness. Krog let it run just a few seconds more, till the sound was full and throaty, then eased in the throttle.

The little plane darted forward and began bouncing over the gravel, Krog steering it from the memory of the field he had gained in more than a day of staring at it. When he felt the tires climb onto the smooth asphalt of the runway, he swung the plane around toward the north and then stood on the brakes and shoved the throttle all the way in. When the engine sounded as though it were running at its maximum, Krog released the brakes. The Cessna leapt like an unleashed dog, roaring and rumbling along the runway, Krog steering toward a distant silhouette he took to be a tree. He had no idea where the other policeman was, and then he did. There was a flash of light, and then another. The damned fool was shooting at him!

Krog fought an impulse to swerve away. Policemen had little experience shooting at moving airplanes in the dark, and Icelandic policemen had little experience shooting at anything. Krog sat hunched forward, his right hand resting lightly on the throttle, his left tightly gripping the control wheel. The next flash he saw through the side window. He was moving past the policeman, past, and away. The Cessna was gathering speed. There was a thunk against the right wing overhead. It could have been a rock he kicked up. It could have been a bullet. He could only hope it had not hit a control cable. What an extraordinary feeling, hurtling along at sixty miles an hour in the darkness.

The Cessna bounced, then settled back to the runway. It was telling him something. He had the control wheel too far forward. He was holding the plane to the ground. He quickly eased the control wheel back. The nose lifted, and the Cessna at once slipped into the air, the noise and rattle of the landing gear abruptly silenced.

Krog flew along the line of the valley until he reached two thousand feet, then made a sharp climbing turn to the southeast, heading toward the sea. As he gained altitude, he regained the twilight. The western sky still had a vivid blue to it, and a faint hint of pale pink at the sharply edged horizon. He looked over the instrument panel—hardly elaborate, but still confusing to a glider pilot. He decided to concentrate on those instruments his own sailplane contained—altimeter, air speed indicator, turn and bank indicator. His only concern with the tachometer, he supposed, was keeping the needle in the middle, in the green. The compass seemed accurate.

His course would take him over the eastern fjords—possibly even Heklafjordur and the little village near his cabin. If he continued on, he'd be headed out to sea, toward the Faroes. And likely a watery grave, for he hadn't the navigational skills required for such a long over-water flight. But they wouldn't know that. And he was supposed to be a desperate man, fully capable of such a rash and reckless act.

Twinkling lights ahead and to the left belonged to some town or village, though Krog could not guess which. He banked the little Cessna toward it anyway, remembering to decrease his altitude by decreasing the throttle. He flew low enough over the place to count two fishing boats tied up at the brightly lit quay, low enough to be heard, if not seen. Then he followed the fjord out to the surprisingly near sea. At the stark silhouette of the final headland—the great dark void of the North Atlantic stretching infinitely before him—he made yet another turn back toward the coast, settling the little airplane on a course that hugged the shoreline. Marked by the faintly visible breaking surf, it curved beneath him, to the south and then to the west.

They would think he was making a mad lunge for the Faroes or Scotland, but he was not going there. He was not going to overfly Iceland and try for Greenland, or make for the Vestmann Islands and snatch an ocean-going boat from one of the unsuspecting fishermen, although that would surely be an intelligent thing to do.

Krog would fly to Reykjavik. That was why he chose the Cessna. The solution to all his problems lay in Reykjavik, he felt sure. Yet they would not expect him there. It was a good chess move.

He allowed himself his first happy thoughts since the beginning of this ordeal, thoughts of vengeance and justice. The Soviets had won the first battle only because of surprise and their cruelty. Now he was prepared for them, prepared for Mr. Rozkowski, whatever his real name.

The running lights of a slowly moving ship appeared below

and passed behind. The unrelenting surf continued its steady guidance. In a short while the glistening icecap of Vatnajokull, the immense glacier, the largest in Iceland, should appear on his right and stay with him for more than a hundred kilometers. A hundred kilometers beyond would come the much smaller Myrdalsjokull, marking the southern cape of Iceland. Then he'd need only swing to the northwest, following a stretch of straight, flat coastline to the hills that overlooked the capital. He felt confident, masterful. Then all at once he did not.

At first he thought that something had happened to his night vision, that its sharp perceptions had been undone by the faint red glow of the instrument panel. But no, the surf below was just as visible, as were the myriad stars that filled the sky out the side windows. Dead ahead, however, there were no stars. Just a great black maw that spread its cloak with every passing minute, slowly enveloping Krog's entire universe. When he was close enough to see the blue electric flashes, he knew. He had taken everything into his calculations but the obvious: Iceland's weather. It had found him as the clumsy police could not. He was about to fly into the center of the most enormous thunderstorm he imagined the world had ever seen.

The rain it carried struck the tiny airplane like a thousand sledgehammer blows loosed at once. There were buffeting winds, and then a violent updraft that caught the Cessna's right wing and flung it over, throwing the aircraft into a roll, and then a dive, and then a deadly spin. Instantly, the instruments were rendered useless, the turn and bank indicator glued to one side. The altimeter dial unwound without pause. Krog's head was pressed against the cabin ceiling with the force of a thousand pounds. He had outsmarted the police, indeed. They would look for his body in the wrong place.

But what about Valkyrie, and all he had discovered? How many millions of people would die with him?

Spencer had taken dinner—lamb and potatoes—at the Hotel Holt, the best place in Reykjavik for lamb and potatoes.

Despite wine, the meal had sobered him, but now he was back in the bar of the Hotel Thor, undoing the food's good work.

He could not find Krog. He would have to compel Krog to find him. Somewhere in Iceland was a bar, a restaurant, a street, where Krog would seek him out. Not in Reykjavik. Krog would not be so stupid as to come to Reykjavik. But somewhere else. Perhaps Akureyri, his hometown.

Spencer drank. He was ruining everything.

Krog would need help. He, Spencer, would be passed out in his hotel room. Gassed. Stoned. Bombed. Drunk.

He lifted his glass, then set it down. Help. He needed help, an anchor, a harbor. Desperately. Soon. Quick.

He threw down some Kronur notes, then hurried to the elevator and his room.

Spencer went through the Reykjavik telephone book listings for "B" three times until he remembered. All telephone listings in Iceland were by first name, a gloriously ridiculous advantage of so small a population. Elisabet Bjornsdottir. On the right street. Would she be in?

"Hello?"

"Hello, Elisabet. This is Jack Spencer."

A silence. "Yes? What do you want?"

"I . . . I'm sorry about my behavior. I . . . I regret that very much."

"As you should, Mr. Spencer. What do you want? It is late."

"I . . . I'm going to Akureyri tomorrow. I want you to go with me."

"What?"

"I want you to come with me tomorrow to Akureyri. It's for my story. I don't speak Icelandic. I need you."

"You can get someone else."

"I don't know anyone else."

There was a pause, another silence. At first it infuriated him, then encouraged him, then pleased him inordinately. She was attracted to him. She was. Otherwise, there would have been a "No."

"Akureyri is a day's drive from Reykjavik."
"Yes. I mean to stay overnight. Separate rooms."
More silence. The longest of silences. Spencer was elated.
"You are a friend of Sonja's and George's. I will help you."
"I'll pick you up at your apartment. At nine."

8

THE HIGHWAY NORTH from Reykjavik followed the twisting curves of cliff and fjord along the coastline and then—after passing the port of Borgarnes—turned up the green, fertile valley of the River Nordura and began climbing the stony hills of the central plateau. The paved portion of the road gave out long before Spencer expected. The hard-packed gravel surface that followed was well constructed but, at the speeds Spencer was traveling, made for rough driving. He had rented a Dodge Bronco, the most useful car for this particular journey. It had four-wheel drive, like many automobiles in Iceland, and was equipped with a two-way radio in case of an accident in the wilderness.

Elisabet leaned back against her door, seemingly unmindful of all the jouncing and swerving, as one might expect from someone who earned her living pouring coffee in heavy turbulence. One particularly bad hole bounced them both against the roof.

He swore, then apologized. "This is going to be two hundred eighty miles the hard way."

"Yes," she said, smoothing back her long hair. "I think you'll find it a much longer drive than it looked on the map."

Spencer grimaced, squinting around a switchback curve that suddenly appeared before them. He had the grandmother of all hangovers, one of the worst he could remember. Furious at himself for the previous day's binge, he had forsworn the requisite one or two curative glasses of whiskey in the morning and now was paying a price. But whiskey and Icelandic roads were not happy partners, and it was even more painfully clear to him that whatever future relationship he would have with Elisabet Bjornsdottir would be almost wholly determined by his intake of the grand good stuff.

Future relationship, indeed. The doctors had not exactly encouraged him to remarry and start fathering more children. He must guard himself against such absurd notions.

"Didn't you know about the airflights?" Elisabet said. "There are four from Reykjavik to Akureyri every day. They take an hour."

"I wanted to see the countryside," he said. "I've never seen the north coast of Iceland before. It will be useful for my magazine article."

"There's a bus, too. One a day from Reykjavik. And the drivers don't make you bump your head."

"I might want to stop and look at something. I wasn't sure a bus driver would indulge me in that." Besides, airplanes and buses could be easily watched. And they departed at fixed times, not when you might want to—or might have to. And no airplane or bus would provide six or more hours with Elisabet Bjornsdottir in complete privacy.

"You could drink on a bus," she said.

He said nothing for a long moment, then thought better of it. "I don't always drink."

They had only cut across a corner of the central plateau and now were descending along the side of a deep northern fjord. The blue water he could see beyond its widening mouth was an arm of the Arctic Ocean. His mind traveled the full distance across it to the polar ice cap at the top of the earth, marveling at the desolation and remoteness. Then he remembered that those waters were full of Russian submarines and ships.

Along the coastal plain the road leveled and gentled, allowing Spencer to increase his speed. Yet, traversing a wide, empty moorlike flat, the road turned away in a long, pointless curve, avoiding no obstacle that Spencer could see, nor any discernible property boundary. It was the third time the highway had done that since they had left Reykjavik.

"Why this curve?" he asked. "Isn't this road long enough?"

"This is an enchanted place," said Elisabet.

"I don't find it at all enchanting."

"Not 'enchanting.' Enchanted. As in the old Norse mythology. Only many Icelanders do not see it as mythology, but as something quite real."

"You mean a home of the gods, Thor, Odin, and all that?"

He glanced at her. She was not smiling. Her wide, gray eyes were quite serious. "The gods dwell more universally," she said. "Here we would likely find some elves and trolls, or possibly a giant."

"Your government believes that? And rerouted the road?"

"It respects the beliefs of those who have them. And as I say, there are many who do."

"Including you?"

"Sometimes."

She still did not smile. Spencer stared at the line of mountains rising ahead, and the dark clouds spilling from between their peaks. After a few weeks in Iceland, he might find himself believing in elves and trolls, too. Perhaps by the end of this trip.

Elisabet uncrossed her legs, stretching them uncomfortably. He took her hand, lightly and briefly, removing his before she would have to make a decision about pulling hers away.

"I'm very glad you've come along," he said. "And very thankful. I was quite amazed when you agreed."

She shrugged. "As I said, you are a good friend of George and Sonja's. And I have been discourteous to you."

"And I, to you."

"Yes," she said. "But I understand that."

"And?"

"Mr. Spencer, we are very forthright in Iceland and I will readily admit I am curious about you. You are something quite entirely outside my experience, both good and bad."

She hunched her shoulders and then stretched her arms at her sides. "There is a small town ahead," she said. "Blonduos. We can get something to eat."

They stopped at a small restaurant in the center of the town, glad to leave the highway that continued on through the mountains to Akureyri. Like so many of the buildings in Iceland, the restaurant was built of corrugated iron. There were paper flowers in small vases on all the tables, and it had a view of the sea. Elisabet ordered for them—a delicious country soup, and a not so delicious dish of boiled fish. He drank beer, and Elisabet let that pass without remark. Quite logically—as Spencer remembered as he tasted, Icelandic beer contained almost no alcohol.

"Tell me again why you are going to Akureyri," she said. "I do not believe that it is merely to look at a power station."

"The Laxa power station, thirty-five percent state owned," he said. "It's on my list of things to see. But I'm also going to make some inquiries about someone."

"Yes?"

There was a fisherman eating at the next table and the young waitress was hovering busily nearby. But it didn't matter if locals learned. That was precisely the idea. "Geir Krog," he said pleasantly.

Her eyes grew even wider. "The murderer?"

"My original interest in him had to do with electricity. The murder suggests a separate story. One my bureau back in Washington might be interested in. About politics."

"How?"

"Geir Krog is deputy leader of the Communists. You're having an election in a few days. This murder could change votes."

"That's crazy," she said. "Krog has been replaced as a parliamentary candidate by his party. No one is going to blame Gunnar Erikisson for the killing. Magnus . . ."

"Your friend the police detective."

"Acting superintendent," she said. "He would find your theory very strange. He would laugh."

"He might find it very strange," Spencer said. "But I'm going to pursue the idea and ask around town. His friends, neighbors, constituents. Nothing like a sex murder to get American readers interested in a story."

"What do you want me to do? All you said was that you wanted me to be your guide."

"Yes, but I need you to help me with these people, too. I don't speak much Icelandic. Besides, I'm an American, a foreigner. With you, they'll be much more willing to talk."

She looked down at her plate. Spencer let his own gaze drop to the smooth skin at the neckline of her blouse, then glanced away toward the window.

"All right," she said. "But it will probably make Magnus very angry."

That pleased Spencer, too.

The rain began thunderously, the iron rooftop of the building rattling as though it were under machine-gun fire. It was nearly dark when they descended the mountains into Akureyri, a big town of white buildings with brightly colored rooftops that sprawled down a hillside to the shore of one of Iceland's deepest and longest fjords. The waterfront was busy with shipping and there was a surprising number of industrial buildings.

With Elisabet's help, Spencer found Geir Krog's street, and then his house. There was a tired policeman in a raincoat and hat across the street, but no one else was keeping watch that Spencer could see. He had no doubt there were others he couldn't.

He drove slowly by, quickly studying the door and side windows. "Nobody home."

"He has no family," said Elisabet.

Spencer had chosen the Hotel Kea. It was a newspaperman's habit to stay at the costliest hotel in a strange town, especially a small one. He had reserved adjoining rooms, each with an excellent view of the huge mountain that towered over the little city—a giant, broad-shouldered mountain, with a line of cliffs trailing across its foot like the hem of a green gown. It was an inspiring view in good weather, depressing in bad. Spencer closed his drapes and, at dinner, suggested that Elisabet do the same.

"Someone might be up there with binoculars," he said.

She smiled with just the slightest turn of her lips. Like Spencer, she had bathed, changed, and relaxed. Doubtless she was tired. He ordered manhattans for them both.

"Tell me why you are so interested in Iceland," she said.

And so he did, as persuasively and charmingly as he could manage. After dinner, he suggested the bar. She quietly accepted, slipping contentedly beside him in a corner booth. He ordered brandy, expensive Courvoisier. There was a soft if melancholy tune coming from a ceiling loudspeaker. She agreed to dance though no one else was doing so. Returning to the booth, they talked of countries they both knew well, of New York, odd memories. She accepted another brandy, and when it was done, they left, their intentions clear.

He kissed her before they reached her door, holding her just close enough to feel her breasts against his chest, but no closer. He was certain he had only to slide his hand from her waist to her buttocks and pull her tight against him, and all that he had thought about for days, all that he wished for whatever weeks or months might be left to him, would be his unhesitatingly. He kissed her as long as he dared, then eased back on his heels.

"I've no choice but to be circumspect tonight," he said. "There's a lot of work I have to do before tomorrow."

He wasn't lying to her.

She pulled back to look at him. Some of her hair had loosened and fallen over her right eye.

"And you are tired," he said. "Very tired."

"Yes," she said.

"And tomorrow is tomorrow."

At that she merely looked at him silently, then turned slowly and reached into her bag for her room key.

"Good night," he said, but she only closed her door softly in response.

Spencer stayed in his own room until he was sure she was fast asleep. Then he quietly called the desk and asked that no telephone calls go to either room until eight A.M. He changed from his sportcoat to a dark sweater and watch cap he had bought in Reykjavik. There was going to be one more sailor creeping about Iceland that night.

He took everything from his pockets but his room key, a penlight, and his old army knife, which held a screwdriver in addition to a razor-sharp blade. If he were caught by the wrong people, he prefered being an anonymous thief to a trespassing American. The hall was empty. Taking the "Do not disturb" sign from the rear of his door, he slipped it onto the front of Elisabet's. The lovers must have their idyll. In a moment, he was walking down the darkened street, just another wandering fisherman. Spencer was beginning to feel less an amateur at this game.

There was no one at the back of Krog's house, just the weary policeman at the front. Spencer supposed that, in a really sophisticated operation, the KGB would have a full-fledged surveillance team here in place, complete with infrared scopes, rifle microphones, poison dart guns, the works. But not in Iceland, in so small a town. Their belief in Krog's return would have to be as slender as the sleepy policeman's.

An IRA man in Belfast had taught him how to pick a lock, but Spencer hadn't practiced the art since he and Chesley had once locked themselves out of their home some two years before. It took him ten minutes to manage Krog's.

Like most of the homes Spencer had been in in Iceland, Krog's was quite expensively and modernly furnished. As he made his slow progress from room to room, Spencer found everything arranged in neat and orderly fashion, but not in a manner that might indicate the objects were much used. The police search had been quite thorough. The kitchen silver was in what was obviously the wrong drawer but set in neat, symmetrical piles.

Cupping the penlight, Spencer ran its tiny beam over the contents of the living room bookcase, looking for loose papers, or books or folders that might contain them. As he feared, he found nothing. No doubt the police had taken everything there was. The same proved true in the study. Returning to the living room, he suddenly realized the anomaly.

Krog apparently subscribed to a number of engineering and scientific magazines. They were all kept in neat and orderly stacks on the bottom shelf of the bookcase—except one. It was in the study, the only magazine in the study, a copy of *Scientific American.* Glancing at the intricate diagram on its cover the first time, Spencer had felt a twinge of recognition. Now he remembered. Turning to the cover article, he saw that Krog had underlined numerous passages throughout.

A noise. The scrape of a shoe sole against concrete. Spencer froze, clicked off his light, held his breath. There was another sound he couldn't distinguish.

With the most careful of treads, he stepped backward, turning, pausing at the study doorway, peering slowly around the side. A silhouette filled the living room window.

Spencer fought his accelerating heartbeat, taking a deep breath, waiting, listening, studying the dark figure at the window. It was the policeman. It had to be the policeman. No one else would be so obtuse. Was he going to enter? Or wasn't he going to bother? What if he did?

Spencer would be no good in a struggle. Despite his height and erstwhile strength, he was a dissipated man, and, though he had been in a few brawls in his time, he would be no match against a trained policeman. There was his knife, his sharpened four-inch blade. Whether he was capable of killing was a question that still fascinated Spencer, but he was not about to answer that question with the life of an innocent Icelandic policeman. No wonder Laidlaw did not want him armed.

So there was only one alternative: surrender, give himself up, sheepishly, foolishly, right there in the house of Geir Krog. And ruin everything. Laidlaw would have him back in Washington within hours.

Could he kill? Wasn't he the terminal man? What had he

to lose? He'd be doing his duty, just as the policeman was doing his. A trained agent would do it.

Spencer would not. The policeman had moved from the window. There was no further sound at the door. There was no one moving around the side of the house. Going to the study window, Spencer saw that the policeman had returned to his unhappy post across the street. Spencer slipped the science magazine under his belt, pulling his sweater down over it. He dared not linger any longer, but he didn't think he needed to.

The article was military in content, highly technical and complicated, something about directed-energy weapons—lasers, and a device called a charged-particle beam projector. Spencer would read it at more leisure.

But the cover had already told him a great deal. The diagram was exactly the one he had seen in the green-covered file on Laidlaw's desk in Langley. All that was missing was the word "Valkyrie."

Spencer's return to the hotel was without incident. Elisabet's door seemed secure, and nothing in his room had been touched. He put the magazine in his suitcase, dimissed the thought of rousing Elisabet, and fell soundly asleep.

Elisabet hardly spoke during breakfast. The inordinately uninteresting tour of the Laxa power plant did not help. Afterward, as Spencer drove hurriedly to Krog's neighborhood, she became more animated. "How do you plan to go about this?" she said.

"Why, I thought I'd go right up to Krog's house and knock on the door."

She smiled, a little.

"I'm quite serious," he said. They parked in front of Krog's house and started toward the door. The policeman across the street—presumably not the one from the night before—was on them in an instant. Spencer at first acted dumb, then belligerent, waving some of his Washington press cards in the other's face. Elisabet, conciliatory, calmed each down in turn, explaining. The policeman scrutinized one of the press cards, studying the photograph as though Spencer might be waving someone else's Washington press card about.

"Talk to whomever you want," said the policeman, handing back the card. "But stay away from this house."

"*Tak*," said Spencer cheerily. "*Tak* very much."

They worked the street, and then a corner grocery, and finally a restaurant. Only a few people were willing to speak with them, but three of these had been fairly friendly with Krog; one, Krog's regular chess partner. All expressed sincere disbelief that Krog could have committed the murder. So, in his responses, did Spencer. He left the strongest possible impression with each of them that he, a visiting American who had appeared out of nowhere, thought that this great and good man had been set up, that it was a gross injustice, that he was distressed about it because he had wanted more than anything to talk to Mr. Krog for his article, that he wished there were something he could do to help Mr. Krog, but that he had to return now to Reykjavik and the Hotel Thor.

As they drove from town, the road before them curving for miles around the shoulder of the huge mountain, Elisabet said what he had been expecting. "I am not a stupid woman, Mr. Spencer."

"Great heavens no, Miss Bjornsdottir. You have a mind as beautiful as the rest of you."

"Just what was going on back there?"

"Just a little American newspapering."

"I speak English perfectly, Mr. Spencer. I am quite familiar with American newspapers. What on earth does 'newspapering,' as you call it, have to do with what went on in Akureyri? You asked crazy questions. You talked more than they did. You didn't seem to care about your political theory at all. What were you doing?"

"As one of the world's great newspapermen, my dear, I learned long ago that you never find anything out by asking someone a direct question. You must be oblique, disingenuous, picking up scraps of this and that, squirreling them away. You mustn't charge but circle like Indians, around and around, till you find your opening. Then move in."

"Move in on what, Mr. Spencer?"

"The story."

"But what story?"

He rubbed his chin, frowning, gripping the steering wheel tightly with his left hand, completely serious now. "I don't know."

She left him alone after that, uncomfortably silent and keeping much to her own side of the seat. He was unhappy about that, yet grateful. He was trying to think.

There was a distraction. It had nagged at the periphery of his vision and his mind for several miles. Finally, reaching the summit of the mountain pass that separated the Akureyri region's valleys from those to the west, he put aside his thoughts to deal with it.

A gray Mercedes-Benz sedan. Sometimes it lagged as much as a mile behind; other times it would surge forward to within a hundred yards, the two figures in the front seat clearly visible as men. Icelandic police would not drive in a Mercedes. The CIA preferred helicopters and milk trucks filled with recording equipment. The KGB couldn't be so obvious.

He calmed himself. This was, after all, the only highway. It was natural that they would speed up and slow down when he did. The road was gravel and wound through mountains. They would understandably be reluctant to pass. Doubtless two Akureyri businessmen on their way south, or engineers. Krog had owned a Mercedes.

Spencer increased his speed by about five miles an hour. The Mercedes did the same.

When at length they passed the village of Blonduos, Spencer abruptly spun the Bronco into a sliding U-turn and headed back into town, pulling up at the restaurant where they had taken a late lunch the day before.

"Coffee," said Spencer to the startled Elisabet. "Got to have some java. I stayed up too late last night." Elisabet, irritated, went off to use the bathroom. He went to the window, as though to enjoy once again the expansive view of the sea, and glanced down the road. They were there. His view of the car was partially obscured by a parked truck, but the color and the outline of the fender and hood were unmistakable.

After his abrupt maneuver, he had gotten an excellent glimpse of the driver and a fair view of the other man. They were not businessmen or engineers. He had seen men with faces like that in Beirut, Belfast—even Saigon, aboard innocent little motor scooters.

He and Elisabet were in trouble—deadly serious awful trouble. There would be just as much danger getting back to Akureyri as there would be continuing on toward Reykjavik. Police from Akureyri would take forever to come, if they would respond at all to such a ridiculous plea. Driving a Mercedes was not illegal in Iceland.

He could use the sanitized line in Glasgow for an emergency call to Laidlaw. But then what—sit and sip coffee till the Marines landed?

He would make a run for it. The big brave terminal man, armed with his deadly army knife-cum-screwdriver, would do the courageous thing. Easy. What was not easy was deciding what to do with Elisabet. Leaving her behind in the village would be foolish. As Laidlaw would put it, she might be viewed as "contaminated." Those two thugs might be just as content to take her first and go after him at leisure. He would have to keep her with him. Certainly, that was what he wanted to do, whatever the risk.

"In the next few minutes," he said, as they got back into the Bronco, "some very strange things are going to happen. Please just do as I say, and worry not."

"Jack, this is becoming tiresome."

"Dear Elisabet, there are worse things than tiresome."

With that, he began turning into the street, nonchalantly, as though they really had just stopped for coffee, as though they had not the slightest notion that the ubiquitous Mercedes might be lurking just down the street. But instead of returning to the road to Reykjavik, he suddenly spun the wheel and roared off toward the north and a side road that swung down along the shoreline. He had studied the map, and this road was ideal. After a few miles, it cut back to a branch of the main highway at a point where he would have a choice of heading north onto the huge Skagafjordar peninsula, east to Akureyri, or south to Reykjavik. There was even a dirt track he could take back up into the mountains. If he could get enough of a lead on it, he could escape the Mercedes completely.

Which is why he did not take that ideal road. The Bronco simply was not fast enough. Instead, as soon as the body of the parked truck obliterated his view of the Mercedes in the rearview mirror, he pulled swiftly between two houses, bumping over the gravel and grass that separated them and sliding to a stop at the rear of the largest. As he hoped and expected, the Mercedes soon went speeding by.

An Icelandic woman was standing at the back door, holding a kitchen towel.

"Is Mr. Olson here?" said Spencer politely.

The woman only stared.

"I'm sorry," said Spencer. "I'm looking for Mr. Olson. I must have the wrong house. *Tak.* Bye-bye."

He drove back out onto the street ever so slowly. Also as he hoped and expected, the Mercedes had vanished.

Clear of Blonduos and once again on the road to Reykjavik, Spencer drove as fast as he could—perhaps a little faster—maintaining the most precarious balance between traction and centrifugal force. Notwithstanding his need to concentrate, Elisabet wanted to talk.

"What is this all about? What was that car?"

"The car was a lovely new Mercedes-Benz sedan, what exact model I can't say. It followed us out of Akureyri. It contained two of the unloveliest gentlemen you have ever seen. And I would not be surprised if they wanted to kill us, or worse."

"What?"

"As to what this is all about," he said, skidding badly in the deep gravel of a curve, "I quite honestly cannot say exactly. The story I came here after does have to do with electric power. Krog is involved. But it's more than that. It started in Washington. I can't tell you the rest. Although it's apparently much more serious and important than I had thought. Our friends in the Mercedes seem to be taking it very seriously."

"Jack, you are a newspaperman, aren't you?"

"I am. I have the liver to prove it."

"But . . ."

"Newspapermen sometimes get mixed up in things. I appear to be mixed up in something."

The Mercedes was behind him again in twenty minutes. Though near enough, the men did not try shooting at him. Once more he began to doubt his own judgment. Perhaps they were only Icelanders, friends of Geir Krog. No. He had seen Krog's quarters, looked at his books, talked to his chess partner. Krog did not have friends like this.

"They're with us again," he said. "The old tundra fox here is not as foxy as he thought."

She looked back, anxious, but not afraid. He could go anywhere with this woman.

"What was that last little village we passed?" he said, flooring the accelerator. "The one with all the goats."

"Sgaggeres," she said, trying to hold the map steady.

"Is there another one soon?"

"Yes, but it's across that little river from us. We won't go through it." It passed to their right, off in the distance, their last help. The Mercedes now filled his rearview mirror. But for some rolling ridges and depressions, the land ahead was relatively flat, and the road should have cut directly through it. But instead it swept to the right in a long curve. Spencer remembered. They were at what Elisabet had called the "enchanted place." Braking sharply, he swung the Bronco off the road and onto the soft, spongy earth. Then, jamming the transmission into four-wheel drive, he ground and lurched up and over the first slope.

"We know that if we keep going we'll reach the road

again," he said. "But they won't know that. They won't know what to do." He was afraid they would just drive on to the next village and wait. But they weren't as smart as that. They were, in fact, quite dumb. They had decided to follow him.

Reaching the top of the first slope, they decided on something that was not so dumb. One of them began shooting.

Spencer pulled Elisabet down onto the floor. She crouched on her knees, her head on the seat beside him. When he wasn't shifting gears, he rested his hand on her hair. But mostly he shifted, spinning and bouncing and swerving the big vehicle over the undulating surface. The Mercedes would struggle on the climbs but gain on him on the level. The goon hanging out the sedan's right window was aiming very carefully.

A bullet—a large nasty bullet—shattered the rear window, but the angle was high. Spencer looked back and saw that it had torn a big exit hole in the roof.

He roared over another ridge, slewing the Bronco from side to side as he descended the following slope. Just ahead was another ridge, and beyond that a huge saucerlike depression. It seemed a different, darker shade of green from the surrounding turf. And its surface was perfectly flat, or seemed so.

"Are there bogs in Iceland?" he said.

"A few," she said, lifting her head slightly to look up at him.

Another shot from the Mercedes missed.

"Like the bogs in the English moors?"

"Yes," she said. "They are all over Iceland. The wider they are, the deeper."

If bog it was, it wasn't for wading. Spencer pressed Elisabet's head back against the seat again.

"Hold on tight." He took that next, last ridge as fast as he could get the Bronco to go, all four wheels leaving the ground. At the same time he slammed the car into reverse, so that when they landed, the wheels spun backward, slowing their mad careen down the slope enough for Spencer to swerve to the right, just missing the oozing border of that ugly, deadly muck. As Spencer churned the Bronco half-sideways along the bank, the Mercedes came soaring over the ridge, the man in the window firing another missing shot. The car landed askew and spun, rolling, into the bog. Fearful of more shooting, Spencer kept going, snaking up the slope and over the ridge until the bog and its new guests were out of sight. Then he stopped, leaning his head back over the seat and breathing heavily, wishing his heart would stop its maniac pounding. Elisabet sat up beside him.

"I'm going to go back and make sure of them," he said, when his breathing had returned to something approximating normal. "Stay here."

She said nothing, but there was a wild, excited look in her eyes.

Spencer trod his ground carefully, remembering the lessons of a dozen army patrols in as many countries. Crouching, he made a slight circle of the great bog, climbing the slope and peering over the rim of the ridge at a point much removed from where the Bronco had left it.

The Mercedes was on its side, two-thirds submerged and sinking. Spencer could not see the driver, but the other man was half out the open window, holding his gun with one hand, clinging to the door frame with the other. He seemed to be trying to get out, but there was nowhere for him to go. The car was ten or twenty feet from the edge. There was nothing Spencer could do, no way to help.

Help indeed. He should be enjoying this. He found that he was at least fascinated by it, in the clammy curious way he had been in Vietnam. How far was he from the sinking car? A hundred feet? A hundred fifty? He could see the doomed man's face so clearly. So stoic, so quiet, looking about vaguely like a dying elephant before his collapse. All was so still.

All at once, the man began to scream. A few moments later, the bog mercifully shut him up.

"What was that?" said Elisabet, when he returned to the car.

"They're gone," Spencer said. "They're at the bottom of

the bog, wherever that is." He opened the rear door on his side and unzipped his suitcase. Never in all his whiskey-sodden days had he needed a drink so badly.

"Can you drive this thing?" he asked. "Get us back to the road?"

"Yes, I think so," said Elisabet. "What are you going to do?"

Spencer dug his hand into the folded clothing until he touched the cold glass surface of the bottle he had yet to open on this trip. Then he moved his hand away.

"I'm going to read a magazine," he said.

Elisabet had surprisingly little difficulty getting them back to the road. As they skidded down onto the gravel again, she shouted something in Icelandic out the window.

"What was that?" he asked.

"I was just saying thank you to the elves and trolls and giants," she said.

He smiled and returned to the *Scientific American*. It was entirely too technical for every word to hold his interest, but he read the introductory passages, and all those Krog had underlined, as well as all the captions. He got the idea. Mankind had come a long way since the crossbow. The particle beam weapon was a crossbow that could hit things twenty-five thousand miles away.

He awakened slowly, not knowing how long he had slept, conscious only of the fact that they were no longer moving. He opened his eyes. They were parked among a great many large rocks near the summit of a bluff. It was late afternoon, but the gloomy overcast that had enveloped their day had pulled apart to admit great shafts of sunlight, suffusing all around him with a golden glow.

Elisabet was outside, standing up at the top of the bluff, her heavy sweater opened to the wind. Spencer joined her.

"Where are we?" he asked. "Why have you left the road?"

"We're not far from it," she said. She raised a finger to her lips. "Be still."

They were overlooking a gigantic amphitheater of a valley, a shallow, mirrorlike lake at its center, the valley's vividly green sloping sides rising to moss-covered rocky escarpments that in turn reached like cathedrals into a sky of towering clouds.

Elisabet stepped back against him, resting her head against his shoulder, taking his arms and crossing them around her waist. Strands of her hair blew up against his face.

"How did you find this place?" he asked.

"There are a thousand such places in Iceland," she said. "You have to come upon them at the right time."

He held her more tightly, pressing his face into her hair. She reached and lifted his hands to her breasts.

"And tomorrow is tomorrow," she said.

He did not hesitate. His body was throbbing so with blood and warmth he could feel none of the cold. Gently rubbing her breasts, he could tell it was the same for her. He kissed the back of her neck through her hair, then took the folds of her sweater and pulled it back and down. Faster, more urgently, he worked at the buttons of her blouse. Her skirt slipped from her legs—he knew not how. Still with her back to him, she moved away, stepping to the edge of the bluff.

Sometime soon, some endless many times, he would share with her the sundry and marvelous tender little secrets he had learned in a lifetime that until this moment seemed so misspent. But now, in this crystalline instant, he would simply take her, with quick, deep thrusts, pressing himself against her until there was moisture between them and then holding her as tightly as this strange mossy earth held these rocks, and then holding her as softly and gently as he knew how, gazing at the light of the golden slanting sun upon her skin, until they felt the cold again, and the wind.

It was many minutes before they felt the cold.

She was so childlike. He could not imagine that he had ever thought her cool and forbidding, that she could ever have disliked him. He stood up and started to look toward the valley.

"No," she said, taking his hand. "It will not be the same."

She had brought a thick Icelandic blanket for the trip and, with the back window shattered, it proved very useful.

He started the engine.

"Your name is John," she said. "Not Jack, but John."

"Yes."

"Then I will call you John."

She had reached the bluff by means of an old summer road. By the time they had retraced its path to the gravel highway, it was dark enough to turn on the lights.

"We have such a long way to go before Reykjavik," she said.

"We are not going all the way to Reykjavik," he said. "We shall go only as far as Borgarnes on the coast."

"And what will we do there?"

"Visit a sea captain."

9

Like their Viking forebears, Iceland's Coast Guard captains were highly independent in their operations, judging their duty where they saw it best. When Captain Ragnarsson heard from his wife that his American newspaper friend from the cod war was in Iceland and wanted to see him, it was a simple matter of anchoring the *Heimdallur* that night off Borgarnes, his hometown.

Spencer had told Ragnarsson's wife he only needed the answer to one simple question. Iceland was a long way to come to answer one simple question, and as Ragnarsson remembered, Spencer was not a man to ask simple questions.

Ragnarsson had had more than a dozen foreign journalists aboard his gunboat during the cod war, including a French woman who attempted to seduce at least half his crew, and an alcoholic Dutchman whose luggage contained little more than Bols gin and Dewars scotch. At one point, Ragnarsson had a BBC television crew aboard, videotaping a battering contest with one of the British frigates and cheering all the while for the Icelandic.

The captain remembered Spencer best. He had been the only American to sail with the Icelanders during that nasty conflict, and he had written about Ragnarsson and his little ship for more than two million American readers—a number difficult for an Icelander to comprehend.

But more than that. As can sometimes happen in the compelling circumstance of a battlefield or a few violent days at sea, the two men became fast friends. They had not communicated much in five years, but the Spencer now sitting on Ragnarsson's couch sipping hot tea was little changed from the man standing boldly on the bridge slugging down whiskey as their gunboat rolled wildly in forty-foot seas.

Ragnarsson's house was a cozy one, lacking only a cheery fire to place it on England's Dorset coast. Ragnarsson had a cozy, cheery wife to match—plump, dark-haired, with a smile that never left her eyes, always busy with something, now bringing more tea.

As she set it down, Ragnarsson looked at Spencer and Elisabet. "I'm sorry," he said. "You would of course like some whiskey."

Spencer, his arm around Elisabet, hesitated, then leaned back against the couch. "No, thank you," he said. He moved his arm to hold her more closely.

Spencer began edging toward what had brought him to Ragnarsson's house. He wished somehow he could talk to Geir Krog. That horrible murder. Could Krog possibly have done it? Could Krog possibly still be in Iceland? Or had he escaped? As a veteran Coast Guardsman, did Ragnarsson think it was remotely possible for Geir Krog to have escaped to sea?

"I thought you had only one simple question?" Ragnarsson said.

"That's it," said Spencer.

"The answer is no," said Ragnarsson. "I was patrolling the east coast that night. There were up to force-twelve winds. No small boat could have survived ten minutes. You remember what that kind of weather is like."

Spencer nodded.

"Could there have been a larger boat?" he asked. "Could Krog have stowed away?"

"We encountered only one vessel putting to sea that night," Ragnarsson said. "A small but very hardy Polish trawler. The *Waldemar Dulski.* It came out of the fjord where the murder was done, but it was not big enough for anyone to have stowed away unseen by the crew."

"Unless Geir Krog had Polish friends," Spencer said.

"We followed them, wondering what they were doing at sea in such a great storm," said Ragnarsson. "They ignored our offer of help, saying they were en route to their home port of Gdansk. Further out to sea they made a rendezvous with one of those big Russian factory trawlers—the kind that your navy finds so suspicious. I think they passed something by breeches buoy. I'm not sure. We watched them for a while, then sought shelter for the night in a nearby fjord. At that point they were beyond my jurisdiction. And I have learned not to meddle with Russians."

"Did you report this to the police?" Spencer asked.

"I *am* the police," Ragnarsson said. "The detectives, the uniformed policemen, the county judges, the Coast Guard—we are all the same."

"Did you report this to those investigating the girl's murder?" Spencer said. "Does Magnus Andersson know?"

"If he checked my report," said the captain. "I file regular reports."

"But you didn't seek Andersson out to tell him this?" said Spencer.

"As I said, Jack, I've had problems with my superiors for meddling too much with Russians."

"Could Krog have been on that boat?" Spencer asked.

"Ask yourself," said Ragnarsson. "Why would he have a Polish trawler standing by so he could kill a girl he had just met a few hours before? Anyway, that Russian factory trawler did not leave the area. It came to Reykjavik. It is in the harbor now. The *Stolypin*, I think."

"Krog must still be in Iceland," Elisabet said.

"Still in Iceland," Spencer said. "And the Polish trawler may have had nothing to do with it."

Ragnarsson remembered the glimpsed face in the window of the wheelhouse, the unpleasant voice over the radio. "Or everything to do with it," the captain said.

The conversation moved on to happier topics. Ragnarsson brought out the bottle of whiskey and poured himself a glass. Spencer and Elisabet still declined. A few minutes later, they went to bed—in a room as cheerful and cozy as the living room, with a curtained window looking out upon the sea and a warm heavy quilt upon the bed. They climbed beneath it naked but did not make love. To hold Elisabet close and warm beneath the thick down quilt—and sleep—was enough for Spencer.

But a dull, thudding throb at the back of his head would not let him sleep. Throb throb throb. Dead dead dead. The blade still hung over him, ever lower.

Chesley was the last woman he had told he loved and meant it. He could have spent the night telling Elisabet a thousand times. But he would not. Not yet. Maybe never.

It was snowing in the morning, and Spencer and Elisabet drove across the new Borgarnes-Akranes bridge unable to see anything but snow and water on either side. When they reached Reykjavik, the sun was shining through the snow. Spencer explained the shattered window and bullet-pierced roof to the rental car agent as some sort of freak accident. The agent appeared to believe him, but he charged him an additional two hundred dollars anyway and warned him it could be more. Spencer had neglected to take out sufficient insurance.

Outside Elisabet's apartment, Spencer only took her hand. "Go to your detective," he said. "If he is not aware of Captain Ragnarsson's report, tell him everything the captain told us. And ask him for protection. Tell him that, thanks to me, you may be in danger. It's the truth."

"I'll be safe," she said.

"When this is over. In the meantime, ask Magnus Andersson's help."

"All right. Do you really mean to go to Egilsstadir today?"

"Yes. I want to see Krog's cabin," he said. "I'll call you as soon as I get back."

"And we shall have dinner."

"And we shall have dinner."

"And tomorrow is tomorrow."

He squeezed her hand. With snow falling into their hair, oblivious to the pedestrians stepping around them on the narrow sidewalk, they looked at each other. There was no need to kiss.

Spencer's next stop was not far—a small leather goods shop on Bergstada Street. It was fairly chic by Icelandic standards, as the price tags indicated. The woman who came out of what appeared to be an office in the rear was extremely handsome—hair so blond it seemed nearly white, pulled back tightly into a tidy Nordic bun. Her blue eyes were wide and friendly, very intelligent, set above wide-boned cheeks. Her skin tanned and weathered from too much sun and wind. Her full figure must have been spectacular when she was a girl. Had there been no Elisabet, Spencer would not have wanted for a female interest in Iceland.

"Mrs. Kekkonen?"

Her eyes discreetly informed him that he was presumptuous to consider her married just because of her age, which was near his own. Her smile forgave him. He liked her at once.

"I am Evi Kekkonen," she said.

"I'm John Spencer. A friend of George Peterson. He arranged for a package to be sent here for me."

"Oh, yes," she said. "It came yesterday. All very rush. Many, many stamps and postage markings." She went back to the office. Through the doorway, Spencer saw what looked to be stairs, doubtless leading to living quarters above.

"It's heavy," she said, setting the package on the counter.

"Books," he told her. This was ludicrous. Why would anyone rush books to a tourist in Iceland—at an address other than his own hotel?

"They must be quite valuable."

"Yes. Have you a bathroom?"

Of course. The tourist would like a bathroom in which to read the valuable books he had had rushed to him from America. But he wanted to open the package there. Outside, or even in his hotel room, it could arouse curiosity.

Evi Kekkonen's lovely eyes were brimming with inquiry,

but she remained courteously discreet. Perhaps George Peterson sent many nutty friends there. "This way, please," she said. For such a large-boned woman, she walked with an easy grace.

Alone in the bath, Spencer locked the door and tore open the wrappings. The pistol was intact and undamaged. He inserted the loaded clip and stuck it into his belt behind his back. The wrapping paper he stuffed in the wastebasket. No one was going to search Evi Kekkonen's wastebasket. All that remained was the disposition of the hollowed-out books. Obviously, they could not go in the wastebasket.

A wonderfully intelligent idea occurred to him. It was a leather goods store; he would buy a briefcase to carry them in and thus explain to any loitering sailor in a watch cap why he had come to Evi Kekkonen's. And if the briefcase were searched? How would he explain the hollowed-out books? He would put something logical in them. He would stop at the government liquor store and buy some pint bottles of whiskey. Wasn't he the alcoholic journalist?

He bought the most expensive briefcase she had—just because he liked her.

The Icelandair flight to Egilsstadir was in one of those small, cramped, and occasionally terrifying commuter passenger planes that Spencer had habitually avoided using in the United States. The view, however, was magnificent, the flight path taking them past the still-smoldering volcano Hekla and the northern rim of the great Vatnajokull glacier. Somewhere in that icy, barren wilderness was Geir Krog.

At the little Egilsstadir airport, Spencer called into town for a hired car. While waiting, he made his daily check-in call to *Perspective* magazine in New York, collect. His conversation with Clepich lasted less than three minutes. All that mattered was Clepich's last comment: The deadline might be moved up. They wanted Spencer's Iceland article as soon as possible.

Spencer left his car and driver in the little village of Heklafjordur and walked up the long hill to Krog's cabin. He was surprised to find it unguarded.

Even the most sensational crimes were solved only through a high tolerance for frustration and tedium. Day after day, Magnus Andersson had examined and reexamined the same details, the same statements, the same evidence—finding nothing new, making no progress. Then a man believed to be Krog—and it absolutely had to be Krog—had stolen an airplane from the Egilsstadir airport and utterly vanished. Andersson had gone to Egilsstadir. He and his detectives had interviewed more than two dozen people. Andersson had studied the ranges and flight characteristics of small aircraft. He had had the surrounding area thoroughly searched. But in the end, all he knew was that Krog had stolen an airplane and vanished.

Andersson was growing to dislike Krog. Even if he were innocent of the girl's murder, as Andersson now strongly suspected, he was otherwise building up a considerable criminal record: unlawful flight, obstruction of justice, burglary, cruelty to animals, assault upon a police officer, and grand theft. The file in Andersson's briefcase was becoming very thick.

Andersson was growing to dislike many people. In the terminal at the Reykjavik municipal airport—blithefully waiting with a small group of Icelanders for the return flight to Egilsstadir—was the American journalist Spencer. What business had he in Egilsstadir? What business had he in Iceland?

But there was a happy moment in Andersson's morning. Elisabet Bjornsdottir was waiting for him outside his office. He took her hand warmly, then escorted her inside, pushing his best chair up to the desk for her. She seemed nervous and slightly flushed.

"I am so glad to see you," he said. "Tonight we shall have a dinner that I guarantee will be without interruption."

"Well, yes," she said. "Perhaps we can. I have to wait for a . . . a call. I'll let you know."

He glanced quizzically at her as he lit his pipe.

"What have you come to see me about?" he said.

Her nervousness seemed to increase, as she looked down at her hands. "I have information," she said, lifting her eyes to his again. "Did you know a Polish trawler left the fishing village near Krog's cabin the night of the murder? Shortly after the murder?"

He nodded, his eyes still curious but noncommittal.

"According to Captain Ragnarsson of the Coast Guard, it was the only vessel in the vicinity that night," she said. "There was a terrible storm, but the Polish trawler put to sea. Later, it made a rendezvous with a Russian factory trawler, the *Stolypin.* It's moored at the Reykjavik waterfront right now. Captain Ragnarsson put it all in his official report, but he wasn't sure you were aware of it."

Andersson shrugged.

"We thought that you ought to know. That it might be important," she said.

"We?"

"I, and John Spencer, the American newspaperman I told you about. We talked to Captain Ragnarsson last night. They are old friends from the cod war."

Andersson sighed. "Elisabet," he said. "We are having enough difficulties without amateur detectives getting in our way. Especially American ones. Especially alcoholic American ones." He paused to relight his pipe. "How did you come upon Captain Ragnarsson? I thought the *Heimdallur* was on patrol."

"It is. He anchored last night off Borgarnes, his home. We stopped there on our way . . . "

Andersson hid his expression behind a huge cloud of smoke.

"On our way back from Akureyri."

"I see."

The ensuing silence lasted until it became most unpleasant.

"Mr. Spencer," she said. "John. He thought you should know this."

Andersson leaned forward in his chair, planting his elbows firmly on the desk and clasping his hands together in the manner of a stern, lecturing professor. "Elisabet," he said. "There were two foreign seamen seen in that village that night. They went directly to the grocery, bought a large amount of provisions, and returned to the wharf and their boat. Captain Ragnarsson's report is altogether logical. As for the foolishness of their braving that storm—well, there are those Polish jokes."

"But the rendezvous with the Russian trawler."

"The storm proved too much for them. Those Warsaw Pact countries like to stick together."

Once again she looked at her hands. Andersson had never seen her behave so self-consciously before.

"There's something else," she said. "On the way back from Akureyri we were followed by two men in a large car, a Mercedes-Benz. They fired a pistol at us."

"What could you have done in Akureyri that would have caused someone to shoot at you? You and Mr. Spencer?"

"I don't know. Nothing. John went there to see the Laxa power plant. He's writing a magazine article on Icelandic energy. I went to help, as a guide."

"It was nice of you to guide him to Akureyri."

She frowned. "John thinks I may be in danger."

"Because of him? Because Spencer is writing a magazine article about the Laxa power plant?"

"It sounds odd. It probably is. He said I should tell you."

"You are surprisingly compliant for an Icelandic woman."

Her frown hardened.

"I'm sorry," he said. "When is your next flight?"

"Not for two more days."

"Why don't you trade schedules with someone? Leave today."

"Leave Iceland? Now?"

"If you are in danger as you say, yes. If it is because of him, as he says, then you should get away from him as soon as possible."

"I'll leave when I'm scheduled to."

She saw the anger in his eyes and returned it. She rose, pushing back the chair.

"I'm sorry I bothered you," she said.

"Elisabet . . . "

"You are a very busy man, busy with this murder. I won't take any more of your time. Good-bye."

She was gone before he could get around the desk. Cursing himself, he sank back into his chair. What a foolish, clumsy, stupid performance he had just given. But he couldn't help it. The woman for whom he cared so much had made him furious—and bitter.

He turned toward the window and for a long time watched the falling snow. He could understand the hatred of the Icelandic Communists for the American base at Keflavik. Iceland would be so much better off without Americans. Or at least one of them.

Reluctantly, he turned back to his desk. He pondered Ragnarsson's report, and why Ragnarsson had made such a point of telling Spencer about it. It might be that Krog had not stolen that airplane. It might be that Krog was aboard a little Polish trawler somewhere in the Norwegian Sea. Or in the hold of a docked Russian factory ship. Or walking the streets of Reykjavik. Russians. Americans.

Andersson realized he had a lousy job.

According to the Icelandic newspapers, Krog's car had been abandoned outside his cabin, stuck in the mud. But walking around the cabin, Spencer could find no ruts or tire tracks or any other sign of automotive struggle. If Krog had abandoned his car, he had done so with calculation, not in frenzied desperation.

The extraordinary view kept Spencer standing for a long moment on the bluff. The cabin was logical as a safe house; it was even more logical as a summer cabin—the far remove from Akureyri and Reykjavik notwithstanding. Elisabet had said there were a thousand such places in Iceland. A few were more breathtaking than the others.

One was the most breathtaking of all. Elisabet nude in the cold wind and golden light. Reluctantly, he took the thought from his mind. There was no one in view or hearing, absolutely no one. He was able to pick the lock of the cabin quickly.

There was the same orderliness as in the house at Akureyri—Krog's neatness, with the thoroughgoing precision of the police superimposed upon it. They had examined everything, cleaned everything, and put everything away. The cabin's three rooms and bathroom seemed altogether sterile, except for the kitchen floor and its faint but still hideous stain.

According to the Icelandic newspapers, Krog had last been seen at the village grocery. Spencer sat down at the kitchen table. Here, they said, Krog had been drinking.

Before, or after? What could she have done that might have so enraged him? Or anyone?

Sunlight filled the cabin. Was there a possibility that the girl had been with someone else? The living room window was large. Standing at it, Krog could have seen everything in the living room and kitchen. But not in the bedroom.

But she had not been killed in the bedroom.

From his chair, Spencer could see the door and, turning, the stain on the floor where the girl had fallen. But someone at the door could not see into the kitchen.

The girl had been surprised.

A cold shudder ran across his shoulder muscles. He looked from door to floor to window to door again. The wind was rising, causing a drumming hum in the cabin's metal roof.

There was no point in remaining further, in browsing among Krog's neatly arranged possessions. There was no point in wandering about the village, plucking at its inhabitants, leaving some word for Krog.

He had to leave at once, as Krog had.

He hurried to the door, slamming it tightly closed behind him. At the bottom of the long hill, in the village, the driver was dozing behind the wheel of his car.

"Terrific view, terrific view," said Spencer, climbing into

the back. "Okay. Back to Egilsstadir. Thank you very much. *Tak.*"

"It is many hours before the Reykjavik plane," said the driver.

"Can't get to an airport too early," Spencer said.

The driver said nothing more until they were well away from the village, following the climbing curves of the gravel highway toward the next fjord.

"You were up at the murder cabin?" he said.

"Yes," said Spencer. "Do you get many people going up there? Tourists?"

"I don't know," said the driver. "I live in Egilsstadir."

The airport, like all airports, no matter how small, would be sanctuary. There would be people. Telephones. The plane to Reykjavik. He tried to remember whether there was a bar—probably not. He opened his briefcase. With exaggerated movements, Spencer took out one of the pint whiskey bottles, unscrewed the cap, and drank extravagantly. Afterward, he managed a careful glance out the rear window. There was nothing. No Mercedes-Benz.

Airports were safe.

The driver left him at the main door to the Egilsstadir terminal. There were ticket blanks in a stack upon the ticket counter. There were plates, cups, and silverware waiting on the counter of the refreshment stand. But there was no one there. It was more than an hour before the plane from Reykjavik. The door facing the runway stood open, the breeze stirring the pages of the newspaper at the top of the stack.

Spencer went to the waiting area, seating himself in the first of several rows of empty chairs. Almost immediately he felt foolish and rose, pacing back and forth a moment, then embarking upon a search of the terminal building.

The manager's office door was unlocked, but the room was empty. The radio and weather rooms were open, but empty. The restrooms were empty. It was as though aliens from outer space had spirited away every human being.

Spencer set down his briefcase and went outside again.

There was no one. Egilsstadir and its airport sat in a wide, low valley. Spencer could not see the town. On one side of the valley was a thick forest of stunted trees. On the other side were bluffs and steep-sided cliffs. Nothing moved on the road.

On impulse, Spencer shouted a greeting—to no one. A pointless, nervous "Hello!"

The echoes startled him. They raced along the cliffs, disappearing behind the terminal building, then resounding, on his left. He shouted again. The sound raced its course again.

He went back inside. There was a gambling machine. He dropped in a fifty-Kronur coin and lost. He kept losing until he was out of fifty-Kronur pieces. He drank from the water fountain. Then he took a whiskey pint and went out the open door to the runway, sipping. As he lowered the bottle, he saw the first of them at the periphery of his vision—a man in a raincoat, stepping out of the forest.

Spencer backed his way into the terminal again, then hurried out the front door—and froze. There were two men coming toward him down the road. Hastening back inside, he looked through the huge north window and saw yet another man approaching from across the field. Only months to live, they had said. But even that appeared to be optimistic.

10

Evi Kekkonen was up late that night, sitting in her nightdress in the office at the rear of her store, sipping Brennivin and listening to radio music as she went over her accounts. She was feeling strangely happy, though she could not think exactly why. The snow that morning had cheered her, reminding her of the coming Christmas. And there had been that funny, good-looking American.

The knocking at the door was low but insistent. Soft rapid raps, a pause, then more, a pause, and more. Evi peered through the curtains of the window at the side of the door, straining her eyes against the darkness, then suddenly giving out a loud gasp. She hurried to the door and unlocked it. The filthy man in the beard stepped in. He looked half-dead and smelled. Shutting the door, she threw her arms around him and hugged him, her cheek roughened by the bristling beard. She hugged him tighter.

"Dear, dear Geir," she said. "I thought you dead."

"I've thought myself dead too," he said.

He stepped back, his large hands on her shoulders.

"You are still my friend?" he asked.

"I am your friend," she said, smiling at him. "Always. You're safe."

He unbuttoned his heavy jacket and lowered himself into the nearest chair. He made it seem ridiculously small. They stared at each other.

"Evi, I did not kill that girl."

"I know that. You don't have to say it. But you are in trouble."

"Very, very serious trouble," Krog said. "I really shouldn't have come. I may only bring my trouble upon you."

It was years since they had been lovers, but a strong bond remained between them. Others had come and gone, but the principal woman in Krog's life was still Evi Kekkonen.

She smiled at him. "We will put your trouble aside, right now you need something to drink, and eat. And a bath. Geir, you are at the moment the least clean human being I have ever seen. Or smelled."

He laughed, for the first time in as long as he could remember.

"A drink now," he said. "That bottle of good Brennivin. Food and a bath later. There's something I must do first. I need my notebooks, Evi. Do you still have them?"

"Of course," she said. "They are in my safe."

She left him with the bottle and his work and went upstairs to her kitchen to prepare something to eat. For a moment Krog simply looked at the stack of notebooks in front of him, as he might have regarded a bomb he had to disarm. But the notebooks were not explosive. They were the key to disarming a bomb, his only key.

Krog knew exactly what he was looking for in the notebooks, and where to find it. He had put the information there, every day, as he had worked and conversed with Rozkowski. He spread the pertinent notepaper out upon the desktop, then went to his pack for the documents he had taken with him from the cabin.

It took only a few minutes. Then he was sure. It was as obvious as the simplest of the equations that had been a part of his every working day. But to know was not to prove or to persuade. Or to prevent the cataclysm from happening.

He sighed and finished the Brennivin. Stuffing the notebooks and the documents into his pack, he then poured another drink and started up the stairs to Evi's living quarters. To bathe, to think.

Krog was not a religious man, nor even a superstitious man, yet he was now half-convinced that he owed his life—and continuing freedom—to the gods. The storm had swallowed his tiny aircraft as a great whale might some small fish. He and the airplane had been tossed up and down, from side to side, shaken and rattled and pummeled, all in blackness, in the midst of a piercing din that sounded like Thor himself was bellowing in his ear. Krog may have been bellowing as well, shouting and screaming his defiant last breaths as a mortal man.

But Thor and the gods and the storm had been kind, or at least not unduly cruel. Half-digested by the great black cloud, Krog had been of a sudden expelled from it—down, spinning and plunging down, into clear air. He saw a faint long line of white below, a distant breaking wave racing across the blackness—far beneath, but nearer and nearer. It disappeared into the shore as Krog jammed his foot against the rudder opposite the tight mad turn of the aircraft. Another wave, much larger, appeared at the left of the windscreen as the Cessna finally shuddered and halted its mindless spin.

There was still the dive. He all too slowly pulled back on the control wheel, leveling the airplane just as a third wave all but filled the window.

He then climbed to a hundred feet above sea level and, thanking the gods and the plane's redoubtable engine, followed the shoreline. It was a circuitous, laborious, and probably unsafe flight path, but it kept him beneath the storms and in the happiest possible airborne circumstance for a sailplane pilot: He could see where he was going.

The weather became generous and cooperative. He was able to follow the coast till he knew he was west of Reykjavik. Reaching what he guessed to be the town of Grindavik, he turned north and inland, and then east again, flying through the starlight in the shadow of a small mountain—a low and gentle slope. Krog had flown this terrain in his sailplane a dozen times or more.

The familiar valley fold in the small mountain's shoulder

was where he had expected it. He lowered the Cessna's nose, pulled back the throttle, and then—on impulse—killed the engine, transforming the aircraft into what was for his purposes a glider. He landed in a rumpled meadow he had used before, though he did not land well. A crosswind almost flipped the wing just after he touched down, and the bumpy ground beat nastily on the Cessna's undercarriage.

When the airplane at length ceased its careening and slewed clumsily to a stop, he flung open the door and began laughing hysterically, gulping for air, cursing and giggling, his head back and his eyes closed, putting aside his black fears and worries, for a long moment of satisfaction.

He was now far in the west of Iceland, more than three hundred miles from the scene of that savage crime and all those policemen, and no one knew where he was. He was only a short way from a good road to Reykjavik, yet he had landed the plane in an obscure place unlikely to be flown over by a search plane. It would be found only by accident. He would be ahead of them all—the police, the Soviets, the Americans—by at least a day, and probably more.

The thought of that small triumph consoled and cheered him as he now sat in the scalding water of Evi Kekkonen's bath. He had been skulking about the Reykjavik area for more than a day now, and, according to the newspaper he had snatched from a doorstep, the aircraft had yet to be discovered. At the very least, he had until the morning to work out his next plans.

Evi entered the room and sat down on the edge of the tub. She took up a sponge and began to soap his back with it. What a remarkable transition that small airplane had brought about. From the maximum misery to the maximum bliss.

"Your food will get cold," she said.

"I am now quite used to cold food. Outlaw fare. I am an outlaw, Evi. I am like Eyvind of the Hills."

"Eyvind of the Hills?"

"It's an old Icelandic legend. You Finns would not know of it."

"It sounds quite romantic. Are you saying we Finns are not romantic?"

He grinned. "Not romantic. Just sex-crazed."

"Yes? It was an Icelander then who wrote 'Finlandia'?" She squeezed a cascade of soapy water over his head. He made the room shake with his laughter.

"I've no right to be this happy," he said.

Evi put her arm around his shoulders. "You've every right," she said.

His expression calmed. "Has anyone come to you about me? The police? Any foreigners?"

"One," she said, kneading the back of his neck. "But he didn't ask about you. An American. A John Spencer. He came merely to pick up a package. He is a friend of George Peterson, the lawyer."

"This man. Spencer. He's been looking for me. In Akureyri."

"How do you know that?"

"I called a friend there. Spencer is a newspaperman. These people are very dangerous."

"He seemed like a very nice man."

"Americans helped me into this trouble. I begin to fear that all of them are with the CIA."

"This Spencer's much too harmless."

Krog still frowned.

"Geir," said Evi. "Perhaps you should see him. He's a friend of George Peterson's. I know you can trust George Peterson. I would trust him with anything."

"I am in need of a lawyer."

"I could write to Peterson. Or contact Spencer."

"No. Not Spencer. If you reached Peterson, would he come?"

"Yes. For me."

He looked up at her.

"Nothing like that," she said. "He is my lawyer. And a friend, a good friend."

Krog put his hands behind his head and leaned back against the wall. Steam still rose from the hot water.

"I'm going to need someone," he said. "I have some important information."

"Do you want me to call Peterson now?"

"No. I will write a letter for Peterson. I'll leave it with you when I go. Call him afterward."

"You will stay the night?"

He closed his eyes.

"Evi, I would stay the year if I could. But I must leave soon. I must be well out of Reykjavik while it is still dark."

She leaned forward, her nightdress opening to reveal most of her breast. He reached with his wet soapy hand. She smiled, then stood and removed the nightdress entirely. In a moment, he had pulled her splashing into the tub with him.

"Your dinner," she said.

His laugh again filled the room.

"Evi, you are food and drink enough for me."

Emil Jahn looked at his watch. He was now very worried about Spencer. Jahn was pursuing confirmation of his conclusions through the assortment of channels available to him, but he already knew enough. Spencer was making suspiciously regular daily phone calls to a number in New York. Spencer was looking for Krog; indeed, he was deliberately trying to attract Krog's attention. Spencer had broken into Krog's home in Akureyri. Spencer had somehow contrived to eliminate two of Jahn's best men—his entire Akureyri detail.

Jahn's initial instinct had been correct. Spencer would have to die. So would Elisabet Bjornsdottir—and the thought of that gave Jahn a nervous, pleasurable shudder. But his second instinct had also been correct. Their elimination would have to wait. Everything must proceed according to schedule. Krog's elimination was the foremost priority. Spencer and his girlfriend could lead Jahn to Krog. As long as Krog lived, Spencer and his girlfriend would live.

But the final resolution was only a matter of days. And, in the meantime, there were other routes to Krog.

"You are giving me reason to be nervous, Colonel Jahn," Gorushchenko had said. "Very, very nervous."

"Everything is under control."

"This new American . . ."

"Is proving very useful."

"You said he was clean."

"I've discovered he is not. That is my job, Herr Botschafter."

"You know that when the time comes we are going to have to get all these people out of the way. We will have enough to contend with at that air base."

"That also is my job, Herr Botschafter."

"You have been very messy at it."

"I intend to be very thorough, Herr Botschafter."

The doorbell summoned Evi Kekkonen from a warm and gentle sleep of several hours. Geir Krog had left her bed almost immediately after they had made love. She had lain there naked and happy, still a little wet from their play in the bath, listening as he moved about downstairs, making his final preparations and finally letting himself out the back door. She had drifted slowly to sleep, wondering in her last thoughts whether—when this awful business of the murder was over—she and Geir might have a relationship again, if they might this time marry.

She was startled by the doorbell. Why had Geir come back so soon? He had said he would contact her again—he hoped within a few days. She looked at her bedside clock. It was not yet five A.M. Evi sat up, wondering whether it might be someone else. But who? Her friends would have telephoned before coming to the door at that hour. Who else? The police? Someone might have seen Geir entering her place and called them. But why would they have waited so long to come?

She decided it had to be Krog, that he was ringing the bell out of urgency, that they might be close behind him, that he needed her sanctuary again, in a hurry, desperately.

Evi threw on a robe and hastened down the stairs. The figure in the window of the door was tall like Geir and wore dark clothing like Geir, but she couldn't see his face. It had to be Geir.

She opened the door and saw the face—a narrow, pink face, a man with pale eyes, thin lips, and no beard. Not Geir.

Before she could speak or cry out or move to shut the door, he stepped swiftly inside, shoved her back against the wall, and—with a hard strong hand—pressed against her neck. She felt an instant of explosive pain and a buzzing numbness, then slumped to the floor.

When she regained consciousness, she was on her bed again, tied to it, her robe removed. There were three men in the room with her—the stranger at the door and two others who looked to be sailors. A gag was stuffed in her mouth and she could not speak. She could scarcely breathe.

The tall, pink-faced one was seated at the foot of the bed. She had to crane her neck slightly to see him, his face framed by her large breasts. He rose and came and sat beside her on the bed. He had a knife in his hand, with a sharp, surgical-looking blade.

"Evi," he said, his voice surprisingly gentle. "We need some questions answered. We have very little time."

She only stared, her eyes wide, bulging. He leaned close, placing the cold blade of the knife against her breast.

"Evi," he said. "I am going to remove the gag from your mouth so you will be able to answer my questions. If you cry out, it will go bad for you. If you do not answer me, it will go bad for you. Do you understand?"

She nodded. Gently, he pulled the gag from her mouth. He set it aside, then showed her some torn wrapping paper. It was from the package that had come for Spencer.

"Evi," he said. "We found this in the wastebasket in your bathroom downstairs. Why was it there? What was in this package? Why did it come to your store?"

"Books," she said, fear causing her voice to falter. "Two blue books. He went to the bathroom. He unwrapped it there."

"His name is John Spencer. He's American. How do you know him?"

"I don't. He is a friend of my lawyer, George Peterson. George lives in the United States. He often has mail sent here. I hold it for him. I held Spencer's package for him. As a favor for George."

"Why would he have books sent to him in Iceland?"

"I don't know. I don't. He bought a briefcase and put them in it. He left. That's all I know."

The stranger nodded. He tapped the knife blade against the side of her breast. "Did Peterson tell you for whom Spencer worked?" he said. "Has Peterson ever said anything to you about doing work for the American government?"

"No. He's just a lawyer. Spencer is a journalist."

The stranger reached and then held something else before her eyes. It was a small tan envelope, addressed to George Peterson by name, but not by address. It had been ripped open.

"The mail you have been keeping for Peterson is very dull," he said. "Legal business. This one, however, is quite interesting."

"I don't know. I'v never seen it."

"I'll read it to you," he said, pulling out a small sheet of notepaper. "It says, 'Mr. Peterson. Thank you for coming. I need your help. Evi says I can trust you. I will contact you soon. It is for Iceland.' "

He leaned close to her again.

"Evi," he said. "This is signed, 'G. Krog.' Geir Krog was here tonight. Wasn't he?"

Her eyes filled with tears, but she said nothing.

"He was here, Evi," he said. "He wrote this note for Peterson and left it with you. He ate and drank here. He took a bath and, I would judge by these damp sheets, made love to you. Your safe is open. He took something from it. You were keeping something in it for him. What was it, Evi?"

She felt a sudden sharp pain in the side of her breast. He ran his finger over the spot and then held it up so she could see the smear of blood.

"What was it, Evi?"

"I don't know," she said, crying. "Some papers."

"What kind of papers?"

"I don't know. I didn't read them. They were all bound together."

"Were they technical papers?"

"I don't know. I suppose so. He's an engineer. They must have had to do with his work."

She wondered whether she was saying too much. Admitting that Geir had been there was already too much.

"Evi, how long ago did Krog leave? A few minutes? A few hours?"

"An hour," she said. It would not hurt for them to know that.

"You must continue to tell the truth, Evi. When is Peterson to come?"

"I don't know. He comes to Iceland regularly."

"Now you are lying, Evi. Krog wants to see Peterson soon. How will Krog contact him?"

"I don't know."

The stranger swung his arm, striking Evi in the face with a sharp, thudding blow. The pain overwhelmed her, briefly blinding her, drowning all her senses. When at length her mind and vision cleared, her cheekbones and nose throbbed. There was a puffy swelling beneath her eyes.

"I have broken your nose, Evi," he said. "It was a very lovely nose, but now it will require a great deal of repair. You must be more cooperative, Evi. Where is Geir Krog? Where has he gone? Where is he hiding?"

"I . . . I don't know." She was sobbing.

"Evi, where is he?"

"I don't know. I don't know. I don't know."

He asked the question four more times. Finally, he picked up the gag and stuffed it into her mouth again. Then he did something strange. He began rubbing her nipple with his forefinger, rubbing it, teasing it, caressing it. In a moment, it was erect.

"We want to know where Geir Krog is, Evi," he said. He held the nipple taut with his fingers. There was a flash of his knife, and sudden burning pain that seemed to fill her breast.

She screamed and raged at him in muffled silence, then craned her head. Incredibly, the nipple was gone. In its place was a small circle of welling blood.

The man looked at his watch, then at her, intently. His eyes had widened, and his face was covered with perspiration. He was breathing heavily. "Tell me, Evi. Tell me."

He pulled the gag from her mouth. She screamed. He smacked the side of her head and shoved the gag back in place. Then, furious, he grabbed her bound hand and pried the little finger away from the others. With another quick flick of his knife, he sliced it off.

She thrashed at him, then fell limp. When he pulled the gag from her mouth again, she only groaned.

"I don't know where he is," she said weakly. "I don't know. I don't know."

He nodded. He looked at his watch, then said something to the other two. In German. Evi did not understand the language, but she knew it was German.

They left the room.

"Where is he, Evi?" the stranger said. "Where is Geir Krog?"

She heard the other two going down the stairs. The stranger glanced after them, then looked back at Evi. His eyes were crazy. He snatched up the gag and crammed it violently back in place.

It was then that Evi realized that her lost finger would not matter, that nothing would matter anymore. He was going to kill her.

He held the knife up before his face, then set about his vicious, slashing work. The waves of pain quickly rose beyond sensation, and she found herself almost a detached witness to the butchery of her body.

By the time he came to the cutting of her throat, she was grateful.

11

Spencer should have known that he was not going to die in a shootout at Egilsstadir airport with four KGB agents. It was too perfect, too glamorous, too much the sort of ending even Chesley would appreciate. He would die, and soon. But not in a gunfight.

He had not even tried to reach for his pistol. He could have killed at least one of them, could have resolved his abiding morbid curiosity, could have died a shared death. Instead, he simply stood foolishly by the ticket counter in the empty terminal, smiling idiotically as they came up to him. It was not until they had him in their car that he had realized they were not KGB but Icelandic policemen.

They had not bothered to search him. One had looked through his briefcase, grinning briefly upon finding the books with the pint bottles of whiskey. Otherwise, they had left him alone. Now, twenty-four hours later, he still had his pistol in his belt. It hurt, but he had no other place to hide it.

He was in a cell—small, antiseptically clean, brightly lit, and windowless except for a tiny pane in the door. The police station was in Kopavogur, a small suburb of Reykjavik. They had taken him to it without explanation and locked him in the cell without explanation. He had been allowed no telephone call and given only two meals. Happily, they had left him his briefcase and his whiskey.

Elisabet. What wretched irony. He had come to Iceland for a last fling of the spear into the universe. Yet all he had accomplished was falling in love. And getting put in jail.

The door opened. Spencer blinked stupidly at the grim-faced policeman.

"Come," said the man. "Bring all your things. You will not be coming back here."

Magnus Andersson was also grim-faced. He motioned Spencer to an uncomfortable chair in front of his desk but offered no greeting.

"I wish you were not in Iceland, Mr. Spencer," he said finally. His voice was as dark as his looks.

"Then why have you made me your houseguest?" Spencer said.

"This is not my home."

"Funny, it suits your personality."

It was a dangerous path Spencer was treading. He smiled as amiably as possible. Andersson did not.

"Unfortunately, you have broken no law. None that we know of. You apparently trespassed on Geir Krog's rented property at Heklafjordur, but for some reason he has not come forward to press charges."

"Why did you have me arrested, then?" Spencer said, ignoring the joke.

"On suspicion," said Andersson. "An aircraft was stolen from Egilsstadir earlier."

"But you've held me for a day. Without charges, or anything."

"It's as long as I can keep you without charges. If the law permitted, I would keep you locked up for a year. Or put you on the next plane to New York."

The pistol in Spencer's belt now felt painful indeed. Bringing arms into Iceland was a serious offense. "Superintendent Andersson, I'm just a newspaperman. I'm just doing my job, researching an article."

"Mr. Spencer. We fought three cod wars against the British and in all of them lost only one sailor killed in a ramming. In one week now we have had two women brutally murdered . . ."

"Two? Two women?"

"Brutally murdered," Andersson continued. "If what Elisabet Bjornsdottir tells me is true, there may be two more bodies to be found in a car somewhere along the road from Akureyri. Four deaths, Mr. Spencer."

"Elisabet is all right?"

"Yes, she is all right! No thanks to you." Andersson hunched forward, holding his hands pressed together before his eyes like a gunsight.

"I don't know what is going on here, Mr. Spencer. I suspect you may be involved. I know Geir Krog is involved. I am sure foreign governments are involved. Funny games. Cloak and dagger. Hide and seek. I don't expect you to tell me what you know about it, but I want you to know this. I'm sick of it. My government is not going to tolerate it. We are a peaceful, civilized country, Mr. Spencer. All we ask is to be left alone. We want no more killings."

"I'm not involved in any murder, Superintendent. I merely became interested in the story."

"And you dragged Elisabet Bjornsdottir into it. You placed her in danger. She has said this herself to me." His hands unclasped as one became a fist. It wavered, then slammed against the desk.

"If she is harmed in any way, I will hold you completely responsible!" Andersson said. "Do you understand?"

Spencer nodded. He stared back into Andersson's dark, boring eyes.

"Did Elisabet tell you what Ragnarsson said about the Polish trawler?" Spencer said finally.

"Yes."

"Does that change things? Do you still think Krog is a murderer?"

"With the evidence we have, he would be found guilty in any court in Iceland."

"Do you think he did it?"

"And now it is even worse for him."

"What do you mean? This second murder—who was it?"

"One of his past mistresses. No one you would know. Or would you? Do you know Krog, Mr. Spencer?"

"I've never met him."

"Did you come here to meet him? Is that why you went to his house in Akureyri? And to Egilsstadir?"

"I've just been pursuing the story."

"You're very meddlesome."

"You said a plane was stolen. Krog's a pilot. Did he take it? Has he escaped from Iceland?"

"The plane was much too small for that. Go now, Mr. Spencer. You are free to go. Your lawyer is waiting for you outside."

"My lawyer?"

"George Peterson."

"He's here?"

"Unfortunately, yes. Another meddler. Now get out."

Spencer rose. Andersson was looking through some papers.

"Who was the woman who was murdered?" Spencer asked.

"Her name was Kekkonen," Andersson said, without looking up.

"Kekkonen? Evi Kekkonen? I—I just saw her yesterday. I bought this briefcase in her store."

"I know," said Andersson. "You used an American Express card. Now get out. I'm very busy. Good-bye."

Andersson decided he would see the justice minister as soon as possible. There were too many foreigners in Iceland now. The situation was getting far beyond the case of Geir Krog.

Even by Spencer's world-weary newsman's standards, George Peterson was an extraordinary man. He had gone into World War II as a teenage sergeant in one of the army's last horse cavalry units and had left it a captain in military intelligence. His father had been a wealthy horse breeder—first in Iceland, then in Maryland—but Peterson had readily abandoned that family interest for the law, which better suited his intricate mind. Though he had graduated from Harvard Law School and had influential friendships in Washington that reached as high as the White House, Peterson preferred to practice in Baltimore.

He had married three times—twice to the same Baltimore woman and lastly to Sonja. He spoke three Nordic languages plus some conversational Russian, German, and French. His Icelandic father had written a book on horsemanship; Peterson was working on a translation of thirteenth-century Icelandic law into English. He grew roses, had been a champion skier, and was—like Geir Krog—a mountaineer and a pilot. He was the honorary Icelandic consul in Baltimore and had been asked to run for the Maryland state legislature.

Sonja called him "my big rock." His face had the planes of a rock, his gray-blue eyes the impassivity. Peterson could be an exceedingly charming man, but his face yielded only two expressions. When he was amused, he would smile. If he felt some other emotion—love, hate, anger, joy, sorrow—he did not smile. The only way to know what George Peterson was thinking was to listen to what he said, and often that provided only the slenderest clue.

He greeted Spencer in the main corridor of the police station with a crunching grip of hand on shoulder. Normally, he dressed quite formally, dark pin-striped suits and the like. Here in Iceland he was wearing a leather cap and a trenchcoat, and a black wool turtleneck sweater. He looked more the spy than Spencer.

As they left through the main door, Peterson bantered on about the universal thick-headedness of policemen, but he became abruptly serious once they were in his rented Audi.

"A 'magazine assignment,' I believe you told me," he said almost acidly. He soon had his rented car rolling at high speed on the road to Reykjavik center.

"I guess you know you came too late for Evi Kekkonen," Spencer said.

"I know. I found her body."

Spencer looked through the rain-streaked side window at a distant gray-green mountain, its lumpy top obscured by a dark, lowering cloud. After a day in that windowless cell, he had almost forgotten where he was. His neck itched with beard. He felt gritty and moldy.

"Superintendent Andersson said it was a brutal murder."

"I met a Marine sergeant once in the war," Peterson said. "He had served in China in the thirties. He showed me some pictures he had taken in Tientsin. They were a sequence, of a man who had been caught stealing. They had tied him to a post, stripped him to the waist, and then cut open the skin of his chest in a huge hole. They then cut out his heart."

He put his hand to his chin a moment.

"Evi was worse than that," he said.

Spencer began to gag. He opened his briefcase and took out the remaining pint of whiskey. It was two-thirds empty when he replaced the cap again.

"I liked her," he said.

"I knew her twelve years," said Peterson.

A yellow Volkswagen came at them in the middle of the road, swerving to the side at the last moment. Peterson reproached it with his Audi's horn.

"Was it Evi who asked you to come?"

"Elisabet," Peterson said. "She called us and told us about your interesting trip back from Akureyri. I had been planning to come over in a few days anyway, but Sonja had me on the next Loftleider flight."

"Elisabet's all right?"

"Yes, yes. As you'll see shortly. We're having dinner tonight together, the three of us. She's worried about you. You seem to have made a fast friendship."

"More than that," Spencer said.

Peterson smiled, but briefly.

"She's one of Sonja's best friends," he said. "Don't get Sonja mad at you."

He turned the windshield wipers to a higher speed—*thickwack, thickwack, thickwack.*

"How did you come to find Evi Kekkonen's body?" Spencer asked.

"I went there for my mail. That's one of the things that bothers me."

"What?"

"There wasn't any mail. None for me, at any rate."

"But she had a stack of it for you," Spencer said.

"So I had presumed. Whoever it was went through her place thoroughly—wastebasket, drawers, her safe. They left her mail, but they took mine. What have you mixed me up in?"

"I don't know yet."

" 'Magazine article'?"

"I'm writing one. I am. The murders are a sidebar."

Peterson slowed the Audi, then swerved it off onto a side road, one that led around a small factory building. Reykjavik was very near.

"Did the police give you a hard time?" Spencer asked.

"Perfunctory. Andersson knows me."

"The son of a bitch locked me up for a day for nothing."

"Not for nothing. Be careful of him. He may be the smartest man in Iceland."

"Smart? He's still proceeding as though Geir Krog were the killer."

"Not really. I think he's chasing whatever you're chasing, except he's not so obvious about it. Was Elisabet right? Did you really go to Krog's house in Akureyri?"

"All part of getting the story."

"You certainly succeeded in attracting attention to yourself, Jack. Don't you think the time has come to explain a few things to me? Lawyer-client relationship and all that? I know only what I've read in the Icelandic newspapers. And what Elisabet's told me."

"I'd think more highly of our lawyer-client relationship if it weren't for all those funny stories you've told me about your other clients."

"I get the strong impression this will not be a funny story."

"Stop the car. Up there by that football field."

"Soccer field. This is Iceland."

They walked, in the rain, to the middle of it. Spencer might be an amateur, but he knew a soccer field was less likely to be bugged than a rental car.

"New navy" or not, an officer could still search an enlisted man's quarters whenever he wished, needing only the CO's permission. But Commander Richards went to Truscott's room without that permission, using a passkey he had pilfered from a CQ. Truscott was away on one of his unofficial jaunts. No one saw Richards enter. He left the light off, conducting his search in the late afternoon gloom from the window.

He looked about casually at first, almost at random. Then he got serious, picking locks, going through drawers and lockers, finding only predictable things, such as magnum bottles of expensive cognac and a cache of Rolex watches. Truscott, as he had guessed, was something of a smuggler.

That they would deal with later. He had looked in all the predictable places. He now tried some unpredictable ones, including the legs of the bunk and behind the plates of the electrical sockets. Nothing. But then, he had not been looking for anything in particular.

Richards rested on the edge of the bunk for a moment, noting the contrast between the gummy blackness of his own shoes and the brilliant sheen of Truscott's. A Prussian army officer couldn't ask for better.

Dirty laundry. Richards himself sometimes hid things in dirty laundry, stashing his wallet in a dirty sock before going to sleep in a hotel room. Truscott's laundry bag was neatly tied. Richards unneatly untied it. There was a roll of magazines inside—no, not magazines. Pornographic picture books. He leafed through one, smiling to himself at the size of the genitals they seemed to be producing in Denmark. The second was the raunchiest example of the art Richards had ever seen. His eye lingered on a truly amazing exhibition of oral sex. Then he turned the page. There was a folded sheet of teletype printout stuck there. Unfolding it, Richards read some classified codings at the top. The message was from Washington, a response from the NavInt computer in the

Pentagon to a query from Keflavik, a query apparently made by Truscott.

Richards deciphered the body of the message easily. It detailed three instances in which Spencer, John A.; M/W; 39; journalist, had performed services for the Central Intelligence Agency. Expense vouchers had been issued.

It was the sort of information that even Richards would have had great difficulty in obtaining directly from the CIA. But the two intelligence agencies shared computer data from time to time, and this had fallen into the navy's. Truscott was a clever lad.

The commander returned the printout carefully to the picture book, and the pornography to its place among the dirty laundry. He looked at his watch, a little number costing at least $1,600 less than any of Truscott's Rolexes. He would be meeting Whelan shortly. For once, they would have something interesting to talk about.

The KGB general and the admiral stepped through a gate in the Kremlin wall into the bright sunlight of Red Square, pausing a moment while the general's car was brought up. A man and a woman, American tourists by the looks of them, were standing nearby, the woman holding a camera. Before the guards could stop her, she stepped closer and snapped a picture of the two high-ranking officers, as though they were part of the local color. Normally, the general would have had the film seized and the guards reprimanded or worse, but he let the incident pass. By the time the woman's film was developed, it wouldn't matter.

"They must think this is our Disneyland," he said to the admiral as they got into the Ziv sedan.

"I'm still not used to all these tourists."

"We are at peace," the general said, smiling slightly.

The car turned around in the Square, the driver steering carefully through the strolling pedestrians and then speeding up as they reached the street and crossed the river by the Rossya Hotel.

"I didn't want to bring this up inside," said the admiral. "But this man you have in Iceland, every member of his team is German. This is very irregular, yes?"

"They were all with him in Africa. They're very good."

"But on such an important project . . ."

"Gorushchenko is watching everything."

"He is very good."

"Too good. I was worried the Americans would become curious why someone so valuable would be given an embassy in Iceland, but apparently they did not notice. That is the only thing I like about Iceland. The Americans pay no attention to it."

"You seemed very confident about that with the marshal."

"If we could penetrate Washington as well as we have Reykjavik, this project would not be necessary."

"I will be flying over Iceland in a few hours. Tonight I will be at sea."

"I envy you. I will be with the marshal again."

"Only a few more days."

"They are very long days."

They fell silent. The general sucked on his lower lip a moment, a nervous habit. Gorushchenko had reported minor problems: a killing, a suspicious American journalist. Colonel Jahn had reported everything under control. At length, the general put Iceland from his mind and turned his thoughts to more pressing matters. A line of trucks was moving down the street in the opposite direction. The general looked at the numbers on the sides. They were beginning the evacuation of the city.

Spencer returned to his hotel room with only minutes to spare before the afternoon deadline for his regular call to New York. Thanks to Superintendent Andersson, he'd missed the previous day. Two missed days and Laidlaw would probably send in reinforcements—or a replacement.

The phone connections were good and he had *Perspective* on the line within three minutes. Jim Clepich was not there.

Nor were any of his assistants. No, there were no messages for Mr. Spencer. Would Mr. Spencer be sending in his manuscript soon? One of the editors had been asking about it. Yes, Mr. Clepich would be told Mr. Spencer had called.

Spencer began filling the deep bathtub with hot, steaming water. After pulling off his dirty clothes, he poured himself a glass of straight scotch and took it to the bath. The water was painfully hot but he wanted the warmth to last. He needed to think, and he had nearly two hours before dinner. Elisabet was still out at the Keflavik airport doing something for Loftleider. Peterson had told Spencer he was staying at the Thor, and also, with "friends." He was now off somewhere with "friends."

Peterson was a happy addition in many ways—as friend, bodyguard, lawyer. Icelandic law was central to Spencer's new plan. Andersson and the police had to be made to see that Krog was innocent. Then Krog could be drawn out of the wilderness. Then Spencer could talk to him. And then . . .

The telephone rang. Spencer dared not let the call go. With a great splash, he rose from the tub, upsetting the glass of scotch.

It was the woman clerk downstairs at the desk. Someone from the American embassy was there to see him. Could he come down as soon as possible?

Swearing, Spencer threw on some clothes—pants, a turtleneck, his jacket. He shoved his bare feet into shoes, saying the hell with socks. He was only going down to the lobby.

The man waiting at the desk was merely an embassy chauffeur. Spencer was being summoned. At once.

The office he was taken to was that of the embassy's deputy chief of mission. Predictably, there was an American flag behind the desk. Spencer had yet to meet an American foreign service officer abroad who didn't think of himself as a modern-day Roman proconsul.

The DCM's name was Fletcher. He was obviously the ranking person in the room, but he contributed nothing aside from an unhappy glance at Spencer's bare ankles. The gathering was dominated by one of his assistants, an attaché of some sort named Whelan, a pudgy little man with too short hair and horn-rimmed glasses. Whelan had one of his own assistants there, curly-haired and rather young, with a very intelligent face. His name was Baker. There was a naval officer in the room as well, a big rumpled-looking man who slouched in his chair. Spencer couldn't tell his rank—he never could with naval officers—but he seemed of some consequence.

They wanted to know why he had been arrested.

"Suspicion of theft of an aircraft," Spencer said.

"What did you say?" said Whelan.

"Theft of aircraft," Spencer said. "I went to the airport at Egilsstadir when no one else was there and the police grabbed me. Apparently somebody had stolen an airplane from there. When they found out I had nothing to do with it, they let me go."

"That's all?" said Whelan. "They kept you in jail for a day for that? For nothing?"

Caution gnawed at the back of Spencer's brain. Laidlaw had been very insistent about his having absolutely nothing to do with the American embassy. Intruders. Moles. One or more of these four doubtless were with the agency. Spencer wondered whether it was the naval officer. Wonderful cover, gold braid.

"Nope," said Spencer. "There was also something about corrupting the morals of a stewardess. I seem to have made off with the acting superintendent's girlfriend."

He had been seen with Elisabet. He would be seen with her again. Very soon, he hoped. If they'd ever let him go.

"Why were you in Egilsstadir?" asked the young Baker.

"Researching a story," Spencer said. "I'm doing a magazine article on Icelandic energy."

"There are no power projects in Egilsstadir," said Baker.

"You also went to Akureyri," Whelan said.

"To the Laxa power plant," said Spencer.

"And to the home of that murder suspect," Whelan said. "Geir Krog."

"I'm working on a news story about the murder, too. Murders. Good story. Political angle. Krog is a high-ranking Communist."

"You're aware of the sensitive political situation we have here?" Whelan said.

"Yes, sir," said Spencer. "Commies want to throw us out of Keflavik. Cold War. Good stuff."

"The situation is serious, mister," said Whelan. "That air base is vital to NATO and your country." He looked at the naval officer, as though for confirmation.

"Vital," said the officer. Spencer thought he saw a slight smile.

"The last thing your country needs right now is for you to be stirring up trouble out here," Whelan said. "Anti-American feelings are running high. There have been protests, marches, anti-American newspaper editorials."

"Right," said Spencer.

"What we're asking for is your cooperation."

"Right. Do you want me to spy for you? A little CIA spook stuff on the side?"

Whelan flushed, with anger or embarrassment. Spencer wondered whether he was the CIA station chief in Iceland. "I'm talking about a little patriotism. Putting your country's interests first."

"Patriotism, right. First Amendment."

The DCM cleared his throat. "Mr. Spencer," he said, leaning forward slightly. "Mr. Spencer, where are your socks?"

"Never wear 'em. *Chi-chi* habit I picked up on the Riviera. Makes packing lots easier. May I have a drink?"

"What?"

"May I have a drink? A slug. A jar. This is an American chancery, isn't it? You should be awash with hootch."

The naval officer was grinning.

"Just a quickie," Spencer said. "Give me a little slug and I promise to be patriotic."

"I think that will be all, Spencer," said Whelan.

The young Baker looked as though he had been about to ask a question.

"Right," said Spencer, rising. "Don't bother to see me out.

And don't bother with a car. Gasoline's expensive here. The walk'll do me good."

Outside, trudging up the street, he cursed himself for his bare ankles. The chilling wind was probably forty miles an hour. Spencer looked at his watch. There was time, barely, and if there really wasn't, then he'd just have to be late. He had to write a story now, for his Washington bureau, the brutal-murders, Icelandic-election, Cold-War story. If his newspaperman cover was to be worth anything, he had to write and file immediately. The magazine piece could wait.

He decided he'd leave very little out of this news story. A good newspaperman put in as much as he knew, and Spencer was still a good newspaperman. That part wasn't cover.

The DCM had left his office almost immediately after Spencer, but the others remained. Commander Richards asked for a drink. Frowning, Whelan had a servant fetch a bottle of scotch.

"I want that man out of the country," Whelan said.

"From the looks of it," Baker said, "it ought to be easy to get him drunk. We could put him on a Loftleider flight to Chicago. He'd be two days or more getting back, if he came back. That might cost him his job."

"I'd like to send him to Antarctica," Whelan said.

Richards accepted a single ice cube from the servant, letting him fill the rest of the glass with straight whiskey. "Had it occurred to you that he might be on our side?" he asked.

"What do you mean?" said Whelan.

"I mean that he might be doing something here for the agency."

"Impossible," said Whelan. "I already ran a tracer through the computer at Langley. Just routine, you know. Drew a complete blank. He's just a meddling newspaperman, but he could cause us some trouble."

"We could pull a snatch," said Baker. "Have him disappear until after the election."

"His home office would start to wonder," said Whelan.

"He could have an accident," Baker said.

Richards took two quick, large swallows of the scotch, then set the still half-full glass on the table beside him.

"I've stayed longer than I should have," he said. "Dinner with the admiral tonight. Please keep me informed."

He had planned to bring up Truscott but now thought better of it. No need to have the boy killed—yet.

"Starkad now urged his men on, and they advanced upon the three on the headland. Sigurd Hog-Head was in the lead, with a thin round shield in one hand and a hunting spear in the other. Gunnar sighted him and shot an arrow at him; Sigurd raised his shield when he saw the arrow curving high, but the arrow went right through the shield, pierced his eyes, and came out at the back of his neck.

"That was the first killing."

Geir Krog lowered his book. He sat wedged in the shelter of a rock crevice on the lee slope of a mountain just to the east of Reykjavik. A cold wind had driven the rain away, and he was reading his now well-worn copy of *Njal's Saga* in the last of the day's light.

"Gunnar shot his second arrow at Ulf-Hedin, Starkad's overseer, and hit him in the waist. Ulf-Hedin fell at the feet of a farmer, who stumbled over him. Kolskegg then hurled a stone which struck the farmer on the head and killed him. Starkad said, 'It's not doing us any good to let Gunnar use his bow. Advance on them more briskly.' "

Krog had taken a bottle of Evi's Brennivin with him, but he had forgotten to ask her for something even more desirable: a newspaper. Reaching this mountain just before dawn, he had spent the day on it, eating a little, drinking the Brennivin for warmth, and reading *Njal's Saga*. His existence in Iceland had become one of a man in another dimension, a man living in another time.

"They urged each other on. Gunnar defended himself with bow and arrows as long as he could, then he threw the bow down, took sword and halberd, and fought with both hands.

It was a fierce and long battle, and Gunnar and Kolskegg killed several men. Then Thorgeir Starkadarson said, 'I promised to bring Hildigunn your head, Gunnar.'

" 'She can't attach that much importance to it,' said Gunnar. 'But you will have to come a lot closer to get it.'

"Thorgeir said to his brothers, 'Let's all rush him at once. He is without a shield, and we shall have him at our mercy.'

"Bork and Thorkel ran forward, ahead of Thorgeir. Bork swung at Gunnar, who parried so strongly with his halberd that the sword flew from Bork's grasp. Then Gunnar noticed Thorkel on the other side within sword-reach. He pivoted on one foot and swung his sword at him. The blow fell on Thorkel's neck, and his head flew off."

Such bloody times. Men reached for sword or axe at the slightest provocation; theirs was a swift and angry justice of severed limbs and heads. Krog envied them, though they were doubtless poor chess players.

"Then Kol fell dead to the ground. When Egil, his father, saw this, he flung himself at Gunnar and struck at him. Gunnar countered with his halberd, drove it through his stomach, and then hoisted him up on the point and hurled him into the river."

Krog read on, as Gunnar sliced off Ottar Egilsson's forearm and Kolskegg cut off Hauk Egilsson's head. After they had killed fourteen of their enemies, they took the body of their friend, Hjort, and rode home. Krog closed the book.

There was a lawyer in *Njal's Saga*—Mord Fiddle, a man more fascinated with the law than with justice. Was Mord Fiddle a name to call George Peterson? Evi trusted him. Krog had no one else to turn to. In a few hours, in the darkness that was now his only home, he would find a telephone and talk to Evi again. She must have contacted Peterson by now.

Krog returned his book to his pack and took out his friend the Brennivin again. It was becoming too dark to read. To the west, lights were going on all over Reykjavik. He would find a newspaper that night. He shivered. The bath at Evi's had made him feel more vulnerable to the weather.

Spencer stood at the window of his hotel room, pondering the now-familiar view of Austurvollur Square and the Althing parliament building, drinking again. He knew he was being watched, probably by more than one pair of eyes. Yet he could see no one. Except for the automobile traffic the square was deserted, the surrounding doorways and corners darkened in shadow. There was no eerier city than Reykjavik at night—not even Belfast.

He sipped his drink, closing his eyes a moment to test his balance—and his sobriety. He was fine, he thought. He was late, very late, but he was exceedingly pleased with himself. He had written a first-rate news story for his bureau—three and a half takes, six hundred words—deftly leading from the murders to the Icelandic election to America's fears about the Russians in the North Atlantic. It was probably the best story he had written in six months. His bureau chief had wired back a well-done.

He was a good newspaperman. He was a good spy. The story, which ought to show up in a dozen papers, shored up all his cover—quotes from Krog's neighbors in Akureyri, a vivid description of the murder cabin in Heklafjordur, a long paraphrase of Andersson's official and unofficial remarks—it justified practically his every movement since arriving. And there was enough, just enough, of what was not yet public fact or public record to reflect a veteran newsman's surmise and digging. He even had a veiled reference to a "secret project" Krog was involved in.

At the very least, he'd confound them. What spy would put his stuff in the public print?

He arrived at the restaurant of the Hotel Loftleider only an hour and five minutes after he had said he would.

Dinner did not go well. Elisabet was as irritated with his tardiness as she was happy to see him, and she was tired from her day at Keflavik as well. Peterson was far from charming, picking at his food distractedly, paying Spencer and Elisabet only the vaguest attention. He might as well have been poring over a legal brief. Spencer glibly kept the conversation going and the wine flowing into Elisabet's glass as best he could, which was good enough. Her irritation subsided into sleepiness. She held his hand under the table.

Afterward, Peterson parted from them outside, expressing an apparently genuine preference for a long solitary walk back to the Thor. He took a long time disappearing into the darkness, a hulking figure in his leather coat.

Spencer and Elisabet took a taxi directly to her apartment. They did not pause to listen to her Django Reinhardt record or have a brandy. They scarcely paused to take off their clothes. Their first time had been a spiritual moment in the cold wild; their second little more than a gentle, cozy interlude. This night, as Spencer had been anticipating all day, became madly and athletically physical. He began by kissing her feet. Before long, he had kissed her body all over—and she his. Afterward, when they lay exhausted, with sheets thrown back, she slept a few minutes, then opened her eyes and turned on her side to look at him.

"Tell me about your Chesley."

"No, Elisabet," he said. "Not now."

"Yes. Please. I want to know."

"She was—she is—very beautiful. She is quite bright. She is rich. Very old family rich. Aristocracy, the American kind, at least. We . . . we have a little boy. Mostly, we were happy. I really loved Chesley, I think. I'm pretty sure of that. But it wasn't enough."

"So you left her?"

"No. She left me. I'm still trying to figure out why. Great blow to the ego, it was. I even cried. I got drunk, and I cried."

She put her hand on his chest, sliding her slender fingers through the hairs.

"Tell me about your ex-husband," he said.

"You know that's unimportant," she said. "You're just trying to change the subject."

"All right," he said. "You're flying where tomorrow? Chicago?"

"Yes. You should come."

"Can't. My magazine article. I've got to get back to work on it. I've been filing news copy."

"I may be gone several days."

"Good."

"Good?"

"The strange men in overcoats in Chicago only shoot at other strange men in overcoats."

The telephone rang, breaking into their conversation as though it were an intruder in the room. She reached across him to answer it, speaking first in Icelandic, then in English.

"It's for you," she said, her eyes as wide as a watching cat's. Spencer felt just as curious.

As he had half-expected, the voice was Laidlaw's.

"Well," Spencer said, at last hanging up. "Tomorrow you are going to Chicago, and I am going to Luxembourg."

Krog had called Evi Kekkonen three times with no answer. After dark, he went to her store but, half a block away, saw a man standing across the street who was unmistakably a policeman. Krog fled. He would have to get back into the hills and try to contact Evi later. He paused just once on his way out of the city to steal a newspaper from a doorstep.

12

The military cemetery is a distillate of war, the only beautiful thing produced by war, the quintessential symbol of the peace that follows—and its price. The American cemetery in Luxembourg lies a few kilometers south of that small country's capital, a quiet greensward walled by thick, somber forest. Its white grave markers stand in exquisite symmetry—a military formation of the dead. Facing them, set at the foot of a broad terrace, is another grave marker, all alone. Below it lies the body of General George S. Patton.

Spencer had chosen the meeting place. Laidlaw approved. They came haphazardly together at the general's grave, fell into conversation, then set off slowly into the long diagonal rows of the other white crosses, talking softly. A fine mist of rain was falling, darkening the trees, making the grass a more vivid green. Only an elderly Luxembourgisch caretaker was to be seen. The air was damp and clammy.

"You must find Krog soon," Laidlaw said. "We're running short of time."

He wore an Irish walking hat, a very old but expensive-looking tan raincoat, and those brown oxfords again. He probably wore them to the beach. Spencer wondered whether Laidlaw ever did go to the beach.

"I got the hint," Spencer said. "All that not-so-cryptic talk about deadlines and hurry up with the manuscript."

"We're under pressure."

"It's still two weeks before the Icelandic election."

"The Soviets are becoming very active. All over Europe. All quite suddenly. Whatever it is that provoked them, they're taking it seriously."

"I know. Two men in a Mercedes engaged me in a little road race coming out of Akureyri. One of them put a bullet through my car roof."

"You seem to have won the race."

"I had a little Icelandic luck. They missed a turn and are now at the bottom of a bog."

Laidlaw paused before one of the grave markers. The buried man had been a captain. On either side of him were sergeants.

"Mr. Spencer," said Laidlaw, staring in his unblinking fashion at the carved name of the captain. "How is it the KGB know so soon you're working for us?"

"It's not my fault. I've followed instructions. I've kept my cover. I've stayed away from your people."

"You spent a night in an Icelandic jail. You visited our embassy half-drunk and, for some reason, without any socks."

"How do you know that?"

"You're not the only spy we have in Iceland. Our regular station people have started reporting on you with some regularity. They find you suspicious."

"Including your friend the mole?"

"No doubt."

Laidlaw lifted his gaze to the distant trees, then turned his head slowly, scanning the cemetery. A young couple, tourists, and probably American, had appeared on the terrace, but they paid Spencer and Laidlaw no mind. They seemed to be looking for Patton's grave, though it was directly beneath them.

"Do you want to pull me out?" Spencer said. "Is that why you're here?"

"I don't want to. I certainly don't. But we may have to do just that. There's some displeasure about you on high."

"I'm doing my goddamn best. I only just got here, you know. And I'm not exactly the only one who hasn't been able to find Krog."

"I don't deny any of that. The problem is some idiotic insistence on the idiotic 'no journalists' rule."

"Are you serious?"

"You're as familiar with Washington as I am."

Spencer scuffed at the grass. It was perfectly mowed and trimmed.

"I'll quit my newspaper job. It's not that much use to me. In the long run."

"It can still be very useful to us in the short run. And it's the short run that concerns me. The shortest possible run."

The young American couple had found Patton's grave. She was taking a picture of him leaning on it. Laidlaw began to walk again, away, toward the rear rows of crosses. Spencer followed.

"Tell me what you know," Laidlaw said.

"I've passed a lot of it on to you already."

"Tell me again. Summarize for me, as you would in a news story."

"Newspaper stories begin with a lead," Spencer said. "My lead is that the Russians have big plans for Iceland—both military and political. Krog, working as a double agent, found out what they are, so the Russians tried to kill him after someone, apparently someone on our side, tipped them off. The girl got it instead.

"Their political plans involve rigging the local election to get the Communists into office. In return for that and God knows what else, the Workers' and Farmers' Party could be expected to pull Iceland out of NATO and throw us out of Keflavik. Judging by Erikisson's reaction to my question, we could expect some sort of Soviet-bloc industrial development—something that uses a lot of electricity. Militarily, the Russians gain a lot just by getting us out of Keflavik. They might cut a deal to get the base themselves and all but push us out of the North Atlantic. There's also a wonder weapon, a neat little ray gun called the charged-particle beam that can hit targets thousands of miles away. It works best from satellite, but it can be deployed on the ground as well. Iceland may figure in that, too.

"Whatever they have in mind, Krog has probably figured it out. In great technical detail. He's supposed to be a very good electrical engineer—a near-genius. The Soviets didn't consider that when they recruited him as an agent. Apparently all they had in mind was having someone in the local Communists to keep an eye on Erikisson."

The American couple were now moving down a line of crosses. The caretaker had disappeared.

"You know about the particle beam," Spencer said. "You had a file about it on your desk. In the house that isn't your house."

"I know about most everything you've told me," Laidlaw said. "Mr. Krog was an excellent informant for me—for a time."

Laidlaw stopped again, this time before a grave on which someone had strewn flowers. They were quite fresh, as though left only moments before.

"If you already know all this and the Russians have my number, just what in the hell am I doing here?" Spencer asked. "What good am I?"

"You are a wild card in this game, Mr. Spencer. A very valuable one. They may know you're in our hand, but they don't know how we're going to play you."

"Well, how are you going to play me?"

"Mr. Spencer. Where is Krog?"

"Still in Iceland. Near Akureyri, or Reykjavik, or somewhere in the wilds. He fled because he had no choice, not because he had anything to do with the murder. The Russians came for him and killed her. We, obviously, can't be trusted. We sent him to that cabin. The Icelandic police won't listen to him. I'm trying to spread the word that I'm the one American who can be trusted, who knows he was set up, who knows he's innocent. I've been going all over the country doing that.

I've also been working on the police. The acting superintendent of detectives seems to hate my guts, but he doubts Krog is guilty. If I can get him to drop the charges, we may get Krog to come in. Still, there's all that evidence. And this new murder."

"Evi Kekkonen. A Finnish woman. A friend of Krog's. Once his mistress."

"You know that, too," said Spencer.

"Our station chief can be very effective—at times."

"Her killer was a real butcher. I don't know why they were so cruel about it. Perhaps they were just trying to provoke Krog. If they did it to . . . to somebody of mine, I'd go berserk. She seemed quite a nice woman. I met her. She's a client of my lawyer, George—"

"Peterson," said Laidlaw, "who is in Iceland. What have you told him?"

"I stayed within my cover," said Spencer, lying. He needed a wild card of his own, and Peterson was all he had.

"He's an old friend of yours," Laidlaw said.

"We still lie to each other."

The young couple were approaching. The man was tall, with long hair and glasses, Jewish or Italian. She was much shorter, a freckled face and red hair gone frizzy in the misty rain. They were dressed like students, though they looked to be in their late twenties.

Laidlaw's glance and assessment of them took a millisecond.

"All these men here died because of one man," he said to Spencer as the couple passed behind them. "Otto Skorzeny. We called him the most dangerous man in Europe, and he was. He almost made the Battle of the Bulge work."

The couple were out of earshot.

"I met him once—Skorzeny," Laidlaw said. "Years after the war." He fell silent, then looked up at Spencer, his glasses slightly fogged from the weather. "Krog," he said. Demanded.

"I really think he's in Reykjavik, or near it," Spencer said. "If he isn't, he will be soon. He's not the sort of a man to hole up in a cave. Certainly not after Evi Kekkonen."

Laidlaw started walking again. "Your story isn't finished, is it?" he said. "It's full of holes. You haven't the half of it, and you couldn't print half of what you do have because you need corroboration. You need to talk to Krog. He's your only source."

"You sound like my editor."

"I am your editor. Mr. Spencer, you must understand the difficulty under which we labor. The Watergate syndrome is still with us. We are still a discredited branch of government. Our best intelligence is dismissed as suspect. We must be as convincing as possible. In this Iceland matter, it is absolutely essential that we convince them."

"Them?"

"The gentlemen in the Executive Mansion. They simply will not pay any attention to the real danger."

"And what is the real danger?"

"Catastrophe."

"That's an ambiguous word."

"The particle beam weapon is the ultimate defensive weapon, Mr. Spencer. It is not merely a toy with which to knock down satellites."

Spencer only kept walking, waiting for the end of the pregnant pause.

"A few of them deployed in the right places would make a nuclear exchange initiated by the Russians extremely one-sided."

Another pause.

"Iceland is one of the right places, Mr. Spencer."

"Why are you telling me this? Do you let all your little operatives in on the Big Picture? Or is this just to inspire courage and resolve? John A. Spencer, savior of the western world."

"You needn't return to Iceland. You are three hours from Brussels. You could be back in Washington by evening."

"You'd let me walk out on you? I might actually write a story, you know. I might put all this in the papers. Tell the world. I've already filed one piece about Krog and the murders."

"It was read to me," Laidlaw said. "Foreign-affairs analysis masquerading as a fairly sensational account of a sex murder. A rather deft piece of work." He walked a few paces more. The mist had given way to drizzle. "It should help your cover with those who still believe in it."

"What about those who don't? What good am I to you if the other side has me marked? How many more days am I going to get to live?"

"I'm sure they are as interested in keeping you alive as I am, especially if they see you as a means of getting to Krog."

"And if I find him?"

"I'm going to provide you with protection, Mr. Spencer. One of the best."

"You once mentioned a Karin Nielsen."

"You'll find her an inordinately attractive woman, in a demure, fresh-faced, rather youthful way."

"She's my protection?"

"I think I can guarantee satisfaction. She's multitalented, but her specialty is being—I suppose the appropriate term nowadays would be a 'hit person.' Very good at it."

Spencer took a sharp, deep breath.

"You're complicating my life," he said.

"You're to go to the EEC this afternoon," said Laidlaw, "to pick up some data on European industrial energy consumption from the information office."

"The information office?"

"From a Monsieur De Vore. He'll have a package waiting for you. You'll have dinner tonight at the Greiveldinger, in the Avenue de la Porte Neuve, arriving after eight P.M. and not leaving before ten. After that, go to the Place d'Armes and a smoky little wine bar called Le Cellier."

"I know it. Wine, cheese, and girls."

"It's a logical place to meet strangers. Karin will join you there. Later, you are to take her to your hotel—in your inimitable fashion."

"And?"

"She will deal with 'and' in *her* inimitable fashion. You're to travel back to Iceland separately. Contact me through her. Do not use the New York number again. If it's crucial, use the Scotland number. Once. The instant you locate Krog, I am to know."

They climbed the steps to the terrace. The rain was coming down harder and there was no time for a prolonged conversation.

"You really do want to keep me on?" Spencer said.

"Yes. Very much."

"What if your superiors won't let you?"

"It will then become very difficult to contact you. It may in any event."

There were only three cars in the parking area. Spencer had rented a Ford Escort. Laidlaw was moving in the direction of a black Peugeot. The other car was a Volkswagen bus.

Laidlaw paused, removing his glove to shake Spencer's hand. "Your efforts will not go unappreciated, Mr. Spencer. I will see you again soon. It will have to be soon."

"You haven't told me what Karin Nielsen looks like."

"She'll find you."

Spencer grinned sarcastically and started to turn, then stopped.

" 'Hit person'?"

"We use another term for it, actually."

"How many?"

"Eleven."

"Eleven?"

"Six of them were on the same airplane. Good-bye, Mr. Spencer. You're in safe hands."

Safe hands. Spencer sat waiting a moment before starting his car, waiting to watch Laidlaw leave, to watch the young couple run by in the now-heavy rain. The tall young man looked at him. What did that mean? Was he going to be sweating Volkswagen buses in his rearview mirror?

He turned the ignition key but let the Ford sit with its engine running. Why had Laidlaw told him so much? Not all that Spencer wanted to know, of course, but more than any regular agent would be told. This was a business in which people were killed just for walking around with rolls of film in their pockets, for passing on messages that meant nothing to them. What would happen if he found himself in some KGB cellar with an electric wire stuck up his rectum? It was his nature, his professional impulse, to reveal information.

Perhaps Laidlaw was right. He was safe until he found Krog, or Krog found him. Then he would be superfluous. They might both be superfluous. In many eyes.

Six on the same plane. Spencer had wondered about the psychological consequences of deliberately taking a human life. What were the consequences of taking eleven?

He wanted to meet Karin Nielsen.

The Volkswagen bus was moving out onto the road. Spencer put the Ford in gear and followed. He'd let the tall young man sweat a car in his mirror.

Peterson was driving his rented Audi extremely fast, even for him, but Elisabet seemed not to notice or care. She was talking about Spencer. She had been talking about him since Peterson had picked her up outside her apartment in Reykjavik.

"You may miss your flight," he said.

"I have faith in you, George."

"It was impossible, just impossible, to get away any sooner."

"I understand."

"You could have taken a taxi, or an airport bus."

"George, as I said. I have faith in you."

Peterson splashed the speeding Audi through a wide puddle. A snow shower marched toward them from the west. Behind it, a weak sun shone vaguely through a screen of thin cloud. Peterson glanced at his watch, calculating how soon he could be back in Reykjavik.

"The flight I'd *like* you to miss is the one you'll be taking back to Iceland," he said.

"What do you mean?"

"Sonja wants me to keep you out of danger. The best way to do that is to keep you out of this country. Skip the flight back."

"And stay in Chicago?"

"Go to Baltimore and stay with Sonja."

"George. This is my job."

"Take an emergency leave. You have enough seniority to do that. If you have any problem, I can call . . ."

"But why?"

"Just to be out of harm's way. Until this blows over."

"Until what blows over?"

She had turned up the collar of her blue raincoat. Peterson reached to the dashboard and increased the heat.

"Until Krog is found and the funny men in Mercedes all go away and John August Spencer goes back to Washington."

"So that's it. You disapprove of my relationship with John. You, who were trying to get us together for dinner at your house just a few days ago."

"It is not for me or Sonja to approve or disapprove of anything. John is our good friend. You are our good friend. John happens to have the sexual habits of an alley cat, which is one of the reasons his wife left him. But if that doesn't bother you, it certainly is none of our business. . . ."

"It certainly is not."

Peterson fell silent, his rocklike face devoid of expression. He pressed harder against the accelerator. The sun itself could no longer be seen, but its light was pouring forth from beneath the layers of cloud, the pools and puddles on the road reflecting it into his eyes.

"Elisabet. This is no time to get mixed up with John Spencer. He's involved in something that can only mean trouble for you. Serious trouble."

"Would you please explain that?"

"I can't."

"That's very helpful."

"Think of Evi Kekkonen, Elisabet. Think of that girl in Heklafjordur."

"Are you saying John is the murderer?"

"What I'm saying, damn it, is that you are plunging headlong into the biggest mistake of your life! You told us you've reached a turning point in your life, that you're thinking hard about how you want to spend the rest of it. Well, John Spencer can offer you nothing for the future. The reason he can be so cavalier about the danger you're both in—"

"He's not been cavalier."

"—is that he doesn't have to worry about the future."

"What do you mean?"

"He's ill. He's very seriously ill."

"I guessed that."

Peterson let the car slow a little. Gray cloud now closed the horizon entirely, and snow was falling.

"He's terminally ill, Elisabet. It has something to do with his cardiovascular system. He has a bad artery in his brain. Very bad. The odds against him are not pleasant."

"Is that why he drinks so much?"

"In part. And it only makes his condition worse."

"Poor dear John," Elisabet said. She squeezed Peterson's hand, then slipped hers away. "Thank you for telling me. I know what friends you are."

"I wish you and John could have met under different circumstances. I truly do."

"It doesn't matter."

"We'll call Sonja from the airport."

"What for?"

"To tell her you're coming."

"Oh no, George. I'm returning here."

"What?"

"I love him, George. I wasn't really able to admit it to myself until now. But I do. I love him."

There were few things as satisfying as a Luxembourg meal. Spencer had passed over the roast thrush and minced liver balls on the menu, settling for a *carré de porc fumé* with sauerkraut, which he washed down not with wine but with several glasses of dark Mousel beer, one of his favorites. Afterward, he ordered a glass of the local firewater, an ultrastrong plum brandy called Quetsch. It came icy cold in a very large glass. He decided to content himself with just one. If Luxembourg was the Grand Duchy of Fenwick in *The Mouse That Roared*, Quetsch was the Q-bomb.

He left at five minutes after ten, having failed to see anyone he even remotely suspected of being Karin Nielsen. The streets were still glistening with the damp, but the rain had stopped and the night skies were clearing. He set off for the Place d'Armes at the pace of a man interested in nothing more than walking off a heavy dinner. It was good to maintain cover. His may have been blown, but there was an advantage in his pretending not to be aware of that lamentable fact. It gave him another wild card.

Luxembourg was a very old city, a onetime medieval fortress on a fairytale hill that overlooked what was for centuries the most important crossroads in Europe. For a brief time, the country had been one of Europe's major powers, just as Norsemen from Iceland had briefly ruled the seas. Such countries were remarkable, not only for being small but also for having survived.

Spencer was fondest of small countries. Ireland was the largest a country need get. It was hard to imagine anyone wanting to die for a country any larger.

The streets narrowed as Spencer approached the square. He passed one street off to the left that was scarcely three feet wide. A claustrophobic dread came over him. He shook it off.

Le Cellier was as smoky as he had remembered, but only half-full, offering an ample choice of seats. He took a table off to the side that had a clear view of the door. Ordering a glass of local Moselle, he searched the room with careful glances. No Karin. No one who could be Karin. No Karin. No Krog. No Evi Kekkonen. No point to all this.

He wanted something stronger than wine. His head was beginning to throb; he hoped only from the Quetsch. This was no time for one of those desperate headaches.

A girl who certainly could not be Karin sat down at the next table. She was blond and dressed like an American tourist—sweater, wool skirt, raincoat, loafers. She was small—five feet three or four, a hundred pounds or less. And so young. It was dark in this part of the room, but she looked for all the world like a high school cheerleader. It seemed a wonder they had let her in. Perhaps they hadn't noticed. He hadn't noticed her enter.

Spencer put her out of his mind and turned back toward the door. It was getting late. And no Karin.

From the corner of his eye, he saw the cheerleader light a cigarette. A second later the lighter slipped from her fingers and clattered to the floor. She leaned over to retrieve it but it was beyond her reach. It was within his. As he bent to pick it up, his head came close to hers.

"Good evening, Mr. Spencer," she whispered. There were lines he had not seen around her mouth and eyes, but she could be no older than twenty-five or twenty-six, he guessed. Eleven dead.

He leaned back and handed her the lighter, a Zippo with some sort of collegiate insignia on it. "May I buy you a drink?" he said.

She smiled—a cheerleader's smile—and moved to his table. "Let's talk about Luxembourg," she said. "I think Luxembourg is really neat."

He ordered a bottle of St. Julien. It went very quickly. She suggested a nearby disco. Following orders, he agreed. He withstood the din for half an hour, then suggested a quiet walk around the square. She shrugged compliantly. It was turning colder, and as they started down the sidewalk she pulled his arm around her, moving close to his side. All he needed was a letter sweater.

"Shall I give you a fill?" he said quietly.

"A fill? Another drink?"

"I'm talking newspaperman talk. I mean, shall I bring you up to date?"

"I'm very up to date, thank you. I've even listened to you talking on tape. You have a really terrific voice. I wondered whether you'd look as good as you sound. You certainly do."

"That's really terrific of you to say."

They walked slowly, almost in step. The shoulders beneath his arm were not frail and bony, as he had expected, but muscular and hard. He wondered whether she played tennis or climbed mountains.

"What am I supposed to do?" he asked.

"Do? You do just what you and Hugh agreed you'd do. You go back to Iceland, you research your article, you maintain your cover, and you find Geir Krog," she said. "Everything else you leave to us."

"Us?"

"Me. I'll need a little while to prowl the ground a bit, but after that, I'll be around you a lot."

"Great."

"I'll need to know some things from you. Stuff about Iceland. I understand you're quite the expert. But we can take care of that later."

"Later," he said. "What do we do now, tonight?"

She looked up at him and smiled sweetly.

"We'll have another drink and then go to your hotel," she said. "I'm really awfully horny." She tilted her head against his shoulder.

He said nothing. The drink part was fine. The rest of it totally unnerved him. It was no more than a dozen hours since he had left Elisabet. His palms began to sweat. "I know a bar," he said. "Charley's, on the Place des Martyrs."

"Charley's. That sounds really neat."

Spencer picked the wrong saloon, although this did not become apparent to him until they were into their second cognac.

Glancing down, Spencer saw the shoes first. Desert boots. Then long, baggy gray flannels. A too-large tweed jacket with a rolled-up newspaper stuffed in one pocket. A rumpled shirt and rumpled British guards' tie, loosened and slightly askew. A thin, bony, but square-jawed British face, dominated by overlong gray hair and thick black-rimmed spectacles.

"Bloody Christ," said the man. "It is you! I was with an AP twit in Teheran last month who said you were dead."

Colin Molyneaux. The last time Spencer had seen him they'd been ducking the aimless rounds of a Patriotic Front sniper in Zimbabwe-Rhodesia. Ducking, and drinking straight Dutch gin from Spencer's flask. An army sergeant finally had blown the sniper up with a grenade.

"Rum tale," said Spencer. "As Mark Twain would say, greatly exaggerated. How are you, Colin?"

Molyneaux pulled back a chair, signaled a waiter, and seated himself all in the same remarkable movement. He didn't sit down so much as fold himself. Pulling his glasses down his long nose, he peered over them at Karin. "All right, you bastard," he said. "Introduce me to your bloody daughter."

Before Spencer, flushed and unsteady, could speak, Karin put forth her small hand to shake Molyneaux's. "I'm Muffy Baldwin," she said. "From Greenwich. Jack and I aren't related. We're just friends. In fact, we just met." She giggled, a demure mew of a giggle.

"Greenwich?" said Molyneaux, as the waiter, apparently from habit, brought him a large whiskey.

"Greenwich, Connecticut," said Karin. "You know, where George Bush is from. My family knows the Bushes. Really great people. Jack comes from just over the state line—Bedford, New York. That's just one of the things we've found we have in common."

"Along with hopscotch," said Molyneaux. "Bloody marvelous." He turned to Spencer, pushing his glasses back up to the bridge of his nose. "Well, Jacko. If you're not dead, what are you doing?"

"I've been buried alive," Spencer said. "In Washington. State Department. Foreign Relations Committee. The stuffed-shirt beat."

"Sounds bloody awful. What sends you this way? You doing the EEC or something?"

"I'm on leave," Spencer said. "I picked up a magazine assignment to pay for the trip. Icelandic energy. Geothermal heating and such like. I've just come down here for a breather and some decent food."

"Iceland," said Molyneaux. "How bloody marvelous. I—"

"Have you ever been to the airport duty-free shop in Iceland?" said Karin. "They have the most terrific sweaters."

Neither man responded.

"And where are you kicking around now?" Spencer said.

"The best," Molyneaux said. "They finally gave me the Paris bureau. It's all ticketyboo, except that occasionally they fling me back to Belfast or some other hole."

Spencer had met Molyneaux in Belfast, in the bar of the Europa Hotel, on one of the nights the IRA wasn't blowing it up.

"There are worse places," Spencer said.

"That's the truth. I'm going to one in the morning. Iceland, in fact. Bloody marvelous coincidence, isn't it? You and I always seem to tumble together in the world's rum spots."

"I don't consider Iceland a rum spot."

"Bloody awful weather," Molyneaux said. "Bloody awful cooking." He turned to Karin, leering. "*Hrutspungar!* Ram's balls! Ram's testicles! A national dish."

"Why are you going to Iceland?" Spencer asked.

"Bloody stupid election. The Bolshies in the Althing. The NATO story. I'm surprised you're not on it, Jacko. That was the line of all your cod war stuff. Perfidious Albion driving the Norsemen out of the Alliance, throwing the Yanks out of their air base, bringing on the Russkies and the end of civilization as we know it. All you need do is put a new lead on your old copy. Only this time it's really going to happen, and you can't blame the Brits."

"The *Bacchus* is tied up at Reykjavik."

"Oh, ho, so you *are* onto it, Jacko. The Red Scare rides again."

"I filed a piece, just to keep my hand in. Remind them I'm alive."

"Right. It's a bloody good story, Jacko. And since you're going to be up there, why don't we tag along together? Just like when I got you that interview with Mugabe. Just like bloody Belfast. You can have one of those gunboat captain friends of yours take us on a little cruise. Hunt the Russkies. Drink a little gin."

He drained his glass and signaled the waiter again. Spencer put his hand over his own glass. Molyneaux's hair was falling over his eyes. He peered through it at Karin, leering again.

"And what about you, Muffyo deario? A gin fizz? *Une limonade?*"

Karin smiled weakly and looked at Spencer. Molyneaux's head fell forward, then snapped back.

"Ram's balls!" he shouted.

Spencer had been deferring his decision about whether he would take Karin back to his hotel. Now he made it, seizing upon the opportunity almost desperately.

"Come on, Muffy," he said. "Time to go. You're over the fence, Collie. You're in need of bedrest."

Spencer took Karin's hand. They rose. So did Molyneaux, after a fashion. His last whiskey must have tipped the scale.

"Bedrest," said Molyneaux. "Bloody marvelous idea. Might I borrow your little blond pillow there?"

"Sorry."

"How about sharesies?"

Spencer reached to steady Molyneaux and hold him at arm's length.

"Sorry, Collie. Some other time. See you in Iceland."

"Too right. What plane are you on? I've got the bloody morning flight. Are you on it? We'll drink a little gin."

"There are two morning flights," Spencer said. "I don't know which one I'm on. It's on my ticket."

"Well, we'll drink a little gin, and everything will be all ticketyboo. Nighto, Muffyo, come 'round when you've grown up."

He turned with a swoop and lunged in the direction of the bar.

"Rum luck," muttered Spencer.

"I think he's neat," said Karin.

Spencer drove the small Ford down the Marche aux Poissons, down the steep hill from the city center and across the River Alzette that curved like a moat at its base. His head was aching, and he was driving badly. Karin was sitting tensely, her hand braced against the dashboard.

"You drink an awful lot," she said.

"It's not that. I'm not feeling well."

"It is that, and I don't like it. I don't like working with drunks. They make mistakes. They cause accidents. I'm low enough on the actuarial tables as it is."

"I'm sorry. I can control it."

"Good."

The street curved back and forth as it passed through the city's outskirts. The houses were tall and narrow, windows dark behind their white lace curtains. He skidded slightly, bumping over some cobblestones.

"Sorry," he said.

"Shit," she said.

"That's out of character, 'Muffy.' "

"Are you kidding? Times have changed, old man. You ought to hear how they talk at Smith College these days."

"You went to Smith?"

"Oh, yes. With scads and scads of Muffies."

"Are you from Greenwich, too?"

"No. I came by my social pretensions like F. Scott Fitzgerald. By way of Minnesota."

"How did you get from Smith College to the CIA?"

"Next question."

"How old are you?"

"Why do you care about that?"

"Old newsman's habit. Name, age, address."

"I turned thirty this year. Do you mind?"

"I thought you sixteen. If that."

"Thanks. I thought you forty-five."

"Thirty-nine. I'm having my midlife crisis early. Molyneaux must be forty-five. Tonight he looked sixty."

The street had become a suburban road. The airport and Spencer's hotel, the Aerogolf, were just a few kilometers distant.

"How well do you know Colin Molyneaux?" she asked.

"Fairly well. Nearly ten years, off and on. Northern Ireland. Rhodesia. Cyprus. Here and there. He saved my life once. A good sort. Drinks too much."

"He wasn't that drunk. What else do you know about him?"

"Middle-class background. Studied at Cambridge. Did some time in the British army. Captain, I think. Married an actress he met in Kenya. No kids. Good reporter. Clever writer. He's never been paid nearly enough."

"Molyneaux is an agent of MI 6."

"What?"

"Don't you think that's really neat?" She flashed a sarcastic smile.

"I know they use their own journalists a lot, but . . ."

"He's a professional agent. They recruited him at Cambridge, but everything else is deep cover. And now he's joining us in Iceland. What fun."

"Does he know you? Did he recognize you?"

"I doubt it very much," she said irritably. "I've never lost my cover. But I'm sure he's on to you. They've stuck him on to you, all right. Shit."

The airport sign came and went. The hotel was just beyond. She leaned her head back against the seat, pressing her fingers against her temples.

"Do you have anything to drink?" she asked. "In your room?"

"Only a bottle of Quetsch, a souvenir. I can call room service for some scotch."

"No, no. Quetsch is just the ticket. I changed my mind. I

want to get drunk. I want to let loose. And I want to get laid."

Spencer wanted only to sleep, to put things out of his mind, to keep them out of his mind.

While Karin showered, he sat slumped in a chair by the curtained window, sipping his Quetsch warm, searching for an excuse. To remain, in Elisabet's sense of matters, chaste. He leaned his head back, listening to a new rain against the window glass and hearing Django Reinhardt's music.

He'd feel a fool saying he had a headache.

She came out of the bathroom, completely naked, dry, and clean. Dropping her towel onto the bed, she knelt before him, reaching for his belt.

"I sense you are a man who needs some encouragement," she said.

He did not resist but merely took a last sip of his drink and closed his eyes. Later, in bed, he did not need any encouragement whatsoever. She was a remarkably artful sex partner, but afterward his most vivid memory was not of her slender supple body or her little girl's face but her hard little hands: With them she was now caressing his neck. With those same hands, she had shot, stabbed, garroted, poisoned, or exploded eleven people. It was like sleeping with death.

He smiled at that. Every night now, he slept with death.

Spencer went to sleep as Karin sat up in bed, chain-smoking and drinking Quetsch in large gulps. In the morning she was hung over but happier. All went well, except when they opened the door to leave and came face to face with two stewardesses coming out of the room across the hall. For a terrifying moment, Spencer thought one of them was Elisabet.

Blood rains
From the cloudy web
On the broad loom
Of slaughter.
The web of man,

Gray as armour,
Is now being woven;
The Valkyries
Will cross it
With a crimson weft.

The warp is made
Of human entrails;
Human heads
Are used as weights;
The heddle-rods
Are blood-wet spears,
The shafts are iron-bound
And arrows are the shuttles.
With swords we will weave
This web of battle.

The Valkyries go weaving
With drawn swords.
Hild and Hjorthrimul,
Sanngrid and Svipul.
Spears will shatter,
Shields will splinter,
Swords will gnaw
Like wolves through armour.

Let us now wind
The web of war
Which the young king
Once waged.
Let us advance
And wade through the ranks,
Where friends of ours
Are exchanging blows.

Let us now wind
The web of war
And then follow
The king to battle.
Gunn and Gondul
Can see there
The blood-spattered shields
That guarded the king.

Let us now wind
The web of war,
Where the warrior banners
Are forging forward.
Let his life
Not be taken;
Only the Valkyries
Can choose the slain.

Krog, hunched beside his cave fire, wearily closed the book and let it drop at his feet. He could not read *Njal's Saga* any further. The blood and gore and fury were endless, a maddening cycle, each reference to severed limb and shattered skull a wrenching, painful reminder of his devastation.

He had obtained his newspaper, all right, stealing a copy of *Kvoldbladid* from a porch step and stuffing it into his parka, not reading it until he was clear of Reykjavik and into the hills. It was now in shreds. For all that day, he had stumbled and staggered about these hillsides in an insane rage.

At one point he began screaming, hurling oaths and curses with the full might of his lungs. He kicked rocks, tore at the soil, threw clods of it at the sky. By killing Evi, by so brutally destroying her beautiful person, Rozkowski had torn to the very primal soul of Krog, had ripped away every layer of human sensibility and civilization. Krog wanted only revenge—revenge as in the olden days. The complex riddles and conundrums that had dogged his mind were now reduced to one simple problem: how to get near enough to Rozkowski to murder him in some foul, cruel, bestial way.

Later, as he lay exhausted on the hillside with the rain of a furious storm pounding upon his face, it occurred to Krog that that was why Evi had died. They had gone to that length simply to provoke him to a rash act.

He calmed. He would give Evi something better to die for. He would go back to the chess game. Putting *Njal's Saga* into his jacket and with his anger cold and tempered, he began to ponder his next move.

13

Mendelsohn had been abruptly summoned to Thorn's office from his studies in the personnel file room. Thorn was not yet there, but his secretary let Mendelsohn wait inside. She brought him coffee and left, presenting an opportunity of which he took full advantage. He did not open any of the safety-taped files and envelopes, but, glancing over their covers, he became aware that Thorn was now involved in much more in Northern Europe than merely Iceland.

Returning to his side of the desk, he lit a cigarette just in time.

Thorn shouldered his way through the door and slammed it behind him. "Sonofabitch!" he said, yanking back his chair and dropping himself into it.

"Are you referring to someone in particular?" Mendelsohn asked.

Thorn took a long cigar from a desk drawer and ripped off the wrapping.

"The Soviets have their second CPB," he said. "A charged-particle beam, deployed and operational. Just west of Moscow. They need only one more."

"This is reliable intelligence?"

"The best, Freddy. It cost us two agents to get it, and we've had to put all of Red One on hold, but it's good. Got satellite confirmation and everything."

"For a man so vindicated, you seem unusually unhappy."

"They don't give a damn, Freddy! I've just been over at the

White House. Fairlington himself sat in. I had the deputy with me. We gave it everything we've got, but they wouldn't listen. They wanted to know about the Russian northern fleet. They wanted to know about Poland. They wanted to know about Spitzbergen Island, for Christ's sake. But when I brought up Iceland and CPBs, they treated me like some kind of nut."

"The new CPB did not interest them," Mendelsohn said.

" 'Strictly defensive configuration,' they said. 'That's the point,' I said. 'The CPB is still classified as experimental,' they said. 'They don't deploy experiments right outside the capital,' I said. They said they'd put some Pentagon brain teams on it. Then they started asking me about the Icelandic election, about how Communist the Workers' and Farmers' Party is. They said they're not going to worry about CPBs until the Russians get one up on a satellite. They said that if the Russians somehow manage to build one in Iceland—ho, ho, ho—then I can come back and talk to them again. Ho, ho, ho."

"The deputy took your side."

"The deputy sat on his hands," Thorn said from behind a sudden cloud of cigar smoke. "Afterward, in the car, he said we've got to lay back on this Iceland thing. He said there are budget cutters all over the place and we can't afford to look stupid. Stupid! They'll see who looks stupid soon enough, only it'll be too fucking late!"

He tilted back in his chair, swiveling slightly to the side to glare at a framed mercator projection of the world on the wall. Except for the map—and photographs of Thorn's family and Thorn himself, dressed in an Air Force uniform—the office walls were decorated with surprisingly tasteful modern paintings.

"I've got to pull John Spencer," he said. "I've got to put Ice One on hold and let NavInt take over. I half-expect that before the day is out I'm going to get orders to shut down our whole fucking station."

"That might be for the best, William."

Thorn ignored this. He tilted even farther back and chewed on his cigar for a long moment.

"You might be wise to leave Spencer in place and just remove Whelan," Mendelsohn said.

"I'm not going to pull Spencer yet," Thorn said. "Hugh went underground in Brussels and we've lost communication. I'm not going to pull an agent without going through his control."

"What will the deputy say about that?"

"I've got the order out. He ought to be satisfied with that. SOP is SOP. How are you coming with our mole?"

"Mole plural," said Mendelsohn. "As Hugh suggests. I detect several. There, here. I believe the navy is involved."

"Jesus."

"I have no names."

"You know why this happens?" said Thorn. He brought his hand down hard on the desk top, scattering cigar ash over his papers. "This happens because all the great minds around here never pay any attention to little places like Iceland, that's why. We're almost as bad as the State Department!"

"I would advise you to shut down Iceland station, Bill. All of it. Immediately. I myself would find it useful to have a conversation with Whelan and that young man of his, Baker. They've let matters get too far out of hand."

"I don't want to do anything until I talk with Hugh," Thorn said, rising. "Come on. Get your files and we'll drive over to the safe house. I could use a beer."

Commander Richards, wearing civilian clothes and jammed into a rented Volkswagen, sat parked half a block from the Polish embassy. In the car and on foot, he had been following Truscott much of the morning. The stops had included the American embassy, which was authorized, and the bar of the Hotel Thor, which was not. Throughout this tour, Truscott had been carrying a rolled-up magazine, which he gripped very tightly.

Making what he hoped was an intelligent guess, Richards

had turned the Volkswagen off the street he had been following Truscott along, sped around the block, and pulled up here, near the embassy of Poland. Truscott had already passed by the Soviet embassy. Perhaps Richards would have better luck here.

Truscott came around the corner and then crossed the street, looking both ways for more than cars. There were no pedestrians in view. Reaching the embassy door, he paused, then darted inside.

He was out again in five minutes, peering around the doorway, then hurrying away. Richards gave him another two minutes, then turned the Volkswagen around in the street and sped away, reaching Keflavik in less time than he would have thought possible.

Even if Truscott were only minutes behind him, minutes were all that Richards needed. He slipped into the petty officer's room, shut the door quietly behind him, and went quickly for the laundry bag. The pornographic books were just where they had been, but the message about John Spencer was gone. Richards checked twice.

Truscott came out of the embassy without that magazine.

Magnus Andersson had been to the hospital to see his superior, who would be back at his job within the month. That was far from soon enough.

They had recovered the car from the bog in the north. There were two bodies in it, as Elisabet had said—the driver a Latvian resident of Iceland, the other a man with a Czech passport. The latter had taken a room in Akureyri for the entire month. In it, Andersson's men had found a suitcase containing two extra pistols, ammunition, several wiretap devices, an infrared night scope, and a small amount of plastic explosive. Either customs or the Coast Guard had been less than vigilant.

Autopsies showed both men had drowned. The car had been rented in Reykjavik, to the man with the Czech passport. That was all Andersson knew.

The airplane Krog had stolen had been found on a hillside south of Reykjavik, near Grindavik. Except for crumpled landing gear and a bullet hole through the upper fuselage, it was remarkably undamaged. Krog was apparently as good a pilot as his reputation indicated. And there was no doubt now that he had taken the plane. His fingerprints were all over it.

His fingerprints were also found in Evi Kekkonen's apartment and store. There was no doubt in Andersson's mind that Krog had been there shortly before her murder and that Krog was now in Reykjavik or near it—hiding with friends or holed up somewhere in the hills to the east, north, or south. Andersson had sent teams of detectives around to those on his list of Krog's known friends in Reykjavik, and they, of course, had found or learned nothing. He had the Coast Guard's Fokker patrol plane and helicopter fly searches over the countryside. As he expected, they detected no sign of Krog. A distant campfire had been sighted by a farmer, but it was put out shortly afterward and could not be located in the daylight. Not since the days of medieval outlawry had anyone been so elusive.

As the newspapers had it, Krog was no better than a medieval berserk. All Iceland must believe that he had gone crazy and was killing women out of some lunatic frenzy. At least two other women Krog had known—and slept with—had asked for police protection and were receiving it. Hundreds of others who had not known Krog were just as nervous. The minister of justice was almost distraught. If Krog was costing the Workers' and Farmers' Party votes, as the American Spencer seemed to believe, his being at large was also hurting the government politically. The minister wanted him apprehended by the election, or else.

Andersson wasn't sure he'd be able to accommodate the minister—or that he wanted to. The two dead men in the bog had made up his mind: Krog was not the killer. But the minister of justice would not find the acting superintendent's surmise exactly sufficient. Neither would the newspapers, and neither, in his hardheaded policeman's way, could Andersson himself. Doubts did not close files.

He went to his office window, clasping his hands behind his back as he gazed off in the direction of downtown Reykjavik. Elisabet was in the United States, but she could be no more distant from him if she were back in her apartment—or sitting here in his office.

Krog seemed an instrument of the gods, the vexing gods. Andersson had had his cold dark life turned warm and bright and beautiful by one evening's encounter with Elisabet. The next morning there had come the murder and Krog, and Andersson's life had been a misery ever since. Krog had brought Spencer to Iceland. And Peterson. Andersson was certain of that. Krog was the reason for the two men in the bog. Krog was the reason for terrible things yet to come.

Bring Krog in and it would all go away. He was sure.

Spencer would go away. He'd see to it.

But now he needed Spencer to bring Krog in. It was the lamentable truth.

Andersson returned to his chair with a weary sigh. Loosening his tie, which he almost never did, he opened the huge file once again. He would do what the wisest policemen always did when frustrated: Go back to the beginning.

He went back to the Heklafjordur reports and statements. He was so tired of them, had read them so many times, that each word brought a vague pain. He let the words blur and began to skim, then suddenly stopped. Sitting up straight, he reread the paragraph he had just finished. It was part of the statement made by the drunken old fisherman down by the Heklafjordur wharf. He said he had seen three strangers come off the Polish trawler. Three.

The grocer had seen just two.

Jahn was still dressed in dirty sailor clothes, for he had just returned from the harbor waterfront, where he had helped excite the daily mob of anti-NATO protesters into a binge of throwing stones at the *Bacchus*. There had been injuries, which were all to the good, and a few arrests, which guaranteed press coverage. Iceland was a piece of cake.

Gorushchenko was late, obnoxiously late. Irritated, Jahn finally got up from his chair and began to pace about the cellar room. A new case of vodka had been brought in. Jahn opened one of the bottles and filled a tall glass. He took it back to the table and began looking through the American men's sex magazine that had come his way that morning. There were a few admitted flaws in the socialist system, and the official opposition to such magazines was one of them.

Jahn pulled out the centerfold just as Gorushchenko came through the door. He laid the magazine upon the table face-up and open. Gorushchenko, frowning, glanced at it without changing his expression. Looking at Jahn's glass, he found one as tall and filled it. He drank a third of it in one gulp, belched, and swore.

"I am due a progress report, Colonel," he said, reaching for his cigarettes.

"We are making progress."

"Ah, yes. The murder of that Finnish woman. An article about this in several American newspapers, written by John Spencer. Have you read it?" He reached into his coat pocket and pulled out a telecopied clipping.

Jahn waved his hand. "I read that," he said. "No worry."

"No worry? Yes?" Gorushchenko's cheeks creased with the faint touch of a smile. He sat down clumsily.

"Both the murder and the news story will attract Krog's attention," Jahn said. "They are provocative. They may bring him to the surface."

Gorushchenko grunted. He looked at the centerfold upside down and grunted again.

"Spencer is without doubt an agent for the CIA," Jahn said. "I have received confirmation of this from our American sources."

"Yes? And you will now finally eliminate this Spencer?"

"I have always had the option to eliminate Spencer. But he

is our best route to Krog. We must keep him alive for that."

Gorushchenko leaned closer. Jahn could see food between his teeth as he opened his mouth to speak.

"Listen, you Prussian bastard," he said. "You are supposed to be the tidy one. Clean and neat, they said. Trust everything to Jahn, they said. He will see you through."

He leaned even closer. "I want things neat and clean and tidy, you prick. I want those people dead, soon!"

Jahn, flushed, restrained his temper. "It's more complicated now," he said. "Spencer has brought a friend here, an Icelandic-American lawyer named George Peterson. He's the honorary Icelandic consul in Baltimore. Spencer has gone to Luxembourg, ostensibly to procure data for his article, apparently to contact more friends."

" 'Apparently'? Don't you know?"

"We had a man on him. He was found in the Alzette River with his throat cut, just hours ago."

"Spencer did this?"

"Possibly."

"Kill him!"

"Not until we have dealt with Krog. Krog knows a great deal, Herr Botschafter. More than I believed. He sent another letter to Peterson which we retrieved from his hotel. It said more than I should like to see written down anywhere concerning postelection agreements for Polish aluminum plants."

"You've recovered this letter?"

"The letter, yes. But that's the last we know of Krog. He named a rendezvous in the letter. We waited there, but no one appeared."

"You should not have killed the Kekkonen woman, you stupid piss brain!"

"Herr Botschafter! Must I remind you of your orders? Of my orders? If I fail, you may stuff me down the crater of volcano Hekla. If all goes well—and all is going well—we shall both soon be enjoying daschas in some warm and pleasant clime."

Gorushchenko glanced down at the magazine. "Does Krog know about our charged-particle beam weapons?"

"I believe so."

"Will you get to him in time?"

"Of course. You know my credentials, Herr Botschafter. I am tired of having to remind you of them."

"You should not have killed the Kekkonen woman. You should not have killed the girl on the east coast. Now that there are people among us whom it is imperative that you kill, you do nothing. You are provoking me, Colonel Jahn."

"You carry out your assignment, Herr Botschafter, and I will carry out mine. There is no need for any more of these meetings. Our conversations are the same. I am going to notify my general of my problems. I plan to request complete autonomy, or transfer."

Gorushchenko glanced one more time at the magazine. Jahn, rising to leave, snatched it away.

14

The Icelandair DC-8 banked for its approach to Keflavik over a west of Iceland basking in deceptively bright sunshine. Spencer stepped off the airplane into a bitterly cold wind that slapped at his clothing. He might as well have been in Chicago.

He wished he were in Chicago.

In Reykjavik he stopped at the bookstore near his hotel for the latest newspapers, then went directly to his room. As best as he could determine with his meager Icelandic, there was nothing new. The conservatives in power were promising drastic action against inflation. Erikisson had made a flat promise to reduce it by half.

Peterson was not there and had left no message. On the odd chance that Elizabet was not still in the United States, he called her apartment, but there was no answer. He stretched out on his bed, looking through the newspapers more slowly, wondering whether Karin would call. Wherever she was, she did not.

Everyone was expecting Krog to come to him except probably Krog, the phantom out in the wilds, who still might not know a Jack Spencer existed. Spencer had a new plan to seek him out—two, in fact, but both required George Peterson, and Karin. And there was a third possibility.

He drained his glass. He would place a newspaper advertisement in the "Help Wanted" columns: "Wanted, electrical engineer; knowledge of sailplanes, chess; travel to America."

If Krog were anywhere in Iceland, he would be reading newspapers. He would be reading every newspaper he could find or steal.

Could the KGB know of the powers of advertising?

Sverrir Axelsson saw Spencer coming out of *Kvoldbladid's* advertising office. There was no avoiding him. Later, over two glasses of Iceland's pointless beer, there was no avoiding the obvious question.

"What are you advertising for?" Axelsson asked. "A house? You'll find there's quite a waiting list."

"Why should I be advertising for a house?" Spencer said.

At first, Axelsson responded only with his strangely boyish grin. "For you and Elisabet Bjornsdottir," he said finally.

Spencer had been thinking about Elisabet much of the time, but he had never thought about a house.

"Elisabet has a very nice apartment," Spencer said.

Axelsson could go and read the ad for himself. Axelsson was a very smart man.

"I placed a help-wanted ad," Spencer said.

"Help-wanted ad? You need help with your story? I will help you." He grinned again.

"Trusting you'll keep this confidential," Spencer said, waiting until Axelsson nodded, "I'm using the ad as a sort of code. I'm trying to get someone to contact me."

"Geir Krog," said Axelsson.

Spencer's hand trembled. "What?"

"Geir Krog, I said," said Axelsson. "I meant it as a joke, but I see by your face that it is not. You are trying to reach Krog."

"My bureau in Washington is very interested in the story," Spencer said. "It's got everything—politics, NATO, sex, the chase. I'm going to try for an interview."

"Once again you involve yourself in our affairs, my friend."

"Strictly business. A good story."

"My paper is running an editorial addressed to Krog," Axelsson said. "It asks him to give up and come in."

"We call that 'ivory towerism' in America."

"It is an appeal to reason."

"Do your people think he's a murderer? Do they know anything the police don't know?"

Axelsson shrugged. "No one thinks he killed the Kekkonen woman. Not even in the Dark Ages was there ever a murder like that in Iceland. But Krog has to come in. People are becoming frightened. It will affect the election."

"That's my theory," said Spencer, "but I can't get anyone around here to buy it."

"I do," said Axelsson. "All this is mixed up with the election, as were the troubles down at the harbor. It's as bad as it was during the cod war."

"Protest demonstrations."

"A near-riot yesterday," Axelsson said. "There may be another one today. I have to go down there now. Would you like to come?"

Spencer couldn't take any more fruitless waiting in his hotel room. "Sure," he said, rising. He stopped. "Sverrir, you won't tip anyone off about the ad? I'm using a box number at your paper for responses."

"If Krog should walk in himself, of course I can't guarantee anything," Axelsson said, smiling. "But if something comes in, I'll let you know immediately. And only you."

Some long low clouds were streaming among the mountains up the coastline to the north, but the strong south wind seemed to be keeping them away from Reykjavik. There were whitecaps in the harbor, even on the sheltered side of the crowded quay. Spencer and Axelsson stood on the black gravel shore opposite, watching the crowd build and press closer to the policemen guarding the frigates.

Spencer had witnessed mob confrontations in the Memphis ghetto, at the 1968 Chicago convention, in Bogside and Belfast, in Mexico City and Teheran. Now Iceland. There was a dreadful, wearying sameness to them, the same theatrics, the same undercurrent of menace and incipient mayhem, the same chants uttered seemingly in the same language.

"There's a rumor the NATO flotilla commander wants to

pull out and end this 'goodwill visit' early," said Axelsson. "But the British captains supposedly will have none of it, not for the sake of these demonstrators."

"Rule Britannia," said Spencer.

The mob grew larger but seemed content to chant and mill about. Someone was carrying a wooden horse's head on a pole.

"I don't think it's going to be so bad today," Axelsson said.

"I hope not. I've got a headache."

"There aren't so many sailors this time."

"Sailors?"

"Trawlermen, from the looks of them. Yesterday they were all over."

Spencer looked behind them, up the street. There was no one there.

"Maybe they're fishing," he said.

There were no messages in his mailbox when he returned to the hotel. Peterson didn't answer his phone. Neither did Elisabet hers. A call to Icelandair produced only the guess that she would be back the next day. He left a message for Peterson at the desk and went to the hotel bar. As in Luxembourg, he found he had chosen the wrong bar—for the same reason.

"Here's luck, it's the toff himself!" said Molyneaux, grabbing Spencer's arm and pulling him to a place at the bar. "A glass of gin? A whiskey? A whiskey! And you can stand us the round, Jacko. At these bloody prices, you'd think the Icies were distilling the stuff from Chanel No. 5."

"I didn't see you on the plane this morning," Spencer said.

"I had the other one, the New York plane," Molyneaux said, lighting a short French cigarette. "You were on the one that went on to Chicago. How was the wee bairn? Was she a bloody good romp?"

Spencer nodded, once.

"You're developing strange tastes in your dotage, Jacko," Molyneaux said. "Have a care, or next it will be little boys."

Spencer had set his wallet briefly on the bartop. Molyneaux

pulled a huge Kronur note from it and waved it at the bartender. Spencer decided he was wrong. No bar with Collie Molyneaux in it was really a bad place—not in Salisbury, not in Belfast, not in Reykjavik. Chesley would have despised Molyneaux, of course, which stood in Collie's favor. Her favorite people were the kind who enjoyed cocktail parties in museums. And if Molyneaux was a professional spy, who was Spencer to think ill of that?

"These bloody Icies are throwing rocks at Her Majesty's vessels," Molyneaux said, "but my office is being altogether nonchalant about it. I don't have to file a word until Monday. So I'm for a couple more of these, a fine dinner of roasted ram's balls, and then a bloody good drunk at the Saga."

"It passes the time."

"Well then."

Spencer stopped at the hotel desk on the way out. Nothing there for him. The evening in the Saga began sedately enough—a few couples dining elegantly in the main room with its sweeping views of the city, then more until it was crowded. Molyneaux and Spencer moved to the second-floor bar. Within minutes, all the stools were taken.

At length, Spencer and Molyneaux gave up all pretense of conversation and drifted apart—Molyneaux into the arms of a large red-haired woman who clutched him to her extraordinary bosom.

A small blond woman backed out of the crowd and into Spencer. She was young, very short, and dressed in dowdy Icelandic fashion—sweater, long black skirt, disheveled blond hair falling over her eyes. She held a bottle of Brennivin—"Black Death"—and pressed back against him until he could feel the separation of her buttocks against his thigh.

"Good evening, Mr. Spencer," she said.

"Muffy!"

"Shhhhh," she said. "How drunk is James Bond?"

"Collie? Very."

"How drunk are you?"

"Sort of. How 'bout you?"

"Cold sober, Mr. Spencer. I've had only one of these awful things. We have to talk. I want to get out of here. Turn me around and kiss me, like you were putting on the make."

"If you insist."

Her eyes were wide open as they kissed.

"We have to stop meeting like this," he said when she finally stepped back. She continued to stare at him.

"I'm very serious, Spencer. We have a major, major problem and I have to talk to you. You have picked me up. Take me to your hotel."

"We can't talk there."

"Certainly not. On the way."

"The penalty for drunk driving in Iceland is worse than the one for murder and treason."

"I'll drive."

"Karin . . ."

"My cover here is Helga Lindstrom. Swede. You may call me Muffy."

"Muffy, Helga. I have a friend."

"I know all about Elisabet Bjornsdottir. I also know she won't be back until tomorrow. Now let's go, damn it! I want to get away from Her Majesty's Secret Service before he sobers up."

"No chance of that."

She drove his rented car in circuitous fashion, making turns almost randomly but at length pulling up where she wanted to, along the shore of Reykjavik's small Lake Tjornin.

"Let's walk," she said.

It was cold but the wind had vanished. The waters of the lake were inky dark and still. As she had done in Luxembourg, Karin put his arm around her and pulled herself tight against him, keeping their pace very slow.

"We're in trouble," she said. "The KGB doesn't have its usual idiot goon squad here. They've sent in some East Germans. An elite outfit—the 'A' team, as Thorn would say."

"Who?"

"Never mind. I've encountered these people before.

They're really bad news. And their presence means two bad things for us."

"Yes?"

"One is that, whatever they're involved in here, it's enormously important. The other is that, the instant Krog turns up, life isn't going to be very easy for us."

"You said you've encountered them. Do they know who you are?"

"If they did, I wouldn't be here. But they're really tough stuff, especially their Number One, Ludwig the Mad."

"Ludwig the Mad? King of Bavaria?"

"That's our little code. His actual name isn't known. He's a KGB colonel. German. He's a little nuts. I'm not at all surprised about that girl in Krog's cabin. He's not always that gentle." She seemed to press even closer to him. "We're going to need help, Jack. A lot of help."

"I'll do what I can."

"You? You just do what you're supposed to. I mean outside help. Reinforcements. With that mole, our assets here are worthless. There's no one I can count on. I've tried to reach Hugh through every channel, but he's gone to ground. I'm afraid to try Washington or London, even Oslo."

A car approached from behind them, prompting Karin to pull Spencer around and kiss him. The car passed without slowing.

"Let's head back now," she said. "Don't hurry."

"What will you do?"

"I wish to hell I knew! Just don't you go starting World War III on your own. Be as careful as you can and keep after Krog and I'll cover your tail. And stay in touch! Don't go wandering off with your girlfriend. I need to be kept informed about everything. Use any of the drop points here that Hugh gave you."

"He didn't give me any."

"Swell." She walked a ways without speaking, her breathing a little heavy. "All right. I'm at the Hotel Esja. Call me there direct to arrange a date, or leave a message. I'm a hot little number you picked up and you like my Svenska brand of nooky. Speaking of that, let's get back to your hotel."

"I don't know that that's wise."

"Wise? Look, Spencer, I've had better and I've had worse, but this is strictly business. We have to maintain cover."

"I've lost my cover. Just ask Laidlaw."

"Well, I haven't lost mine!"

"You don't understand. It's nothing personal. I mean, my friend . . ."

"Shove your friend! Look, you came here to do a job, not advance Icelandic-American relations. Knock off the swain act."

"I'm sorry."

"Look, Jack. I'm not really in the mood myself. I'll curl up in your chair or something. But I'm going to your hotel room. We have to keep this going."

He pulled her around and kissed her forehead.

"Okay," he said. "Don't worry."

She laughed, not happily.

They turned off the lights in his room. He undressed to his underwear, then got into bed. She stood by the window for a long while, staring down at the square, then sat in his armchair for the longest of times, her head silhouetted against the windows. Finally, Spencer sat up and threw back the covers.

"Karin," he said. "Come here."

She sighed. "All right," she said, rising. "Just to sleep."

Later, toward morning, Spencer awoke to something. She was facing away from him, her warm back against his chest. And, gently, she was sobbing.

15

WHEN SPENCER WOKE again, it was late in the morning. The frail Icelandic sun had risen above the rooftops and was shining through the window. Two days in a row with sunlight, Spencer thought. What extraordinary weather.

There wasn't a trace of Karin in the room. Spencer lay back again and gazed for a time at the place where she had lain on his bed—where Elisabet had also lain. A troubling juxtaposition of memories.

The telephone rang, setting his nerves ajangle. It was not Elisabet but Peterson.

"Where the hell have you been?" Spencer asked.

"Visiting friends," Peterson said. "Drumming up business. Have you ever seen the statue of Leif Erikisson they have here in Reykjavik? By the church on the top of the hill?"

"Only from a distance."

"Well, it's even more striking close up. Why don't you meet me there in twenty minutes?"

"Thirty," Spencer said and yawned.

Standing on the hilltop at the base of the huge sculpture, looking down at the sweep of the city below, Peterson looked something like a statue of Leif Erikisson himself. Unusually cheery, he took Spencer around to the back with its surprising inscription; the statue had been a gift to Iceland from the people of the United States in 1930, marking the one-thousandth anniversary of the Althing's founding.

"Hands across the waters," Peterson said. He looked up at

the statue's enormous shoulders. "I've talked to Geir Krog."

"You what?"

Peterson smiled. He was amused, but he seemed perfectly serious about Krog.

"As I suspected, he and I have mutual friends," Peterson said. "They took some finding, but I found them. They arranged for me to talk with him over the phone."

"A safe phone?"

"Oh, yes. This was up north of here, in a place where you wouldn't expect there to be a phone."

"Did this have anything to do with a newspaper ad?"

"Newspaper ad?"

"Yes. Did Krog say he was responding to an ad in *Kvoldbladid?*"

Peterson studied Spencer warily.

"Er, no," he said.

"I've got to see him," Spencer said. "As soon as possible! Is he willing to meet with me?"

"He's willing to meet with me," Peterson said. "It seems we had a very close mutual friend in Evi Kekkonen. Krog is a very angry man. He wants revenge and he would appreciate my help."

"Damn it, George, this is my show. There's more at stake here than Krog's revenge."

"Indeed, although you haven't made it perfectly clear to me precisely what is at stake."

"Later. Will he agree to see me, too?"

"I think that can be arranged. It's all for the good of Iceland. Isn't it?"

"When are you to meet with him?"

"Tonight."

"Where?"

"He hasn't told me yet. Undoubtedly someplace near. He gave me the strong impression he's hiding out near Reykjavik."

Peterson was no longer looking at him but was gazing out across the city toward the sea. A large freighter was moving slowly toward the harbor. Beyond it, a few fishing trawlers were headed for open water. The remaining NATO vessels, as far as Spencer could determine, were still moored at the quay.

"Did Krog mention me at all, George? At all?" It was Spencer's show, all right, but Peterson was writing the script. Spencer might just as well have stayed in Washington and sent Peterson in his stead.

"Yes," Peterson said. "Briefly."

Two sailors were coming up the hill, one of them wearing a pea jacket and black watch cap.

"You make Krog nervous," Peterson said.

They walked back to the Thor, riding the slow, old-fashioned elevator to their floor. Peterson went to his room to rest and wait for the message from Krog that was to be relayed by his friends in the north. Spencer returned to his own chamber elated, and yet depressed. Once again, he had nothing to do. It was a dreary business, being a spy; he was always waiting upon others.

One drink—a weak whiskey and water—wouldn't hurt. He took it to the armchair and sat sipping. This way, at least, he wouldn't have to look at Karin's chair. However, it was hard to keep his eyes from the bed.

He got up and began to pace back and forth. Then he looked at his watch, hesitated, and went to the phone. He had called Elisabet just before going to meet Peterson at the statue, but the phone had rung on and on without answer. Now he tried again. There was a click, and then a buzzing busy signal! Twice more he tried, with the same result—a happy result.

The fourth time, she answered.

"Elisabet," he said. "It's Jack. Jack Spencer."

She hung up without a word.

Swearing, Spencer stared into his drink for a long moment, trying to assess the depth of his trouble. Those damn no-good stewardesses in the hotel in Luxembourg.

He dialed again. She picked up the phone quickly but said nothing.

"Elisabet?"

Another loud click, and the dial tone.

The next time he called, he got the busy signal.

It had been Commander Richards' clear duty to have Truscott arrested immediately, but his instinct was to wait a while. His instincts now told him time was running short.

He had switched Truscott's schedule to the day shift to keep him on the base—and away from his interesting friends. He had just now visited Truscott in the situation watch room, chatting harmlessly about the sudden lack of Soviet naval activity in the Iceland area—there was nothing but the trawler *Stolypin* in harbor and a couple of subs prowling the upper reaches of the Denmark Strait. Most of the Russian northern fleet had shifted far to the north of Britain. It hadn't been so quiet in months.

Richards was now in his office, his door shut and locked, dialing a code into his scrambler phone. In a moment, Whelan came on the line.

"Richards here."

"What's up? Another funny?"

"Not even a rowboat. It's this newspaper guy, Spencer. I got a rumble from NavInt that he may be working for you guys after all. Are they keeping you in the dark?"

"I checked with Washington and Grosvenor Square. There was nothing."

"Well, maybe there was a computer error," Richards said, writing on a piece of notepaper. "Why don't you try again? I'd like to know where we stand. NavInt is never wrong."

Whelan paused. "Right," he said, finally. "I'll get back to you."

"I'll be at the officers' club," Richards said. "Preparing for lunch. Roger dodger, over and out."

Two martinis later—two very nice, crisp martinis—the message center summoned Richards back to his office and the scrambler phone.

"Yeah," said Whelan. "I can confirm. He's working with us."

"Thankee, old buddy," Richards said. "We'll keep out of his way." Hanging up, he tilted back in his chair, propping his long legs on his desk. There was no way Whelan could have gotten that out of the agency computer. Richards had made a run at that first thing that morning. As he had expected, it came back clean. Spencer's only CIA tag was that interesting little note in Truscott's laundry, out of the navy computer.

Funnies, indeed.

He would have to get to Spencer soon. But first he had to neutralize Truscott.

Richards called in four shore patrol before summoning Truscott to his office. Numbers were intimidating—especially wearing .45 automatics. They took Truscott down to a secure room in the basement. Even the admiral sat in.

Truscott was easily intimidated. As Richards had suspected, his motive had been merely money, surprisingly little money. The KGB could be real cheapskates.

The young man, nervously smoking cigarettes, backed off in stages. He pleaded innocence and ignorance until confronted with the NavInt message. Next he claimed that he was working for the CIA and only following orders. Then Richards confronted him with his visit to the Polish embassy. As Truscott pondered that, Richards recited some of the more exciting provisions of the Uniform Code of Military Justice. He also chanced to mention the provision of the new Thurmond Act that restored the death penalty for treason. Just for laughs, Richards threw in the years at hard labor a smuggling conviction could bring.

Truscott told everything he knew—which wasn't really very much, but certainly enough.

"Why were you so dumb as to walk straight into the Polish embassy like that?" Richards asked. "Why didn't you use a drop?"

Truscott stared down at his brilliantly polished shoes.

"They wanted it in a hurry."

"They?"

"Whelan said so."

"Mr. Whelan at our embassy?"
"Yes, sir."

There was, unfortunately, a slight jurisdictional problem. After a brief conference, Richards and the admiral agreed they'd have to shunt the matter to Washington. Richards coded the long, top-secret, EXDIS message himself. He aimed it very high in the intelligence bureaucracy. According to Truscott, Whelan had some protection in Washington. High up.

Spencer raced out of the Hotel Thor into the early night. Peterson had received the call from his friends and then called Spencer back, arranging to meet immediately in the upstairs bar at the restaurant Naust. It was only three blocks away, but in Spencer's hurry, it seemed three miles.

He started down the walk, startled suddenly as a red Volkswagen pulled up to the curb beside him. "Mr. Spencer," said the driver. "I need to talk to you."

Spencer glanced at the dark figure inside without pausing. The voice was American, but he was not about to get into any car with a stranger. He was not about to stop for anyone.

The Volkswagen spurted ahead, then halted at the curb again. The driver leaned across the seat and stuck his head out the open passenger window. "Mr. Spencer, please. This is important. It concerns your life."

His life. What a thing to threaten him with.

Spencer only vaguely recognized the face, but the voice brought recognition. The American naval officer. The one who had been at the embassy. He was dressed in civilian clothes. Spencer continued on a few paces, then stopped. Never turn down information. Never pass by a possible source. A prime rule of journalism.

He got into the car. The naval officer reached into his breast pocket. For an instant Spencer thought he was going to pull out a gun. Instead it was his wallet. He flashed his military ID. Commander James L. Richards, it said.

"I remember you," Spencer said. "Drive around the square, slowly."

"You're with the agency," Richards said, putting the Volkswagen in gear. "You're here for the CIA."

"I'm a simple journalist trying to get a simple story about Icelandic energy, and I am very, very tired of being hassled by my own government."

"You've worked for the agency in Mexico, Northern Ireland, and Iran," Richards said. "That much I know as absolute fact. It's my strong belief that you're working for the agency now. I had an enlisted man in my section arrested today who fingered you. He also fingered someone else, a man in our own embassy, as a KGB agent."

Spencer said nothing. He sat with his arms folded. He and the officer were so big for the car that their shoulders touched.

"The embassy man is named Whelan," Richards said. "He's the CIA station chief here."

"The mole," said Spencer.

"I've no doubt of it, but the only proof I have is the enlisted man's statement. I've alerted my people in Washington, but I can't move against him myself. It'll take awhile to get through channels. I thought you'd want to know about him."

Spencer exhaled through his teeth. Things were moving too fast.

"I do," he said. "I appreciate it."

"Can I drop you anywhere? You were in a hurry."

"Yes," said Spencer. "The restaurant Naust, in Vesturgata. No. No, take me to the Hotel Esja first."

He would have to tell Karin immediately. He wished she hadn't seemed so frightened.

16

Gunnar Erikisson closed the drapes of his study windows against the night, and prying eyes. Sitting at his desk, he opened the folder before him. The papers within were full of figures—trade balances, export volumes, inflation rates, gross national product levels, per capita income, and considerably more—all of it going back to the founding of the republic in 1944. Economics delighted Erikisson; it was politics he found unpleasant.

When the door opened, he thought nothing of it; he did not even look up. His housekeeper came and went like that, as she pleased. He presumed it was she and said nothing. Finally, when he heard no further movement, he glanced up. He blanched. That Erikisson's skin could become any paler seemed a medical impossibility, but it did. Every last drop of blood was sucked to his vitals. He trembled. He felt faint.

"Geir?"

"Calm yourself, Gunnar," said Krog. "I'm not here to harm you."

Krog moved to a leather chair next to Erikisson's desk, lowering himself slowly but heavily into it. His eyes never left Erikisson's. Krog smelled awful, but Erikisson was too terrified to notice.

"Are you armed, Geir?"

"I have a knife. But it's not why I've come, Gunnar. I've come to plead with you."

"Plead with me? For help? You killed that girl. You killed your own mistress."

The expression of rage that at once contorted Krog's face might better have accompanied a thundering bellow, but he made no sound. He gripped Erikisson's arm and yanked him near.

"I have killed no one," he said through gritted teeth into Erikisson's face. "If I had, I would not be here. Do you understand? I have killed no one!"

He relaxed his painful hold on Erikisson's arm, letting him fall back weakly into his chair.

"Gunnar," Krog said. "I want you to call off your agreement with the Soviets. That's why I have come."

Erikisson grimaced and looked away.

"Please, Geir," he said.

"I'm going after them, Gunnar. I've made my plans carefully. I have friends. I know where the Soviets are vulnerable. I am going to get them, for what they did to those two poor women, for what they've done to me, for what they are doing to Iceland. But win or lose, Gunnar, succeed or fail, I want to know that you will end this agreement."

"I have given my word."

"Your word? You would betray Iceland, for your word?"

"We have argued this too many times, Geir. You are ardently patriotic, but you are not sensible." Erikisson gestured at the papers in the opened folder. "Iceland's inflation rate at the end of this calendar year is going to exceed seventy-five percent, Geir! The economy is utterly out of control. We are on the brink of catastrophe. Are you forgetting what happened in Germany after World War I? My mother grew up so poor she never saw money until she was twenty-one. They bartered fish and potatoes. Do you want Iceland to return to that?"

"Your scary stories again, Gunnar. You ignore the point."

"I ignore nothing. There are five political parties in our little country, Geir. Everyone has had their chance but us.

The Independence Party, the Progressives, the Labor Party, the People's Alliance: They have all tried—and failed. Individually, and in coalition. Now it is our turn. We—the Workers' and Farmers' Party, Iceland's true Communists—can win this election and we can succeed."

"But at what price?"

"Price? I will be able to reduce the cost of all our oil by fifty percent!"

"Not you, Gunnar. The Soviets are the ones who will reduce the cost of their oil. What you will do is give them whatever they want in return."

"How many years have you and I wished for what they want? To have the Americans out of Keflavik? To have Iceland out of NATO? To have Iceland free and independent at last? You are working for the Americans now, Geir, but once you shared my dream."

"I don't work for the Americans now. If I did in the past, it was only to stop the Soviets. A free and independent Iceland is my dream, too. But I see no freedom and no independence in the filthy deal you have made."

"Filthy deal? An aluminum plant?"

"If it's so honorable, why do you keep it such a secret?"

"Geir, the election . . ."

"If your agreement is indefensible now, how can it be defensible after the election?"

"It's only an aluminum plant! I'm not offering them any bases. It's just an aluminum plant. We already have one of our own. What's wrong with another? It's to be run by Poles. There are no Russians involved. And in return we get so much."

Krog jumped to his feet and pulled Erikisson to his.

"You fool!" he said. "Can you be that naive? Have you no idea what they are going to install in that aluminum plant? What they really plan to do with all that electricity? I have figured it out, Gunnar! The Russians may seem like buffoons, but their military technology is the finest. They are going to use it for a weapon, Gunnar. They are going to use Iceland to make war!"

He threw Erikisson back into his chair. "I have stayed too long," he said. "I hope you will come to your senses and stop this despicable thing you have started. If you won't, I will. I will. You will not be prime minister, Gunnar Erikisson."

"What? What do you mean?"

"Stop your trembling, you damn fool! If I were going to harm you—if I were all the things they say I am—you would be dead. Do you understand that?"

"Yes," said Erikisson. "Yes, I do."

"I'll go now. Don't interfere with my escape."

"I won't."

Krog took a bottle of aquavit from the side table and set it down sharply in front of Erikisson. "Here," he said. "Have a drink." He walked out quickly, shaking his great bearded head. For a long moment, there was no sound. Then there was the slam of a door.

Erikisson took the bottle, filled the glass, and drank—nothing timid about his sip. He drank, emptied the glass, filled it again, and drank again. He reached for his phone, resting his hand on the receiver. Gorushchenko would want to know about this.

Gorushchenko would have to deal with his own problems, he decided. Erikisson would do his duty as an Icelander. He picked up the receiver, dialed, and asked for acting superintendent Magnus Andersson. He got a sergeant instead. Andersson was away from the office, the man said. There had been a breakthrough in the Geir Krog case.

"No Krog," said Spencer, once again looking at the luminous dial of his watch.

"It's only been fifteen minutes," Peterson said, rubbing his hands against the cold. "Let us not be so demanding."

Spencer grunted, huddling deeper in his trenchcoat. They

were sitting in the utter dark in a hollow in the ground, their backs against the cold mossy earth.

"What do you call these things?"

"Booths," said Peterson. "Originally, they were quite deep, like the trench dugouts in World War I. During the medieval Althings, people would live in them—as they might in Holiday Inns. Lawyers would do business in them."

"Instead of under rocks."

"Be more charitable. Law is the foundation of all civilization."

"Right, and look at the state of civilization."

Peterson let the remark pass, and they sat in silence for several minutes. Unseen puffs of wind chased each other about the dark valley around them. Their eyes had become accustomed to the faint starlight, and the severe outline of the rocky mound in front of them was clearly delineated. They were at Thingvellir, the site of Iceland's first Althing—a parliament founded three centuries before Magna Carta. The mound before them was what remained of the Rock of Laws. Thereon had stood the Law Speaker, a man unique for having memorized all the nation's laws in a time of no writing. Here were all disputes settled—marriages dissolved, property transferred, punishment meted—with banishment the worst punishment of all.

Spencer shivered. "You're sure this is the right place?"

"Jack. There is only one Thingvellir, and only one Rock of Laws. It's like arranging to meet at the Washington Monument. You wouldn't go to Annapolis instead."

"There are houses across the lake. All those lights are on. Perhaps they've scared him off."

"It's a hotel. It's on this side of the lake. And I'm sure Krog was well aware of it when he arranged to meet here. It's almost pitch dark up here."

"I still don't understand why he sought you out instead of me. I've been all over the country making myself available."

"My father was Icelandic. It's as simple as that."

"Just like the Order of the Falcon."

"Yes."

The wind suddenly rose and blew steadily against the backs of their necks for a long moment, then subsided.

"George, I have a pistol with me."

"I know. I saw the bulge."

"I mean to bring Krog back with us whether he wants to come or not."

"Then you may have to shoot him."

"I don't want to do that."

Karin had seemed relieved by Richards' revelations about Whelan, but she had insisted on staying in Reykjavik. She wanted desperately to get in contact with Hugh. If she didn't hear from Laidlaw by noon the next day, she said they would have to move on Whelan—especially if they were going to be taking Krog out of the country.

Spencer wished she were here at Thingvellir. Small blond girl, Muffy.

"Elisabet's back," he said.

"Yes," said Peterson. "I talked with her."

"I tried to. She hung up on me. Three times."

"You must have displeased her in some way."

"What did you tell her about me?"

"Nothing of any real consequence. Just that you're a philanderer, an alcoholic, that sort of thing."

"You did?"

"That you have a serious medical condition, that you're up to absolutely no good here in Iceland, and that she would be out of her pretty mind to have anything more to do with you."

"Damn you, George."

"And, just as I expected, it made absolutely no difference. If anything, it whetted her appetite." Peterson coughed, covering his mouth carefully to confine the sound. "She told me she loves you, John. Aren't you lucky."

"Loves me?"

"That was three days ago. Before you found a new friend. A Swedish friend. At the Hotel Esja."

"George, what did–"

"Not a word. You apparently were more than a little indiscreet in Luxembourg. And you picked the wrong hotel. Stewardesses are a sorority, Jack. Especially with a little airline like Loftleider."

Peterson rose and stretched, then reached in the pocket of his leather coat and pulled out a flat metal tin of small Dutch cigars.

"Would you like a Schimmelpfennig?" he asked.

"I gave up smoking, remember? For my . . . health."

"Oh, yes."

Peterson struck a match.

The sound of a mere gunshot is not that terrifying. What is harder on the nerves is the sound of a gunshot combined with the sound of the bullet, the bullet whizzing by, the bullet striking home. Peterson dropped to the ground. He swore. Spencer dropped beside him.

"George? Are you all right? Are you hit?"

"I'm fine. I–"

There was another shot, then a hesitant echo of it, and then two more. After that, there was mayhem–a rolling explosion of return fire from the other side. That was returned. The tits begat tats.

Spencer remembered two things from his wartime experiences. One was that at night one's tendency was to fire high. The other was never to strike a match in the open.

"You're not hit?" he said to Peterson, hugging the ground as he crawled next to him.

"No," said Peterson, waiting for the next spasm of gunfire to spend itself. "I guess Mr. Krog will not be joining us tonight."

"Why did you light that match? You know better!"

"A foolish lapse."

"Back to the car," Spencer said. "Hurry!"

It wasn't where they had left it. Behind them, there continued sporadic firing. At the distant hotel, more lights had gone on; then abruptly all of them went out. Spencer and

Peterson had to grope their way along the road. The car was not where Spencer remembered leaving it. It was not anywhere.

"We've got to run!" Spencer said. "Get away from here!"

"Good idea!" said Peterson, lurching off into the darkness. It occurred to Spencer that his friend was smiling.

Spencer had been looking back over his shoulder. He didn't expect headlights to come on in front of him. He froze, then leaped into the shallow ditch to his right. Peterson stayed where he was, blinking at the bright light. The driver, gunning the car's engine, leaned out his open window.

"Jacko, you twit," he said. "Get your bloody arse in here!"

"Collie!"

Peterson and Spencer ran, stumbling, and clambered into the little automobile, Spencer into the rear seat. Before he pulled the door shut, Molyneaux had the car grinding into reverse.

"This is my car, Collie."

"And aren't you glad I had it here waiting for you?" Molyneaux said. "It would have been shot full of bloody holes where you left it."

"How did you get here?" Spencer asked, as Molyneaux roared off down the road.

"Taxicab," Molyneaux said. "Discreetly. Followed you out here. You looked like you might be going someplace interesting. It makes me pissing mad, don't you know, to get scooped."

"With this story, you'd have been better off being scooped," Spencer said.

"Did you see who that was shooting at us?" Peterson asked.

"George Peterson, isn't it? Well, I did that, Peterson. At least half of them are Icelandic police. As to the others, I wouldn't have the faintest bloody idea. Would you, Jacko?"

Spencer said nothing.

"Well, I'm for a drink," Molyneaux said. "We'll go to my hotel. The Esja. By the by, Jacko, I ran into your litle friend Muffy there. And isn't it amazing? She's turned Swedish."

17

THORN STORMED OUT of the deputy's office, picked up Mendelsohn at the library, drove his Ford station wagon at breakneck speed up the Georgetown Pike to Virginia's Riverbend Park, and rented a rowboat.

"What shall I sing?" said Mendelsohn, lowering himself gingerly onto the aft seat. " 'Row, Row, Row Your Boat' or 'The Volga Boatman'? " Wearing a baggier-than-usual three-piece suit, he sat awkwardly, his knees pressed tightly together, his hands holding the sides of the boat. Thorn moved the boat into the river and then began pulling—appropriately, Mendelsohn thought—upstream against the strong current. They were only about a mile above the roaring cascade of Great Falls.

"Our last conversation was overheard," Thorn said. "And recorded. It's hard to bug a boat."

"Then I don't need to sing 'The Volga Boatman.' "

"They found our mole, Freddy. The goddamn navy found our mole for us. They traced Whelan through some enlisted man at Keflavik who got bought by the KGB."

"Whelan, using incompetence for cover. He was near the top of my list."

"Yeah, but not high enough. Anyway, I've got priority flashes flying all over the place to Karin. She's to take Whelan out. Immediately."

"And then?"

"It's all over, Freddy. We're shutting down Iceland One and turning everything over to the navy. I've even got to close a section in London and pull more than a dozen agents out of Norway and Denmark. Everything Whelan got dirty."

"Spencer?"

"The deputy made that very straight. Karin's to take him out, too."

"And Karin?"

"She comes home. It's time, anyway. She gets a nice desk here in Langley."

"And Hugh?"

"Out. The deputy is very displeased about Hugh."

"Good."

"You're out, too, Freddy. You've performed your last assignment for the agency. I mean, shit. The navy."

Mendelsohn shrugged.

"And the 'window of doom'?" he said.

Thorn gave a hard sloshing pull on the oars, then let them rest above the water a moment. "Wide open," he said. "The satellites picked up truck and bus convoys moving out of Moscow and ten other cities last night. The 'strategic bathtub' is full."

"They've practiced evacuations before," said Mendelsohn. "They do it very regularly. It's required once a year for every Russian county."

"They've started icing our agents en masse, Freddy. Confined foreign journalists to quarters. Said it had something to do with Poland. Satellites have picked up stuff along the Chinese border, too." He began rowing again. The Potomac was very clear in these upper reaches. Peering over the side, Mendelsohn could make out the dark, sharp-edged forms of enormous rocks, their tops barely penetrating the surface.

"The deputy doesn't care," Mendelsohn said.

"He cares plenty. But he isn't buying our line. He's thinking China. The Asia section really has its hand in his pants."

Mendelsohn lit a cigarette, putting the blown-out match in his pocket in habit. "That is idiocy," he said. "By neutralizing the United States, they may dispose of China at leisure. That is the principal point of neutralizing us."

"The deputy," said Thorn, glancing along the riverbank,

"can be thick of head sometimes." They rowed a ways in silence until they had cleared the north end of a long, rocky island.

"He has one point," Mendelsohn said. "It takes months to build one of those particle beam things."

"Maybe," said Thorn.

"We could be wrong, Bill."

"I think we probably are wrong. I hope to hell we're wrong. What keeps me awake at night is that we may be right."

"How much time will you give Hugh?"

"None. As soon as he surfaces, out he comes. I may have to go in and get him out. Then, go navy."

"Whelan had a protector on this end."

"So you've said. The choices are limited."

"I have it down to Hugh, you, or me."

"Yeah."

"The deputy is aware of this."

"No," said Thorn. "Not yet. He's pissed enough as it is. I think the best I'm going to get out of this is a transfer to Uganda."

He stopped rowing and, using the oars only for occasional guidance, let the boat slip back toward the dock in the current. It moved very fast.

"Bill, what if Karin and Hugh lay hands on Geir Krog?"

"And spring him? Then maybe I won't get transferred to Uganda. But I ain't exactly going to count on that."

The KGB general was in an office he kept away from the Kremlin. Instead of at a desk, he sat next to a long table covered with reports and communications. He had asked to see only priority messages, but they were coming in great volume. One he had set aside. The marshal wanted to see him yet again.

The weary general had little doubt as to the reason. He had himself seen the report on his East German colonel in Iceland just an hour before. Without prior consultation or authorization, Jahn had dispatched members of his Iceland team to

Europe and Latin America. He had sent messages to others who had been with him in Africa and were still operating there, in no code the KGB had on file.

It was the general's practice to allow his better operatives the widest possible latitude in the field, and Jahn was his best man. But there was nothing within the scope of the Valkyrie project or any of its ancillary operations that involved Switzerland, where three of Jahn's people had gone, or Latin America. The report suggested Rio as the probable destination. They had no active business in Rio except for a few local terrorist cells. There was nothing pertinent to Jahn's mission in Africa. The report troubled the general.

He pushed a button on the telephone beside him. In a moment the door to the room slid noiselessly open and a secretary entered, the older one whom he trusted completely, not the one he slept with.

"I want to send a message to Gorushchenko in Iceland," he said, waiting until the door slid closed again.

Gorushchenko could handle things. The general would tell the marshal everything was under control.

Quickly, he dictated his message, then rose. He was running late. Smiling, the general considered the possibility that the marshal was not interested in Jahn at all. The plan the general had devised for diverting American attention to Norway and Spitzbergen Island was working. The marshal might only want to congratulate him.

The general was an excessive optimist, but it helped him keep his sanity. So many of his colleagues had ulcers or worse. A few were certifiable paranoids.

Not so his friend Anatoly, off on his strange little ship. It was so odd for an admiral of his rank to be going to war in such a drab, defenseless vessel. He could have remained at his headquarters in port, or on one of the flag vessels in the northern fleet, but Anatoly had insisted on commanding the Valkyrie ship personally. He was like that.

The general, taking the elevator down to the street, wondered if he himself should be in Iceland taking charge, but he shook the thought from his mind. Optimism, always optimism.

Fearful of Andersson's police, Spencer and Peterson spent the night with two of Peterson's friends in a country house north of Reykjavik. The friends were an older couple—pleasant, discreet—treating this sudden visit as though it were nothing out of the ordinary.

Molyneaux had gone back to Reykjavik, promising to send Karin Nielsen out as soon as he could find her. She pulled up to the house in an old British Morris Minor station wagon. Dressed in her Icelandic woolen cap and sweater, she looked about twelve. Waving Peterson back, Spencer took her hand and they went for a walk on the moor behind the house.

"I brought you a clean shirt and socks," she said.

He laughed. "Thank you."

"And some messages." She dug her small hand into the pocket of her sweater. One said simply that Elisabet Bjornsdottir had called. Spencer put that into his pocket without comment. The next stated that a Mr. Clepich had telephoned and wanted to talk to him urgently.

"That's out of date," she said. "I've talked to Hugh. He has orders to return to the United States at once. I have orders, too. As soon as I've dealt with Whelan, I'm to go home."

Two large birds, larger than gulls, wheeled into the wind above them, calling. "They're shutting everything down," she said. "The agency is pulling out of Iceland."

"And me?"

She looked away, biting her lip. "Thank you very much, but your services are no longer needed. The project is canceled. You may, however, keep your expense money."

"How generous. What about Geir Krog?"

"If you happen to have him in your back pocket, take him back with you. Otherwise, forget it."

He put his arm around her, as she had had him do in Luxembourg and by Lake Tjornin. "I'm not going back," he said. "Not yet."

"I didn't think you would. Hugh isn't either. I have to; I always follow orders, or try. Anyway, they've got a quiet little job for me at Langley."

"I'll buy you a drink some lovely night in Georgetown," he said, squeezing her shoulder. "Are the police looking for us in Reykjavik?"

"One of them came around asking for you at the Thor, but he didn't hang around. Molyneaux got pulled over in your car. They let him go. I wish you'd keep him with you. He's getting in my way."

"Has he figured out what happened at Thingvellir?"

"No, but I have. You were set up. You, the police, the KGB. You were all set up. Your friend Krog has quite a sense of humor. One policeman was killed. So were two 'unidentified gunmen.' "

Spencer unfolded the third message. It was from Sverrir Axelsson. There had been a reply to his advertisement.

"I stopped by and picked it up," Karin said, reaching into her other pocket. "I opened it. It's in English, but I don't understand it." She handed it to him, her touch lingering.

" 'I know who you are,' " Spencer read. " 'Know who I am, and you shall find what you seek. Eyvind of the Hills.' "

"I have to go now," she said. "With luck, I can be on the evening plane." She turned within his arm and lifted her head to kiss him.

"Luck," he said finally.

"That wasn't for cover."

"I know," he said.

"I'll be looking for that drink, some lovely night in Georgetown. Some lovely night damn soon."

Colonel Jahn, as Rozkowski, sat in his hotel room with the blinds drawn. He was entirely naked, gulping nervously from a glass of vodka, holding a small American air pellet pistol—a toy that fired what was called a BB, with hardly enough force to penetrate a magazine. He was aiming it at a magazine, an American men's magazine, opened to a picture of a nude, reclining woman. Sweating, Jahn squeezed the trigger. A hole appeared in the center of her right breast. Another then appeared in her left one. His third shot hit her thigh. Correcting his aim, he obliterated her pubic area with his fourth. He kept firing until he had riddled her torso, then he moved the pistol and put a hole in the middle of her forehead. Finally, he dropped the little pistol and began to masturbate. When he was done, he lay back sweating and gasping for breath. His hands were trembling. He drank vodka until that stopped.

Jahn was losing and the Americans were winning. It was as simple as that. Four of his men were dead. The Icelandic police and the Coast Guard were on full alert. The American Truscott had been arrested, and if Whelan had not yet been, he would be soon. New American agents were arriving in Iceland. Erikisson was weakening. Krog, who must by now know enough to wreck everything—a one-man obstacle to the most ambitious enterprise in the history of warfare—was still at large, still capable of arranging such masterful coups as the bloody encounter at Thingvellir.

In two days, if Krog could be kept out of the reach of the Americans, if everything could be kept under control, none of this would matter.

Or would it? Jahn knew Gorushchenko had been sending back negative reports about him. He had intercepted one that all but called him psychopathic and dangerously unreliable. Jahn was about to accomplish something worthy of the great Otto Skorzeny, yet all he might get for his reward was a bullet through the back of his head in some cold Moscow basement.

He must dispense with Mr. Rozkowski.

He was showered, dressed, and packed within fifteen minutes. Leaving his bags at the desk with instructions that they be sent to the Keflavik airport on the next bus, he paid his room bill in cash and went into the bar. After a quick vodka, he slipped out the door, arriving at the Polish embassy a few minutes later.

Rozkowski disappeared in quick stages as Jahn shaved off all his hair, darkened his eyebrows, and inserted dark-brown contact lenses to hide his pale blue eyes. He added a pair of heavy-rimmed glasses. There was then a final clever touch. Years before, Jahn had had all his upper teeth pulled. A change in upper plates could alter the shape of his face dramatically. Rozkowski had a long, narrow face. Choosing another denture, wider and with a much shorter bite, Jahn instantly transformed himself to a round-faced man with thin compressed lips and an oddly cast jaw.

After changing his clothes and slipping into his coat pocket the passport and wallet of a Horst Erlanger, anthropologist from Leipzig, he moved to the embassy of the Democratic Republic of Germany, his new headquarters.

Karin lolled in the warm steamy water, closing her eyes a dreamy while, then opening them again to the incongruous sight of Reykjavik as seen from an outdoor swimming pool in late fall. A few flakes of snow were falling, yet here she was in a bikini. This was one of the wonders of Iceland, an outdoor public pool filled with the hot, mineral-rich water from the underground springs that heated all the city. Karin splashed water over her face, then lowered her small body till the water rose to her chin. She was all atingle, but it had nothing to do with the water. She was always this way, before.

Whelan was across from her, a pudgy, unattractive man wearing his glasses even in the pool. His habit was to come here daily and swim thirty minutes, never more or less, a break from his office routine. He was nearly done and would shortly be returning to the men's dressing room to change. Karin left the pool, pausing only to pick up the canvas carry-all bag she had left at the edge. She would attach the silencer in the women's room.

Whelan would be her very last one. She was sure of that now. She let her mind leap ahead to the afternoon plane—and, briefly, to bars she knew in Georgetown. Spencer would live. She would see to that.

18

Spencer and Peterson had borrowed a car and were driving east onto the central plateau, following a gravel road that wound near places Spencer had hoped to take Elisabet—and had thought of taking Karin—Geysir, which had given its name to all the geysers in the world, and the extraordinary waterfall Gullfoss, with its bewitching golden mist. There was no stopping for either of them. Peterson was driving calmly but insanely fast. He was convinced Krog would meet them at Hveravellir, the legendary redoubt of Eyvind of the Hills.

"He can be at no other place," Peterson said.

They arrived well in advance of the early sundown. There were only two structures at Hveravellir—a travelers' hut and an isolated weather station. The only inhabitants were the man and woman who operated the station. Polite but not talkative, they pointed the way to the site of Eyvind's dugout, then returned to whatever it was that—all by themselves in this empty, rock-strewn wilderness—they had been doing.

There was no Krog half an hour later, nor an hour later. Spencer and Peterson sat on the rim of Eyvind's dugout—a rock-lined depression about the size of two bathtubs—their legs dangling. The central plateau here was high, a broad saddle between the glaciers Langjokull and Hofsjokull, but the terrain surprisingly flat, a rolling windswept moor without a mountain crest in view. Spencer would not have believed there could be a single spot in Iceland without a view of a mountain.

"I feel like I'm sitting on the edge of a grave," he said.

"Don't be morbid," Peterson said.

"It comes easily these days."

Peterson looked away, squinting at the horizon. "Just how bad is your condition, Jack?" he asked finally.

"If I were to topple into this hole within the next minute, my doctors wouldn't be surprised at all. I imagine they're surprised it hasn't happened already."

"Then why are you here? Why are you going through with all this?"

"What should I be doing, sitting in a rest home back in Washington? Going to Singapore and renting a pallet in a house of the dead? No, I've come to terms with it, George. I go day by day. If it happens here in Iceland, all the better. I thought of that coming in on the plane, when we were making the approach into Keflavik. The immortal sea and all that. The strange green mountains. You can look eternity in the face here."

"Iceland isn't a grave, Jack. I'm sure the CIA doesn't care what happens to it, but I hope you're not putting it in jeopardy just so you can have your own personal little Valhalla."

"You know how I feel about Iceland."

"I know how you used to. I know how you used to feel about Elisabet Bjornsdottir, until the first fluffy blonde came along."

"I still feel that way about Elisabet. The other girl—that happened for another reason. She's a special case."

Peterson smiled, but he was not amused. "Elisabet didn't find her so special," he said. "But maybe that's all to the good. Sonja's right, Jack. Elisabet needs an Icelander. It wouldn't work out with you two even if there wasn't a thing medically wrong with you."

Spencer had been scuffing the heel of his shoe back and forth against a rock slippery with moss. "Elisabet tried to reach me when we were out at Thingvellir," he said. "She left a message at the hotel."

Peterson said nothing. He lit one of his small Dutch cigars.

The sun was setting, and the match flared brightly in the shadow of his cupped hands.

"What happens now?" said Spencer. "Do people start shooting at us again?"

"This will be different," Peterson said. "I have great faith in Geir Krog."

"On the basis of two telephone conversations?"

"On more than that."

"I can understand how the KGB got on to us at Thingvellir," Spencer said. "If Collie Molyneaux could follow us so easily, it certainly wouldn't be beyond their talents. But the police were tipped off, George. Who did it? You? Me? Krog?"

"Krog has a complex mind."

"Yeah, and a goddamn fiendish one."

"Jack. If the police hadn't been there at Thingvellir, you and I would probably be dead now."

Spencer sat silently, staring at the bank of the dugout opposite him. In the slanting last light of the day, the rocks without moss stood out in relief, forming a sort of circle. Someone had been digging there.

"All these killings," Peterson said. "You've no idea what a traumatic effect they're having on Iceland."

Spencer took out the reply to his advertisement from his pocket.

"You can't begin to understand Iceland," Peterson said, "until you realize how passionately these people want to be left alone."

Spencer paid no attention, staring at the dirt bank.

"'Know who I am and you shall find what you seek,'" Spencer said, reading the reply aloud. "Krog is 'who' I'm looking for, but he used the word 'what.' George, we're not going to meet Krog here."

Peterson looked up at the fading light.

"Maybe after dark," he said. "We should wait until after dark."

"No," said Spencer, sliding forward and standing. He began to pull rocks out of the opposite bank–carefully at first, then faster, then furiously. In a moment, he had pulled forth a small bundle wrapped in waterproof cloth.

"You were right about the Eyvind of the Hills business, George. You and Krog do think alike. But Krog never meant to meet us here."

He unwrapped the cloth. Inside were several notebooks, some files, and a thick sheaf of papers.

"What is that?" Peterson asked.

"It's better than Krog," Spencer said. "It's what I'm supposed to bring back. It's what Krog knows."

Peterson picked up one of the notebooks.

"It's in Icelandic," he said.

"You can translate," said Spencer. "It can't be any more difficult than thirteenth-century legal codes."

"It's going to take a while."

"We'll need a place to work. Will that couple in the weather station help us out?"

"I'll show them my Baltimore honorary consul's card," Peterson said. "I'll tell them I'm with the Icelandic government."

It was many hours before they were done, well after midnight. But they were indeed finished. Now Krog was irrelevant. Spencer knew all that there was to know.

The weather station couple had gone to bed. Spencer and Peterson sat at their kitchen table, Krog's papers strewn all over its top, an extra notebook filled with an English shorthand version of what the others contained in front of Spencer. He snapped it shut. "Now we go back to Reykjavik," he said. "I give this to Karin and I'm done. A day ago I was feeling like the most incompetent mope on the planet. But now I've done it. It's all over."

"You have everything in your notebook now," Peterson said. "What will you do with Krog's papers?"

Spencer shrugged. "Stash them somewhere for safekeeping," he said. "Why?"

"I'd like to turn them over to the Icelandic government. They have a stake in this, too."

"No, George. Not for a while, anyway. This is hot stuff. I

want it exclusive. Now, can you manage this road in the dark?"

"I can manage any road in Iceland."

"Good. Let's go. I want to get this over with."

Did he? As they roared, bounced, and slid their way along the gravel track leading south and west, he asked himself that. There was a hard draw to make. If Elisabet would have him, could he contemplate for a moment leaving Iceland without her? Was he to return to Washington, to his pointless job, to his alcoholic prison?

The twin beams from the headlights rocked and skittered over the bleak night landscape as Peterson ground the car around a curve. Spencer reminded himself that matters were not quite concluded—and wouldn't be until Karin had his notebook and was on a plane.

"I'm bothered by something," Peterson said.

"The long hours?" Spencer said. "Or is it that you're not getting paid for this?"

"I won't charge a fee for saving Western civilization. But that's just it. I'm not sure that's what we're doing. There's something that doesn't make sense. The Russians will do everything they can to help the Workers' and Farmers' Party win the election. If that happens, they'll reduce the price of their oil by fifty percent. In return, Erikisson will let them build an aluminum plant. And the aluminum plant is to be just a front for a secret laser weapon, yes?"

"For a charged-particle beam," Spencer said. "One of three the Soviets must have in place before launching a preemptive nuclear strike."

"But how could they construct such a thing without Iceland's finding out about it?"

"That would be easy, with Erikisson's cooperation. And he would only know what they told him. Iceland would be a neutral country, if not a friend of the Soviet bloc. And we'd have no way of knowing whether the weapon had been installed. We wouldn't know when to make our move."

"That's where I have a problem, Jack. *When*. The election

may be only a week away, but even if Erikisson wins, they'd be months getting a project like that through the government. Construction couldn't begin until spring."

"The 'window'—our strategic vulnerability—we're going to be exposed to that a long time, George. They have time."

"Precisely. Why all this urgency then?"

"I'm not really sure. I'm not sure at all."

The sky was beginning to lighten. Spencer turned on the car radio to a woman singing another of those mournful Icelandic songs. "When we get to Reykjavik," Spencer said, "could you go on to the police station and do something to distract Andersson for a while? I need time to find my friend."

He didn't need that much time at all. In the hall outside his hotel room, his nostrils told him something was wrong. He stepped inside, clutching Krog's papers, but didn't touch the light switch. The faint dawn light from the window was enough.

Karin was sprawled on her back on his bed. She was naked, but it hardly mattered. A bloody line around her throat showed that it had been cut. That was the minor wound. Spencer had never before seen someone so thoroughly murdered.

Reeling, he stumbled out, shutting the door. He started down the hall, having to stop, to lean back against the wall, alternately gagging and weeping. The killer's name was in Krog's papers—Rozkowski. Karin had called him Ludwig the Mad. Tough customer.

Eyes closed, Spencer waged World War III in his mind, vaporizing entire nations. But there was no undoing the horror behind that door.

When he regained control, he had the desk clerk call the police, without telling her why. Then he fled.

The sky was growing bright in the spaces between the clouds. The air was bitter cold. Spencer, his eyes filled with tears, clumped along the street. Here he was, half a madman himself now, oblivious to where he was or who might be following him, having no idea where to go. The police would shortly be after him. Ludwig the Mad would be after him ever so much more serious than before. With Laidlaw out of reach, Karin had been his only link with the agency. He dared not try the clean line to Glasgow. If they had gotten to Karin he could trust no one.

Yet his information must go where it was needed, where it was so implausibly, urgently needed. What was left to him? Going to the post office and dictating a fifteen-hundred-word telegram? Should he and Peterson just get on a plane?

Telegram. Telex. A bit of wire copy. It was the best way in the work to transmit information. He turned around abruptly and began walking the other way. The offices of *Kvoldbladic* were just a few blocks away. He would write a news story, the best of his career. He would put it all in print.

The sleepy and somewhat startled night editor telephoned Sverrir Axelsson at home. Arrangements were quickly made to provide Spencer with a typewriter and an office where he would not be disturbed. Axelsson arrived when Spencer was halfway through his story. Spencer shoved the first takes at him but kept typing. When he was done, he sank back in his chair and closed his eyes. Axelsson brought coffee, then produced a half-full bottle of scotch from a desk drawer. Newspaper offices were the same around the world.

Spencer drank and fidgeted while Axelsson finished reading. He wanted to be off, to find Peterson and Elisabet.

Axelsson set the pages down very carefully on the desk, a look of wonderment on his face. "If this is true," he said, "it will make our election very interesting."

"Here's your confirmation," Spencer said, placing the cloth-wrapped bundle beside his copy. "Krog's papers. The whole works. It's yours. Can you send my story for me? To my bureau in Washington?"

"Of course. Right away." Axelsson picked up the bundle. "We hit the street, as you would say, in ten hours. Is that enough to protect your exclusive? There's an AP stringer here and UPI has a contact here too."

"If my bureau chief doesn't put this on the wire as soon as he gets it, he'll have only himself to blame," Spencer said. He stood up, stretching, his shirt sticking with perspiration to his back. He had not written a story this fast in years. "I'll talk to you later," he said, reaching for his coat.

He found the police waiting outside.

19

Magnus Andersson was surprisingly serene—serious, as always, but not at all stern. He spoke with courtesy, and Spencer supposed that he could find ways to like the man. He and Peterson were sitting stiffly side by side, like repentant schoolboys before a headmaster. Spencer's suitcase, packed by some policeman, was in the vestibule, along with Peterson's. His pistol was in his belt, still unnoticed by these otherwise efficient detectives.

Andersson was staring at him, his black eyes thoughtful—if not friendly, at least devoid of their former anger and malice. He largely ignored Peterson. "The Polish engineer Rozkowski is known to us," Andersson said. "We have a unit that watches all the foreign embassies, and Rozkowski has been a frequent visitor to the Polish one. He was observed entering it yesterday. He was not observed coming out. From all reports, no one has seen him since."

"He's the murderer," Spencer said. "He killed the girl in Heklafjordur. He killed Evi Kekkonen. He killed my friend."

"I believe that is probably the case," Andersson said. "I am simply telling you what we know at this point." He swiveled slightly in his chair, glancing at Peterson, then returning his steady policeman's gaze to Spencer. "I believe you did not kill the young woman in your room," he said, "although there's ample evidence to charge you with anything from complicity to the deed itself." He paused and leaned forward. It seemed to Spencer almost as if Andersson had rehearsed this speech.

"I won't charge you," he said. "Though you are extensively involved in these matters before us, I won't detain you. I'm going to let you go. You may consider this in part official gratitude for what you did for us during the last cod war." He paused again, carefully folding his hands.

"But you must leave Iceland," he said. "You, and Mr. Peterson. There's a flight to New York this afternoon and you must be on it. Your continued presence complicates things for me. It causes too many problems."

"You can't deport people on your own authority," Spencer said. "I have a valid passport."

Andersson glanced at Peterson again. "No, I cannot do that," he said, looking back to Spencer. "But I can tell you this. If you are not on that plane, I will put you in jail. If you linger here, the courts may require me to do that anyway. I will have you driven to the airport. You must go, Mr. Spencer! Do not try me any further."

They were assigned as escorts two policemen trusting enough to let them have the back seat of the car while they themselves took the front. With hours before the flight's departure, they drove slowly. Several times Spencer turned to look back at the retreating city. Then it was gone, with only its background mountains to be seen.

Peterson handed Spencer a small unsealed envelope. The note inside was from Elisabet. There was only one line. "I want to talk to you before you go," it said.

Spencer read it over, then reached for the door handle. Just as quickly Peterson gripped his arm, saying nothing but shaking his head. "Call her from the airport," he said. "There's no point in doing anything else."

Flat, soggy, open ground stretched away from both sides of the road, offering no chance to hide. He might be shot dead in seconds.

"Did you read this?" Spencer asked.

"No," said Peterson. "She told me what it said. I stopped to see her before joining you at the police station."

"Damn. Damn this whole thing. I should have called her immediately."

"Jack. She'll be on a flight to America next week. I expect she'll be coming to our house."

"Does she know what happened to Karin?"

Peterson shrugged. "I didn't bring it up," he said.

The two policemen accompanied them into the terminal, one taking up a station at the main door, the other following them through customs control to the passenger area. Once there, he let Spencer and Peterson wander where they would but would not permit Spencer any telephone calls. He was very insistent about that and finally got very rude when Spencer continued to argue. There was luck in that. When the bar opened a few minutes later, he refused to sit with them and stood off by himself, out of earshot. It was a very small bar, with only four stools, and that early in the day they had it all to themselves.

Peterson ordered a club soda; Spencer, a beer. Having no other customers, the bartender then went off on some brief errand.

"I don't feel like leaving Iceland just yet," Spencer said, watching the policeman over the rim of his glass.

"I imagine not."

"I'm not going to."

"Jack. Elisabet's coming over next week."

"You're not lying to me about that? You've been less than candid at times."

"I may have respected some lawyer-client relationships other than our own, but I haven't lied to you. Certainly not about Elisabet. And I haven't lied to her about you, either."

"It's not just Elisabet, George. I don't want to get on that plane because I'm not sure I've finished my job. I don't think we know all that Krog knows. There was a line in one of his notebooks: 'Rozkowski's calculations on the schematic tell all. He must be stopped at once.' That was a message to himself. I'd like an explanation. He can't be talking about the Icelandic election. I want to get an answer to your question, George, about why there's all this urgency. I want to talk to Krog in person. I want to get hold of Whelan, if Karin didn't get to him. I want to get hold of Rozkowski."

"What about our policemen friends? They're not going to let you just walk out the door."

"I don't propose that we go out the door. We'll walk out through that gate."

"But that'll take us to the airplane."

"It will take us to the ramp. On the other side of the field is a genuine U. S. navy air base. They can't get us there, George. They'd have to go through their foreign ministry and file a formal protest or something. It would take days."

"But what's the point of getting ourselves marooned on a navy base?"

"It's in Iceland."

The New York-bound Icelandair DC-8 arrived late from Luxembourg, but—as Spencer had hoped—the passengers were allowed a few minutes in the terminal for some shopping in the duty-free store. Spencer and Peterson moved to the head of the line at the gate just as the announcement was made that the plane was ready for boarding again. The New Yorkers crowded behind them. When the gate opened, Spencer waved good-bye to the policeman.

Once clear of the outer door, Spencer paused, letting some of the passengers push past him to the aircraft door. He grabbed Peterson's sleeve and pulled him under the DC-8.

"All those passengers can see us," Peterson said.

"Doesn't matter," said Spencer, as they emerged on the other side. "I could start strangling you and they wouldn't give us any notice. Now let's walk over behind that fuel truck. Not too fast."

"We'll never make it, Jack."

"They haven't started shooting."

From the fuel truck they made their way to a parked DC-3, and from that to an idle navy P-3 Orion patrol plane. No one was behind them. Only a short walk in the open separated them from a navy hangar. They started toward it, Peterson lagging behind.

"I said not too fast," Spencer said. "But you've been positively dawdling."

"Sorry," said Peterson, looking back at the terminal.

"I don't want you to violate any lawyer-client confidentiality, George," Spencer said. "But why did you inform the police we were going to Thingvellir to meet Krog?"

"Why do you say that?"

"Because I didn't do it. And Krog certainly didn't do it. And there was no one else. The police knew our exact location. Hell, they were deployed like an infantry squad, with a perfect field of fire to provide us cover. Or to trap Geir Krog. What was that match? A signal to them?"

Peterson glanced back at the terminal again.

"And how, George old friend, did you cut this deal with Magnus Andersson to drop all his paperwork against me in return for my immediately leaving the country? I mean, I was once a police reporter, George. That's not how you handle murder one in any country."

"Magnus Andersson likes you."

"Right. And that nice little touch of no phone call to Elisabet. Did you arrange that, too?"

"No. I suspect that was Andersson's idea."

They were getting closer to the hangar. Spencer could see another P-3 Orion inside, with several enlisted men in fatigues working on it.

"You'd much prefer for us to be on that plane to New York, wouldn't you?" Spencer said. "Who is your client in this case, George? Are you working for the agency? You certainly can't be working for the KGB—I'd be in the same shape as Karin by now."

"I'm not working for either of them. And I in no way wish you any harm, Jack."

"Well, who then? Are you doing all this for the fun of it? Are you on retainer as an informer? Are you some kind of Icelandic junior G-man?"

"You said Iceland couldn't afford an intelligence service. That's incorrect. It has such a service, consisting of one man. And it doesn't cost them very much. I only charge for expenses."

"Right," Spencer said. "Is Elisabet a spy, too?"

"No. She is just Elisabet, which is why I've been trying to keep her away from you."

Spencer stopped. "George, I'm going into this hangar," he said. "If you want to go back to your Icelandic friends, fine. I'll see you back in Washington, and you and I and Sonja can have a lot of drinks and laugh about all this some night. But if you want to stick with me for the rest of this thing, our lawyer-client relationship is going to have to be full time. I don't want any more exciting surprises like Thingvellir. I don't want to talk to another Icelandic policeman until I'm really ready to leave."

"Fair enough. My word on that."

"Okay. Let's go join the U.S. navy. Maybe they know what they're doing."

One of the naval airmen in the hangar immediately took them to the flight operations room, where another enlisted man summoned Commander Richards, as Spencer requested. He arrived very quickly, smiling, his manner almost like that of a party host. "We were expecting you," he said, escorting them down a corridor.

"How's that?" Spencer asked.

"We watched you crossing the field."

There was another officer in the room Richards led them to, a shorter, much older man who stood with his back to them, staring out the window at the darkening sky. Despite his age, he looked to be only a lieutenant commander. His uniform was ill-fitting–worse even than Richards'.

"There goes your plane," he said, over the sound of distant jet engines. "Why aren't you on it?"

He turned around. It was Laidlaw. "Why aren't you?" he repeated.

"I haven't finished here," Spencer said.

"I believe you have. What can you tell me that I don't know?"

"Karin Nielsen's dead."

"I am extremely unhappy about that."

"We got to Krog. At least by telephone. George here–"

"I am familiar with Mr. Peterson, and his sideline."

"We got Krog's papers," Spencer said. "They substantiate everything, the *quid pro quo* with Erikisson, the particle beam weapon in the aluminum plant. The head KGB man here is a Polish engineer named Rozkowski."

"His name is Emil Jahn," Laidlaw said. He seated himself gently in a wooden chair next to Richards' desk. "He is a KGB colonel."

"He killed Karin—and Evi Kekkonen, and that girl."

"Yes."

"I sent the story to my bureau in Washington hours ago."

Laidlaw took off his glasses, staring at Spencer grimly.

"You put it all in a news story?" he asked.

"Yes. And I gave Krog's papers to a columnist friend at *Kvoldbladid.* I'm sure he's done a story, too."

Laidlaw began cleaning his glasses with his handkerchief. "You gave them to a columnist at *Kvoldbladid,*" he said.

"He's dependable," Peterson interjected. "He won't compromise you."

Laidlaw glanced at him, moving only his eyes, saying nothing.

"Whelan's the mole," Spencer said. "Karin went after him. I suppose he's dead. Or escaped."

"He's not," Richards said. "We picked him up. We're holding him just down the hall."

Spencer stepped toward the door.

"Sit down," said Laidlaw, carefully putting on his glasses again. "I have enough problems without any more of your impulsiveness."

"Now look—"

Laidlaw raised his hand.

"I'm being churlish," he said. "Please forgive me. The situation is not pleasant. As Karin may have told you, Washington has become very nervous about this operation and ordered everything shut down. We're as good as fugitives—from our own government."

"I got a telex from my headquarters," Richards said unhappily. "They're very serious about this. If we run across you, we're supposed to flash Washington immediately. If we can, we're supposed to put you on ice until they can get a plane here for you."

"I've lost Karin," Laidlaw said, looking from Spencer to Peterson, "and gained you two. A regrettable trade." He turned to Richards. "I need time. How much can you give me, Commander?"

"Not much," Richards said. "Whelan's an entry in one log book and these two in another. If you were to leave immediately, I'd still have a lot of explaining to do. And, reading between the lines, I wouldn't be surprised if there was a plane from Langley here in the morning. The best I can do is slip you off the base tonight, and the sooner the better."

"I need time," Laidlaw said, "and a haven. Yet all that's out there is police, KGB, lava rock, and the sea."

"There's your answer," said Spencer.

"What do you mean, Mr. Spencer?"

"The sea. We'll find a haven on the sea."

"I'm afraid the navy can't help you out on that one," Richards said.

"No, but the Icelandic Coast Guard can," Spencer said. "One of the captains is a friend of mine, someone we can trust." He looked at Richards. "If you can get a message to the patrol vessel *Heimdallur*, I think we may have a place to go. For a while."

Captain Ragnarsson's signal came back almost immediately. He named a rendezvous point up the coast and promised to be there within four hours. Procuring a van from the motor pool, Richards got everyone through a rear gate and drove them up the coast to a point where the road left the shoreline and cut across the peninsula toward the town of Sandgerdi. He stopped the van, then turned it so that the headlights shone down toward the sea.

"This is the rendezvous," Richards said, handing Laidlaw a flashlight. "He'll signal and send in his inflatable. You're lucky; the surf's low tonight."

Laidlaw, Spencer, and Peterson got out. Whelan, his hands bound behind him, sat sullenly in the rear seat.

"I forgot to ask," Richards said. "Are any of you armed?"

"I am," said Spencer. He pulled out his pistol. It was the first time he had held it in his hand with any degree of purpose since he had arrived in Iceland.

Richards shoved Whelan out the door with such force that he fell face down in the mossy dirt.

"Good luck," Richards said.

Ragnarsson's gunboat was late, and then later. They bore its tardiness patiently, sitting huddled in the dark. Because they did not want to talk in front of Whelan, they bore it silently. Laidlaw, hunched in his naval officer's overcoat, staring out at the deeper darkness that was the sea, would not have been very talkative in any case. He reminded Spencer of a historian's description of Frederick the Great sitting at a campfire with his troops, except there was no fire, and few troops.

Peterson took out one of his Dutch cigars and lit it with a long wooden match. Laidlaw paid no attention. Spencer kept his eyes on the match, wondering from how far it could be seen. Whelan quietly got to his feet and began to run. He was yards away before anyone noticed.

Laidlaw whirled around, the flashlight on in an instant, its small circle of illumination dancing on Whelan's receding back.

"Get after him!" Laidlaw said.

Spencer scrambled, trying to run before he fully stood. He stumbled, lurching into Peterson, the collision knocking them both to the ground.

"Shoot him!" said Laidlaw. "It means our lives!"

Spencer gripped his pistol with both hands, sighting it with both eyes. The dancing circle of light was now quite large, but very faint.

There it was, a human life. A squeeze of the trigger and a small lead projectile would fly into that human back at supersonic speed; flattening; tearing through muscle; shattering the spine; rupturing spleen, kidneys, and liver; emerging in an explosion of bone, blood, and tissue. Spencer was a very good shot, a function of his boyhood in the wooded countryside of upstate New York. He had scored "expert" with both rifle and pistol in the army.

"Shoot, damn it!" said Peterson. "Shoot!"

Spencer's finger trembled, but the muscle would not contract. He put the sight of Karin's body in his mind, but by then Whelan was all but out of range.

Peterson snatched the pistol out of Spencer's hand, dropped to one knee, and fired two quick rounds. Whelan had vanished into the dark. In the echo of the gunshots, there was no cry or scream, no sound of a body dropping. Spencer thought he heard the sound of hurried footsteps on the gravel road.

Suddenly, surprisingly far away, a car's headlights were turned on. A small silhouette that could only be Whelan halted in front of them, spun around clumsily, and, arms behind him, ran toward the edge of the road. A tall figure got out of the car and fired one shot. Whelan dropped. The man from the car walked quickly up to him and fired five more shots in rapid succession. Lowering his gun, he seemed to turn in Spencer's direction.

"Come along, Jacko!" he shouted. "Everything is all tickettyboo!"

They hurried up to the road and the car's headlights, old Laidlaw moving the fastest. He flicked the flashlight over Whelan's contorted body, then on the newcomer.

"Well, now, what a bloody fine reunion," said Molyneaux. "Hugh Laidlaw. Been a few years, hasn't it? Thought you were retired. Shouldn't have thought I'd run into you here among the Icies."

"Good evening, Mr. Molyneaux," Laidlaw said. "I seem to be in your debt once again."

He turned the flashlight back on the body.

"The face'll need a bit of tidying up," Molyneaux said. "We ought to soak it for a time in the sea." Whelan no longer had a face. Molyneaux's five rounds had turned it into a bloody pulp.

"Jacko," Molyneaux said. "Sorry about the wee bairn."

Commander Richards, drinking yet another cup of coffee, wandered about the situation watch room. Just idling, of course; another boring night in Iceland. A good night to watch the Russians, however. They had a large part of their northern fleet out and were cluttering up the maps of the Greenland Sea and the Denmark Strait on the navy computer screens with every size and shape of blip imaginable. The operations officer had put on an extra crew to cope with all the traffic.

Richards, sipping from his cup, strolled to a video display terminal being manned by a young ensign. "Switch to shore radar, Mr. Neikirk," Richards said. "Let's have a look at the local stuff."

A few seconds later, the familiar outlines of the Seltjarnarnes Peninsula appeared on the screen, Keflavik at the center. A small blip was approaching the shoreline just up the coast from the base.

"He's not making any ident, sir," said the ensign. "Do you think he's an intruder?"

Richards leaned close to the screen. "No," he said. "It's just one of the Icelandic patrol boats. By the looks of her, I'd say it's the *Heimdallur*."

"Jeez, Commander. How can you tell that?"

"It's an acquired skill," Richards said.

20

THE BEEFY HAND that clamped itself on Mendelsohn's shoulder needed no introduction. Mendelsohn closed the file in front of him—Karin Nielsen's—and looked up into Thorn's unsmiling face. "What now?" said Mendelsohn. "Another rowboat ride? Or shall we go bicycling?"

"The deputy and I are wanted at the White House," Thorn said. "This time we get to see number one." He turned back the cover of the file, then let it fall closed again.

"She was quite an athlete in high school, that little waif," Mendelsohn said. "Her father was killed in the Korean War, murdered as a prisoner of war. That's how we got her."

"Yeah, I know," Thorn said. He glanced quickly about the room. Two women clerks were busy at the other end. "The stuff has hit the fan, Freddy. Our boy Spencer got to Krog, all right. But instead of sending his stuff through channels, he put it out over the news wires. It's good stuff. Looks like he got all there was. But he put it in the *newspapers*. The White House is at maximum panic. The President is making nasty comments about whether the National Press Club is running the CIA."

"What are we to do now? Send everyone back into Iceland?"

Thorn shrugged. "Who knows?" he said. "Karin missed Whelan, you know. He went over the wall. I'd bet all my beans he's in a Russian trawler or sub right now. Spencer gave the police the slip, and for all I know he's with Krog. Hugh's completely vanished. They may have gotten to him in Brussels. Karin sent an advisory there was a British MI 6 agent on the ground in Iceland."

"The sum of our assets," Mendelsohn said. "A paltry sum."

Thorn looked at his watch. "Time to go. They're sending a chopper from Anacostia to pick us up."

"Have a pleasant flight. The White House lawn is very scenic this time of year."

"You're coming too, Freddy."

"I? To see the President of the United States? Whatever for? I am a mere pensioner, brought back to rummage here in the dusty bins."

"There's a lot of high-level curiosity," Thorn said. "How come our mole got fingered by the navy, instead of us? Who was helping him on this end? How come so much has gone wrong? Young Baker's turned up dead, you know, in an alley behind a gay bar in Alexandria. He didn't even have a chance to tell us how he liked his flight back from Iceland."

Thorn clamped his hand on Mendelsohn's shoulder again. "There's a high-level feeling you can relieve a lot of this curiosity, Freddy."

Ambassador Gorushchenko disliked going to the East German embassy for any reason. It was doubly unpleasant going there with Emil Jahn as his host. They ushered him, with little deference, to a small windowless room in the rear. It contained only a desk and two chairs, and Jahn, as though exercising territorial imperative, had already taken the one behind the desk. A bright but shaded light hung from the ceiling, Jahn's newly shaven head glistening in its glare. Gorushchenko was impressed; the man had utterly transformed his face. Jahn poured refreshment: schnapps, as Gorushchenko noted with disgust. In retaliation, the Russian lit one of his cigarettes, disregarding the closeness of the room. He pulled a copy of *Kvoldbladid* from his coat pocket. "These meetings are unnecessary, Colonel," he said. "To follow your activities, I need only read the Icelandic newspapers."

Jahn glanced down at the front page. There was a photograph of Erikisson. The Icelandic term for aluminum was in the headline. The byline read "Sverrir Axelsson," whom Jahn remembered from his list of Spencer's reported contacts in Reykjavik.

He dismissed the article with a small wave of his hand.

"The American, Spencer, planted it," he said. "*Das macht nichts.*"

"The American seems to have gotten to Krog—as you have not. Yet he was to lead you to Krog; isn't that so?"

"Krog is all but irrelevant now, Herr Botschafter. There is nothing in the newspaper article we need fear."

Gorushchenko sipped the sweet liqueur and made a face. Jahn seemed very pleased with himself, yet nervous, a card player on the verge of a big win that was not yet in hand.

"It suggests incompetence, Colonel," Gorushchenko said. "I wonder at your reputation. Krog is still alive and at large, as are this American Spencer and his lawyer friend. Your sailor has been arrested and our friend Whelan is a fugitive at best. And that young woman—"

"Agent."

"You were excessively brutal. So messy. So unprofessional."

"It was necessary. That little killer bitch . . ."

"It was provocative! One of the reasons Iceland was so attractive to us was that the Americans paid such little attention to it. Now you are rubbing their noses in the place."

"Herr Botschafter, you insist upon looking at the black side. Krog remains a fugitive. Spencer is an amateur. He is on the run and can do us no further harm. The Icelandic police are falling all over themselves trying to find those two and cope with three murders. The American sailor knew nothing. Whelan is expendable. The CIA has reacted to his case like crazy men. They've shut down everything they have in Iceland. The elimination of that girl, one of their best, will only disrupt them further. The American navy is preoccupied with all those vessels from our northern fleet."

Jahn leaned closer, ignoring Gorushchenko's cigarette smoke.

"And everyone is worried solely about the election!" he said. "The newspaper article only reinforces that fixation. Everything I have done reinforces that! All is well, Herr Botschafter. All is *Volkommenheit.* And in twenty-four hours none of this will matter!"

Jahn was very agitated. Gorushchenko sat silently a moment, waiting for him to calm down. "I do not mean to be overly critical, Colonel," Gorushchenko said. "About tomorrow, then. Your preparations are complete?"

"All is in order, Herr Botschafter."

"You don't need any more men? More weapons teams?"

"No. There is no need. Everything has been arranged."

"The timing must be precise. Exact. We have only a few hours to put everything in place."

"I am aware of that! All is in order!"

Gorushchenko, wheezing slightly, leaned back in his chair and gestured at the bottle of schnapps. Jahn refilled the glasses, fighting the trembling of his hand with a tight grip on the bottle.

The Russian took his glass and stood. "To success," he said. "To our fathers."

Jahn got to his feet and they both drank, emptying their glasses in a single swallow. Jahn wondered at the toast. His father had been killed at Stalingrad.

"I will be less nervous if you are not so complacent about Krog and the American," Gorushchenko said. "Take some precautions. Provide us with some insurance. Good luck," he said as he opened the door. Jahn would need it. Gorushchenko had received permission to have Jahn arrested as a dangerous psychotic at the conclusion of this operation. It would mean confinement in an institution in the Urals at the least, possibly the injection of a painless but fatal drug. If the Iceland operation failed, of course, he could have Jahn killed outright.

"*Gluck*, Herr Botschafter," Jahn said as the other turned down the corridor. He smiled to himself. He had already ordered Gorushchenko's assassination at the hands of his agent in the Russian embassy. There was no countermanding the instructions. Gorushchenko was a walking dead man.

Jahn refilled his glass, this time with vodka from a bottle hidden in the desk.

Dawn found the *Heimdallur* moored to the quay at Borgarnes, bow to shoreward, the cold waters of Borgarfjordur mirror-still and beginning to glimmer with a pinkish light in the first flush of the rising sun. It had rained heavily during the night, but now the pale sky was empty of clouds. Spencer went back to his cabin for a thick blue sweater before continuing up to the bridge.

Throstur, the bearded young second officer, was in command, if idly so. Captain Ragnarsson was still ashore, presumably at his house.

Spencer accepted a huge mug of coffee from a crewman and went to the forward windows of the bridge. Laidlaw was down on the foredeck, at the prow, wearing nondescript sailor's clothes. Ragnarsson had not been enthusiastic about having an American naval officer visible on his deck, especially a bogus one. Spencer filled a second cup of coffee for Laidlaw, then went down to join him.

"You're very thoughtful, Mr. Spencer," said Laidlaw. He sipped without taking his eyes from the shore and the little town beyond. The quay the *Heimdallur* was moored to was at the side of a small island separated from the shore by a narrow channel. The bridge that crossed it led directly to Borgarnes' main street. "Where is the captain?"

"Still ashore. His house is up on the hill there," Spencer said.

"How did you two leave matters last night?"

"He'll do one of three things: Arrest us. Put us ashore somewhere. Or put himself and the *Heimdallur* at our disposal—at least for a day or two."

Laidlaw stared down at the water.

"If he agrees to the last," Spencer said, "where should we go? What shall we do?"

Laidlaw sighed. "I don't know," he said. "To be perfectly candid, at this point, I'm not sure what we should do. Last night I all but decided to cast everything aside, go back to Washington, and let them do with me what they will."

"Go back? After all this?"

"All what, Mr. Spencer?"

"After all we've found out. After all the lives that have been lost. For God's sake, Laidlaw, do you want me to tell you in detail what they did to Karin? It was what biology students do in laboratories, except I think they started when she was alive."

Laidlaw turned suddenly and gripped Spencer's arm, so tightly that Spencer's hand went numb. "I am not insensitive," Laidlaw said. "I knew Karin Nielsen for a very long time. I knew her very well." His face was flushed and mottled. He relaxed his grip and looked back at the water. "There are many dead people in my memories," he said. "I am very unhappy about Karin, but this hasn't been our costliest operation. As for all that you say we've found out, I knew nearly all of it weeks ago."

"What do you mean?"

"Krog sent us everything he learned as soon as he got it. While he was piecing it all together, we were piecing it together. I think we came to his conclusion before he did."

"Conclusion? About what?"

"About the particle beam accelerator."

"If you knew that, what in the hell was the point of my coming here?" In his anger, he spilled coffee on the deck.

"You did what you were supposed to, Mr. Spencer. You performed a very valuable service."

"My story. All these killings—Karin getting her guts ripped open—just so I might file a goddamn story?"

"Yes."

"I don't believe this. You make all those squalid rotten stories about the CIA ring true. Jesus."

"Mr. Spencer, if your article proves to be all that brings this crisis to the attention of the White House, all that gets the

White House moving, don't you think that's performing a valuable service?"

"Why didn't you tell me?"

"You wouldn't have believed me. And you wouldn't have done it."

Some gulls wheeled overhead, calling aimlessly. There weren't many. Borgarnes was a farm town, one of the few ports in Iceland that wasn't involved in the fishing industry.

"Well, now that I've completed my 'mission,' I guess there's no point in my hanging around, is there?" Spencer said.

"Yes, there is. We have to keep at this. I don't know what the White House will do. I've lost Karin. All I have is you—and Peterson and the Englishman."

"But you don't know what you want to do."

"We shall grope."

"Grope?"

"Grope. Make guesses. Scratch at shadows. That's all we ever really do, isn't it? Stumble through dark rooms? Wrestle with people from the other side doing the same?"

"You make it sound so clumsy."

"Espionage is clumsy. It's like any other form of warfare. The side that is the least clumsy and the most lucky wins."

He turned his back to the rail, looking off at the mountains across the fjord. "Consider the stupidity of our situation, Mr. Spencer. We are confronting something truly dangerous. Iceland is a fulcrum that could lever the unthinkable nuclear war. But the government we are trying to save only obstructs us. Do you know, I would not be surprised if Langley had ordered my arrest, perhaps my execution."

"Execution?"

"I have sinned against the agency. As defined by the revised statutes of the United States, I've committed treason. I was Whelan's chinaman, Mr. Spencer, the 'friend' in Washington."

"What do you mean?"

"Whelan's incompetence was not feigned. He was a typical

KGB recruit—not very bright, and greedy. I got on to him quite quickly, but I did nothing. Whelan was a window I could reach through. When Krog learned too much, and Whelan informed the KGB, I let it happen. I let them go for Krog. I had to. I had to keep Krog from scaring off the Russians. I wanted them to get started with what they had in mind for Iceland."

"So you'd have something to show the White House."

"It was a mistake," Laidlaw said, "as Krog could have told me. The Russians are not behaving as I expected. I let Whelan linger on too long."

"And Karin died."

"That was not my intent, Mr. Spencer."

An unseen wind, far out in the fjord, ruffled the slick surface of the water.

"You really think they might want to kill you?"

"It's a possibility I must consider. I had protection of my own, the man assigned to learn the identity of the mole. He got on to me, too, but he didn't take any action. He dragged his feet. To an excessive degree. I'm sure they're on to that as well. Thorn, the man in charge of this project, is really quite bright."

"Why are you telling me all these things?"

"Because you have no future, Mr. Spencer, and neither do I. This is our last fling, no matter how it comes out."

The sun was full in the sky now, glittering off the veins of snow and ice on the slope of the mountain directly across the fjord. Their breath was vapor.

"I can see the Vikings here," Laidlaw said, "in one of those small wooden ships. Thirty men rowing out to the sea, going wherever they want. England, Ireland, Spain. America."

"What can we do, Laidlaw? If Captain Ragnarsson agrees to help, what can we do?"

"We know what the Russians eventually plan. Krog was trying to find out where. I want to know when. Do you trust Peterson?"

"With my life, but short of that, I'm not sure. He's very very strong on Iceland."

"Iceland, unfortunately, is expendable. If we had to destroy the entire country, it would be a small price to pay to stop the Russians."

"George Peterson would disagree."

"What's your opinion of Molyneaux?"

"He's very, very strong on Britain."

"That may be a help. How good a friend are you of Ragnarsson?"

"He picked us up at Keflavik, didn't he? The only problem is that he likes being a Coast Guard captain and he's not about to sacrifice his job for our fun and games."

Laidlaw turned back toward the shore. "Do you have Krog's notes on possible sites for the aluminum plant?"

"Yes. They're all near the coast. A couple of them are fairly close."

"I want to look at them, if your captain friend will agree. Krog was very urgent. Very urgent."

"He's a bright man," Spencer said.

"There's another reason for visiting those sites—I can't think of anything else to do."

Spencer glanced up at the ship's bridge. Peterson was there, looking down at them, and another figure was visible just behind him.

"Our friends," Spencer said. "Shall I call them down?"

"Not just yet, if you don't mind."

"If I don't mind? Am I in control now, Laidlaw?"

"If you like."

"I like. I would like to talk to my friends now."

"Just one moment. There's something I want to ask you, Mr. Spencer. Karin had no father. I was . . . Mr. Spencer, did she fall in love with you?"

"No. There was something, but not that. Not so soon."

"What about you?"

"Yes," Spencer said finally.

"But the Icelandic girl."

"Both."

"You would have had to choose."

"Now I don't."

A figure was moving down the hill on the road. A man. Spencer recognized him as Ragnarsson long before he reached the bridge across the channel.

"Are there police in this town?" Laidlaw asked.

"I don't know. The captain is technically a policeman, you know. They have rifles and pistols up on the bridge. Anyway I don't want to go against Ragnarsson. If you want to try that you go against me."

"As you please."

Ragnarsson called them all to his cabin, a carpeted, well-furnished chamber that included a television set and short-wave radio. Throstur came with them. He had a pistol in his belt. "I have talked by telephone to my superiors," Ragnarsson said. "There is much foreign naval activity off our western and northern coasts. I am to resume my patrol." He lit his pipe. "I did not mention you people," he said. "I was told that, if I came across you, I was to put you under arrest. Very well. You are all under arrest."

Laidlaw was staring at Throstur's pistol, but he remained motionless.

"But we must be several days on patrol," Ragnarsson said. "There is no point in your being locked up. You shall have the freedom of the ship. And in making course changes, I think I might appreciate your advice." He smiled, but fleetingly.

"This patrol could be serious," he said. "Two of your interceptor fighters shot down a Russian Bear bomber over Greenland this morning."

21

It developed as Jahn had hoped. Erikisson turned out as large a crowd as he could muster—more than five hundred. They milled about on the Reykjavik waterfront, then, as though on signal, began to press toward the quay and the NATO ships. The policemen pushed back, holding their clubs with both hands, but the mob was too large. The police retreated. When they halted briefly, unsure how far they dared fall back, the mob pressed even harder. A man fell with a loud splash into the harbor, and the shouting grew louder. A shot was fired and screams were heard among the shouts.

Jahn and his men got busy.

Jahn moved toward the front of the crowd, anonymous in his watch cap and sailor's coat. A man stepped in front of him, an old, heavyset man. Jahn fired his pistol, held in the pocket of his coat, into the small of the man's back. The pistol had a silencer in place, and the only sign of his firing it was a dull thud, a wisp of smoke, and a gush of blood from the man's mouth as he was flung forward. The bullet was of the softest lead.

Jahn moved away. As a woman saw the dead man and screamed, he slipped sideways, then forward again, relentless. A younger woman, shouting and shaking her fist, was at the front of the crowd, swearing at a policeman. The policeman turned and fled. Jahn aimed his pistol at the woman's buttocks and fired. She shrieked as she fell. The crowd went crazy. More people fell into the water. A British seaman on the gangway of the *Bacchus* panicked and began firing into the mob. In the pandemonium that followed, Jahn cut him down; his body tumbled into the water beside his ship.

Jahn moved away, finding respite behind a piling. This would turn the election around, though that did not matter. It would infuriate Gorushchenko. Though that did not matter, either.

Sverrir Axelsson had rushed to the harborside, but he went no farther than the street above. As a reporter, he was better off at this vantage point. As an Icelander, he was much too close. He found the whole of it appalling, terrifying, stupefying. With this carnage, the Workers' and Farmers' Party would have the upper hand again. They would win the election. NATO would be the only issue.

He wondered whether Spencer were still alive. So much death, in a country that had had the least of death of any country in the world.

He found tears in his eyes.

Gorushchenko rang for an embassy maid. He had taken lunch at his desk and now wanted his plates cleared away. Reports of Jahn's staged riot at the harbor were being brought in on small notes. He already had a large pile of them. To say the least, the Icelandic government was going to be distracted for a while. The American government would be confused; he had to grant Jahn that.

It was not the maid who responded, but Ludmilla Rashevsky, wife of his deputy. She came around behind the desk, standing at his side as she stacked everything on a tray. The curve of her hip was at his shoulder. He suppressed an urge to pinch her, forcing himself to look away. She was blond, wide in the hip but comely.

Something pricked the side of his neck. With a startling swiftness, his mind went numb, his body limp. As he fell backward—ever, endlessly backward—he looked up into her staring blue eyes. A shiny cylinder was in her hand. When he was almost dead, he heard her suddenly, deliberately, fraudulently, scream.

Andersson stood at the desk of his ranking sergeant, taking calls from the three telephones he had set up before him. The crowd at the harbor had backed away from the ships in fear of further gunfire, but it had not dispersed. It could surge back, Andersson had no doubt. Whoever had organized this catastrophe had planned it well.

He stared down at his opened notebook. He had written four names, four dead: one drowned, one shot by a British sailor, two shot by someone—possibly a NATO sailor, but probably someone else—from behind. The woman's wound had been terrible. He was reminded of the three murders.

Surely Krog was not in that crowd. Surely not. The policeman in Magnus Andersson had no doubt about that.

He had stationed men at roadblocks all around Reykjavik, in part for Krog, in larger part for the Americans who had disappeared from the Keflavik airport. Impulse nagged at him to call in those men, to send them to the harbor and break up the crowd for good.

But it was too late for that. Whoever had arranged the riot had done his work and gone. He picked up the phone and called the minister of justice.

The minister got immediately to the point. "What can stop this? I want no more deaths."

"Contact the admiral, sir. The NATO fleet must leave at once. Even if they only stand off the coast, they must leave the harbor."

"We are a member of NATO, Superintendent."

"They have to go. The situation is out of control, sir. Out of our control, if not someone else's. Two of these people were deliberately murdered. We have some agitators here, sir, and I don't think they're Icelanders."

"I would hope to God not. All right, Superintendent, I'll try to send away the ships. It won't help the political situation."

"I am concerned with the security situation, sir."

"I understand. I'll get back to you in a few minutes."

Andersson hung up slowly. Here he was, as much as giving orders to the minister of justice. He picked up the phone again and called Elisabet.

"John?"

"This is Magnus Andersson."

Elisabet paused. "I'm sorry, Magnus."

"Elisabet, we're having serious trouble down at the harbor. I want you to stay in your apartment. I'll get a man over there to guard your door as soon as I can."

"That's not necessary."

"It is, Elisabet. It's extremely serious. Please stay where you are."

"Where is Spencer? Did he fly back to America?"

Andersson wanted to say yes. "He disappeared, Elisabet. He and George Peterson disappeared from the Keflavik airport. I don't know where they are, but I'm sure they're in Iceland. Elisabet, stay at home. I'll get over there myself as soon as I can."

"All right, Magnus. I thank you."

How formal.

"Good-bye."

Elisabet had been ready for her bath and so was naked. She set the telephone receiver down carefully. Something bothered her. She was standing in her living room. There were no windows opposite that looked into hers, but up on the hill there was a street.

There was a figure on that street, a man. The early evening was upon the city, and he was standing in the shadows, but she could see him. A sailor.

She ran up to the window and drew the curtains closed quickly. A glance at her clock showed that the evening news program on television had started. She turned on her set and stood, suddenly cold, watching with mixed horror and fascination the riot scene at the harbor. It could not be true. It could not be Iceland.

After a moment, she snapped off the set. She poured herself a brandy and went to her phonograph. Django Reinhardt again. She eased herself into the tub. Lifting her glass, she thought about Spencer. There was no doubt about the little blond girl. Elisabet's friends had seen them together in Luxembourg.

And now the little blonde was murdered, too, more horribly than the others.

Was Spencer fighting against this, a lone figure against the terrible forces that had been loosed upon Iceland? A truly heroic man, as in the old sagas? Or was he something else out of Iceland's mythic past, a figure of doom, a harbinger of evil and of trouble? The time of darkness was settling once again upon Iceland, and it had brought John Spencer.

There was a creak of a floorboard. A strange man was standing in the bathroom doorway, a tall man—bald, with glasses, in sailor's clothes. She knew at once that he was the man from outside, from down on the street. There were others with him, in the next room.

She threw her glass at his face and screamed.

22

Commander Richards had entertained his guest at the officers' club—in the navy's gin-filled fashion—and now was taking him along the corridors and through the pass gates to the situation watch room.

"Sorry about the girl," Richards said.

"It happens," Thorn said.

"Unnecessary roughness."

"The KGB has a real sicko here."

"This used to be the dullest post in the navy. Lately it's been like living in the South Bronx."

"We'll get the bastard. That's a high-priority item."

"I really am sorry about Whelan."

"We're not shedding any tears," Thorn said. "They sure shot him up, though. The forensic boys will have their work cut out making a positive."

"I would have detained Whelan longer, but your friend Laidlaw had some heavy credentials."

"Yeah."

"Would you like some help from the navy?"

"You've got your hands full with this alert. Anyway, I brought help. A lot of help."

They paused at a pass gate to show a Marine guard their IDs.

"The election's as good as lost for us," Richards said as the gate slid shut with a bang behind them. "That harbor riot queered it for good."

"Maybe," said Thorn. "We'll see. There's time."

"Not much."

"We've been through these things before. Even if their guys win, we still have a lot of ways to keep the Russians out of here."

"None that Mr. Erikisson would approve of."

Thorn shrugged. "How accidental was that Bear bomber shoot-up?" he said.

"Not very. We've been having these fly-bys for months. This time one of their waist gunners opened up. A long sustained burst."

"Jesus," Thorn said. "A prop reconnaisance bomber, firing on an F-15 with a machine gun. What the hell's goin' through their minds?"

"Beats me. What we're trying to decide now is whether this fleet movement of theirs is in response to the Bear bomber incident, or whether the Bear bomber was part of all this."

Showing their IDs again, they stepped into the large, darkened situation watch room. It was busier than it had ever been in the entire postwar history of Iceland Defense Force. It would have been even had Washington not called a Def-Con Two, which put every American military unit on the globe on high priority combat alert.

The Russian northern fleet was out and running–all of it–more than one hundred seventy surface ships and submarines, streaming into the North Atlantic to either side of Iceland. The eerie green screens of the computer video display terminals were dotted with flecks of light and numbers. Each looked like an air controller's radar screen at Chicago's O'Hare Airport–only busier.

"You'd think they were deliberately trying to attract our attention to Iceland," Thorn said.

"Or away from it," Richards said. "All our course projections show them well south of here in a few hours, heading for the transatlantic sea-lanes."

He moved to one of the VDT consoles, with Thorn following. The man at the keyboard was a lieutenant j.g. With the

DefCon Two, there was a double shift of officers in the watch room that night.

"Any funnies?" Richards said. "I mean, aside from the ocean full of funnies."

"Yes, sir," said the lieutenant. "I've got a few inbounds." He worked his fingers quickly over the keyboard, erasing the wide-area map from the screen and, with a flicker, punching up one showing only the west coast of Iceland. Three blips with small glowing numbers appeared on the left side of the screen. "You got two Oscar-class jumbo subs entering Faxaflo Bay, Commander," he said. "They're on converging courses that ought to bring them together just off Reykjavik harbor."

"What?" said Thorn.

"They pull this all the time," Richards said. "Nerve games. Just as we sound all our alarms, they turn back. Keeps us from dozing off."

"Don't they know we're on DefCon Two?" Thorn said. "And a little trigger-happy?"

"Beats me," said Richards. "But they want us to look at them. What else you got, Lieutenant?"

"A trawler, Commander," he said, pointing at the third blip, much to the north of the submarines. "He's a brand new one, just come into the area, so we don't have an ident, but he's a big bastard."

"I hate them," Richards said to Thorn. "We know they're up to their gunwales in surveillance gear, and they know we know it, but they carry on like happy little fishermen anyway. The Icelandic government even lets them harbor here."

"He's heading for Breidafjordur, for the north shore of the Snaefellsnes Peninsula," said the lieutenant, "probably looking for shelter for the night."

"The weather's not that rough."

"Maybe he's got engine problems, Commander. His speed's down."

"The hell with him," Richards said. "What have we got at Reykjavik to intercept those subs?"

The lieutenant's fingers flew over the keyboard again. "No

much, sir. Two British frigates from the NATO goodwill fleet, standing offshore. Everything else is off tracking the main Russian fleet."

"Okay," Richards said. "Flag those two subs and message operations 'urgent.' Just in case they haven't noticed."

At Spencer's request, Captain Ragnarsson had taken the *Heimdallur* all the way up the coast to the new hydroelectric power plant at Arnarfjordur in northwest Iceland. In his notes, Krog had cited it as a good prospective site for the Soviet aluminum plant, but they had found nothing, not a trace of anything untoward. Ragnarsson had sent Second Officer Throstur to talk to the power station crew chief. Nothing again. The man had treated Throstur as though he were slightly crazy.

Now the *Heimdallur* was returning south, rounding the Latrabjarg headland and entering the broad expanse of Breidafjordur, at fifty miles wide the largest fjord in Iceland. Throstur was at the helm, Ragnarsson and the others gathered back at the bridge's chart table. The captain pulled the overhead lamp down closer to the map, its bright white light glaring on the paper. Reading from Spencer's notebook, Ragnarsson drew a small red X at the mouth of Hvammsfjordur, a smaller fjord that emptied into Breidafjordur just east of the town of Stykkisholmur.

"There you are," Ragnarsson said. "Less than three hours' sail away. We are lucky the weather is calm."

"There's just a transformer there, a junction point in the electrical grid," Spencer said. "Krog's notes said the terrain isn't any good for heavy construction, nor the road."

"Are you suggesting we pass it up?" Peterson said.

"I, for one, am getting a bit bloody bored with this wandering about," Molyneaux said. "And I am getting a bit bloody low on gin. If we must take this scenic cruise of this godforsaken island, let's stop for a load-up of the grog."

"Krog did include this place on his list," Peterson said.

"We could be wasting time, valuable time," Spencer said.

"Krog said the next site down the coast, the one near Akranes, was the likeliest of all."

"I could not get you there until tomorrow," Ragnarsson said.

"Let's not deliberately pass anything up," Laidlaw said. "Let us try to be methodical about this."

Ragnarsson looked at Spencer.

"Okay," Spencer said. "We'll check it out."

"Three hours, is it?" said Molyneaux. "I'm for my cabin, then. Does this Stickyholm have a liquor store?"

"Stykkisholmur has a convent," Ragnarsson said. "The nearest state liquor store would be in Akranes."

"Bloody barbarism," Molyneaux said. "A nation full of raving alcoholics and no bloody liquor stores."

Ragnarsson had once told Spencer that he had saved the lives of some fifty British seamen in his career in the Coast Guard. He was looking at Molyneaux as though there would never be a fifty-first.

"Mr. Molyneaux," said Laidlaw. "In times of scarcity, we must share. I have a small bottle of whiskey in my cabin. I should be happy to offer you a small glass. I would like to talk to you about something."

"Princess Margaret's love life, no bloody doubt," Molyneaux said, but he moved toward the stairs to below.

"I must go to my own cabin and bring my logbook up to date," Ragnarsson said. "I'll have to be inventive to explain your presence."

"I'll help you," Peterson said. "We lawyers have a way with euphemism."

Left alone, Spencer went to the forward part of the bridge. The faces of Throstur and the helmsman were only faintly visible in the red instrument lights that were the sole illumination.

"Too bad it's dark," Throstur said. "Breidafjordur is one of the most beautiful parts of Iceland. Near Stykkisholmur there are many, many islands."

"I've never been here before," Spencer said.

"Many come here because of Mount Helgafell."

"Is that one of your high peaks?"

Throstur laughed. "Oh, no. It is a very small mountain near Stykkisholmur, less than a hundred meters high. But it is a very lucky place. It is said that if you walk up Helgafell for the first time without looking back or speaking a word, you will be granted three wishes. But they must not be evil wishes, and when you make them you must face east, and you cannot reveal your wishes to others."

"I'd like to climb it," Spencer said.

"Shall I change course?"

"Another time."

Spencer's pupils had dilated sufficiently for him to see the wave tops and the horizon. Off the starboard quarter were some faint lights—a ship perhaps, or a village. He gripped the forward rail with both hands, leaning closer to the cold window glass. The seas were calm, but there was still a slight roll to the deck beneath his feet, and the powerful, throbbing vibrations of the *Heimdallur*'s two engines.

Two weeks before he had been pointlessly taking up desk space in the Senate press gallery, aimlessly stumbling through his empty days and terrifying nights, through bars and stupid parties and women whose names he could not remember. Now he stood upon the sea, beneath a limitless night sky, with all the world before him, all the world dependent upon where he decided to go and what he decided to do with this strong little ship and his good friends. He felt what he had never before felt in his life, the heady freedom of command. What was the line in *David Copperfield?* "Whether I shall turn out to be the hero of my own life . . ."

"Why are you carrying that pistol?" Spencer asked Throstur.

"Orders from Reykjavik."

"Have you ever used that? Have you ever shot anyone?"

"This is Iceland, Mr. Spencer. During the cod war, I think Captain Ragnarsson had the deck gun fired at a British ship once. It was a hired ram-tug trying to smash the *Heimdallur* when we had many sick men below. The captain became very angry. But that's the only shooting I've ever seen."

"Did he hit anyone?"

"No. He just had the gun fired twice across the tug's foredeck. It turned away."

Spencer looked again through the forward windows. The lights he had thought might be those of a town had moved—slightly closer, and considerably forward.

"Is that a ship?" he asked.

Throstur looked at the radar screen and turned the scan to a shorter range. "Yes, Mr. Spencer," he said. "It's a big ship for these waters, a trawler or a freighter."

Spencer joined him at the radar. "Icelandic?" he asked.

"I don't think so," Throstur said, studying the screen. "If it's a trawler, it's a factory trawler. And we haven't anything so big. The only freighters we have this large belong to Eimskip. And there wouldn't be an Eimskip ship in these waters."

"Eimskip?"

"The Iceland Steamship Company. The only port near here is Stykkisholmur, and this ship is not on a course for Stykkisholmur."

"Could it be Russian?"

"They are the only ones who have had factory trawlers this size near Iceland," Throstur said, "but there has been no report of one near Breidafjordur. I don't know where he could be going. There is no need for him to seek shelter."

"I want to get nearer. Very near."

"I'll have to ask Captain Ragnarsson."

"Do."

Throstur said something to the helmsman, a man close to Spencer's age with a thick moustache and sideburns. Then he left. Spencer leaned very close to the radar screen, amazed at the clarity of the images—islands, shoals, rocks, enemy ship. Glowing dials against the inky darkness. It had to be the enemy, the Russians, the murderers of Karin. He was at war again, at war in a ship, at war in a machine. He had at last found what he had come to Iceland for.

The lights on the other ship had gone out.

Colonel Jahn was hot, sweaty, and excited, driving the van crazily along the gravel road. Despite the deep scratches in his face, he was happy, almost joyous. He was just a few kilometers short of his destination—of the culmination of all his plans.

He glanced again at his rearview mirror. His entourage—two cars from Reykjavik, two more from Akranes, a truck from Borgarnes—was following along, making every turn without lagging. Four more vehicles would meet them at the site. With the weapons he would have at his disposal, he could withstand any sort of armed force Iceland could bring to bear for days. There would be no repeat of any of his misfortunes. All was again under his control.

Jahn had an armed man in the seat next to him, two more in the seat behind. Behind them, on the floor, was the Vietnam-era U.S. army body bag in which was Elisabet Bjornsdottir.

She was still alive—for now. Still naked, bound hand and foot and doubtless perspiring greatly in that bag, she had only the few inches of unzipped opening he had left her to breathe through. As he had impressed upon her, if she disturbed or displeased him in any way, he had only to zip the bag closed to kill her—swiftly, silently, and awfully.

The woman was insurance—against Magnus Andersson and the Icelandic police, against John Spencer and whatever CIA help he had left with him in Iceland. Neither man would move if it meant this woman's life, Jahn was sure of that.

He was exceedingly pleased about what he had done to Karin Nielsen. They had been after each other all across Europe for years. Once she set a bomb for him in his toilet, which he found only just in time. He had kept her alive in Spencer's hotel room as long as he could. She had kept herself alive, defiant—cursing him through her gag, cursing him with her eyes. Jahn felt so good that she was gone.

He had sent his first radio message just before leaving Reykjavik. Confirmation had come from his associate in Moscow while he was on the road. When he reached the transformer site, he would receive word of the Kremlin's response.

There was no real doubt what it would be. They had no choice. They could not get to him. He had taken out Gorushchenko. The two agents the KGB had put on him—man and wife—were dead with their throats cut in the cellar of the Polish embassy. All the men Jahn had with him were fiercely loyal Germans, and there was no one in Iceland who could countermand his orders.

The Kremlin had no choice. Five hundred thousand English pounds deposited immediately in the specified bank in Rio de Janeiro. One million two hundred thousand Federal Republic Deutsche marks deposited immediately in the specified bank in Geneva. And to be deposited within three hours in a safe deposit box in a bank in Johannesburg, a case containing forty-two million American dollars' worth of diamonds.

If the stupid Russians wanted their surgical nuclear war, they would have to pay for it.

Jahn had a submarine—its crew completely loyal to him, its captain about to be dead—en route to a rendezvous near Akranes. He had an American business jet waiting in Scotland. Within forty-eight hours he would be in Angola, ready to vanish into the wonderful sanctuary that was Africa. There was no better place on the planet to disappear. All he had to do was permit the Russians to have their little war.

There was no one in Europe, no one in history, so ingenious. Skorzeny would have approved.

The policeman Magnus Andersson sent to watch Elisabet's door had not reported. Andersson called her on the telephone. There was no answer. He tried twice more, then grew anxious and angry. Summoning a car, he raced to her apartment, finding her door ajar. Inside, furniture was overturned, a phonograph record smashed. Water, still slightly warm, remained in the bathtub, though much of it had been splashed onto the floor. On the bathroom wall were several streaks of blood.

Andersson knocked a table over picking up the phone. He called his headquarters, demanding at once reports from the checkpoints he had set up on the roads leading out of Reykjavik. Had there been any cars registered to one of the Warsaw Pact embassies? Had there been any cars rented to them? Had there been any rental cars at all?

Within minutes, he heard. Two rental cars and a rented van had passed Andersson's checkpoint on the road leading northeast from Reykjavik.

A few hours later, he heard again. The cars he had sent in pursuit and the helicopter he had requested to shadow reported that the three vehicles—joined by several others—had pulled up just east of Stykkisholmur. Leaving just a small reserve at the harbor scene, Andersson ordered every policeman he could lay hands on to the north.

He would save Elisabet. He promised that to the gods. He would save Krog, or try. Krog was indeed a wronged man.

The KGB general was given a copy of Jahn's outrageous signal. He knew at once that it was not a joke, that its terms could and would have to be complied with, and that he would be held responsible. The quarters he and his staff had been assigned in the underground bunker on this extraordinary night were on the same level as the war command room and the marshal's elite security troops were stationed in every doorway. There was no point in thinking of escape.

He was standing, adjusting his uniform tunic, when the two armed officers appeared at the door. He came toward them, nodding, making it clear that they need not even speak. They took him past the war command room to a smaller chamber down the hall. There were a chair and a table with a tape recorder atop it. He was pushed down into the chair with little deference for his high rank. A moment later, the marshal and several aides joined them. A major quickly turned on the recorder. Everyone seemed to be sweating.

"I have only a few minutes to deal with you," said the marshal. "This comes at an inconvenient time." He smiled at his own sarcasm.

"I am sorry to inconvenience you," the KGB general said.

"Did you know about this?" said the marshal, glowering as he held up his copy of the Jahn message.

"I guessed he was up to something. I was going to have him removed after tonight."

"Too late."

"Yes. Much too late."

"Can he do this? Can he be that well prepared?"

"Yes. He is—was—my best man."

"Is there any way he can be stopped?"

"Yes, but not without stopping Valkyrie."

The marshal turned and began to pace, then stopped.

"If we provide the funds, will he do as he promises?"

"Yes, I think so. We haven't much choice."

"Does he realize how long it will take to carry out his instructions?"

"He probably has it timed to the minute."

"After Valkyrie, I could have all of Iceland blown up just to get him."

"That would destroy the weapon. He's probably counting on the chairman not wanting you to do that."

The marshal resumed his pacing. The general avoided the eyes of the other officers, feeling humiliated. In Stalin's day, he would by now have been hung upside down on a meathook.

For a fleeting moment, he wondered if he and the marshal were sharing this same thought: Jahn might be doing them a favor. By compromising Valkyrie in this way, he was giving them an opportunity for postponement, a chance to reconsider, a chance to spare millions of lives. There had to be a better way. The general had thought that from the beginning.

"We will do as he says," the marshal said. He stood over the general, who did not lift his eyes. "We will hunt him down. You, general, will be fully interrogated. At the least, you are guilty of the grossest incompetence."

The general knew what that meant, and what "fully interrogated" meant.

The marshal ordered everyone from the room. "In a few minutes, you will be taken from here," he said. "Compose yourself. I must return to my duties. Good-bye."

The general glimpsed three or four armed guards in the hallway before the door closed. He sighed. He would not need a few minutes to "compose" himself. The marshal was being kind. As the general bit down on the capsule he always carried, his last thoughts were on how the war would come out. He would be one of its first casualties.

23

THE *Heimdallur* had drawn much nearer the big trawler. The foreign ship was still running without lights, still invisible to the eye, but on the radar screen it was clearly delineated in bright, yellow-orange light upon the dark green, moving resolutely up the fjord.

Captain Ragnarsson was certain it was Russian. Only Molyneaux disagreed, holding out the possibility that it could be British. "Our trawlers still fish in these waters," he said, "with the kind permission of the Icelandic government."

"You have nothing this big," Ragnarsson said. "Only the Russians and Japanese have trawlers so large. And we have had no Japanese for months."

"Well, you could bloody well be wrong," Molyneaux said. "So have a care what you do to that ship."

Peterson laughed, his eyes and teeth shining weirdly in the red light. "What harm could this little boat do?" he asked.

"It's built like a bloody tank," Molyneaux said. "They all are. Came close to drowning bloody half our fishermen in the cod war."

"We only cut trawl lines!" said Ragnarsson. "If some of your frigates got in the way, it was not to be helped."

Laidlaw coughed impatiently. "The captain is right," he said. "The trawler can only be Russian. Whether we can do anything to it or not, we must follow it. It is heading for that transformer site."

Ragnarsson glanced at the radar screen, then went back to the chart table. He nodded.

"That is a very good guess, Mr. Laidlaw," he said. "The course they are taking leads only to a channel between the islands. The transformer is all there is at that anchorage."

"What in hell would they be up to?" said Molyneaux. "Are they picking someone up?"

"They'd use a submarine for that," Laidlaw said. "I think that trawler may be full of construction material. I think they may be starting on that particle beam emplacement without waiting for the election."

"It would still take them weeks," Molyneaux said.

"Days," said Laidlaw, "if everything was prefabricated."

"They'd run the risk of detection. Satellite photos."

"It might be a small risk, for a few days," Laidlaw said. "Iceland's cloud cover is inordinate. We don't normally make satellite photo scans of Iceland. It would take a special order from Washington. And the transformer's already here. New construction wouldn't look that suspicious."

"They're increasing speed, sir," said Throstur.

"Do the same," said Ragnarsson. "Close with them."

"What if some Icelanders came upon them," Peterson said, "while they were setting up that thing?"

"They'd probably kill them," Laidlaw said. "They've been doing quite a bit of that lately."

Spencer moved to a window in the dark, seeing the trawler only in his mind's eye but seeing it vividly—a long silhouette, low and menacing, sailors in watch caps along its rail.

"Too bad it's not a bloody vacuum cleaner," Molyneaux said. "They could sail right up to that transformer and just plug it in."

Peering into the darkness, Spencer saw that the trawler *was* low in the water. Of course! How obvious! As a newspaperman, Spencer had early on taught himself that the first thing to look for was the obvious. Why had he forgotten that?

"That's it!" he said. "It *is* designed like a vacuum cleaner! It doesn't have to be built! Krog put in his notes that they could install the thing almost anywhere in Iceland's electrical grid. Krog just failed to see the implication."

They all stared at him without expression.

"That trawler *is* the particle beam weapon! All they have to do is throw a line ashore and hook it up! That's it! That's all they ever intended to do. Everything else was distraction. The election, the harbor riots, the murders, sending out their fleet. All they ever wanted from Krog was to learn the best place for a hook-up. The rest was just to confuse him. And us."

They were still expressionless.

"Damn it!" Spencer said. "It's in that ship! World War III is in that ship!"

"It's possible," Laidlaw said. "And at this juncture, if it's possible, it's probable."

"How close can they come to shore there?" Spencer asked Ragnarsson. "They'll have a deep draft."

"Very close," Ragnarsson said. "This fjord is very deep."

"You have to stop them," Spencer said.

"What bloody with?" asked Molyneaux. "You've got two bolt-action rifles, a few pistols, and that Boer War surplus deck gun. Are you going to stop World War III with that?"

"We can stop them," Ragnarsson said in a low and even tone.

"Don't be reckless, Captain," said Peterson.

"George!"

"I'm speaking only as a lawyer," Peterson said. "I would not like to see Iceland unilaterally declare war on the Soviet Union."

"I represent the police," Ragnarsson said. "These are Icelandic waters. I will enforce our laws. If they resist, I will stop them."

"But for God's sake, man," said Molyneaux. "How?"

"The same way we stopped you in the cod war," Ragnarsson said.

It had been months since Thorn had carried a firearm, years since he had done this sort of thing. But it all came back to him; the weight of the automatic pistol now felt natural under his arm. In any event, there could be nothing easier than a car snatch in Reykjavik—dark streets, narrow sidewalks, few pedestrians.

"Is that him?" said Thorn's driver.

The man walking toward them was wearing a long overcoat. He walked hurriedly, with a strange dragging gait, his collar up, head down, wispy white hair flying in the wind.

"He looks like Ebeneezer Scrooge," Thorn said. "Yeah, that's him. That's Erikisson." Thorn glanced back at the darkened chase car parked behind him, noting the low small cloud of exhaust. He pulled out his pistol. "Let's get him."

Colonel Jahn had reverted to the strictly military officer he had once been—the very excellent military officer. He deployed his small force around the perimeter of the transformer site for maximum effect, giving the automatic-weapons men the broadest fields of fire, positioning the sniper scope teams in the rocky clefts above the transformer hut, and one in the high-tension tower beside it. The American claymore shrapnel-throwing mines he liked so much he set not only facing the approaches to the site but also along the road. This would indeed not be another Thingvellir. He could wipe out half the Icelandic police force if he wanted to—and he would if he needed to.

His perimeter also touched the fjord. If the trawler crew tried to come ashore, they'd have to fight and die for it. He could deny them the transformer connection no matter what. Jahn had wired enough gelignite to the transformer hut to vaporize every piece of metal in a millisecond.

He had left Elisabet Bjornsdottir alone in the hut, still in the body bag, with a guard outside at the door. As he had made clear, she could suffocate herself if she thrashed about. He did not want a guard around when he and the girl had their private dealings. And they would.

Jahn walked his perimeter, hands in his pockets, pausing finally atop the highest bluff at the site, looking out to sea. There was no sign yet of the trawler, no riding lights, no distant silhouette. Or was there? A glimmer off to the west caught the corner of his eye. He thought he detected a faint light.

One of his men came running up the slope.

"Message for you, Colonel! At the transmitter."

Jahn had ordered the transmitter truck parked at the farthest reach of his perimeter to avoid interference from the transformer's enormous electromagnetic field. He stumbled once completing the distance, bloodying his shin.

The message was what he had expected. The Kremlin knew him well enough to know that they must comply. He was sure they were preparing countermeasures to stop him, to hunt him down wherever he might go. But they had complied with all his requests, every one. There was nothing—absolutely nothing—they could do to him now until he had complied with all theirs.

"Send this signal to the trawler," he said to his radioman. "Proceed. All is prepared."

The light within the transformer hut was barely more than a glow, and little of it came through the small opening in the thick, sticky bag in which Elisabet lay imprisoned, half-sick from fear and discomfort. But she was fully aware of her surroundings and knew that she was alone in this strange room. When she heard a sliding footstep near her even though the door had not opened, she knew that whoever was there had been there before she and her captors arrived.

A large hand momentarily blocked the opening, then abruptly enlarged it, pulling down the zipper. It was a man, a large bearded man.

"I am Geir Krog," he said. "Don't be afraid."

Magnus Andersson pulled his car up on the bumpy ground where his men had parked the others, in the shelter of a long low ridge that shielded them from view of the transformer site. A sergeant came up to him, a young man with a pale, unhappy face.

"We've lost two men, Superintendent," he said. "One of them had his car blown up by a bomb or a mine. The other was shot trying to get close. There are many of them, and they have many weapons."

"Is Elisabet Bjornsdottir with them?"

"Yes, Superintendent. They announced that to us over a loudspeaker they have. At least one of them speaks very good Icelandic."

"Is she all right?"

"They say she is. They have her in the transformer hut, rigged with explosive charges."

Andersson got out of his car and climbed to the top of the ridge, the sergeant following. Lifting his head slowly, he could see a few small lights here and there about the area, but the hut and the high-tension tower were in darkness. He could see nothing moving on the fjord. Above the mountains to the east was a dancing line of northern lights.

The shot came with a sudden ringing snap, the bullet striking the ground just a few inches from his face, stinging him with dirt. He shoved himself, rolling back down the slope.

"They see in the dark," he said, brushing off his clothes.

"An infrared scope," said the sergeant.

"Infrared scopes," said Andersson. "Land mines."

"And automatic weapons. They've fired a few bursts at us."

Andersson sighed. "We have only rifles and pistols."

"We have more men on the way, Superintendent. And we have the helicopter."

"I don't want to lose it. I'm wondering if I should call in the American military for help. They have well-armed Marines."

"This is an Icelandic police matter, Superintendent. The kidnapping of an Icelandic citizen and the seizure of Icelandic government property. And you would need permission from the justice ministry."

"It would take all night just to explain it to them," Andersson said. "Have you tried to reach any of the Coast Guard vessels?"

"I made contact with the *Aegir*," said the sergeant, "but it is on the other side of the peninsula, in Faxafloi. The *Heimdallur* is supposed to be near, but I cannot contact her."

"What do they want, these people?" Andersson asked.

"They said only that we are to leave them alone until morning," the sergeant said. "Otherwise, they will kill the girl."

Andersson leaned his head forward, burying his chin in his hand. "I cannot call in Americans," he said.

"We have this advantage, Superintendent. We have them surrounded. They cannot escape from here."

"Except by sea," said Andersson.

The *Heimdallur* had come close astern of the big trawler, the silhouette of the ship's strange rigging now so visible against the aurora borealis to the east that they no longer needed the radar to follow it.

Ragnarsson picked up his radio microphone, switching the set to an open-channel frequency. "This is Icelandic patrol vessel *Heimdallur*," he said. "You are in Icelandic waters. Heave to, and identify yourself."

There was no response, just the faint crackle of static.

Ragnarsson repeated his message in Icelandic, and then in Danish. "Going by the book," as he said afterward. Again no answer. "Throstur," he said. "Get the Very pistol and fire a flare over his stern. I think it will carry that far."

Throstur went to the storage bin and unlocked it. Molyneaux peered over his shoulder. "Here's all your bloody rifle ammunition," he said.

"Break it out," said Ragnarsson. "Break out the pistols, too. Where are the shells for the deck gun?"

"Down below, sir," said Throstur. "There's just the one crate of twenty-four shells. They're supposed to last us two years."

Ragnarsson picked up the microphone for the ship's public address system, growling a few words of Icelandic into it. A buzzer rang through the ship. In a moment, they could hear the thud and clang of feet running throughout the little vessel. Three seamen huffed up onto the bridge, two of them going for the rifles.

"Let me have one of those," Spencer said. "I don't know

ow experienced your Icelanders are, but I rated 'expert' in he army. Give the other to Peterson. He's even better than I m."

The captain nodded. The seamen took up pistols instead, rom an odd collection that included some old American .45 utomatics and a huge British Wembley revolver. In short rder everyone on the bridge but Laidlaw was armed.

"Throstur!" said Ragnarsson. "Fire the flare!"

The young man stepped out onto the open bridge wing, aised his arm high, and fired. The trajectory was perfect, the hell exploding high above and just aft of the trawler's stern. As the flare fell, burning bright red with a sputter of white parks, the name on the stern became legible.

"It's Russian," Ragnarsson said.

Laidlaw took the captain's binoculars, translating the Cy-illic letters.

"The *Kosygin,*" he said. "A special honor."

Ragnarsson went to the radio.

"Trawler *Kosygin,*" he said into his microphone. "I order ou to heave to. We are going to board you."

This time there was a response. A distant staccato clatter nd a few darts of flame, followed instantly by some thuds in he metal roof above them and a shattering of glass in one of he windows. They all went sprawling to the deck floor, most f them moving quickly to the protection of the thick metal ulkhead beneath the forward windows. Ragnarsson and the elmsman remained, crouching, at the wheel. One of the eamen had been hit, the seaman whose rifle Spencer had aken. He was groaning and whimpering miserably. Spencer ad never gotten used to the sound of brave men suffering rom their wounds.

"Bear off!" Ragnarsson shouted to the helmsman. "Bear off o port!"

"Are we turning back?" Spencer asked. The falling flare ow filled the bridge with light. Ragnarsson ignored him, eaching to jam the speed control forward to "full ahead."

Again the bridge was raked with machine-gun fire. It took

out two more windows and demolished a barometer abov
the helm.

"Are we turning back?" Spencer asked again.

"No!" Ragnarsson said. "I want to pull abreast of him! want to come at him from abeam!" He began swearing i Icelandic, words Spencer only vaguely recognized.

Throstur was standing at one of the shot-out windows, ab surdly firing at the trawler with one of the pistols.

"Throstur!" Ragnarsson shouted. "Go below and get tha deck gun working! Hurry!"

As the young man hurtled down the stairs, Peterson too his place at the window and began firing slow, careful, wel placed shots with his rifle, pausing after each. Spencer crawle out onto the bridge wing with the other rifle. He wasn't sur of its make or model, but the clip slipped into the magazin with ease. The bolt chambered the first round without a snag He found the safety and clicked it off, then lowered his chee to the stock and lined up the sights as best he could, aimin for the trawler's superstructure and what he hoped was th bridge. He pulled the trigger, surprised at how quickly th rifle fired, and at the pain of the recoil.

He clicked back the bolt, his nostrils filling with the burn ing scent of gas and powder as the empty shell fell to the dec with a clang. He eased another shell into the chamber, the sat back on his heels, hesitating. This was a mistake. His tin bullet had gone flying off through the darkness, striking what A slab of metal? A human chest? Absolutely nothing? Mayb Peterson was that good, but he was not. Firing like this wa not combat; it was rhetoric.

The small darts of light appeared once more. The *Heim dallur* apparently was pulling abreast, for this time the flail o bullets broke up the windows on the side of the bridge, show ering Spencer with a blizzard of glass.

His hand was cut. The back of his head was beginning t throb, so violently he could almost hear it. Spencer went t his knees, tottering a moment with his eyes closed, the looked through the open door to the bridge. Ragnarsson an the helmsman were still at the wheel. Someone else had been hit. Molyneaux was kneeling over whoever it was. Peterson was still firing in his slow, methodical way through the forward window. Wires and paneling were hanging down from the ceiling.

"Hard starboard!" Ragnarsson shouted. "Hard! Full ahead!"

Spencer felt the *Heimdallur* lurch and stagger in its steep, high-speed turn. The water was calm, but a heave of spray came splashing over the rail.

Ragnarsson was going to ram. He was hurling his tough little gunboat at the trawler as fast as it could go, the seas peeling back from the bow and the waterline with a loud continuous swoosh. Unless the Russians had some weapon capable of blowing the *Heimdallur* out of the water, they were set on their course, resolute, relentless. The Vikings had been the most fearless people in all European history and the Russians were about to discover that all over again. If they killed every man aboard, the *Heimdallur* would still bear hard on her mark.

And if they killed Spencer? Spencer, the walking dead man? If one of those machine-gun bullets came faster than sound, sharp as a needle, harder than rock, smashing his nose, squashing his face, ballooning his head, and emptying out his skull? Well, then, here he was at last, face to face with it.

He lifted himself up to the rail and snapped off three quick, smooth shots at the nearing trawler. Someone had fired another flare, then another. The two floated down in tandem, coloring everything a fiery pink and red. There was more rifle and machine-gun fire, and a new sound—a higher-pitched, whizzing explosion. Spencer looked over the rail, craning his neck. Throstur was firing the deck gun. The trawler, looming closer, showed hits with bursts of sparks on its steel plating. But its guns still fired.

Spencer shot off two more rounds, emptying his clip. He wanted Chesley to see him now, ending his life in this violent fashion, ending it the way she liked least. Balaclava, Agincourt, the Scots grays at Waterloo, Pork Chop Hill. This spectacular dancing with death was the ultimate experience, as the soldiers had told him. More than sex, more than childbirth, more than any discovered wisdom. To die while living, to live while dying, and to have a reason for it. *Flight to Arras.* What had Antoine de Saint-Exupéry written? "Those who died served as bondsmen to the rest."

Smoke now, colored by this strange pink-red flickering light. More cries and groans. Chesley in a white Connecticut summer dress. Figures rushing past the windows. Peterson firing, slowly, like a machine. Ragnarsson's voice, hoarse in shouting. Laidlaw standing at a window, shooting the huge clumsy Wembley revolver. The trawler was so near, so big. Spencer could see figures along its rail, figures in the windows of its bridge. He raised his rifle, inserting another clip.

Bang! Slide, click. Bang! Slide, click. He used up the clip and then inserted another.

There was a sailor at the trawler's rail, shooting at them with some hand-held automatic weapon. Spencer was careful now, aiming low, holding his breath, squeezing slowly. The sailor vanished. Had he killed someone? Finally?

He looked into the *Heimdallur*'s bridge, but no one was paying him any attention. Ragnarsson had taken the wheel. Laidlaw still stood ghostlike at the forward window, holding the huge revolver. Peterson was still shooting. One of the seamen was on his knees, firing a pistol.

Looking over the rail, Spencer saw Cullie down on the foredeck, working the gun by himself. Throstur was lying beside the gun, dead or wounded. Two sailors were lying nearby. Slam the shell into the breach, Swivel and aim. Yank the trigger. He was hitting things on the big trawler. Useful things. The machine-gun fire stopped. The Russians were using only small arms now. Many sailors were crowding the rail. Spencer fired slowly at them in target-practice fashion, moving from one to the next to the next. Two of them went down. Had he killed them? He made the amazing discovery that he hoped he had. Avenge Karin. Evi Kekkonen. Vengeance.

More smoke. More noise. More shooting. The hull of the

trawler was very near. His eyes, his mind, were taking it in so slowly. It seemed like a ballet. Would Chesley hear of this?

Spencer was struck by a tearing, exploding pain—at the back of his head, at the side of his head. It had happened, just as the doctors had promised. Too much stress, and the fragile blood vessel had ruptured, filling his skull with blood, numbing that dying quarter of his brain. He fell again to his knees, and then onto his side, the noise and light fading. He had won. Death may have come for him as they promised, but he had run to meet it.

A thought of Chesley. Clutch a thought of Chesley. But why? Her only value to him now was that she represented so many years of his life. Karin Nielsen. He had felt an overpowering affection for her that was based entirely on pity, and now she beckoned from out in the great black void, beckoned with hard little hands.

Elisabet. Luminescent gray eyes. Long dark hair. Soft hands. Beautiful voice. Beautiful mind. That cold, golden afternoon in the hills returning from Akureyri; he had loved her more intensely than he had ever loved a woman, than any man had loved a woman. It was only a moment, but it was his most wonderful moment. In the end, what was life but a moment?

Spencer did not hear the rending crash as the *Heimdallur*'s bow plunged into the hull of the trawler, tearing an enormous hole and buckling steel plate for a hundred feet to either side. Nor did he hear the screams.

The instant he saw the first distant flare, Jahn knew there was serious trouble. The sound of gunfire that followed was almost expected. Jahn hurried down to the transmitter truck, though not so fast as to alarm his men.

"They caught up with the Icelandic Coast Guard, Herr Oberst," said the radio operator. "One of those gunboats."

"Gunboat? One of those little patrol vessels?"

"*Ja*, Herr Oberst. They've opened fire on it with a machine gun. The gunboat's firing back."

A machine gun. Here they were, the key to what would be

the most consequential military undertaking in the history of mankind, and they had equipped the trawler with machine guns. Jahn swore and leaned close to the radio operator's face, speaking through his teeth.

"Tell them to ignore that little gnat and proceed here as fast as possible," he said. "Once they've tied up here, the gunboat will be no problem."

The operator nodded, hunching over his set. Finally, he leaned back, taking off his earphones. "They are attempting to do just that, Herr Oberst," he said. "They will signal when they reach the channel."

"Very well," said Jahn. "Signal Moscow that all is well."

"*Jawohl,* Herr Oberst."

Jahn began pacing beside the truck, his hands clasped behind his back. He had always expected that the Icelanders might be something of a nuisance, that one of his vehicles might pick up a police tail, that some civilian might stray on to the transformer site. But the police in Reykjavik were supposed to have their hands full with the harbor troubles. There were only six patrol boats in the Icelandic Coast Guard, and, counting fjords, they had thirty-seven hundred miles of coastline to cover, even though the country was just three hundred miles across. It should have been possible to stage another Normandy invasion without their noticing.

Yet here he was confronting an army of policemen across his perimeter, with more no doubt on the way. And one of the gunboats had turned up in the worst possible place at precisely the worst possible moment—a place it had no logical reason to be.

But he was still in control. The Icelanders could not penetrate his perimeter—and would not as long as he had Elisabet Bjornsdottir. This lumpy piece of shoreline was still his for several hours, and that was all he needed. Once the trawler was moored and its device energized and operational, half an hour was all he needed.

"Moscow affirms your signal, Herr Oberst."

If all went as planned, if the "great glorious socialist military enterprise" succeeded, there was the slightest possibility that the Kremlin might let him get away with his little extortion, might not pursue him so hotly, might let him disappear. If everything failed, they'd track him down like Trotsky—though much more swiftly.

He was prepared for that. Jahn, as always, was ready for a number of eventualities. And, if worse came to worst, the money he carried from his operating fund was enough to keep him comfortably hidden in Africa or South America for several years.

"Signal from the *Kosygin*, sir," said the operator. "They have been rammed."

"What?"

"Rammed, Herr Oberst. They're listing and taking on water."

The ocean pouring in on all those billions of rubles of extraordinary equipment, on Moscow's crowning technological achievement—the one area of weaponry development where the Soviets actually had surpassed the United States!

"Can they make the rendezvous?"

The operator bent over his set again. "*Nein*, Herr Oberst. They say negative. They are trying to make for shore."

The ultimate incompetence, handing themselves over to the enemy. "Come with me," he said to the operator.

Jahn had a motorboat at anchor just off the beach. Its mission was to guide the trawler in to the shore, but its crew would follow Jahn's every order, and his order would be to proceed to the rendezvous with his submarine.

"Take three of the men with automatic weapons and go down to the beach," he said to the radio operator. "We're going to go aboard the boat. I'll join you in a few minutes."

"*Jawohl.*"

He would now deal with Elisabet Bjornsdottir, and so would deal with all Iceland. Her presence would prevent the police from trying to halt his escape, would hold off any gunboat that tried to intercept them. But she would be present only in the most clinical sense of the term. If Iceland defeated him, it would be at some cost. She was the most beautiful woman in Iceland, they said—not for much longer.

He took the radio detonator from his pocket to make sure that it was not activated, then started up the slope to the transformer hut. Ordering the guard to take a position on the perimeter, Jahn paused with his hand on the door latch. He was beginning to sweat, beginning to make himself angry. He waited until his breath was coming fast and heavy, then pulled the long-bladed knife from his boot and pushed open the door.

He could see the body bag in the faint light, just where he had left it, but there was something strange about it. Stepping nearer, he realized it was too flat.

His eyes searched the huge jumble of equipment in the room for more than a minute before he caught sight of her cowering in a corner, her nakedness largely covered by a heavy outdoorsman's jacket, her hands and feet free.

Jahn realized something was wrong just as the two great fists came down hard upon the back of his neck. There was a white pain, and then his mind went black. He felt the knife drop from his hand, felt himself falling forward, over and over.

He was unconscious when he hit the floor, but it lasted only a moment. He came to with Krog standing over him, holding the knife, the dim light playing grotesquely over the big man's enraged face.

Krog put his heavy booted foot on Jahn's neck. "Vermin," he said.

"How are you here, Krog? How can you possibly be here?"

"I can think, Rozkowski, or whoever you are. I thought it out, as a good chess player should. So I am here."

"Krog, I have two dozen men outside. I have this building wired with explosives." He began coughing from the pressure of Krog's foot.

"You killed Inga, and Evi Kekkonen, and so many others You were going to kill Elisabet Bjornsdottir."

"Krog, you cannot get out of here alive unless I let you. I'll do that—you and the woman. All I want is to leave this place, to leave Iceland. Now."

"Leave Iceland? I know what you plan to do, Rozkowski. I know it all."

"That's over. The Soviets have been stupid. It's all over. Everything is undone. We are leaving Iceland."

"You think I would let you go? After all you have done? That I would let that pass unavenged?"

Jahn looked at the girl, who had drawn nearer, pulling the jacket close around her. "Think of her, Krog," he said, half-gasping. "Do you want her out of here alive?"

Krog glanced back at her—a mistake. Jahn grasped his foot, pulling and twisting. Krog went sprawling. They came together again, lunging and clawing, beating and punching. They rolled against a heavy piece of machinery, Krog's head striking a corner. Jahn kneed him hard in the groin and shoved himself free. When both got to their feet, Krog, bleeding from the head, held the knife. Jahn, still gasping, had taken the radio detonator from his pocket. With his thumb, he activated it.

"You know what this is, do you not, Herr Engineer?" he said, holding it out in his hand. He moved his thumb again, depressing a button at the top. "If I lift this, none of us will escape. Stalemate, Krog. Stalemate!"

Krog stepped back and flung open the door behind him.

"Go! Quick!" he cried to Elisabet. "Hurry! Run! Run!"

She touched Krog's arm, stealing a quick look at his extraordinary face. She did not look at Jahn; she did not want his image in her mind ever again. Then she ran, out the door and down the slope, crazily, clumsily, falling once, the dirt alternately slippery and painful beneath her bare feet. She ran till her breaths were coming almost as fast as her pounding heartbeats. Then she saw a man with a gun rise up in front of her and she dove for the ground, pressing her face against the earth.

The explosion split the sky with searing light, a shattering roar, and heat, then a rumbling of the ground and a great scatter of falling debris.

Elisabet looked up to see the man with the gun clutching at his chest, falling. The transformer hut had vanished but for flame, and the tower beside it was crumpling and falling.

There was gunfire. She pressed her head to the ground again and did not lift it until long after the gunfire had ended.

Men were standing around her. One knelt down. Magnus Andersson, his eyes sadder than she had ever seen, sadder than she imagined any man's eyes could be. He lifted her to her feet, gazing intently into her face and repeating her name over and over. Sobbing, she pressed herself against him, holding tightly, so glad when his own arms came around her.

Dying on the deck. Who lay dying on the deck? Nelson, dying at Trafalgar. But was it on the deck, or in his admiral's cabin, thinking filthy thoughts of Lady Hamilton? Thinking filthy thoughts of the First Sea Lord? But Spencer was lying on the deck, and he was not dying, and this certainly wasn't Lady Hamilton peering into his face.

"George," Spencer said. He put his hand to the pain at the back of his head, feeling puffy flesh beneath the hair and a stickiness he assumed was blood.

"You took a bang," Peterson said. "Ricochet, or a metal fragment."

"We thought you among our dead," said another voice. There was a face to go with the voice. White hair. The distinguished Mr. Laidlaw.

Spencer slowly sat up and ran a hand over his face. He was indeed not among the dead, not yet. He opened his eyes, blinking. The *Heimdallur* had lights on, lights on all over. Two great searchlights atop the otherwise ruined bridge were trained forward on the water.

"It's over," Peterson said. "Captain Ragnarsson is picking up survivors. The Russian trawler went down, Jack."

"Our dead," Spencer said, turning to Laidlaw. "How many?"

"Two dead," Laidlaw said. "Seven wounded."

"Who?"

"A sailor, and Mr. Molyneaux," Laidlaw said, pausing. "Dead. Six Icelanders, including Throstur, wounded. And you."

Spencer got weakly to his feet and stood gripping the rail. His head ached terribly. His hearing was complicated by stuffiness and a ringing.

Molyneaux's body still lay by the gun, curled backward grotesquely. His glasses were missing. His long hair was dark with blood where it touched the deck.

"He died for Iceland," Peterson said.

Poor Collie. No posthumous Victoria Cross for him. But maybe there would be.

Spencer became aware of something burning in the distance, a bright yellow flame far down the shore. "What's that fire?" he asked.

"We don't know," said Laidlaw. "There was an explosion. The captain thinks it may be the transformer site. We've been preoccupied with other things."

He gestured at the waters off the bow. The area illuminated by the searchlights was filled with swimming men and debris, the two boats from the *Heimdallur* working among them. Ragnarsson was up at the prow, shouting through a bullhorn. The trawler had in fact vanished. A moment before, it had filled Spencer's eyes. Now it was gone.

"We did that," Spencer said. "All our conversations, Mr. Laidlaw. It came to this."

"The trawler was making for shore when it went down," Laidlaw said. "The captain says the water is shallow enough for divers to get at it."

"Do you have any doubt there's a particle beam weapon inside?"

"None at all. But it will be best if no one has any doubt."

Iceland was quiet, at peace. What of the world thousands of miles away?

"Have the Soviets done anything else?" Spencer asked.

"We radioed Reykjavik," Laidlaw said. "There's been nothing."

"Are you still convinced they were planning a nuclear strike?"

"I'm still convinced that was a strong possibility."

"This is a great victory," Spencer said.

"A small victory," said Laidlaw.

"But we may well have prevented nuclear war," Spencer said.

"For now," said Laidlaw softly.

24

ELISABET HAD SLID the door to the balcony fully open and now stood before it, her head back, eyes closed, savoring the strong warm ocean breeze that enveloped her. She wore a thin robe, nothing else. The wind blew it billowing away from her body.

"Someone may see you," Spencer said from the bed.

She smiled. "Here I am not so afraid."

She smiled again and stepped out onto the balcony into the sunlight. She lingered at the railing for a moment, then eased herself into a lounge chair, tilting back her head as she reclined, closing her eyes again, seeming to lift her body slightly as though to aid her skin in drinking up the sun.

Hawaii was having a buoyant effect upon her, at times a narcotic one. It was exactly like Iceland, she agreed—the mountains, the volcanoes, the sea—but there was endless sunshine, and warmth and trees and hot sand.

Their hotel room was on the tenth floor but the waves sounded as though they were breaking beneath the balcony.

The package.

It had come just a few minutes before, delivered to his door. Since only a very few people knew he had gone to Hawaii, its arrival puzzled him, and he let it sit on the table unopened for a time.

If it were going to explode, it would have done so by now. He snatched it up and ripped it open, the parting paper revealing a book.

A travel book on Hawaii. The author, Hugh S. Laidlaw.

With a slight smile, he opened it and thumbed through the pages, coming almost at once to an envelope.

A rum job, Collie Molyneaux would have said. Spies didn't just stick letters into books.

It was a letter, typed on an odd, slick, plasticized paper.

Dear Mr. Spencer,

This is not quite so obvious as it seems. The bellman who delivered this package is not a bellman but an old associate of mine. This paper, now that you've exposed it to the light, will disintegrate in approximately fifteen minutes, so do not tarry.

You may find the travel book useful. It was favorably reviewed. I've decided my next one will be on Iceland. What an amusing time the KGB will have with that.

We were deprived of an opportunity to talk after my friends from the agency came aboard the *Heimdallur*. For a time, I was afraid I was going to be deprived of an opportunity to talk with anyone ever again. But our success has produced the reward of forgiveness, and I have been allowed to quietly retire once more, with the proviso that I maintain my usual circumspection and reticence. This letter is a small violation of that, so I must rely on your discretion.

I mentioned to you a colleague in Washington who had been protecting me. I never liked him. He was a homosexual and an extreme reactionary. But he helped me until the very end. There remains much they don't know or still blame him for. I have the unpleasant feeling he may have done this out of some attachment to me, but in any event the *beau geste* proved foolish, for the poor man has now disappeared.

Thorn, whom I also mentioned to you, has been quite handsomely promoted. This had less to do with the outcome of our little enterprise than with his success as a diplomat, if I may use the term, in persuading Prime

Minister Erikisson to be so generous with NATO. As you undoubtedly know, the Keflavik base is to remain ours for the indefinite future. As you may not know, Great Britain will shortly announce a contract to supply Iceland with low-cost North Sea diesel fuel for its fishing fleet.

This is the second time the United States has twisted the English arm on behalf of Iceland, and, interestingly, the second time you were involved. Who knows, you may end up in the British archives along with George Washington, Wolfe Tone, and Rudolph Hess.

You were pressing me as to what we have accomplished. My sources within the agency are no longer what you would call the very best placed, but I'm fairly reliably informed that the particle beam equipment recovered from the trawler, and generously forwarded to us by the Icelandic government, has delighted some of the better minds in the Pentagon and elsewhere and will be very helpful in our own efforts to duplicate or surpass it.

As for what the Soviets were about to do, we can never be totally certain. But it was an extremely extensive operation. They had, we now discover, evacuated ninety percent of the population of Moscow and some three-quarters of the population of Leningrad and Volgagrad. We know that our activities—yours and mine—disconcerted them greatly. The latest estimates I've heard concerning Soviet preemptive strike capabilities now put any next effort at three to nine months away, if then.

If three months seems rather pitifully small to you, bear in mind that our efforts at least equal the battle of the Coral Sea. Bear in mind also that our former President lost the civilized world between two and three years of safety with his neglect of defense.

Congratulate yourself. If it were not for my extremely enforced retirement, and your medical problems, I should happily embrace the prospect of working with you again. I would say that you missed your calling, except that I persist in thinking your calling and mine are much the same.

Your friend Peterson need fear nothing, not even a requirement to register as a foreign agent. The United States government views honorary consuls kindly, especially those who have risked their lives on its behalf.

Of Molyneaux, I can only say that I am grateful for him, as I had occasion to be several times before.

As you may have gathered—should have, but perhaps did not—my relationship with Karin Nielsen was more than I may have indicated. Her loss is the greatest I have suffered in this career. I am pleased that she knew you. I very much mean that. She was ordered to kill you, I discover. She was insubordinate.

I congratulate you on your lovely Elisabet. You are a uniquely fortunate man, Mr. Spencer.

I must close, before this disintegrates in your hand.

Which, in a moment, it did.

Spencer stared at the last few dark wisps as they were blown away by the breeze from the balcony door. He had wanted to read the letter again, over a drink, an old habit of his when reading things.

An opened bottle of gin and one of scotch stood on a dresser top, untouched since the cocktail hour the evening before. He left them that way.

His "medical problems." It was now precisely three days since he had passed the six-month mark—the barrier, the deadline, the limit. Yet here he was.

He looked down at the veins in his arms. He felt his pulse, finding the throbbing steady and normal. He closed his eyes, driving all manner of thoughts from his mind. But not all. Karin had saved his life, had spared his life, but for what?

"Elisabet," he said. "Please come here."

"Do not take me from the sun."

"Please. It's important."

"If it's important, John, then you come here."

There had been another letter—from Connecticut. He had been carrying it for days. Chesley wanted him back. She almost demanded it.

"Elisabet. I want to marry you."

"What?"

"I want to marry you."

She rose from the chair, the robe barely clinging to her shoulders.

"What did you say?" she said, standing in the doorway.

"I want to marry you, Elisabet. You're all I look forward to now. I want you. For as long as I live."

She walked slowly to the bed, kissed him, then sat down beside him.

"Dear John," she said. "Dear Jack."

"This place is crawling with clergymen. We'll have it done at once."

She pulled back slightly, her wide gray eyes staring into his.

"Dear Jack," she said. "No."

"No? Am I hearing you?"

"Yes, and I am saying 'no.' "

"Pardon me for being confused."

"Jack. I love you, but I cannot marry you."

"My illness."

"That doesn't matter."

His eyes sought a place to rest—the ocean, the hotel wall art, the two liquor bottles, her gray eyes.

"Karin Nielsen," he said.

"That matters," she said. "That you did that to me after we had . . . that you might do it again. That matters very much. But it would not prevent me from marrying you."

"What is it, then? I mean, damn. Elisabet. What?"

"Iceland."

"Iceland?"

"It is everything between us, Jack." She put her hand on his shoulder, then began gently rubbing his back.

"Elisabet, there is no American fonder of Iceland than I."

"That is true, Jack. But you would not be happy staying

long in Iceland. You would not want to live there. Not for long. And I cannot be happy staying long away. I love Hawaii. But already I want to go back to Iceland. There is no life for you there, and it is the only life I know."

"But . . ."

"Please. Be truthful with me, with yourself, as I am being. I do love you. You will always be in my mind. But I cannot marry you." A great wave crashed against the sand below, then another.

"What will you do, then?" Spencer asked. "Will you continue to fly for Icelandair? Will I ever see you in the United States?"

"Of course. You will see me whenever you want."

"But when you are in Iceland . . . ?"

Her eyes brightened and became wider still.

"I am going to write a book," she said. "In the pocket of the jacket he gave me to wear, Geir Krog had a copy of *Njal's Saga.* It is Iceland's most famous saga. I thought, that terrible night, that someone ought to write a *Geir's Saga.* About all that he did. I cannot. I don't know enough about what he did. But I can write an *edda*—a poem book—about Geir Krog, that great good man. I will do that."

"And Magnus Andersson. Will you see him again?"

"Of course."

"Elisabet . . . he will ask you to marry him."

She stroked the back of his neck.

"Yes," she said. "That is a possibility. But do you understand, Jack? That changes nothing for us."

She leaned forward and looked into his eyes.

"That is a matter for tomorrow, Jack."

Then she lay back upon the bed, pulling him after her.

"Today is today," she said.

FICTION

GENERAL

☐ Chains	Justin Adams	£1.25
☐ Secrets	F. Lee Bailey	£1.25
☐ Skyship	John Brosnan	£1.65
☐ The Free Fishers	John Buchan	£1.50
☐ Huntingtower	John Buchan	£1.50
☐ Midwinter	John Buchan	£1.25
☐ A Prince of the Captivity	John Buchan	£1.25
☐ The Eve of St Venus	Anthony Burgess	£1.10
☐ Nothing Like the Sun	Anthony Burgess	£1.50
☐ The Memoirs of Maria Brown	John Cleland	£1.25
☐ The Last Liberator	John Clive	£1.25
☐ Wyndward Fury	Norman Daniels	£1.50
☐ Ladies in Waiting	Gwen Davis	£1.50
☐ The Money Wolves	Paul Erikson	£1.50
☐ Rich Little Poor Girl	Terence Feely	£1.50
☐ Fever Pitch	Betty Ferm	£1.50
☐ The Bride of Lowther Fell	Margaret Forster	£1.75
☐ Forced Feedings	Maxine Herman	£1.50
☐ Savannah Blue	William Harrison	£1.50
☐ Duncton Wood	William Horwood	£1.95
☐ Dingley Falls	Michael Malone	£1.95
☐ Gossip	Marc Olden	£1.25
☐ Buccaneer	Dudley Pope	£1.50
☐ An Inch of Fortune	Simon Raven	£1.25
☐ The Dream Makers	John Sherlock	£1.50
☐ The Reichling Affair	Jack Stoneley	£1.75
☐ Eclipse	Margaret Tabor	£1.35
☐ Pillars of the Establishment	Alexander Thynn	£1.50
☐ Cat Stories	Stella Whitelaw	£1.10

WESTERN — BLADE SERIES by Matt Chisholm

☐ No. 5 The Colorado Virgins	85p
☐ No. 6 The Mexican Proposition	85p
☐ No. 7 The Arizona Climax	85p
☐ No. 8 The Nevada Mustang	85p
☐ No. 9 The Montana Deadlock	95p
☐ No. 10 The Cheyenne Trap	95p
☐ No. 11 The Navaho Trail	95p
☐ No. 12 The Last Act	95p

WESTERN — McALLISTER SERIES by Matt Chisholm

☐ McAllister and the Spanish Gold	95p
☐ McAllister on the Commanche Crossing	95p
☐ McAllister Never Surrenders	95p
☐ McAllister and the Cheyenne Trap	95p

SCIENCE FICTION

☐ Times Without Number	John Brunner	£1.10
☐ The Dancers of Arun	Elizabeth A. Lynn	£1.50
☐ Watchtower	Elizabeth A. Lynn	£1.10

WAR

☐ The Andersen Assault	Peter Leslie	£1.25
☐ Killers under a Cruel Sky	Peter Leslie	£1.25
☐ The Serbian Triangle	Peter Saunders	£1.10
☐ Jenny's War	Jack Stoneley	£1.25